The
Portico
Thief

Dolcy Stone

Published by Little Red Dog

Copyright © 2022 Dolcy Stone
All rights reserved.
ISBN: PB 978-1-7391714-1-4

The Portico Thief by Dolcy Stone

Dolcy Stone has asserted her rights under the Copyright Designs
and Patents Act, 1988, to be identified as the Author of this work.

To KT, who believed in The Portico Thief since its first draft and without whom I would never have finished.

To Little Rea for offering her support through tummy rubs, for which I am the most privileged person alive.

CHAPTER 1

St Albans

THE gun aimed at his face.

Elbows bent, palms forward, Sidney Knight raised his hands.

He listened to the heavy breathing beneath the intruder's mask.

Sweat dripped off his thinning hair, trickling down Sidney's neck along the bony bumps protruding from his back. It was too fucking hot. Even the air conditioning unit couldn't ease the suffocating humidity. The study windows – closed – trapped the heat as the walls pulsated like a smouldering fire. But maybe that was just his skin, drenched from the heat and the shitty effects of his chemo.

He'd had guns aimed at him before, but never in his own home. Watching the trembling barrel in front of him, it occurred to Sidney that the man behind the mask had probably never shot a gun before. And it was the wrong kind of gun for a professional. Revolver. No silencer. Shiny. Smoothbore. Its power would kill him for sure, but it wasn't a professional's gun.

Did he care? Like fuck he didn't.

The ache in his muscles spasmed. His legs juddered, whacked from his chemo, under his fragile body as the beat in his chest jumped around like a kid on two dozen packets of loaded gummy bears. If only the shit holding the gun would ask for what he wanted.

The light from the hallway trickled into the room, and Sidney scrunched his eyes, trying to make out the man's shape. His size. He guessed him to be tall but slight – finely framed. The darkness hid the colour of his eyes, yet their glint showed they were staring – startled.

It was the light thud on the kitchen tiles that had caught Sidney's attention as he lay awake, waiting for his next shot of morphine. His mind had been twisting – was this shit ever going to end? At the bottom of the bed, the two Labradors had woken simultaneously, too hot and old to care about the noise, their heads rising slightly before flopping back into a lazy slump of snoring. They were used to Agi, the housekeeper, mooching around for midnight snacks and finding ways to deal with her insomnia. For once, Sidney was grateful they were too fat and old to follow him down the stairs.

Why wasn't he speaking, asking, demanding? Isn't that what

intruders did: demand something? Or was he just there to kill him? Think. He had to think … but his brain was fried, and his next shot of morphine was due. His body fucking ached like someone had poured acid into his veins. Any strength left in his legs faded. His hands, still raised in the air, trembled as more sweat trickled on his skin like fire – down his spine and into the waistband of his cotton pyjamas. The summer air choked his lungs, and his brain spun. What did it matter? He was dying anyway.

Slowly, his hands lowered. It was a better way to go than lying in a hospice bed, not able to beg for the drugs that would kill him more quickly. For fuck's sake. In a week or two, he'd be soiling the bed and reeking of decaying, sweaty flesh. The toxins in his body would build up, back up, and reach his brain. Then he'd hallucinate – pluck cherries from the air. And, in front of his children, he would struggle like something possessed. Maybe fate had intervened, and this was his way out. Everything was prepared for his death: it didn't matter if he went now or next week. It was done. His affairs were ready.

'What do you want?' he asked.

'You know what we want,' the gunman replied.

'You!' Sidney laughed. 'Jesus fucking Christ. You think I'd give it to you?'

As he said those words, his body was pain-free for the first time in months. The dizzy morphine haze that had haunted his every waking moment had disappeared. Fate stepped in. His thoughts couldn't have been clearer. All he had to do was make the intruder shoot him. Easy, he thought and walked calmly towards the trembling gun.

CHAPTER 2

St Albans

SHE froze. Shit. Muffled voices came from the study. The old man was meant to be upstairs sleeping. She glanced back at the window she'd jimmied open only ten minutes before. Run, she whispered in her head – but she didn't. Instead, she turned her face towards the study she'd only just left.

As she moved back along the shadowy corridor, the voices grew louder. The old man's breathing rasped like the death rattle she'd heard in her mother's lungs. She leant her head gently on the doorframe, her eyes focusing between the crack. Two men, one masked and gunned up, the other old and yellow with death. She knew that look. She knew the clammy sweat beading on his forehead as if it were her own. And she could smell it. Jesus Christ. She didn't want to see it, a dying man killed, even if he was Old Bill.

Through the slit between the door and its frame, she watched the old bloke slowly lower his hands and walk towards the gun. What the fuck was he doing? What the fuck was he doing! He moved across the room. The end of the gun trembled. He walked straight at it, into it – right up against the fucking thing. Fucking, fuck. Her voice screamed inside her head.

The sound, the bang, wasn't how she'd imagined it would be. It popped like a tiny canon, not some ricocheting sound effect that would have woken the entire neighbourhood. And his body didn't do what she'd seen in the films. Instead, he slumped over – fell forward. There was no stumbling around, no hand grasping at the bullet wound. No. The old man just slumped. Her breathing stopped. Time stopped. Sidney Knight lay motionless. The gunman froze.

She was frozen too, yet her blood pumped so fast she could hear it in her ears. She could hear her own breathing as if someone had put a microphone to her mouth. Jesus fucking Christ – she had to run. Was the gunman behind her? The breath lunged up from her chest – shallow and fast. Flinging herself back through the jimmied window, she tumbled onto the gravel, landing on her knees before stumbling to her feet. Regaining her balance, she ran across the lawn and into the trees that hid her faithful Triumph. With the kit-bag on her back and the stolen envelope inside, the envelope George insisted his client was desperate for, she flicked up the motorbike's stand and pulled out into the country lane.

Her thoughts tumbled like a blanket of ash falling from the sky. Police cars would be there in minutes. The old housekeeper would have heard the gun pop – her heart plunged to her stomach. What if the gunman had known about the old lady and killed her too? She needed to turn back – she couldn't turn back. She needed to phone George, but she couldn't do that either. The taste of blood tingled across her tongue as she bit into her bottom lip. Job one of seven on the Red List, and an old man was fucking dead. The prick of tears stung her eyes.

In his fucking pyjamas!

The blues of the police cars flashed in the distance, and she slowed down. There's a fucking posse of them, she thought, taking the bends gently as her gaze darted ahead. Reaching a curve in the road hugged by trees, she slipped behind them and turned off the bike's lights. Jumping off, she removed the helmet – her dark auburn hair dropping to her shoulders. A deep breath. The blue strobing lights flashed past. It was more than a posse. There were too many to count. Marked and unmarked. What the hell had the gunman been thinking? Who the fuck would shoot a Scotland Yard big-nob?

Checking her watch, she noted the time. It would be an hour before she'd get back to London. An hour on the road with the image of the old man walking towards the gun, wanting to be shot. Her mind played back the tinny echo of the gunshot.

Despite knowing she shouldn't, she lit a cigarette and leant back on the breast of the Triumph. The smoke spiralled upwards. What was she now? A witness to the murder or the main suspect?

George hadn't told her who the client was or what was in the envelope. He hadn't even told her who the job either – his name. But she knew it. She knew the name of every job she had done or planned to do. She'd known Sidney Knight's name since the first time George had told her about the Red List. She'd researched every one of the seven – curious. And after the research, she'd been into their houses and nosed around. What did they have? What made them untouchable?

She flicked ash into the dirt. Over the past few weeks, George had changed – become quieter, more thoughtful. His mood was gloomy, distracted. Burying the cigarette butt deep into the ground, she turned and straddled the motorbike, sliding the helmet back on. At least George would be pleased she'd done *exactly* what his client had requested. He hadn't wanted anything else from the job – just one specific envelope, and she'd followed the strict orders – not to be tempted to steal anything else.

As she pulled out into the country lane, her senses recalled the smell of the old man. Tree shadows played in the dawn's light – whizzing in the distance. She'd recognised that smell as soon as she'd snuck over the threshold. Cancer. The house harboured the fucked-up poison but didn't hide it. The smell had saturated the air like the leech that it was. Fuck the speed limit.

Harley whacked open the throttle and let the sound of her bike boom behind her.

CHAPTER 3

St Albans

SHE knew what they were doing inside as she sat in the police car outside the St Albans house, waiting for her siblings Zeb and Rosa. They were due within the hour, and she didn't want to leave, but Angus had said they needed to speak before the police took statements – before her brother and sister arrived on the scene – it was her father's wish. His wish. But what did that mean?

The ball in Emily Knight's stomach knotted tightly as the restlessness in her legs became too much to bear. She slowly got out of the car, breathing a deep breath that refused to feed her constricted lungs. Out of habit, she ran her fingers over the light sweater that warmed her from the late evening breeze and straightened the crumples in her linen trousers. Dark long strands of hair fell loosely over her face, and she brushed them back – wet from tears. Her gaze searched into the gathering of police, both uniformed and plain-clothed, to find the Detective Inspector. She resisted the urge to cross the police tape that created a barrier between her and the house – their family home for over twenty years. The barrier between her and her father. Her father. He was in there, without her, alone. Blue lights bounced their flash against the sandy-coloured bricks and reflected on the windows: on the skin of strangers all congregating before the house that was now a stranger too. Their home. He was in there. Alone. The knotted ball in her stomach tightened.

Emily knew what was going on, what it looked like inside. She knew how his body would be slumped and examined, how men and women would be leaning over him: flashbulbs zapping and paper-white forensic feet. The colour drained from her olive skin, and her hand reached out to the cool metal of the police car, her fingers pressing against it.

'I need to speak with the DI,' she said quietly to the young female officer.

The PC crossed the blue-white plastic line and spoke to the middle-aged DI, who left the cluster of suited men. She moved her way through the jumble of uniforms, all standing around with no real purpose … except to be at the murder scene of a retired Deputy

Commissioner of Scotland Yard.

Emily didn't wait for the DI to reach her before she said, 'I wondered if I can be taken to the Fox & Hounds. My godfather's just arrived.'

The DI brushed a strand of red hair away from her sweaty face. 'Of course, Miss Knight. PC Morrison will drive you and wait for as long as you need her.'

Fox & Hounds

Through the car window, Emily watched the orange streetlights whizz past in a haze of sunset colours, blurred by the heat of the evening sky. Blowing a slow, deep breath from her lips, she closed her eyes, the tears shining on her thick black lashes. Her mind turned to her father. It can't be true. Someone would tap her shoulder soon and tell her it was a mistake – he wasn't dead.

When the police car pulled up outside the pub, she rubbed her sweater sleeve across her face and sniffed it in … the emotion that was silently taking over.

'You look better than I expected.' Angus kissed her cheek.

Feeling smaller than she'd ever felt, she sat down opposite him. 'I have a police officer waiting for me outside, and Rosa and Zeb are due to arrive soon.'

'Then we must be quick.' His long, knobbly fingers quietly drummed the top of the table as he leant forward. Lamplight shadowed his carved, sharp face. Finally, he whispered, 'You need to go to the drawer in his desk, Emily – not the one everyone knows about, but the one hidden under that one. There should be an envelope with your name on it. Everything you need to know is in there.'

Acidic bile burnt the back of her throat; her voice barely audible as she asked, 'What the hell is going on?'

'There are things I can't tell you because there are things only your father knew.' His hands reached across the dark wooden table and entwined gently into hers. 'I'm sorry, Emily, I really am. I wish I could have helped him, but I only knew what he needed me to know. My job now is to help you.'

'I don't understand. Why would anyone want to kill a man who was already dying?' She waited to hear his response, but none came.

Her gaze studied him – her godfather, one of her father's most trusted friends, as well as his solicitor – and yet he had nothing to say. He had nothing to say. Her fingers withdrew from his.

How was she going to manage without her father now? First her mother and now her father. She was expecting him to leave her soon, too soon, but not like this. Not with a bullet in his heart. That's what she'd said, the DI, a gunshot wound to his heart. Emily wasn't ready. Wasn't prepared. The doctors had given him a few more weeks, maybe months. That would have got them through the summer at least, possibly even to Christmas. Maybe. She'd hoped for one last Christmas with him. Time with all the family together. Time to say all the things she wanted to say.

Her gaze stayed on the man opposite her. Yet, he had nothing to say after seventy years of friendship with her father. She knew there were so many questions she needed to ask him, but they didn't come. Her brain and mouth had disconnected.

CHAPTER 4

East Ham: Nelson Street, The Primrose Estate

'WHAT'S she gonna do with a bloody law degree! Ain't like she's got the brains to be a lawyer.'

'The girl needs to go, Debra. She can't be under your feet for the rest of your life.'

Joanna glanced up from under her fringe at her mother, trying desperately to hide her face. She'd been waiting for months to hear whether she'd been accepted.

Her uncle watched as Debra reached for the packet of fags and continued. 'You're probably right,' he agreed, 'but at least she won't be hanging around the house all the time, and you know what, she'll probably get a student loan every year, which can help with your bills.'

Hiding her smile, Joanna's head hung even lower. If anyone could talk money with her mother, it was her uncle.

Debra Evans grunted, lit the fag, and plucked a piece of tobacco off her thinning pale-pink lips. Peppered grey hair, spilling out of the loose bun it was tied in, tumbled down over her cheeks. She turned to her daughter. 'If it was up to me, I'd have you working more bloody hours.'

'It's a lump sum.' Joanna's uncle said quickly.

'How much?'

'I don't know without checking, but around £15,000.'

Joanna waited. She waited for the information to sink in, for it to dart around in her mother's brain and for her to work out how she could spend it: how much drink she could buy, how many bets she could place, how long it would last. Debra exhaled a rattling chesty cough before taking a slug of vodka. For someone who drank constantly and smoked so much, her skin looked as creamy as a glass of milk. Tall and slender, she leant back in the chair as her light blue eyes set coldly on her daughter's.

'You need to pay your keep with that money, d'you hear me?' Joanna nodded. 'And I don't want you coming back here full of yourself, not like your shit of a father.' The girl nodded again. 'Now piss off. Me and your uncle have things we need to talk about.'

Closing the door behind her, Joanna heard her mother's voice turn down to a hushed low as she asked whether there was any more news. Although the girl wanted to press her ear to the door and listen, she couldn't help but bounce up the stairs grinning. *Finally*. For a few extra hours every day, she could escape. With university and her job at the local pub, she would never be at home when her mother was. And she'd never had to be around the consistent smell of cigarettes, fried food, and cheap body spray. Something lifted in the girl's spirits. Freedom. The air in her lungs moved with ease, and the heaviness in her limbs started to dissolve.

Joanna flung open the bedroom door and threw herself onto the bed. Underneath the frame, hidden, were all the books she'd been secretly buying over the past six months. She'd stashed pens, paper, notebooks, textbooks, a red pencil case, and best of all, a second-hand law dictionary. Hanging over the side of the mattress, she pulled it out and unwrapped it from the jumper that hid its existence. Her nose pressed against the old leather binding – the smell of all its years breathing into her soul.

Lying on her bed, facing the old glow-in-the-dark stars on the ceiling, Joanna let the smile come. Maybe she'd make some friends – ones that her mother wouldn't bitch about. Maybe, she thought, just maybe, she would meet someone who wouldn't think she was odd. She wished she already knew someone like that, someone to share the news with that she'd been accepted at university. She wanted someone to know, someone to tell her they were proud of her.

Reaching for her next favourite book, the one she loved and hated, she rolled onto her stomach and stared at the picture of the author on the back. Professor Emily Knight – beautiful, composed – elegant. Joanna had studied her repeatedly: one of the best barristers in the country – admired and respected. Now she'd be a student in her class. Her mother didn't know it, but her uncle did. He'd helped her choose which university to go to, helped her with the application, and used a friend in the admissions department to get her application through each part of the process.

Opening the book, its pages already worn, she started at the beginning – again.

CHAPTER 5

Oxford: Richard Seal's Residence

WOULD this be the job to excite her again? She sighed and breathed in, adjusting the boob-flattening strapping designed to disguise her. Everything she wore, every tool she used, was made to specification – made for precision. With a final calming breath, she pulled on her leather gloves and shot out from the dark hollow into the surrounding shadows of the trees. As she ran, she thought about her last job and the old man. The police hadn't reported two intruders in the house that night; was she in the clear?

In the darkness of the night, only the glistening of her green eyes could be seen beneath the balaclava. There were no streetlights around her, no moon to catch her shadow as she charged towards the garden wall and jumped, her strong hands grabbing the top as one foot pressed hard into the moss-covered bricks. The toe of her pump crunched against the wall as she vaulted over it onto the cushion of a well-manicured lawn. Jesus, she thought, as her knees crunched a little with pain. She was getting too old for this shit.

Within seconds, she was running again towards the house, its imposing silhouette casting an inky shadow. A window at the top was slightly open, as she knew it would be. Between the study and master bedroom, at opposite ends of the house, a spaniel slept in the kitchen – more effective than any alarm she had ever encountered. Her stomach turned slightly. It didn't matter how many times she staked a place out, there was always room for error, especially when dogs were involved. Everyone seemed to have dogs these days, she thought, except her. She missed that bond. That friendship. Maybe, when she retired, she could get one.

Harley Smith smiled to herself at the thought, calmed her breath, and focused her attention on the alarm's bell-box fitted to the wall above the window she needed to enter. Running up the height of the house was an old cast-iron drainpipe; she wobbled it to check it could take her weight and pulled her body up, wrapping her soft pumps against the cold cast iron as she moulded the shape of her feet around its curves. Winding, she pulled herself upwards. A weave of sweat traced down the back of her neck – she liked it – wanting it all over her body just like the old days.

Reaching the top, she roped herself to the pipe's brackets and released her hands to work on the alarm. With finely gloved fingers and a fine wire-cutter, she flipped off the white plastic bell-box cover and snipped through the coloured strands, wishing for something that would test her skills – something that would excite her.

With everything back in her knapsack, she curled like a snake in its slither, twisting herself over the window ledge and slowly through the open space. Landing feet first onto the dense weave of the carpet, she lowered into a pouncing position, listening. Nothing. Harley's eyes scanned the shapes hidden in the shadows, allowing herself a moment to map the study in her mind, to compare it to Ben's detailed diagram but most all, to her own memories from years ago, when she had secretly visited number two on the Red List – Robert Seal – Dean of Oxford University.

With light silent steps on the thick carpet, she morphed into a dark outline – a phantom. Tapping her fingers along a wooden desk, she listened to the echoes until they turned to a dull thud. She bent her knees to the floor. Why do they all think a safe is safe? People like her knew the truth … nothing was ever protected. Even her safe, hidden in the rafters of her bathroom ceiling – buried above the light fitting – was as vulnerable as any other to a thief with knowledge.

Closing her eyes, she held her breath and listened to the nuances of the dial's clicks. The more it had been turned over the years, the easier it was to hear the gentle sounds of its combination.

A deep and distant grumble from downstairs broke the silence as metal clanked against metal, ringing an echo into the night's stillness. Harley paused. Seconds passed. Then a minute. Another noise. A heavy sigh and a thud in the kitchen below – the dog midnight snacking.

Her fingers methodically began again, and the safe door released. Inside, the velvet pouches, boxes full of individual jewels, and money held in money clips touched the tips of her fingers. She knew the contours of treasures as if they were part of her body. Systematically, each item went into her knapsack. Underneath it all, a flash of cream caught her eye. The envelope George's client wanted. Unassuming. Casually tossed beneath the thousands of pounds worth of jewels. Just like the one at Sidney Knight's house. Plain, A4, cream. But not one bought from just any kind of stationery shop – this type was familiar to her. She knew the quality, knew the make because she used the same herself. Fighting the impulse to slit it open and peek inside, Harley slid it into the knapsack.

Back at the window, she glanced behind her, making sure she'd left nothing behind. Her body slid like a light breeze over the windowsill, gliding down the drainpipe. Within minutes, she was running again. Sweat trickled over her skin under her black clothing as she weaved between the trees, her breathing fast yet controlled. Every inch of her skin stuck to her clothes as she hurled herself back over the garden wall and ran to the bike hidden in the bushes. Another one done, she thought, and no one had died.

Tarmac whizzed under the broad wheels of the Triumph, beaming little blasts of reflections from the cats' eyes. Navigating the country lanes, she drove for over an hour, constantly checking the empty reflection in her mirrors.

Thoughts tumbled through her mind as the engine purred its rhythmical hum. The Red List – seven untouchable names. A spark of electricity ignited in her stomach – a slight fizz in her veins. They were suddenly allowed, her and Ben, to hit the names on it, which meant something was going on that George wasn't telling them. Things were about to get interesting, she thought. Life wasn't just about stealing and selling or making money. Even if going through the motions was just the same, at least there was a different reason for the jobs. And how much money did she even need? She had so much in her safe and different bank accounts that she didn't know what she was worth. If she wasn't doing it for the money anymore, what reason did she have? She sighed beneath the helmet.

And then there was Sidney Knight. Number one on the Red List. The image of him still lingered in her head. The news had covered nothing else the next day: Sidney Knight, retired Deputy Commissioner of Scotland Yard, murdered while undergoing chemo for prostate cancer. She'd known that – the cancer thing – but she hadn't known how seeing him walk to his own death would continue to vibrate its image in her mind when she least expected it.

But the news still hadn't reported that there were two intruders that night or that he'd purposely walked into the gun. It hadn't reported anything stolen because the police wouldn't have known about the envelope she'd taken. Perhaps his family didn't either. Harley's stomach turned. Were the police looking for her? Just her? They had no idea she wasn't the gunman – how could they? She was many things, but a killer wasn't one of them. And if nothing else but the envelope had been stolen, what the hell was the gunman there for?

Around 2.00 a.m., she pulled into a private parking bay at Westminster. Tony, the night concierge, shot up off his chair as she entered the building. He smiled. 'Miss Harley, did you have a good night?'

'Good to be home, Tony,' she replied. Normally she loved chatting to him, but if she engaged, she'd be trapped. Pressing the glowing blue button for the lift, she closed her eyes, longing for sleep.

'It's been rather quiet here tonight,' he said. 'But Miss Davies arrived about ten minutes ago, so I let her in.'

The lift clunked its doors open and with a clenched jaw, Harley entered its small space. Waiting for it to deliver her to the tenth floor, she thought of Aimee being there, making her jaw clench even harder.

Before she could put the key in its lock, Aimee opened the door wearing a dark-blue lace bra that pushed her breasts into a rounded cleavage, rising and falling with her breath. A glimmer of sweat beaded on her supple-tanned skin. As she leant on the edge of the doorframe, her hair fell over her angular shoulders like a torrent of silvery gold, shimmering under the lights reflected in the corridor's mirrors. She whispered, 'I need fucking.'

Harley sighed and shoved past her, through the entrance hall and into the lounge. Throwing her helmet on the sofa, she slumped down next to it – the knapsack still on her back. 'What are you doing here?'

'I thought you'd like fucking after the job.'

'Really? I wasn't expecting you. What's wrong?'

'Nothing. Why? Does something look wrong?'

Lighting a cigarette, Harley glanced up at the tall half-naked woman standing before her – her lean limbs caressed by the subtle shadows of the lamps. Despite Aimee's soft, athletic beauty, Harley didn't feel like fucking. In fact, it was the last thing on her mind; she needed to speak to Ben.

'I'm shattered. Go to bed, and I'll be in soon.'

★

A sleepy voice mumbled, 'Jesus, it's nearly bloody three in the morning.'

'I've got it,' Harley whispered.

'Where are you? You sound like you're under water.'

'The bathroom. Your sister turned up.'

'She's always turning up.' Ben yawned. 'You okay?'

'Yeah, just buzzing a bit to be doing over another name on the Red List.'

'I know, it doesn't feel right, does it.'

'Has George said why yet?'

'Nope, just that it's what the client wants.'

'Don't you think it's odd that Sidney Knight was murdered the same night I was there?'

Ben sighed. 'D'you want me to come over?'

'No.'

'Then *what*?'

'I don't know… I just needed to hear your voice.'

Westminster

The view of Westminster didn't hold her attention as she paced before the closed doors to the balcony. Usually, it brought peace in its quietness while the world slept – stillness in its beauty.

The post-job buzz bubbling in her mind mixed with the vision of the old man again, his pyjamas turning red and the sound of his body thumping to the floor as he fell. The Red List. He'd been at the top of it – number one – and yet, the night she was instructed to do his place over was the night someone else had held a gun to his face. Harley stopped and stared through the window at the London lights. It made no sense, she thought. If the gunman had just wanted Sidney dead, he would have shot him immediately. She leant her head against the cool glass as she looked at the view. Did the gunman want the envelope? Her brain ticked over. If it was the envelope, then they didn't know what George knew – where it was. 'But they came for something,' she whispered to herself. 'And they didn't get it.'

George had never told her much about the Red List, yet she knew the names on it by heart. When she'd broken into all their homes years ago, it was out of interest, belligerence – rebellion. She'd been young and hadn't paid much attention to what she found – or hadn't. And she'd just assumed that the names on the list were George's friends, but they weren't. 'No,' she mumbled to herself. There was no way a man like George, coming from a working-class estate in East Ham, and doing what he did, would get to know some of the highbrow men on it – an accountant, a Dean at Oxford University, and even the Director General Nuclear. George probably had more money than most of them would ever see, but that didn't make him *their* kind of man. More importantly, it didn't make them *his* kind of men.

As she moved away from the window, her gaze scanned the rows of neatly lined bookshelves, looking for something to shut down her mind – something she had read so many times that she didn't need to concentrate – didn't need to read. She needed something she could just scan the words of until her eyes closed. Plucking out Nelson Mandela's biography, she quickly turned the well-read pages. Her mother had always said she needed to slow down and would never learn if she read so fast. Yet Harley would spend her pocket money on more books every week – books her mother had never heard of. Turning the page, she heard her mother's words drift into her memory.

'You'll go blind if you keep reading under there,' her mother said as the glow of the torch lit up under the duvet. It was her voice that Harley missed the most – soft and melodic. Gentle. When her mother said her name, it was like the safest pair of arms. If her mother smiled when she said it, everything in the world was right: she didn't need to feel scared. Her voice … the words of the book drifted into a haze of printed fogginess as Harley's mind glided towards her mother singing: she couldn't sing like an angel, but it was still beautiful, and music always filled their home. As Harley's eyes closed, she floated weightlessly and melted into the softness of the sofa.

'What are you reading today, darling?'

Harley looked up at her mother. 'Nelson Mandela. He was released from prison on my seventh birthday. Did you know that?'

Smiling down at her daughter, Elizabeth replied. 'I did, and you still are seven.'

'Actually, I'm seven and 364 days. So that means he's been released for 364 days. I wonder if he's getting used to being out of prison. What do you think, Mummy?'

'I think you need to rest that wonderful brain of yours and get some fresh air. Come on, up you get. You can take Flint out for a walk while you're about it.

CHAPTER 6

St Albans

SHE shouldn't be there, in her father's once forbidden study – in the leather chair moulded to his shape, not hers. Emily sighed. *She shouldn't be there.*

The cream A4 envelope and the key her godfather, Angus, had told her to find, lay on the desk before her. The secret drawer. How long had he needed such a place? Nausea stretched its tentacles up from her stomach into her throat, which ached as she tried to swallow. Placing everything else to one side, she stared at the envelope addressed to just her – then smelt it. There was no lingering scent of him, but he'd touched it with the hands she adored – the beautiful hands she loved.

The acid in her stomach gurgled as she tried to fight the tears pricking their daggers in her eyes. It was in his writing – her name. Her name. 'The last time,' she whispered and plucked her father's gold engraved letter-opener from the pen-pot to slice the envelope's creased seam. Slowly, her fingers pulled out the papers.

For the first two weeks after he'd been murdered, she'd been fighting to get through the police line into the house, to the desk. But her fight had weakened. There was nothing she wanted to fight for anymore. The only thing she wanted was to stay in her pyjamas all day, every day, and under the duvet. Food hadn't tasted like food. Alcohol had left her even heavier. Even cleaning her teeth had been too much effort some days, and although Emily couldn't ever admit it to her friends, there were days when she didn't clean them – or herself.

The days had made her eyes puffy. The nights had made her head ache in the mornings. The pit of her stomach never seemed to settle or ease – like a plague of shitty little bugs constantly gnawing at her insides. And when all that was happening, she couldn't catch her breath either. The oxygen was going in, but it wasn't doing anything while it was in there. His funeral hadn't helped – it was a lie that it would bring closure: whoever said such a thing had never been to one. All it brought was more exhaustion, having to play hostess to all the upset relatives, friends, and hangers-on who revelled in their grief. And then there was the after-grief. The real grief. The kind of grief that no one ever expects or can explain, that doesn't have a solid form. It doesn't have a pattern, a rhythm, or any kind of logic to it. It's the emotion that attacks from behind when no one is looking. Emily never knew when it would come. It didn't creep up on her. Instead, it was like a smack to the back of her head that made her burst into tears as she made a coffee, poured a whisky, or did something completely irrelevant and unconnected to the loss of her father.

Life had stopped until Zeb, her brother, intervened and dragged her to the mirror, showing her how thin she'd become.

'You look shit,' he'd said, and she believed him. But he didn't know what she knew. Did she know anything? Emily sighed. Maybe she should just tell him. Maybe she should just hand the letter over to the police. But she couldn't. It was time to get a grip, crack on, and deal with the envelope her father had left her.

Hearing her father's live-in housekeeper, Agi, pottering in the kitchen, Emily unfolded the two sheets of paper. Tears hung in the corners of her eyes. His writing. Ever since she'd been old enough to read, he'd always written her little notes, and now, in his usual style, he started the letter with My Dearest Darling Emily. The tears dripped.

His words ran neatly across the page. One line after another as she read them over and over, taking none of them in. How could she concentrate? How could he be gone? Emily exhaled a slow, trembling breath, wiped her nose, and tried to read the letter again.

My Dearest Darling Emily,

Before you begin to read further, I want you to know that I am prouder of you than you can imagine. I only hope that after reading my words, you can somehow maintain a sense of pride in me also, for all the good I did and not the mistakes I have made. There have been many. It has taken me several attempts to write these words because I do not underestimate the enormity of what will inevitably be your disappointment in me. These are the hardest words of my life, which has now ended.

I cannot write about the things I have done or the situation I found myself in. To do this would be against all my understanding of how written words can be traced, tracked, and used. So, trust in me this final time, Emily, and know I never intended to leave such a complicated trail or woven mess for you to unravel. I say you *because I know that I cannot ask Rosa or Zeb to untangle this. They are more than capable, but the outcome would not be one I wish for you all.*

You will discover things about me you never knew. They will go against everything I taught you and will be things that make you question everything you thought you knew. At some stage, I know you will even question yourself and resent me for the burden I am about to place on you. Through this, do not stop until you find the truth. It is only this that will enable you, I hope, to forgive me.

With these words, I include a key. I cannot put in writing what it opens, but I know you will work it out if you can remember the long summer evenings when we used to sit and study together for your bar exams. Do you remember them, Emily? Long nights fuelled with whisky and idealised debates on the morals and ethics of what law meant to us both. When you find the truth, you will know what to do. I wish I could tell you more, but this isn't the right time, nor the right way. Forgive me.

It is time for me to say goodbye. I have written these words so many times. Long paragraphs recounting my love for you, Rosa, and Zeb, but none can encapsulate the joy and love you have all brought to my life. Know that I will never leave you entirely and that I carry you all with me, as I hope you will, me.

You must speak with Thomas, Emily and do not go to the police.

Forever your proud and loving father,

Dad

Her fingers trembled as her heartbeat thumped under her skin. With his instructions branded into her memory, she slipped the key into her jacket pocket and left his study. It was time to head back to London. Students would arrive in under twenty-four hours, and she needed to sort herself out.

Throwing her bag onto the desk, she glanced around her office before sitting on the familiar chair and staring at the lines of books filling one wall. Amongst them were some of her father's on police procedures, notorious cases he'd worked on, and guidance on evidence collection. His name glowed on them all, like a beacon drawing her eyes to look. Emily frowned as she stared at them.

Sighing, she leant her elbow on the arm of the chair, resting her cheek in the cup of her palm. Who was she going to talk to now? Who would understand the nuances of her day? Her hands ran across her trousers to smooth them down.

Sitting didn't help, so she stood, shaking out the irritation in her legs before walking over to the view from her window: the canal below. Murdered. That's what he was, she thought. Murdered. 'Why, Dad?' she whispered to herself. 'Why would anyone want to kill you now?'

Turning, she glanced at her desk. There was so much to do – so many things to think about. Summer had always been spent preparing for her law classes, researching for a new book, and enjoying time with her family at the house in St Albans, but she'd barely done any of it. Rosa and Zeb had withdrawn into themselves, and none of them wanted to be at the house without their father. If only she could see his hands again – watch them as they peeled carrots for a Sunday roast. How on earth could she feel anything less than pride for him?

The letter still meant nothing more than the words he'd written, the words she had read. He'd told her to talk to Thomas Crowe, his accountant, but Thomas was away on business. Waiting for him to come back was like waiting for a tooth to be pulled.

Emily looked down at the key her father had left her. What was she meant to do with it? And what if it revealed truths she didn't want to hear? The thump of her heart increased. And there'd been no clues in the house of where the key would fit; she'd hunted every crevice, been distracted by old photos, the smell of his clothes, memorabilia he'd stashed in shoe boxes at the back of the wardrobe. But nothing had caught her attention as something she would be ashamed of him for.

There were things between her father and mother that had never been discussed in front of them, but they knew, all three siblings, that bad things had happened. Rumours were whispered at school amongst the teachers, and there was a time when her mother's face was always red and patchy from crying. But Emily's memories were vague. As the youngest, she was more out of the loop than Rosa and Zeb, but she couldn't ask them – he'd told her not to.

A knock on her office door jolted through her body. She brushed the loose hair strands back from her face, ran a finger under the rim of her eyes and took a deep breath. 'It's open.'

The door squeaked on its hinge. 'I thought you might need a strong coffee and a doughnut.'

'You're too kind,' she said quietly. It didn't feel right, but she smiled as her friend and colleague, Ammon, handed her the hot cardboard cup.

CHAPTER 7

East Ham: The Eagle Inn

DIMLY lit, with dark wood and faux oil paintings on the walls, The Eagle Inn was George's local. She always found him there, with its dirty pink velvet stools framing the dark varnished bar cluttered with drip trays, ale pumps, and ice buckets. Growing up just around the corner, George had never left the area. Despite his wealth, he lived in the same house his parents had once rented and drank in the same pub, along with most other families from his childhood. It was a safe pub: everyone knew something about someone within it.

Just turned sixty, he was lightly tanned, slim but with an endearing little podge for a tummy. Despite this, he looked good for his age, with gentle wrinkles around his lips, light laughter lines circling his grey-blue eyes and a mop of silver hair so thick it stood up on its ends like an old Elvis quiff.

A smile spread inside Harley's body as she watched George, sitting in the corner cubicle, lean forward and say something to his son, Ben. When she sat beside him, his aftershave, mixed with the musky mead of his cigars, filled her heart with warmth.

'What's the urgency?' she asked.

George gave her one of the three glasses of whisky. 'Can't I call a meeting of my employees without a bloody reason?'

'You have delusions of grandeur, old man.' Ben grinned, his blonde hair flopping over his bright blue eyes – eyes that were identical to his sister's.

George sipped his drink before lowering his voice. 'I need you to do something, Love.'

East Ham: Park Avenue, The Primrose Estate

When she'd met George, she'd been high on cocaine, eighteen, and trying to steal his neighbour's car to earn cash for her habit. Stealing cars was easy money back then. She'd swap them for wraps filled with sparkling fine crystals.

It was around 2.30 in the morning. She was huddled over the driver's door with a wire coat hanger. A red Mitsubishi sportscar, shining under the moon as if it were the lights of a showroom. If she could steal it, she could score enough cocaine to last at least a couple of months. That's all she needed and wanted – to know that she had her next few lines to get her through. It wasn't like anyone cared.

With his head dipped but his gaze on the horizon, George had walked around the corner. For a moment, they both froze, but then he walked up to her and casually said, 'You won't get into that car with a coat hanger, Love. It's not some shitty Ford.' Staring at him – still high – she rammed the wire hanger in even deeper: he was right, her attempts were useless. She hissed a fuck and kicked the car with her heavy boot.

Holding out his hand, he said, 'Give it here.'

'Fuck you.' She ran the point of the hanger into the red of the car, causing a sharp gouge along its door.

'I'm not going to call the Old Bill, and I'm not going to kill you with it,' he said gently. Harley handed the hanger to him, watching as he bent it over several times until it was a small, wiry shape in the palm of his hand. He sighed. 'Listen, Love, being out here at this time of night ain't safe, and whatever you're on ain't safe either.' Watching her, he asked, 'What's your name?'

'Harley …' She stopped and smirked. 'I'm not that fucking off it.'

'And this is what you do, is it? Half-inch cars to feed your habit?' Rummaging into his pocket, he pulled out a scrappy piece of paper and pen, scribbled on it and handed it to her. 'Come and see me here tomorrow.' Without another word, he dipped his head again and walked towards a garden gate. Gone. Harley ran – away from George and away from her father's voice in her head, telling her she was a *fucking* waste of space.

The next day, she woke around 2.00 p.m., found the scrappy piece of paper screwed up next to the packet of cigarettes, and after two cups of coffee, left her bedsit to meet the weirdo. What did she have to lose?

East Ham: The Eagle Inn

'Love, are you listening?'

She smiled at him. 'I am. What is it? Another envelope job already?'

23

'Nope, although we've still got five more of those buggers to get. Nah, this is something urgent. Like Eddie Ranking urgent. Diamonds from Europe.'

'Europe.' The pitch of her voice rose as she spoke. 'Smuggling, for Ranking?'

'It's a one-off. We need your help.'

She chewed the inside of her bottom lip. Smuggling. If she got caught, she'd be locked up for years in a foreign jail; she could just as easily be killed as caught. 'Who's we?' she asked impatiently.

Ben ran a hand through his mop of blond hair. 'My sister fucked up.'

Harley's voice rose again. 'Aimee?' She glanced at George's face for confirmation and then back to Ben. 'What the hell has she done?'

'She did over Eddie Ranking's gaff, and he caught her.'

'When? *Jesus.* Eddie? Since when has Aimee been doing jobs?'

Ben sighed. 'She's not, not with us anyway. She's shit at them. But she's got some idea in her fucking head again that she should be part of the business. Stupid bloody cow.'

'But when? She's been at mine nearly every night lately!'

'The night you did the second envelope job.' Ben replied. 'Robert Seal's place.'

Harley looked at him. 'No, she was at mine when I got back. Don't you remember? I phoned you, and you asked why I sounded like I was under water when I was sitting in the bathroom.'

George interrupted. 'This ain't getting us nowhere. We've got to clear up the mess. We don't want shit coming at us from all sides right now.'

'What do you mean by that?' Harley asked.

'I mean, we've got to get these envelopes, and these ain't like normal jobs.' He sighed. 'Some of these places we're going into ain't exactly your usual run-of-the-mill gaffs.'

'You've got that right,' Ben mumbled beneath the palm of his hand as he rested his chin on it. 'Fuck knows why you've got us hitting the Red List after all these years.'

Harley glanced at Ben, then George. 'He has a point, George. And why can't Aimee do it herself? If I'm going to help, I want to know all the details.'

George rubbed his sun-wrinkled forehead and frowned. 'Ranking asked for you to pay the debt.'

'Me? But he doesn't even know me!'

Pulling a piece of paper from his pocket, George scribbled an address on it. 'It's going to take a while to sort out the plans, so for now, I need you focused on the envelopes. You'll need to go to this address when we're ready.'

CHAPTER 8

Westminster

'NEVER again,' she whispered in her head. The early morning sun streamed through the bare window into the lounge, shining across Harley's closed eyes. In the distance, an alarm echoed from the bedroom, waking her from the heaviness of sofa-sleep. In yesterday's clothes, she sat up – stretched – her body aching from the sleepy curl she'd been in for a couple of hours.

Rubbing her face, she yawned, stood up, groaned and stretched her slender limbs again before ambling into the bedroom. Damn noise. Her head banged, and her eyes felt like gritty shit.

Silver-gold hair tufted out beneath the duvet onto the pillow as Aimee slept, oblivious to the beeping racket of the alarm and the thud of its demise as Harley whacked it dead. She glanced down at the dozing woman, sighed, and headed for the shower. What on earth had she been thinking? How the hell could one girl be so stupid? Didn't Aimee know that Eddie Ranking was out of bounds? 'Of course she did,' Harley muttered as the steaming water rained down on her face.

To make things even worse than Aimee fucking over Ranking, the flutter in Harley's heart was tapping a storm under her ribs as she dried off and dressed in dark-blue jeans and a white shirt.

In the mirror, reflections of the sun seeped through the bedroom blinds behind her, catching on the dust particles floating like smoke trails against the whiteness of the crumpled sheets on the bed – and Aimee, who was finally stirring. Turning away from her reflection, Harley quietly exhaled. 'Do I look okay? Is my makeup too much? God. I don't even know why I'm doing this.' She sighed. 'Why the hell has George got me doing this?'

Stretching, Aimee's arms reached out from beneath the duvet – hands and fingers uncurling. Finding the dark wooden post of the bed, she let the stretch work every muscle of her body. Her voice was soft – sleepy. 'Babe, you look too good to go.' Slowly, her hands ruffled into her hair as she shifted from sleep into the day. 'Undo a button.' She yawned. 'You've got boobs worth showing off.'

Harley slipped on her mother's wedding ring before leaning over to kiss Aimee's smooth cheek, making the sleepy woman tremble. 'I need to talk to you about Eddie Ranking.' A residue of red lipstick lingered from the kiss, and with a gentle movement, Harley's thumb brushed it away.

'Do you have to go?' Aimee asked, sliding the duvet from her naked body. 'Come back to bed.' The length of her slender legs opened, and her hand slid between them. Finding herself, she trembled under her own touch. A tingling wave pulsed between Harley's legs as Aimee's fingers found her own wetness and pushed into it – a smooth glide into the warmth. Harley's senses spun with a rush that fed heat into her veins. 'Jesus, Aimee. I'm supposed to be talking to you about Eddie Ranking,' she said quietly.

The woman on the bed closed her eyes and immersed herself, tipping her head back against the cool white cotton sheets. The pleasure lengthened her neck into an arch, her body elongating as her free hand reached backwards, finding the pillow to grip. The slow rhythm of her fingers fucking made her breasts gently bounce with the movement: rounded and soft, with light pink nipples that stood hard and erect – beautifully formed in their youthful sway. The wetness glided onto her fingers as she moved them … slow then fast, towards an uninhibited fucking. Her body rode the penetration with careless expertise until Harley whispered 'fuck' and fell to her knees, yanking Aimee towards her and onto her tongue. There was a cry of pleasure in the otherwise silent room as Aimee clenched her entire body and then held still. With a gasp, she tensed, shuddered, grabbed Harley's hair, and slumped into a languishing heap.

★

East London: University

The air inside the lecture theatre was sour and spicy. Standing on the stage before a panel of academics stood a woman dressed in a black suit – her white shirt open just enough to reveal the dip of her cleavage. The line of her back was straight – stoic. Her hands clasped together before her lap as her gaze scanned the room.

Students talking in pockets of excitement slowly quietened. Harley glanced behind her, assessing the room as much as the woman on the stage. When she returned her gaze to the front, the woman was looking at her – impassively. The silence was broken by her voice: effortless and purposeful.

'This lecture started at precisely 10.00 a.m. It's now 10.12 a.m.

which means you took twelve minutes to calm yourselves and acknowledge our presence. If you feel this is acceptable behaviour, you will irritate every professor, every client, and every judge with the misfortune to teach you, instruct you, or hear your arguments in court.'

Harley's skin tingled.

Introducing herself as Professor Emily Knight, criminal law lecturer and Moot Mistress, she stood linear: a sculpture of impenetrable blackness. In that hour, before 252 students, her hands stayed locked in their position. Harley examined every inch of her, noting how the Professor stood so still when she herself had trained for years to control every movement. With the stillness came a steadfast intention, as if the Professor had memorised a list of bullet points and nothing could deter her from its delivery. Every question Harley had in her mind disappeared as the woman methodically went through one topic after another.

The outline of the Professor's shape beneath the light drifting through the high windows drew Harley's attention too. Impressive. Toned. Slender, yet full of curves beneath the tightness of the shirt. Tightness. It wasn't what Harley expected: a contradiction from the woman who stood so guarded – a contradiction from the woman Harley had researched and read all about.

'For those who are my tutees, I'll be in my office until 16.45. You must see me by this time and no later.'

The Professor left the stage and exited through the heavy double doors that creaked as they swung back and forth after she'd gone. Harley turned her head back to the front of the lecture hall and closed her eyes for a few seconds – the whisky from the night before still flowing through her veins. There were another two hours of induction ahead, and the new speaker's words floated distantly into her ears. Her head dipped forward, the weight inside plunging to her forehead. Her eyes rolled – she was gone.

A hand on her arm jerked her awake. She could barely shake herself into consciousness as slender, pale fingers slid a packet of sweets along the lecture bench towards her. Instinctively, she took one, but the sugary sourness hit the back of her throat, and she stifled a sharp choke of a cough. Glancing to her left as her eyes streamed, Harley saw a pale, pretty face with a soft smile. She half-smiled back as finally, she heard the Dean of the Law School close the induction session.

Ecstatic to escape, she grabbed her things and rushed through the doors, down the echoing corridor and into the cooling air. Why the hell had she agreed to George's suggestion of doing a law degree? Dashing through the crowds of students, Harley headed towards the canal that ran through campus. All she wanted was a quiet place to smoke, a place for her brain to recover from all the information thrown at it.

Lighting a cigarette, she sat on the bench and stretched her legs. A moment to herself. No George. No Ben. No Aimee. No one asking her to do something – be something.

The lecture theatre had been airless and muggy, but she knew it wasn't that making her chest tight. Sometimes, she didn't feel like she could breathe. The irony, she thought, as she inhaled the nicotine and blew its smoke into the air. *But it wasn't that.* She gazed down at the neon-green water covered in moss and full of discarded student indulgences from beer and cider bottles, kebab wrappers and sandwich cartons. *No, it wasn't that.* It was something deeper inside that she couldn't quite grasp, but whatever it was, it made her lungs feel shallow and her chest tight. Was she always going to be a thief? She sighed. Was she always going to be with Aimee? Harley shifted further back on the bench. Wasn't it time to be someone else? To be the woman her mother had wanted her to be.

'Hey.'

Interrupted, Harley frowned a little and glanced up. The girl standing before her was in her early twenties with faded blue jeans, a red coat and a thick red woollen jumper covering her slim body. Her bag and shoes matched red too, and around her neck was a red scarf. Strands of light blonde curly hair tumbled around her face, loose from a ponytail. 'Hey,' Harley replied. 'Sorry, I rushed out without saying thank you for the sweets. I was desperate to get some air.'

'Air? Here?' The girl smiled and sat down. 'I'm Joanna.'

'Harley.'

Joanna wrapped her hands into the cuffs of the jumper that poked out from the sleeves of her coat, and then she began to babble about how she'd decided to study law, thanks to her uncle, who'd encouraged and helped her. She giggled as she babbled – at things Harley wasn't sure would be funny even if they were delivered differently. She watched the girl's hands constantly twiddle at the jumper's cuff ends and how they never stopped twiddling while she was talking. Harley usually avoided such a person, but there was something different about her: simplicity and vulnerability. Or maybe there was something familiar about her: reassuring, with an accent so similar to George's and Ben's that she could almost hear them in the conversation. Whatever it was, Harley agreed to meet the next morning for a coffee before checking her watch and muttering 'shit.'

★

Muffled voices came from Professor Knight's office as Harley sat outside on a worn leather chair. It was 16.30 exactly: she'd made it. The frayed seam of the chair's arm snagged under her fingertips as she waited, yawning.

Her eyes closed for a moment. Diamond smuggling for Eddie Ranking wasn't exactly the excitement she was looking for in her life. There'd be no question about doing it if it was a straight smuggle for George – but Eddie Ranking – he was a cheap shit of a thug.

Weightlessness floated over Harley's body, and her fingers stopped fiddling with the chair's worn threads.

'Don't be late, Emily.' The strong Middle Eastern accent made Harley's eyelids spring open. The man lingering in the Professor's doorway was the same man that had been sitting behind her in the lecture theatre. The Professor affectionately smiled at him before turning her gaze to Harley. The expression changed.

With glasses perched on the top of her head, the Professor asked. 'Are you here to see me or to sleep?'

Harley shot up from the chair, her bag falling off her lap and to the floor. 'You,' she replied, quickly picking up her bag and following the Professor into the office.

Trying to bring her brain back into the immediate world, she scanned the room's content. She liked it; neat rows of organised books and a random collection of artworks with a print of the suffragettes taking main stage. And the office smelt lovely – fresh air and perfume.

The Professor, composed and measured, indicated with her hand where Harley must sit. She wanted to smile because every fence she met, every forger, bent copper, and money launderer had the same air of aloofness to them. It was like they were walking in the shoes of someone they thought they should be. But she's not pretending, Harley thought, as she did as she was told and sat in a chair where hundreds of students had sat before her. A little buzz fizzed in her blood.

Taking a silent deep breath, her gaze followed the woman who moved to a large oak desk in the corner of the room. As the Professor sat down, their eyes finally met. Knight's were dark, the kind of darkness seen only in a night sky, where even stars couldn't pierce through the blackness.

Wanting to speak, Harley waited – letting Professor Knight's silence command the room. In the silence, her mind wandered to the next job she'd planned with Ben and how they would find the time to train if she was inundated with homework.

'Your name?' the Professor asked with the kind of accent Harley expected from someone so educated. The woman's eyes locked them together with an invisible thread of steel – pulling Harley into the depth of their darkness. She fidgeted in the chair, pulling her hair round to her right shoulder. The Professor's eyes were so dark that the pupils merged into the irises. It wasn't just the darkness that was unsettling; it was their concentrated intensity.

'Harley,' she said. 'Harley Smith.'

'You're one of my academic advisees, Miss Smith, so I will see you every two weeks. I've studied your timetable and slotted you in at 17.30 every other Friday. I expect you to be here, on time, and not half-asleep as you were outside just a minute ago. I have a busy schedule, and you need to give me twenty-four hours' notice if you can't make it. I don't accept excuses such as headaches or period pains as a reason for your absence. Do you understand?'

Harley nodded.

'I will discuss how you are progressing in your studies and any concerns regarding your workload. I won't engage in conversations about your personal problems, such as husbands, wives, boyfriends, or girlfriends. If you need that kind of assistance, we have a counsellor on campus trained in such matters. Do you understand?'

She nodded again as Knight's eyes remained as indifferent as two lumps of coal on a snowman.

'I expect all my tutees to work hard and maintain a high level of commitment to their chosen profession. In return, it's my job to ensure you complete your degree. If you struggle, I'll push you harder. Do you have any questions?'

There had been many questions in Harley's mind, but she shook her head. Knight stood up – the conversation over.

CHAPTER 9

East London: University

EMILY sighed. The first day had been more difficult than she'd expected. Drawing her scarf tighter around her neck, she tucked it into her black winter coat and pushed through the swing doors that opened onto the busy London street, lined with fried chicken shops and dirty poster-covered windows. On the main road running through the East End, sirens screamed as they always did. She stopped at the top of the Law School's steps, glancing at the passers-by on their way towards their Friday nights and the weekend.

For the first time in her career, her mind wasn't in the same room as the young minds who needed it to be. The day had been heavy and painfully drawn-out. Her clock-watching had become the enemy, and she was tired. Tucking her hands into her pockets, she moved into the flow of pedestrian traffic, her step heavier than usual.

Islington: The Wine Rooms

Leaving Angel tube station, Emily's gaze scanned all the faces, and then she smiled. There he is, she thought, as a man walked towards her, his short arms outstretched and ready for an embrace. After squeezing her tightly, Thomas Crowe stepped back and pressed his tubby hands onto her shoulders as he smiled back. 'You look as lovely as ever.'

'And you must be in love to say such a thing.' Emily slipped her hand into his. It was soft and plump – never a day of manual work to coarsen it. Accountancy suited him. 'I've been waiting for weeks to finally have you back in the country. So, where are you taking me this evening, Mr Crowe?'

Together, they walked arm-in-arm as Thomas guided them through the Friday night rush-hour crowds. He steered Emily down a side street to a tall Victorian townhouse and its plain grey front door with a silver lion-head knocker. He tapped, and the door opened. Inside was a rustic wooden bar surrounded by old sand-engraved mirrors sparkling with fairy lights. Small reflections bounced from wall to wall, and candles floated within decadent glass lampshades hanging upside down and cascading from the ceiling. Small, intimate tables made from driftwood furnished the space, each with its own flickering candle that reflected further against all the glass and mirrors.

Thomas led Emily to a secluded corner table where a Pinot Grigio was already submerged in ice. The gentleman that he was, he eased her out of her coat, pulled out her chair and waited for her to sit before he, too, made himself comfortable.

'You look stunning tonight, Emily,' he said gently.

'I can't concede to feeling it at the moment.'

'I can see your tiredness, but that could never take away your beauty. In fact, I think it just adds to it.' His fingertips touched against hers, and she felt his warmth radiate onto her skin. 'Do you know how much I love you?'

'I do,' she replied quietly. 'And I love you more than any man I know, except my father.'

Sadness crept across his little round face – still tanned from his recent trip to Spain. Despite all his money, his teeth were cigar-stained and crooked, his lips plump and fleshy. 'And your brother and Ammon, which makes me fourth on the list.'

Emily rolled her eyes. 'You know what I mean. Don't be such a diva.'

'That's my job … to be your diva. What else am I good for? I'm just an old queen these days.'

'Well, you're my old queen. And besides, I know that look, you're in love or lust. Come on, who is he?'

Thomas laughed and beckoned the waiter with a click of his chubby fingers adorned with a heavy gold ring embossed with a coat of arms. 'Let's eat first.'

As they waited for their food, she listened to him recount the story of how he'd met his new lover, how gorgeous the young man's body was, how he'd danced like he was in his twenties again, and how his fat old body was wilting under the strains of such a hedonistic lapse in his sense of responsibility. Emily smiled affectionately. She loved Thomas and his sense of freedom and fun, but he was right, his body was wilting. The glow had gone from his hazel eyes, despite his current lust-interest, and his face, once plump but taut, was flabby and bloated. Even his hair, once a silver crowning mop, was nearly all gone.

But she loved him and how he never took life seriously, even though he was one of the most intelligent men she had ever met, except for her father. He might not be her godfather like Angus, but he'd been part of her life for just as long and one of her father's most trusted friends, as well as his accountant.

Yet, her brain fuzzed over despite his usual animation and embellished storytelling that normally had her fixated with anticipation.

Thomas's face hovered before her as she drifted to another place and the memories of her father. Memories of the last summer in their old house before her parents bought the new family home in St Albans. Before then, they'd had vibrant summers of barbecues and parties where all her father's friends joined them every weekend, sharing the joy of playing swing-ball or football with the children. Buckets full of ice housed the cans of beer and fizzy pop. There was always meat roasting on the smoking flames of the rusty old barbecue her father never wanted to replace.

Women, mainly mothers, congregated in the small East Ham kitchen and garden; children either screamed from play or irritated each other. A cranky old radio covered in paint used to take up the remainder of the silence, and on Sunday evenings, they would all sit together under faded umbrellas, listening to the Top 40 chart.

Thomas waved his plump hand extravagantly in the air, and Emily smiled vacantly at him. He was nothing like he used to be back then, she thought, svelte, striking, and mischievous. He still had that, at least – the mischievousness. Back in those days of youthful fun, no one knew he preferred men. Coming from a generation where it had been illegal, Thomas hid his sexuality until he was in his sixties. It had never bothered her father because he'd believed it wasn't his business until Thomas wanted it to be. She loved her father even more for that.

But those summers ended abruptly, and Emily couldn't recall when or why.

As the food arrived at their table, Thomas took her hand and asked, 'Where did you just go?'

Their gazes met gently. 'I need your help, Thomas.'

'I know, sweetheart. I've been waiting for you to ask.'

★

34

Islington

Her numb fingers wrapped tightly around the phone in an attempt to keep them warm as she hurried back along Islington High Street and into the side roads. Why did he always take so long to pick up? 'Finally!' she said as she heard her brother's mellow voice say hello.

'It's late, Emily. Is everything okay?'

'I've just had supper with Thomas.'

'Is he well?'

'He's in lust again, so looking a bit worn out.'

Zeb laughed, and Emily warmed inside her veins. It was a laugh that swept her back to when they were children and up to no good.

'Did you call just to tell me that?'

She swapped the phone to her other ear and dug a freezing hand into her coat pocket. 'I'm not sure why I phoned. I think I just wanted to hear your voice.'

'Have you been drinking?' he asked softly.

Emily smiled to herself – he couldn't possibly judge her. 'A little, but that's not why I called.'

'You don't know why you called. You just said so.'

The humour in his voice made her grin so hard that her cheeks ached in the chilled night air. 'You are such an irritant sometimes.'

'Are you wearing your Louboutins? I can hear them on the street.'

'How on earth do you know the sound of a Louboutin?' She laughed. 'Jesus, it's freezing out here.'

Zeb sighed. 'You phoned for a reason, Emily. What's wrong?'

The sound of her stilettoes ceased, and she paused to look at her reflection in a shop window. 'I miss him, Zeb ... I can't believe he's gone.'

'I know,' he said quietly.

'I should let you go back to sleep.'

'I wasn't asleep, but I need to be. I've got a Ministry briefing first thing.'

With the phone tucked back into her bag, she buried her hands deep into her pockets. His voice calmed her – it always calmed her. They were closer in age than she was with Rosa, but it wasn't the reason she felt closer to him. Zeb was, reluctantly, a double of her father. He always denied it, but Emily saw it more and more as they grew up – as Zeb became a man. They didn't look alike; none of them looked like their father. All three siblings were olive-skinned and chocolate-eyed like their mother. Sidney Knight had been blonde in his younger days, with pale blue eyes and a full mop of floppy blonde hair slicked back into a shining peak when he was out of uniform or at home. No, it wasn't the way Zeb looked; it was his intellectual strength, his measured responses, and his commitment to duty and family.

The sound of Emily's Louboutins rang on the pavement once more as she hurried toward home. Pulling the coat's collar tighter around her neck, she thought how lucky she was to still have Thomas in her life – someone who knew her father as well as she did. The short little man with bloated fingers and a flamboyance to envy felt like the only person she could share her secrets with.

As she reached the front door to her house, the warmth of the wine had worn off – her blood shivering beneath her skin.

CHAPTER 10

East Ham: Nelson Street, The Primrose Estate

THERE was no doubt in Joanna's mind that her mother wouldn't notice a tidy kitchen, but she would sure as hell notice a dirty one.

Hearing the hushed voices in the lounge, she'd tiptoed past the door and into the kitchen to get a glass of water. The worksurfaces, covered with an assortment of Chinese takeaway cartons whose contents had been scooped onto plates in a hurry, made her heart sink. Closing the door quietly behind her, she stared silently at the mess – at the leftover food.

With the thin walls of the two-up, two-down, she focused on the voices – muted and deep – of her two uncles. She enjoyed them being there because, for those moments, her mother's attention was elsewhere. And she knew that Uncle Tom would leave a small gift on her bed before he left, as he always did when he visited. Sometimes it was money, but lately, it was a law book or something she could use for university. He would often message her and ask what she needed, then sneak it to her room when he popped to the loo – her mother never knowing. Joanna had hiding places, clever ones, where her mother wouldn't dream of searching. She liked having them – secrets from her mother.

She tried to keep focused on those voices as she tidied away the leftover Chinese, but the urge inside her was pulsating its control in her stomach and then her mind. Scrubbing the work surface harder than it needed, she turned her gaze away from the Chow Mein and towards the dried rice scattered on the floor. Before she bent down to pick it up, she reached over with her fingers into the carton half full of the Chinese noodles and chicken and hurriedly stuffed a handful of it into her mouth. Her cheeks ballooned like a hamster.

Her stomach had rumbled all day, but there'd been no time to eat – and no money. Even though her new friend, Harley, paid for most of her meals when they were together, Joanna could eat for a whole family in one sitting if the food was available. Closing her eyes, she savoured the flavours. Her mother never allowed her to eat with them when her uncles came round. And Debra Evans never ordered extra, either.

The noodles and chicken melted on her tongue, especially when she poured the sweet and sour sauce into her open and full mouth.

Groaning in pleasure, she tipped her head back and munched as fast as possible. Sauce dribbled from her lips, trailing its sweet stickiness along her cheek and chin. 'Heaven,' she groaned in her head.

Engrossed, she didn't hear the kitchen door open.

The carton of noodles in her hand flew upwards as her mother smacked it from below. Joanna's eyes sprang open just as a slap landed on her cheek, and the snap of her mother's voice hit her ears. 'Did I say you could have that!'

Joanna dropped to her knees, to the noodle chaos on the floor. 'I'm sorry, Mum. I thought you'd finished. I was just tidying up.'

'You were stuffing ya fat face like you always are.' Her mother snapped as she reached into the cupboard for a bottle of cheap Russian-labelled vodka. 'Clear up the fucking mess you've made, girl. Look at the state of ya; you've got fucking noodles all over ya face.'

Joanna rubbed her cheeks with her jumper cuffs before trying to scrape the noodles off the floor with her hands. She couldn't leave a trace. If she did, her mother would leave it there until the morning, making a point of letting it dry in. Debra left the kitchen, her daughter still on her knees.

With the kitchen door closed, the girl scrubbed the floor as if her life depended on it. There weren't any tears. There were rarely any tears these days. And she knew it was her fault – for eating something that wasn't meant for her, especially with her mum in the next room. She mumbled to herself, 'pretty stupid move, Joanna' as she scrubbed and cleaned.

Closing the door quietly behind her, she tiptoed along the hall so her mother wouldn't hear her pass. Joanna moved silently to the bathroom so she couldn't be heard on the creaking floorboards – she knew where every creak was – she'd learnt them like they were part of her own breath.

Joanna bent over the loo and shoved her fingers down her throat.

CHAPTER 11

East London: University

DIAMOND smuggling. The tips of Harley's fingers tapped gently against her top lip. The clock on the wall said 8.35. Joanna was late. Why had she agreed to meet the girl so early? The wooden stirrer sank into the cardboard cup as condensation trickled down the café windows.

George. She sighed. There was something different about him since they'd started the Red List jobs. His legs were always bopping up and down under the pub table when they met as if he'd taken some kind of amphetamine. And dark shadows were lingering under his eyes. When he thought no one was looking, his mouth straightened rather than smiled.

George. She owed him so much: she was rich because of him and possibly even alive. When they'd met, the cocaine had soaked into her system to such an extent that she had to go through the hells of detox. George had made her go through it. Body shivers. Tremors. Sweats. Dying with the persistent stomach cramps.

Day and night, he'd sat with her, cooled her with damp towels, hydrated her, changed her sweat-sodden sheets, and fed her soup that his wife had made. He'd heard her delirious ramblings and soothed her uncontrollable tears as she rocked with pain – physical and emotional. He'd changed her soiled clothes when her bowels had released themselves – when the shit had literally burst out of her body.

At the end of it all, when she was physically and emotionally clean, he'd paid for her education to become a gemmologist. After a year in Antwerp working with a contact who sold George's gains, she returned, and he taught her his trade. By twenty, it was as if cocaine had never been in her system, except for the never-ending need for the same adrenaline rush.

She knew George had got an insight into her emotions, her memory, her detachment from the world, and that she didn't give a damn for herself. What was the point?

When he started to teach her, he understood her body's ability too. She could stand still for hours, holding her breath silently like she was dead, staring at anything without fear. Although she showed a poker face to the outside world, every raw emotion that poured out during detox showed George who she was underneath all her shitty bravado, why she was the way she was, and why she had the skills she needed for his business.

The scraping of a chair on the tiles jolted Harley awake, and her eyes flashed open to see the girl.

Dumping her heavy bag on the floor, Joanna asked, 'Late night?' before heading for the coffee machine without giving Harley time to reply. She's too thin, Harley thought, with her blonde bed hair knotted in curls and her clothes too big for her, as if she'd lost weight or lived in the hope of putting it on. The girl turned and walked back with her coffee, eyes puffy, circled by dark rings. They weren't traces of a good night out, Harley noted.

A coffee in one hand and a breakfast flapjack in the other, Joanna sat opposite her and compared their timetables, suggesting that as mature students, they should stick together and support each other. Harley nodded to every suggestion, her thoughts turning to the upcoming trip to Antwerp. Joanna was just what she needed to make sure she didn't miss any lecture notes. Although, she thought, did it matter if she did?

Joanna's pencil tapped against the timetable sprawled out across the table. 'Crap.'

Glancing down, Harley saw Professor Knight's name. 'What's wrong?'

'I've got a friend in the second year who has the Dark Knight as her academic adviser. She's a real bitch, apparently.'

'The Dark Knight?'

'That's what everyone calls her, the Dark Knight. I'm not in your criminal law tutorial, so we've got to ask her to swap one of us over. I don't know what's better: to ask if I can join your group or you can leave and join mine.'

'Well, she's my academic adviser too. If I ask to leave, it could cause me problems, so perhaps we should ask her if you can join my tutorial group.'

'Would you do it?' Joanna asked. 'I'm terrified of her.'

'Then why would you want to be in her class?'

'My uncle says she's one of the best briefs in London.'

'How does your uncle know what a brief is?' Harley looked at her and wondered how the girl knew what one was too.

Joanna shrugged. 'D'you fancy checking out the union bar

tonight?'

'I can't.' Harley replied. Noting the disappointment on Joanna's face, she added, 'But hey, I'm definitely up for it another time.'

Hertfordshire: Ethan Edwards' Residence

Standing at the bottom of the stairs, Harley calculated their ability to reveal her presence. Although solid oak, she didn't doubt how their age would creak in the night's silence. The quietest place of any stairs was away from the centre and away from where people were prone to walking.

Moving slowly, one step at a time, she listened. In the shadows of darkness, her footsteps were like whispers and her breath … as silent as a grave. She crept to the top and then along the hallway to the main bedroom, where the owner was sleeping. The breathing inside the room was heavy, guttural and rhythmical. She glanced in and thought how much she hated the sleeper jobs. Why couldn't George wait until the man was away? Politicians were always away!

Ethan Edwards, Cabinet Secretary, one of the most senior civil servants in the country, was snoring so hard his breath kept catching in his throat. Harley's stomach flipped – the reality of who he was dropping a line of amphetamine into her veins.

Silently, she placed one black pump across the threshold of the room, took a ghostly step in and let her feet lightly brush over the thickly woven carpet. Her leather-gloved hands opened the pouch around her neck – ready. Along with the envelope, George wanted her to get, there were Victorian jewels that her fences would pay good money for. 'Damn the client,' she whispered in her head. If she was going to take such big risks, she needed some kind of reward.

A slight squeak came from its hinges as she opened the wardrobe doors. Pausing, she waited. There was no change from Edwards, so she swiped a small device across the face of the safe, magnetising the electronics inside, shutting down the beeps of the keypad. As it swiped across, it read the internal memory and flashed up each security digit, one by one. A small purple light blinked six times. The safe opened.

It didn't take much to crack a safe – the electronic ones were the easiest. Harley's safe, despite being hidden in the best place, had a tri-protection system of a key, a dial, and a keypad. Not even Ben knew where it was or what systems she used to protect herself from people like them. She smiled to herself and wondered if he'd ever tried to find it; he probably had, just for the sheer fun of it, but she didn't mind.

Piece-by-piece, she took the jewellery and gently placed it into the pouch, still dangling around her neck. Ethan Edwards shifted his feet. Glancing over her shoulder, she waited for the rustle of the duvet to stop before sliding the envelope from the safe, closing its heavy door and leaving the room. Outside in the hallway, she tucked the pouch beneath her black sweater and placed the envelope in her knapsack before reaching the top of the stairs.

From the bedroom came the sound of smacking and scraping – dashing towards her, skidding along the oak floorboards. Then a high-pitched yap of excitement. A small, dark puppy flung itself against her legs. It yapped again. Footsteps followed behind it.

'Frankie,' a voice whispered gruffly. 'Frankie, come here.' The puppy yapped harder and pushed its little butt playfully into the air. It yapped at her feet as Edwards' footsteps thudded on the wooden floor.

Slipping back into a doorway, Harley froze, whispering 'fucking shit' as she concentrated on the pulse in her neck, breathing her pulse slower. It sounded so fucking loud, and the voice was getting closer.

'What are you doing, you little sod?' The naked man bent down and picked the puppy up. It woofed high-pitched puppy woofs frantically as its little face turned in excited delight at the stranger in his new house. Its owner turned too. His eyes were dark, staring at Harley hiding behind the blackness of her balaclava in the shadow of the doorway.

Calmly, Ethan Edwards, Cabinet Secretary – naked – placed Frankie on the floor. As he did, Harley pushed into him, trying to knock him off his feet so she could pass. But Edwards grabbed her arm, pulling her backwards – yanking her into his hold – trying to control her. Curling her body over, she spun around to face him, anticipating what would come next. His grip wrapped into her neck, pressing into her windpipe like a clamp before he slammed her backwards. Her spine punched against the hard brick of the wall. *Jesus fucking Christ.* Pain bounced up Harley's back. *Fuck.* Fuck. But she couldn't cry out – she couldn't let him know she was a girl. Holding the need to scream in her mouth, she bit down on her bottom lip. Fear trapped her. 'How to get out. How to get out,' she whispered in her head. But she didn't know how to escape his hold, his grasp – a clamp with ever-increasing pressure.

Lifting her off the floor, his hands pushed further around her throat, blocking air from going in or out of her lungs. Her eyes bulged as her mind chased in every direction. What would George tell her to do? She was too old for this shit – too fucking old.

With all the power she had, she thrust her right knee upwards, high between them. As she did, her leather-gloved hands twisted and dug into his hair, yanking his head ... down. That'll fucking get you, you bastard, she thought, as all the power of her knee rammed under his chin. She shoved his head down further and slammed it against her kneecap.

Ethan Edwards buckled over, releasing the pressure of his hold, and Harley slid out from him. In his panic, he swung a fist blindly into the air, the flat smack of his knuckles catching her face, knocking her sideward. She whiplashed onto the oak doorframe – a sharp hot-poker missile propelling itself up her back and neck. Another gasp of pain caught on her already bleeding lip – the taste of iron on her tongue. She fell to the floor, landing on her palms. The jolt snapped in her wrists. Harley wanted to scream.

Drawing on all her determination not to cry, she closed her eyes and took a deep – deep – breath, trying to take her mind away from all the stabbing shocks inside her body.

Scanning, her eyes searched in the darkness, looking for her escape and assessing Edwards as he crumpled over. While he slumped, she drew on her strength to balance back up on her feet. Keeping her knees bent and her body low, she pulled in her core muscles and swung out her right leg – low on the ground – swooping it around, outwards, and back towards herself. Catching his ankles with speed, her leg whipped into his, and he stumbled again, his knees hitting the floorboards, his orientation lost. In that second, Harley leapt from the shadows and jumped over him. Hurling herself down the staircase, she leapt through the open window.

Running. Dripping with sweat. The blood seeping beneath her mask. Her feet pounded across the ground, protected only by soft pumps that didn't cushion against the sharp stones. She stumbled over plants and flowerbeds, bolting faster than she thought she could ever go, knowing she was leaving a trail behind her. There was no time to put her leathers back on, no time to put anything into the secret places on the Triumph. If she didn't get out, the police would be on her.

Harley's brain went into meltdown – a mashed-up Eton Mess being jolted around inside a concrete mixer.

Kicking the chrome stand up, she pulled out from behind the trees. The pain in her head, the pounding in her face, and the spasms up her spine were irrelevant. She didn't – couldn't – think of anything except responding to the instinct of her adrenaline. 'Slowly, girl,' she whispered to herself between the quick short breaths. Slowly, Harley Smith.

For the first thirty minutes of her journey down the dark country lanes of Hertfordshire, her blood was boiling with adrenaline that brought with it nausea, rising from her stomach into her throat. She struggled to control it, but the acid burn rose higher and higher. Pulling over onto a grass verge, she yanked off her helmet and balaclava. The sickness swam upwards into her mouth. Her roasting skin turned cold – drained of blood. Bending over, she retched, gasping for air through her mouth. Between spasms, she tried to slow her body down, trying to reduce the havoc inside.

In the darkness of the desolate lane, knowing the police would be looking for someone of her description, she pulled off her black polo sweater and unravelled her breast strapping. Naked from the waist upward, her hands scrambled in the left saddlebag on her Triumph for her emergency clothes: a white t-shirt and a pale-pink cashmere sweater. Untying her damp hair from its tight knot, she weaved her fingers through it, bringing it back to life and put the pouch of jewels into a small hidden under-pocket on the right saddlebag. The knapsack, with her kit and the envelope, tucked into the left – hidden. There was nothing she could do about her stinging face or bloodied lip, but everything else was hidden for now.

Harley sat on the edge of the bike's seat. She knew she should leave and get out of the area, but she needed a minute. Just a minute, she thought. She flopped over and gripped her fingers into her scalp. 'Fucking fuck,' she whispered. 'Fucking fuck fuck fuck.' Harley's knees buckled, and she fell onto them into the dirt. 'You stupid fucking cow. Jesus Christ. You stupid fucking cow.' She blew out a long slow breath and stood up. 'One day, you're going to get yourself killed.'

Pulling her phone out of the saddlebag, she dialled Ben's number. 'It's me.'

'Did you get it?'

'No, yes, fuck! Everything went wrong.'

'What d'you mean? Are you okay?'

'No. Everything just fucked up.'

'Come to mine. Don't stop anywhere and keep to the speed limit.'

East Ham: Pinnie Street, The Primrose Estate

Harley lowered herself slowly into the almost scalding water. Her body curled over – knees tucking to her chest as her forehead rested lightly on them. Tear salt stung on the split in her lip as steam droplets weaved along the black shimmering tiles in Ben's bathroom.

She couldn't cry; she couldn't. If she cried, she'd show her weakness – her father hated weakness. He hated it so much that his shouting mouth would get closer and closer to her face until his spit would cover her small body with a blanket of fear.

Harley's eyes closed as she remembered Flint running towards the front door in excitement and against her little legs as her mother opened it. The wobble of the glass in Harley's small hand. The drop. The crash of it against the skirting board. Her father propelling himself off his armchair. The onslaught of rage that made his face twist into a boiling red. She'd tried desperately to keep still, to show no emotion, but the tears disobeyed her ... and him. They'd rolled silently from her eyes.

Her mother reached gently out to his arm as she quietly said, 'Darling, I've bought your paper.'

'She's bloody snivelling again. Look at her. She's always bloody snivelling.'

Elizabeth smiled softly down at her daughter. 'Why don't you take Flint out for a walk, sweetheart.'

Red from the heat of the water, with all the blood bathed away, Harley padded into the lounge wearing Ben's boxers and a t-shirt. Looking up, he smiled. 'Why do girls always look so sexy in men's clothes!'

As she smiled back, her fingers touched the split in her lip, stopping her from replying.

'It really didn't happen for you tonight, did it?'

Lowering herself awkwardly to sit next to him, she sighed. 'I was careless. I should have done a final recce.'

'Why didn't you?'

'Homework. There's so much of it.' She slowly tucked her legs under her body and lit a cigarette. 'I really don't know why I'm bothering to make an effort with this bloody law degree.'

'That's the old man for you.' Ben sighed. 'Let's see the envelope.'

Harley passed it to him, her movements painful. Slow. 'Definitely a document in there,' she said, as his fingers took it from her.

'Do you remember all the names on the list?' Ben laughed. 'What a stupid bloody question. Maybe we can work out why we're suddenly doing their gaffs over?'

'Why do you want to know? If we get them all, George is happy, right?'

'This is different. Something isn't right. I don't know … but my gut doesn't like it. Dad is acting really odd these days.'

Harley sighed. 'I've been thinking the same too, but what's made you think it?'

'He keeps disappearing in the evenings, and it ain't to The Eagle. Even Mum's worried, and that ain't like her.'

'Do you think he's having an affair?'

Ben sat up straight. 'Fuck off, he wouldn't do that to me mum!'

'Then you know what you need to do, right?' She gazed at him and the confusion on his face. 'Jesus! You've got to follow him, you idiot. It's the only way you'll know.'

Ben leant back into the soft cushions. The blonde fringe he tried to sweep back fell a little over his blue eyes as he closed them. He's tired, too, she thought, and leant back in the same way, so her shoulder could rest against his. It felt hard and muscular – solid and safe.

They sat in perfect silence for a while, just the sound of their breathing in the air. They had spent over half their lives breathing together. Their bodies had learnt to read each other's, learnt to recognise the nuances of movements, the expressions in the quietness of their eyes. There was nothing they didn't know about each other, nothing they couldn't see or read. Together, they moved, thought, and worked as one. They were each other's shadows. Harley was always at her most peaceful when she was with Ben, inside her soul, even when they were working.

CHAPTER 12

East London: University

Daggers stabbed along her spine as she heaved her body upwards. The clock flashed 11.30. Ben was gone from the bed, but his scent, fresh soap, lingered in the air. It took a while for her eyes to focus and for her body to unravel from its tightness. Beside the bed, her phone flashed with messages – she groaned. She was late for meeting Joanna and was in trouble with Aimee.

Fifteen minutes late for the property lecture, Harley decided to sit in the corner of the campus café instead. The mug of hot chocolate warmed her hands as the October rain drizzled its fine mist on the dirty window. There was no point in arriving at the lecture late: Dr Shah was just as uptight about lateness as Professor Knight. Exhaling, she leant back in the chair and closed her eyes – tired again. At least she'd be on time for the criminal lecture. Not that it really mattered. None of it mattered.

She hurt even when she didn't move, and her lips throbbed like hell as she sipped from the warm mug. Thoughts of her father shouting drifted back to her mind. She knew what he'd have called her for messing up so badly. Every time she failed at something, his voice was in her head. His face close to hers – his breath warm and damp on her skin. He would have disapproved of her work without question, but more than anything, he would have disapproved of her failure. Sighing, she thought about what her mother would say if she knew what she was doing for a living. She'd be horrified, Harley thought, and pressed her eyelids tighter together.

'May I sit?'

She knew the voice. It was light and soft – a melody on the air – with a beautiful musical tone that made her heartbeat speed up. She opened her eyes and drew herself up straighter, trying hard not to show that little blades of pain were stabbing at her with every move. 'Of course.'

Placing her coffee cup onto the table, Knight asked, 'Do I need to suggest pastoral services?'

Harley's brain froze for a second, and then it registered: her lips, cheek, and bruises. She quickly shook her head, but the movement caused a bastard stab that lunged up her neck. What a fucking sight, she thought, wanting the world to suck her under so she could hide.

'Thank you,' she replied quietly. 'It's nothing.'

'It doesn't look like nothing.' Knight said as she removed her coat and placed it neatly on the back of the chair.

'I'm fine.'

'I'm really not sure that you are.'

Harley's hands clamped the mug a little tighter. 'I didn't think it was in your rules to be interested in your students beyond their academic work.'

A slight glimmer of amusement flashed in Knight's eyes. 'Quite. But then I don't find most of my students hiding in the campus café, missing lectures, and with a face the colour of a plum.'

'A plum? Is that how I look?' A smile passed between them, and for a moment, a gentle fizzing bubbled inside Harley's body. In the flash of a second, the women held each other's gazes longer than social etiquette normally allowed. A warm burn rushed to Harley's cheeks, which were obviously already flaming. Just as she was about to reply, a man dashed to the Professor's side with a dishevelled air and said, 'I'm so sorry I'm late.'

Harley diverted her eyes to the tall, flustered man. The warmth in her body dropped like glass crashing on a concrete floor as his hand gently touched the Professor's shoulder. It rested there after a discreet squeeze. Knight glanced up at him and smiled. 'I hadn't noticed, Ammon. I was just chatting to one of my students.'

Ammon. So that was his name. Ammon. With his white and yellow gold braided wedding ring encircling his slender finger. Ammon. The man who was leaving the Professor's room the day of their first meeting – the man she'd seen walking by the Professor's side across campus on several occasions. Ammon. Pulling himself out of his heavy grey duffle coat, he sat down and glanced at Harley.

'I hope the other person is worse off than you.' He grinned – his perfect white teeth clashing with the black frames of his heavy, round preppy glasses. Although designer, his jumper was threadbare just enough to make him look less pretentious. Slightly unshaven, his face was chiselled below a mop of thick blue-black hair. With his flawlessly manicured nails and his genuine antique Cartier watch, Harley's jaw clenched a little. The side of his arm gently – and unknowingly – drew to Knight's like a magnet and stuck.

Harley stared at him. 'I don't understand your comment.'

'Your face.' He replied with a bright, boyish smile that Harley wanted to slap. 'I hope the other person is worse off than you, although, by the looks of it, I'd imagine they'd be in hospital if they were.'

'I'm not sure that's funny.' She snapped. 'What if my husband had done this?'

'I'm sorry.' Ammon hesitated. 'I was just trying to make light of what looks very painful.'

The Professor touched his hand and looked at Harley. 'I doubt Mr Hassan meant anything by what he said, Miss Smith.'

'As a woman, I'm surprised you can be so dismissive over such a flippant comment.' With slow, awkward movements, Harley began to put her coat on.

'I really am sorry.' Ammon said again. 'I didn't think.'

Knight glanced at him. 'You don't need to apologise a second time. Miss Smith is obviously feeling a little sensitive about the subject.'

Using the table as support, Harley pulled herself up: her cheeks burning red. 'Is that how you approach clients who might have suffered domestic violence, Professor? Only, it's a bit archaic, don't you think? The woman is being overly sensitive.' As she turned to leave, the Professor stood up, her chair scraping on the tiled floor.

Harley turned, frowning, as Knight said, 'You may not always agree with someone's choice of words, Miss Smith, but there are better ways to express yours.'

The thought of sitting for two hours in a lecture theatre, with Knight standing sanctimoniously on the stage, made Harley's insides tighten as she made her way across campus. Joanna would be there, she thought; she could pick up any notes. Harley slid on her helmet, slowly straddled the Triumph, and pulled out onto the busy main road. 'Fucking knobhead,' she mumbled as she accelerated.

Abney Park Road

At Abney Park Road, she slowed down to scan for number 146. It was just like Ben had described, an unassuming semi-detached: not the place Aimee had tried to rob in North Essex.

Parking up, she sat for a moment, making sure Eddie didn't have any of his thugs loitering, before sliding off the Triumph and sauntering across the street. Her black leather-gloved finger pushed against the bell, its ding-dong chiming in the distance. Footsteps padded on wooden flooring, and a plain-looking woman opened the door – plump and busty. Ranking either loved her, or she knew too much, Harley thought.

'I'm here to see Eddie.'

Ranking's wife tossed her chunky hand in the direction of the room at the end of a large white hallway. Harley stepped across the threshold and followed the woman toward the kitchen. Cigarettes, tea, bacon, and vanilla air freshener wafted under her nostrils. It was almost too much for her empty stomach.

Eddie Ranking, the man with a massive reputation – and a stomach to match – was sitting at the end of the long thin breakfast bar, rolling hand tobacco into skinny and perfectly formed cigarettes. Buttonholes on his pink shirt stretched to almost popping from their holes. As his wife left and shut the kitchen door behind her, Harley studied the man – fat-faced, unshaven, and ragged. Another knob, she thought.

Eddie glanced up. 'George finally sent you then?'

Standing still, Harley waited for him to say something less obvious. Ranking lit one of his many pre-rolled all placed neatly in a silver tobacco tin – his plump lips inhaling slowly.

'You can bring them in, can you?'

'You asked for me, so I'm guessing you think I can.'

'Your face looks like you're shit at what you do.'

Harley sighed. 'Your alarm bell-box outside is fake. The real alarm, which is silent, is set in your loft, triggered by sensors you have in each room. You've done this because when the alarm is triggered, your neighbours and the police won't know about it. The electronic panel in your loft sends a message to you by text, telling you which room has been entered. You also have three CCTV cameras positioned on the front of your house and probably as many on the back, even though you don't keep anything on the premises. Your business acquisitions are in a lock-up, not registered in your name but your wife's, as is your second house in Essex, no doubt.

Your security system there is just the same as here, but it's ineffectual for someone like me. I wouldn't need to enter the loft to disable your alarm or your cameras so I could find your valuables hidden behind the baseboard of the white mirrored wardrobes in your bedroom. Of which, the mirrors are something you despise because every time you look in them, you realise you are not the man you were thirty years ago.' She stared at him. 'As to diamonds, the ones your wife has in her ears are fakes; only she doesn't know that does she? I'm guessing that most of the jewellery you buy her is fake. After all, you don't want all your assets tied up in just one woman, do you?'

Leaning back in his chair, the man in front of her stared with his small dark brown eyes. It was a look that left her unsure of what he'd say next, but she was starting not to give a shit. This was Aimee's mess, not hers. And she hated Eddie Fucking Ranking.

'So, you're Harley Smith, eh? I've heard a lot about you. You'd better sit down.'

CHAPTER 13

Mayfair: The Temple Club

'WHAT'S going on between you two?' Zeb asked.

Emily held the phone between her ear and shoulder as she rummaged in her bag for ID. Smiling, she handed the driving licence to the concierge and signed in as Thomas' guest. She used to sign in as her father's, she thought, as she watched her hand scribble her name in the oversized leatherbound register that always smelled musty.

'We're just catching up, that's all. I have things I want to ask him about Dad.'

'What things?'

'Just things, Zeb.' She sighed. 'I'd better go. Thomas hates it when I'm late.'

The Temple Club was a place she knew well: its fustiness mixed with cooking from the kitchen and the creaks in the floorboards as she walked. She'd spent her teenage years waiting in the old dust-musty foyer for her father at the end of the evening. And in her adult years, she'd joined him as his guest as they sat by the fire, going through her early cases as a barrister, her teaching methods in academia, her love life, her dreams. But as Emily moved between the rooms, past the bookshelves lined with old leatherbound books worn at the spines, she realised that those moments had always been about her, and no matter what her father's day had been like, he'd always given his time to *her*. The realisation didn't feel too good.

Emily didn't need the concierge's help to find Thomas in the smoking room because it was where she had always sat with her father, drinking whisky, debating the law and enjoying the roaring fire on winter nights. After her mother had died, The Temple Club was where Sidney spent most of his evenings when in London, but now Thomas was sitting where her father had once sat, smoking the same brand of cigars. She could smell it in the air – the scent of mead warming her heart yet making it ache too. God, she longed for her father's scent again – and the vision of his hands, manicured and deft, able to write beautifully and yet still strong enough to build shelves from old pallets.

As she walked towards her father's old friend, he stood, struggling a little to straighten, and opened his arms to her, like he always did. They embraced before she sat opposite him, her whisky glass already waiting on the worn and polished table. The fire raged a wonderfully skin-burning heat, and for a moment, Emily leant forward and warmed her hands. She shivered. 'It's freezing out there.'

'I've been here most of the day, working. I'm lovely and toastie and full of fine foods.'

Emily smiled at him. 'How long have you been the accountant for this place now? It must be years.'

'I guess about twenty-two or twenty-three. God, that makes me feel so old.' He laughed. 'Come to think of it, Paolo makes me feel old too.'

Sitting back in the chair, Emily smoothed her hands over her trousers. 'Well, I'm not surprised; he's what? 32?'

Thomas grinned. 'And gorgeous.'

'I still need your help.' Emily said, pulling an envelope out of her bag and passing it to him. 'He wrote me this, and I don't know where to start with it.'

The chubby little man opened the envelope and read the words of his old friend. Emily stared at the skipping flames of the fire as he did, sipping her whisky and allowing herself to be mesmerised by the heat and the burnt shades of orange that trailed up the chimney. She knew the letter Thomas was reading by heart, the *'I only hope that after reading my words, you can somehow maintain a sense of pride in me also, for all the good I did and not the mistakes I have made. There have been many.'*

She wanted to know what her father had meant by that, what mistakes he'd made. There was nothing he could have done to make her not feel pride in him. She sat quietly, desperately, waiting for Thomas to finish, her slender fire-warmed fingers playing with the thread of the scarf that rested on her lap.

Finally, he glanced up. 'We have a lot to discuss, but I don't know if you can take it all in.'

'Why did he think I wouldn't be proud of him?'

Placing the letter on the table between them, he sat back in the chair, the whisky glass in his hand. 'Have you heard of The Domino Set?'

Emily nodded. 'Over the years, yes. I've had the occasional client mention it – one of the most organised criminal gangs in the South.'

Thomas leant forward. In a hushed voice, he said. 'Your father was part of it.'

'I don't understand.'

'I need to explain a few things.' Slowly, he started to unravel what Sidney had told his daughter. 'If you've heard of The Domino Set, you'll know what they do and how they do it. When they started out, they named themselves The Domino Set because they wanted to make sure that if one went down, they all went down – always protecting each other through necessity. Despite being a policeman, your father made sure none of them were ever arrested. They started small, like any gang, but as their confidence grew, so did the scale and complexity of their jobs. Bigger and bolder, the Set flourished and, over time, took on more jobs and needed more crew. It became a network of twenty-eight highly skilled criminals, fences and protectors. They had a romantic notion of twenty-eight being their crucial number.'

'Twenty-eight dominoes.' Emily said quietly.

Thomas nodded. 'That's it. There were more on the periphery of the main Set itself. They called them Pips – like the dots on the Dominoes. You can't run an operation like they did and not have an army behind it.'

Emily gazed at him. Surely he was talking about someone else, not her father. She crossed her legs and adjusted the scarf still on her lap. 'So my father, was he one of these Pips?'

'Did he give you anything else? Like a string of digits or a key?' Thomas before sipping at his whisky.

'Well—'

'Thomas Crowe!' A voice projected from the entrance of the smoking room. 'Good to see you, old boy.' Zeb grinned as he made his way across to them. 'Emily mentioned you'd be here this evening, so I thought I'd drop by to say hello to my favourite godfather.' Thomas smiled, not standing for his usual welcoming embrace.

'I thought you were working late?' Emily said as she stood and brushed the rain droplets off her brother's black cashmere coat.

'I was supposed to be, but the Chief decided we all needed to be in at 5.00 tomorrow morning, so we've been let out early.' Then, rubbing his hands together, he beamed. 'I've not interrupted anything, have I? God, I'm starving. Does anyone else want some food? I haven't eaten here since, well, since meeting father before he got ill.'

After ordering from the menu and taking a long sip from his gin and tonic, Zeb glanced at Thomas. 'How are you, old man? It's been a long time since I've seen you.' His long, lean leg crossed over the other as he sat back in the stiff leather armchair.

Thomas half-smiled. 'Life is good. And how are you? Last time I talked to you properly, you'd just been promoted at the MOD and were working on a case that had you travelling to Berlin.'

'Gosh, that's got to be about three years ago.' Zeb grinned, but Emily could see that it didn't quite reach his eyes. 'I don't recall seeing you at the funeral, Thomas, but then it's all a bit of a blur.' He ordered another G&T as the waiter whizzed by. 'Things are good, despite the obvious. I'm up for promotion again, and my partner should be getting his divorce soon.' He smiled at Emily. 'Shouldn't he, Sis.'

'Oh, well, I guess that depends on the wife!'

Zeb laughed – his dark eyes gleaming until they focused back on Thomas. 'So, what are you two doing in this stuffy old place? Actually, don't tell me; if I know you, you're up to no good, Thomas Crowe, and I don't need to be privy to it. I swear the Ministry is always watching us watchers.'

'Are you staying in London tonight or going back to Surrey?' Emily asked.

'London. I've booked my usual room at The Forge and given the driver a couple of hours off so I could join you.' His hands smoothed down the creases in his trousers before resting on his lap. 'I was thinking of you this week, Thomas.' He looked up. 'I found some old photos of you and father together, along with some familiar faces and ones I don't recognise. I'd say you were somewhere in your early twenties. It all looked rather jolly.'

'Burn them' Thomas frowned before taking another sip of his whisky. 'I don't need to be reminded of my youth.'

CHAPTER 14

East London: University

THE Professor stood on the stage – watching. Splinters of sunlight threaded through the narrow windows high above, filling the stage around her like ribbons of light. For a moment, Harley saw one ribbon catch the Knight's profile, illuminating her face. Radiant. At that moment, she looked velvety: revealed. Strands of dark hair, slightly wavy, framed her face. It had fallen free from the loosely bundled knot at the nape of her neck, where the concentration of hair made it even blacker against her slightly olive skin. As the ribbon of light changed under a passing cloud, her high cheekbones softened – sharp to delicate. Harley thought how beautiful she was – exquisite.

The students at the front of the lecture theatre quietened – their silence seeping upwards towards the back until everyone was hushed. At 3.16, anxious faces aimed their gaze down at the Dark Knight. Once again, the Professor glanced at the clock on the wall above the door.

'Sixteen minutes this time. You are getting progressively worse.' Her eyes skimmed their gaze over the faces of her students. 'Let me clarify something: it's my job to ensure you all leave here with qualifying law degrees. If you wish to learn, I will teach you: if you don't, I won't. The next time we're due to meet for a lecture, I expect you to be on time and silent at precisely 15.00 hundred hours. Those who fail to do this will be asked to leave.'

There was a nudge against Harley's arm: Joanna rolled her eyes and feigned boredom. Of all the places for Knight to look, it had to be on the girl. 'Do you have something you'd like to share with us, Miss Evans?'

The girl jerked at the sound of her name and flicked her head back towards the Professor: her neck blotched red. There was a fleeting icy glance from Knight to Harley before the Professor said, 'Good. Now we understand each other, I'll begin.'

Scribbling secretly on the girl's notepad, Harley wrote, how does she know your name? But Joanna ignored it – her head down and her pen poised.

After two quick hours, Knight glanced up at the clock. 'Our time has ended. Please prepare for your tutorials on this subject.' But before the woman reached the entrance of the lecture theatre to leave, Harley shot from her seat – running down the steps as she called, 'Professor.'

'Miss Smith.' Knight stopped and looked directly, impassively, at her.

'Can I talk to you for a moment?'

'Can't it wait until our office hours next Friday?'

Harley's mind stumbled. Her cheeks flamed hot as the blush rose on her skin. It wasn't just on her face; she felt it fly through her body with a tingle – a flutter in her stomach. 'I wanted to ask you something before the tutorial group on Thursday.'

'Then come to my office. I don't revel in the experience of loitering after lectures have ended.' Knight glanced briefly up towards where Joanna was sitting, then left.

Hurrying out into the breezy, late October evening, the wind caught itself in Harley's hair, whisking it into an untamed mess as she ran down the busy street towards the Law School. A little flushed, she knocked on the office door without hesitation. Knight's stilettos echoed on the wooden floor: the latch clicked – the door opened. The Professor walked away and indicated where Harley should sit. She obeyed silently. Unlike the first time they'd met, the Professor sat opposite her, crossing her legs and smoothing her hand over the black trousers before resting both on her lap. Then, with measured consideration, she said, 'You have a question.'

Thrown by the sensation of flight in her stomach, heat rose to Harley's cheeks again. Pulling her hair to one side – trying to smooth it down – she mentally paused. Tension soaked the air as the Professor sat, looking internally coiled. There was an invisible zone around the woman, and Harley wondered whether it would omit an electrical buzz if she touched it – whether it would make her jump with a jolt? Her curiosity was desperate to find out.

The light in the office was dim, muted. The late October sky trickled sluggishly through the window and into the room, which had the subtle permeations of the Professor's lingering perfume. Harley settled on the edge of the seat and caught the woman's gaze that was watching her expectantly.

'I wanted to ask if Joanna Evans could join the Thursday tutorial group I'm in with you?'

'Why do you ask?'

'There are very few mature students on the course, and it would be beneficial for us both if we could study together and maybe help each other out.'

Uncrossing her legs, Knight stood up and moved to the window. She gazed down at the view of the canal with her back to the room and her arms crossed over her chest.

'Today was an example of how you interact together. Despite Miss Evans scribbling notes profusely, I'm not sure you've developed your concentration levels enough at this point.' The Professor turned. 'I saw you write nothing during the lecture.'

Harley's mouth opened then closed. She tried again. 'I didn't need to write any notes, but I can tell you almost everything you said and in what order you said it.'

Leaning against the edge of the desk, Knight's hands slid into the pockets of her trousers. A glint entered her eyes, but it was hard to read. Whatever it meant, it irritated Harley. It irritated her, even more when the Professor said, 'Really? I'd be suitably impressed if you did that. Perhaps you should try.'

Harley's eyes narrowed as she looked up at the Professor. 'You'd like me to impress you? I don't particularly have the need to do that.'

Tilting her head slightly, Knight gazed back at her in silence: an unfaltering look that pushed Harley to say, 'However, at 3.32, you were talking about the act of consent within a sexual relationship and explaining the reasoning in the case of R v Brown, 1994 House of Lords. At 3.46, you discussed the connection between desire, motivation, and intent and how the mind considers them the same, but the law does not. At 4.15, you moved on to *mens rea* and *actus reus*, which will be the main topics for our tutorial discussion over the next three weeks. Finally, at 4.23, you stated that if we couldn't grasp these concepts early in our degree, we would fail to understand the basis for much of the UK criminal justice system.

You looked at the clock on the wall three times, perfectly timed to the beginning, middle and end. You prefer the twenty-four-hour clock to state such timings, but I prefer those hours in their written form rather than their oral and have chosen not to bend to your preference.' With a slight pause, she asked, 'Would this be a suitable demonstration of my ability to concentrate, Professor?'

The muscles in Knight's jaw visibly tightened under the soft skin of her cheek. The blackness of her eyes had remained steadily on Harley, their indifference squashing the wonderful moment in the lecture theatre where the shards of sun had streamed silver threads over the Professor's face. There was nothing illuminated about her now – nothing warm. Silence sat awkwardly between them as Harley waited, expecting the Professor to tell her to leave for being insolent. But instead, an amused expression brushed momentarily across the woman's eyes. At that moment, Harley felt pulled towards her, the space between them disappearing as if a whirlpool had sucked them down together – removing all distance. The power of the swirl created an explosive tingling in her blood – her body almost too hot to bear.

'Whether you need to impress me or not, Miss Smith, you've done so. I concede. You've obviously developed your concentration levels beyond my expectation and my judgement.' She continued, 'I'm therefore willing to give you the benefit of the doubt regarding Miss Evans. If you prove me wrong, she will be removed, and you must work even harder in your tutee hour to ensure you've not been distracted. Despite your aptitude for concentration and detail, I think this is a mistake. Now, do you have more questions?'

Shaking her head, Harley stood up, knowing that the conversation was over.

★

Westminster

'Miss Davies arrived about an hour ago.' Tony said as he buttoned the top of his shirt, lifted his collar and slipped on his tie. 'And you need someone to take a look at your face.' He half smiled, his green eyes glinting as his lips curved around uneven yellowish teeth. Wrinkles creased on his face – a craggy yet handsome face. Thick grey speckled hair, interspersed and sprinkled with black, matched the light stubble around his chin. It was always there, but then, he was always on a night shift.

His age defied her. There were times when he appeared somewhere in his late fifties and moments when his youthful, vibrant twenty-year-old self frothed with mischief. His voice, soothing and soft, was as charming as his cragginess – an East End lilt polished from all his years as a concierge.

'It's fine, Tony. Just a bit sore when I smile.'

'Have you seen today's paper?' He asked, pulling it from the drawer under the desk.

'I was going to read it on my tablet in bed. Why?'

'There's an article about how there's a trend in high-end burglaries. Paper reckons nearly fourteen million has been stolen in the past two years alone.' Tony ruffled the pages straight to show it to her.

She leant in and began to read. 'They say it's the Panthers.' The scent of his aftershave wafted to her nose. He smelled good. He always smelled good. She liked being close to him; he was familiar to her, with his rough hardworking hands and perfectly pressed concierge uniform that hadn't changed over the years.

Tony snorted. 'They get too much credit. I don't think they could have pulled this lot off. They only seem to like the big stunts, like Hatton Garden.'

She wanted to read it in more detail, but he'd moved the paper away. 'Oh, to have the brain to do something so exact,' she said.

'I knew you'd enjoy reading it. You might be defending a gang like this one day.'

'Or prosecuting.'

'You'll never be a prosecutor.' He frowned.

'May I borrow this? I prefer reading the paper than my tablet.'

Without waiting for Harley to remove her coat, Aimee leant in towards her, pressing her tongue into her mouth with a plunge that made Harley want to pull back, not just from the pain of her bruised mouth, but she wasn't ready for Aimee's needs. She wanted to talk about Eddie Ranking and the diamonds she had to smuggle, but Aimee whispered, 'I need you.'

A second kiss landed on Harley's lips. This time she pulled back from the sting. 'Jesus.' Pushing past, freeing herself from the grip of Aimee's hands, Harley threw her bag onto the floor and unravelled herself from her scarf and coat.

Aimee slumped on the sofa, her blonde hair falling around her face just like Ben's. 'You never seem to want to fuck these days.'

Harley leant against the bookshelf. 'Have you seen my face? Only, it's a bit bloody painful at the moment.'

'Yeah, of course, but that doesn't mean you have to stop wanting to.'

Harley sighed and headed towards the kitchen to find the bottle of wine chilling in the fridge. Aimee trailed half-heartedly behind her.

'What did you do at school today?'

'I had a lecture by Professor Knight. I'm hungry, are you?' She asked as she poured them both a glass of Chardonnay.

'Starving. I've not eaten all day. Your face looks like shit, by the way.'

'Fancy some bread and cheese with the wine?'

'I need to lose a few pounds, but yeah, fuck it, why not?' Sitting on the high stool by the breakfast bar, she watched Harley potter. 'What's the Professor like? Male or female?'

Distracted, Harley cut through the bread with a sharp knife and replied, 'Female, they call her the Dark Knight.'

'Great name! Or not.' Aimee laughed as she plucked an olive from the bowl and popped it between her teeth.

'She's got a reputation for being a bitch. I had to see her after the lecture to ask if Joanna could join my tutorial group.'

'Is Joanna the one who colour coordinates everything?'

'Yep.' The slices of bread lined up neatly on the heavy wooden slab next to the grapes. 'She gave me a hard time for asking, but I seemed to talk her round. I don't know how because I thought she'd have a go at me. Then she said I'd proven her wrong, and she'd concede.'

Aimee frowned. 'Who uses a word like concede? Is she like some old spinster who wears flats and thick tan tights?'

Sitting on the opposite stool, Harley completed the spread of cold meats, bread, cheeses, grapes, and olives. It was more than she'd intended to make, but the preparation eased her thoughts. 'She's not, no.'

'Then what's she like?'

'Interesting.'

'That doesn't sound particularly good.'

Putting her hand over her mouth as she ate, Harley shook her head. 'No, I mean it in a good way. She's unusual. And top of her game. I was reading that she's studied at Cambridge and Harvard. That's pretty cool. And she's won loads of cases at the Old Bailey and Court of Appeal.'

Aimee's glass clunked on the countertop before she picked up her fork and lanced an olive and cheese cube together. 'Sounds pretty vanilla to me.'

'You would say that! But she's not – far from it.'

'I spoke with Ben earlier.'

Harley glanced up. 'And?'

'You need to call him about your flight to Antwerp.' Aimee chewed slowly.

There were things Harley wanted her to say, to admit. Would she ever mention what she'd done at Eddie's, or why? Ever since Harley had worked with George, certain names were off-limits – Eddie was one of them. You don't 'crap on your own doorstep,' as George would say. Aimee knew that too. Even though she wasn't part of the business, George never hid what he did from his family or who he worked with and Aimee had watched her and Ben being drilled, trained, pushed, and polished. There was never any question that she didn't know the rules they lived by.

Unable to hold back any longer, she asked, 'What the hell made you choose Eddie Ranking's house?'

Aimee placed the fork down on the plate and poured herself another glass of wine. Taking her time to clear her mouth of food – something she didn't normally do – she sat back on the kitchen stool, crossed her long legs, and sighed. 'You hate me for getting you into this, don't you?'

'I don't hate you, but I'm not happy I've got to take such a risk.'

Aimee smiled. 'You love a risk; you know you do.'

'That may be the case, but now Ranking will get his claws into me, and you know damn well that your dad has been trying to keep us apart for years.' Harley sighed. 'Why Eddie? I mean, did you do it because you knew it would piss your dad off or because you thought it would impress him?'

Aimee jabbed a piece of cheese, the metal fork hitting her teeth as she took a bite. Harley waited for a reply, but there was none.

'You know I've got to bring ten over, don't you? And where those ten have to go, right?'

Still, Aimee didn't respond.

'If I mess this up, Eddie will make me do more for him, or he will want some other kind of payback from George. You know what he's like. He'll get heavy-handed with one of us. Are you ready for that?'

'I could come with you,' Aimee said.

'You're the cause of all this.' Harley stood up and pushed the plate with the half-eaten food away from her. 'I'm going to go for a run.'

Hyde Park

She ran until she reached Hyde Park: wet grass wafting into her lungs as she followed the route around its edge. A damp mist hovered in the air, moistening her skin as streetlights reflected on the wet pavements – residual puddles from the earlier rain. Car tyres splashed their spray with a whizz as she ran towards Birdcage Walk. The vibration of her feet hitting the concrete pleased her – urging her on. With its increase, her breath became faster and more laboured. She liked to hear it, to see it in the cold air and to know she was pushing herself beyond her limits.

The coldness of the air faded as her muscles warmed with sweat. Finally, she headed down to the Serpentine at the centre of the park and stopped for a moment, breathing heavy and fast. George had taught her how to calm it – her breath; so she stood in silence, closing her eyes to hear its rhythm, visualising the slowness of the pulse in her neck. After a few minutes, she opened her eyes – her lungs silent.

Before her stood a little duck, its orange webbed feet resting on the edge of the grass. Slowly, she sat down so as not to scare it. 'I wonder what you're called in your world?' Harley whispered. It said nothing in reply. 'You look like a Betty.'

She smiled to herself. 'You've lost the plot, Harley Smith.'

There was something peaceful about Betty – uncomplicated. She wanted that too, an uncomplicated life. Harley sighed, recalling the summer picnics down by the Serpentine before her father had changed. Despite his wealth, he'd never let her mother spend more than necessary.

Picnics were made of lemon curd sandwiches and cheap fizzy pop. It didn't matter to Harley: it had been time with her parents – hours spent with them when she was home from boarding school. She'd loved and hated school. It gave her access to book after book after book, and she was rewarded for all her studying by being voted Head Girl for her year three times in a row. Each time her mother kissed her with pride, Harley swore she would be even better the following year because she loved that kiss more than anything in the world.

When her father died, school continued, but her mother changed. Elizabeth fought battles with his family over things Harley didn't understand at the time. When she went home, her mother would look drawn – weary. Harley would hear her arguing on the phone and then the hushed voices of her mother and Mrs Chandler, who lived next door and was a permanent fixture in their home. It was only when her mother died that Diana, Mrs Chandler's daughter and Harley's closest school friend, told her what had been happening.

That was the night she snorted cocaine, letting the drug block out everything until the noise in her head had gone. The need to do it again – to rebuff all her emotions – came almost instantly. The hurt, the disappointment, and most of all, the anger were obliterated with a simple snort of the drug up her nose. When she wasn't snorting, she was tearing herself to pieces with a cocktail of self-destructive thoughts. The cocaine stopped all that. It brought her peace – in a way.

Westminster

Damp with sweat, she flopped onto the side of the concierge desk. 'How's your daughter's dog now, Tony?'

'Oh, he's much better. Katie said to say thank you for the pet hamper you sent her. I'm not sure who enjoyed it more, the dog or Katie showing it off to her friends.'

'I'd give anything to have a dog again.'

'I don't know why you haven't. It'd be the fittest dog in London. How's university?'

'Ask me in a month! Right now, I haven't got a clue about any of it!'

'Well, I'm proud of you. I'm sure your mother would be too.'

'I wonder if my father would. He didn't seem to like me much.'

'From what you've told me, the tumour changed him.'

'It's hard to remember what he was like before all of that; it seems like such a long time ago.'

East Ham: Pinnie Street, The Primrose Estate

Ben's angular body bent over. Swearing in frustration, he picked up the bow he'd thrown on the ground. Harley watched him, her back leaning against the cold wall. He took another shot and missed.

The evening light was fading as they stood in the long garden at the back of his house. Still, it wasn't an excuse – they needed accuracy, whatever the lighting.

'For fuck's sake.' He snapped. 'Why the hell do we have to work with bows and fucking arrows! I'm not bloody Robin Hood.' His blonde hair flopped over his face. 'These envelopes are a pain in the arse. We've only done three and still got four of them to go. Whose gaff is next?'

'Stuart McKenzie.'

'Remind me who they all are. My brain is fucked today.'

Harley sighed. 'Sidney Knight, Richard Seal. Ethan Edwards, Stuart McKenzie, Sami Khan, Lucas Orchard, and Robin Goldsmith.'

Ben threw the bow to the ground.

'What's with you tonight?'

'My bloody sister, that's what!'

She picked the bow up. 'What's Aimee done now?'

Stepping to the side, Ben ran his hand through his thick blonde hair. 'How do you put up with her?'

'It's easier than finding someone who wants to know what I do for a living.'

'Ranking is being a shit because of her fucking stupidity.'

Ranking. He was everything George wasn't, yet they'd grown up on the same estate and were once even friends. Her life was entwined with him because of his history with George and now even more so because of Aimee's mess. Harley understood why Ben was pissed off – she wasn't happy herself. Once Eddie Ranking had his claws into something, he didn't ever want to lose control of it.

Pulling the string back to just behind her ear, she aimed and released. The arrow whooshed into the air, causing a breeze over her skin. 'That's being dealt with now, right?' She said as she revelled in the pleasure of the leather-shooting glove and breastplate. The quills of the arrows thrilled her too, but most of all, the whoosh … bullseye.

Ben ran his hand through his hair. 'Now you're pissing me off too!'

Handing him the bow, she stepped back. 'Well, perhaps you should take your angst out on the big red dot in the middle, you know, the thing you keep missing!'

The bow's string pulled back in his right hand as the muscles in his arm went taught with the strain. He frowned. 'Ranking won't go away. You know that don't you? Not now he has something on Dad.' The arrow missed the red target by an inch, and he threw the bow to the floor again. Harley leant down and picked it up, handing it back to him. Ben sighed. 'If she ever bothered to listen, she'd bloody know they hate each other.'

'Again, Ben. We haven't practised in weeks and need to get this right.'

'I can't concentrate.'

'You need to. You've seen McKenzie's house. We can only get in on the third floor. If we can't shoot accurately, we're fucked, and I won't have time to shoot for both of us.'

'Dad saw Ranking last night. I turned up just as he was leaving.' Holding the bow level to his chest, he aimed again. 'I swear he looked like he'd seen a ghost, you know. He was white as a sheet. I've never seen him like that.' The arrow plopped off the bow onto the ground. 'For fuck's sake.' He kicked it across the concrete paving.

Leaning down, she picked it up – again. 'Breathe properly, like you've been taught.' She smiled playfully at him. 'Maybe you're losing your touch.'

'Fuck you.'

'Look, George said he needs the envelopes, right? So, concentrate.'

'With all your gadgetry, haven't you got something that can scan the contents of the envelopes without opening them?'

'We're not bloody MI5!' Lighting a cigarette, Harley leant her back against the garden table. 'Who's the client for the envelopes?'

'He said I don't need to know.'

'Well, I guess you don't. It's not our job to know, but if you're going to obsess like this, I suggest you find out.' She glanced at him. He had a point. Even though they had grown up together, George and Eddie hated each other. Maybe that's why they hated each other. Why would George even entertain Ranking in his house? It wasn't just hatred between them – it went beyond that. Yet Eddie was in his life again, just as the envelope jobs had started.

'Lift your elbow up. You're getting sloppy.'

Ben turned to her. 'Don't you think it's weird? Ranking going to see Dad and us doing over the people on the Red List?'

'If George thought we needed to know, we'd know.'

THE PORTICO THIEF

CHAPTER 15

Mile End: The Blue Cat

CHILLED drops of water ran down the sides of the half-empty wine glass. Her head felt fucked. Her father's key sat on the bar before her, a familiar shape, but she had no idea where from. Fucked. She was dreading the afternoon ahead. Everything was fucked. Joanna Evans was everywhere she went, and so was Miss Smith. They were joined at the hip and on her mind all the time.

The key was on her mind too, and so was Thomas. All the things he'd told her were swirling around in her head. How could any of it be true? Her father wasn't the man Thomas had described. And The Domino Set was practically a myth. No one knew who they were, how it started, how far its reach was. Clients had mentioned it to her a few times with respect and awe. Emily sunk her head into her hands. What the hell was the key for?

Sitting back up, the glass came to her lips, and she downed the remains. The barman poured her another for the fourth time. She wanted to cry, but half laughed instead; her tears would be just as fucked as everything else. Repeating it over and over in her head, the word fucked gave her some relief. Even court was fucked – losing her first legal argument that morning in nearly five years.

Gulping down the fresh glass of wine, she sighed and ran her hand through her tumbling hair. He'd been right – her father. Everything she knew about him – thought she knew about him – had disappeared. The man who had sat up all night revising with her for her Bar exams, including the subject of ethics, was allegedly part of one of the country's largest criminal gangs. Questions tumbled in her mind. Did her mother know? The muscles in her jaw clenched. Why would he do that to her? Why would he pretend to be something he wasn't?

The result of the morning's case drifted back to her mind. Had she lost because she was too distracted or because her client's case wasn't as strong as she'd believed? Either way, the outcome had taken her to the bar she always relaxed in, where she could be herself.

Five years without losing. She'd prided herself on such success, but now … now she'd lost, and so had her client. Ordering more wine and thinking about just how fucked her life was felt like the only thing she was capable of. She hated self-pity, but everything was too messed up – fucked – not to allow a moment of it.

In the mirrors behind the bar were the reflections of women drinking – in couples or groups, except one. One was on her own, sitting in a booth and drinking a glass of wine. Their gazes met in the mirrors. The young blonde smiled. Emily diverted her eyes back to the key.

To add to the fucked-up feeling inside her head, the Detective Inspector had left a message on her phone while she was in court. There was no news. No more leads on who had shot her father. All they knew was that a motorbike had been seen in the area soon after her father had been shot – seen on CCTV from the gated entrance to the neighbour's house. They'd lost track of it behind the masses of trees. Months had passed, and the investigation was just as fucked as her head.

'You look like you need company.'

'Am I that sorrowful?' Emily smiled at the blonde now by her side.

The woman smiled back, tucking the wave of her falling fringe behind her left ear. 'I can think of a way to make you happier if you dare.'

Emily laughed. 'If I dare? I'm possibly too old for such a proposition – and for you, no doubt.'

'I've been watching you, and I get the feeling that it's just what you need.' She leant towards Emily's ear and whispered, 'I like being fucked. Hard. You're welcome to join me. Otherwise, I will just have to do it myself.'

East London: University

What the hell? Groaning, she dipped her head into her hands and closed her eyes for a moment. Lunchtime drinking didn't suit her anymore. Even worse, she'd done it during teaching hours. Following the blonde woman into the bar's loos and doing something she hadn't done since she was seventeen was not a good idea.

A mint melted in her mouth. The woman's name evaded her. Woman. She laughed. Woman. The age gap between them must have been nearly twenty years. Sitting up straight, she brushed the hair from her face and twisted it up into a loose knot at the nape of her neck. With her makeup retouched, she studied herself in the small mirror on her desk. 'You look like shit.' she mumbled.

Although her colleagues usually complained at the start of a new academic year, Emily never did – she enjoyed the newness of it all. Seeing young faces generally eager to learn fed her need to teach the subject she loved. But this year – every day – it was like a heavy lump sitting in her chest that wouldn't shift, not even with a deep cough or a clearing of her throat. It was so embedded. Grief had never done that to her before. It wasn't just sitting there – inactive – it was sending out fluttering shockwaves making her heartbeat faster – yet she couldn't breathe. She tried a deep breath to see if it would satisfy her lungs, but it didn't. And seeing Joanna Evans almost every day was making it worse.

There was nothing Emily could do to stop the girl from applying to study law at the same university she worked at, but she'd done everything not to have her in her tutorial groups ... and then came Harley Smith. Why would such a woman want to study with someone like Joanna? And to refuse the swap of classes would have caused questions and raised suspicions. She didn't want that.

Looking at her watch, she sighed. Seeing Joanna in every Friday lecture was a torment she didn't have the energy for, but every damn Thursday too – in close proximity – was something that made the lump in her chest embed itself even deeper. Of all the universities she could have chosen. And she was always there: lingering in the doorways of the school's corridors or sitting on the leather chair outside her office. Why didn't she say anything? Why didn't she ask for whatever she wanted? But she knew ... Emily knew what Joanna wanted.

The pressure in her head throbbed again, and she quickly swallowed two painkillers with a large gulp of water. She wasn't sure what she needed to make her mind clearer and her body less heavy. The random anonymous fuck hadn't helped. The woman had made everything worse when she'd said she had a girlfriend waiting for her to get home. Emily recoiled.

Sleep wasn't helping either; in fact, sleep wasn't happening, not since her father had been killed. It was impossible to settle her mind. It wasn't just the grief talking to her all night, it was all the possibilities of what he'd become involved in – something so messed up that he was killed for it. Lying in bed just made her mind whirl even more. Nothing would silence the thoughts, not midnight runs, alcohol or even the occasional smoke of weed her brother had given her.

The alarm on her phone beeped. It was time to go – to face her Thursday students. To face Joanna Evans.

CHAPTER 16

East London: University

'ARE you okay, Joanna?' Her skin was sticky and colourless, and the irritating tapping of her leg under the desk – up and down – was rubbing against Harley's thigh. Shuffling her notes for the third time, Joanna nodded.

Dressed in black, with a small silver circle on a fine black lace around her neck, Knight entered the room with her glasses perched on the top of her head. Closing the door, she handed a bundle of papers to the nearest student and turned a chair back-to-front. Leaning against it, she surveyed the room. Her cheeks were redder than normal and her makeup, although near-perfect, was heavier – a redness to her eyes.

'Today, we'll discuss the subject I lectured on last Friday. Your tutorials will always run this way, so the lecture can provide you with a strong grounding for our discussions. You should have all read the cases for week one in your tutorial packs. Is there anyone who didn't?'

No one raised a hand.

'Good. Can anyone tell me what *mens rea* is?'

Silence.

Glancing around the room, she focused on Joanna. 'Miss Evans, you have extraordinary looking notes in front of you; what do they say?'

A flush rose to Joanna's face as she stared hard at the pages before her. She didn't speak: her head dipped as a red blotch rose on her neck.

'With all those colours and lines, I'm sure you must have something to say. No? Then Miss Smith, would you be able to tell us all?'

Shit! Nowhere on her notes had she defined *mens rea*. Her blood pulsated in her veins, and she flushed as red as her friend next to her. Raising her gaze to the Professor, she replied, 'It's Latin for guilty mind, but really it means intention. Looking at Joanna's notes, I can see she's also written that intention isn't the same as motivation or desire.'

Knight ignored the dig and continued. 'Not a bad answer, but what does it mean?'

'It means there needs to be an intention to commit a crime. Motivation alone isn't enough. A person can be motivated to kill someone but might not intend to.'

Without acknowledging her answer, Knight moved on to ask the next question to the next student in her firing line – James. Sitting opposite Harley, the plump nineteen-year-old's cheeks became ruddier under his ginger fringe. Stuttering, he answered her question before she moved on to the next student and the next. The class was exhausting, and Harley was relieved when it ended.

Joanna slipped her arm through Harley's and pulled her rapidly along the corridor as they left the classroom. 'I hate that woman.'

James followed behind them, his face still as ruddy as before. 'She's intense, isn't she?' He mumbled in a North Essex accent.

Joanna turned and smiled at him, a pink flush rising to her pale cheeks. 'You answered, though. That's more than I could.'

'Why didn't you? The answer was in your notes, and you told me all the answers this morning.'

Harley smiled to herself – the two of them must have met for coffee before the class. It pleased her. Joanna needed friends at university and needed the confidence having them brings.

As they walked towards Library Square together, Joanna slipped her arm again through Harley's – linking them together as if they were old friends. Harley wasn't sure if it was sweet or unnerving.

James, with his strong fleshy limbs, followed behind, making jokes about Knight that made the girl giggle in delight. A little out of the loop, Harley remained quiet so the pair could carry on their innocent flirtations.

The Embankment

There was never a definitive reason why she chose the routes she ran, but there were ones she preferred, depending on her mood. When she wanted something peaceful, she ran the Hyde Park route; even though it was always busy, it had a slower pace than the commuter streets. But the park wasn't what she needed. She wanted something hard, something to tire her physically and hurt her muscles. She wanted the pain in her body because at least then she'd be feeling something.

Running past Big Ben, she chased the thumping of her heartbeat down towards the river Thames, hitting her feet fast on the tarmac as the evening rush hour belched its fumes around her. Weaving between office workers, she played a game of dodge that made her senses wake up and sharpen – pushing her to bend in different ways and making her feet decide their movement mid-step.

As she zigzagged and crisscrossed, her heart raced beneath her ribs. The more she sweated, the more she pushed herself to the edge. That's what she wanted, to be taken to the edge of something. Despite all the years of not taking cocaine, she still wanted, needed, that edge: she wanted to burst with sensations. Forcing herself harder, she ran until she was by the river's edge, along past Blackfriars, under the bridge whose underbelly lit up with neon blue. She ran to the next bridge and the next until she was close to Tower Hill – her marker. Turning back, she pressed her body harder than it could usually take.

Life was changing, she was changing, and as she ran, she thought about all the possibilities before her. Could she make it through the law degree? Could she ever give up working with George and Ben? What if their biggest clients wouldn't let her because she knew too much? But what did she know? George was the only one who met with them: she didn't even know their names. Each footfall brought with it another thought, another question that made her pound harder with the impact of the concrete shuddering through her feet, up into her limbs and into her heart which beat hard as the sweat dripped down, drenching her skin.

As she ran, the words of Diana, her old school friend, flooded her mind – words that had made her life feel worthless. They'd hit her like a giant fucking demolition ball, knocking her internal balance into oblivion for years. Just an hour before Diana's sixteenth birthday party at boarding school, as they were getting ready in Diana's room, her friend dropped the bomb. 'He wasn't your real father, you know.'

Those words sucked out the last speck of Harley's emotion. She was empty. The memories of her childhood had been smashed, and so was her trust in her mother: the one person she loved without question. How could she have done that? Made her believe that David Smith was her father? When he died, why didn't she tell her then? When he was shouting in her face, making her stand still without showing her tears or her fear, why didn't she pick her up

74

and say, don't worry, he's not your real father...

In the last five years of his life, Harley irritated her father, and his anger was all her fault. She wasn't intelligent enough, couldn't stand still long enough, her room was too untidy – despite her having spent hours organising it. When he asked her questions about books she hadn't read, she read them. The next time he'd ask her something else she didn't know, so she would go away and read something new, trying again to please him. It became a vicious circle she could never be a winner in.

Too young to understand what a brain tumour did to a person, she internalised his anger as her own. In her only outlet, sports at school, she'd kick or punch, hold her breath underwater for longer than any other girl, and challenge herself to a point where the PE teacher would dive in and pull her out of the pool. Everything she did became a challenge against herself, a dare to conquer, a fear to beat.

Her young mind rationalised that if she could conquer every fear, read every book, know every answer, she'd eventually win him round again. All she wanted was to have the father back she'd once known and loved, the man that would read endlessly to her for hours as she sat on his lap or teach her the piano – his love, his career. Nothing worked, but as a child, she kept innocently trying until the moment he passed away.

Diana was high when she'd told Harley. Lines of cocaine were being offered around on pink-framed mirrors. She'd always said no in the past, never wanting to disappoint her parents – her mother. But as the line was offered, she'd thought, there's no one left to care. Her remaining grandparents didn't. So she'd snorted it up her nose with a sharp inhale, with determination – every brilliant little grain of it. Her mind had flown away, free from itself.

Westminster

Fried garlic and roasting chicken wafted in the air, intermingling with the faint scent of shampoo. Scraping her hair loosely back, she quickly towel-dried and threw on a t-shirt with a pair of cut-off shorts. By the time she reached the kitchen, she was ten minutes late, but Aimee didn't mind; she was busy laying plates on the breakfast bar.

'Good day at school, babe?'

Nodding, Harley filled a glass full of iced water and asked, 'How was work?'

'Oh, you know, usual. My bitch of a manager finally agreed to me having time off over Christmas.'

'So, you're actually going to the Maldives?'

'What about school?'

'We had our criminal tutorial today.'

'Was that with the Dark Knight? How was she today?'

'She looked a bit dishevelled, although I don't think her version of dishevelled is like yours or mine.'

'What d'you mean?'

'I don't know … like she'd been drinking or crying.'

Wiping the hair away from her face, Aimee glanced up from the cooking. 'Doesn't sound very professional.'

'She was still top of her game, though, although Joanna doesn't seem to like her.'

Aimee scraped the chicken onto the salad and tossed it around. 'Well, there's a reason she's got that nickname; she's probably a right bitch,' she said, plopping the bowl down and sitting opposite.

'I enjoy her teaching, she's interesting.' She watched Aimee put a piece of chicken into her mouth, expecting her to respond, but she said nothing as she ate. 'I can't imagine ever being that intelligent.'

Aimee drained the wine glass of its contents. 'Or that boring,' she said as she poured herself another.

'I have to go out in a bit.'

'Is Ben with you?'

'It's not a job. I've got to meet Ranking.'

'I thought you'd sorted all the plans for Antwerp?'

'Would you pack my bag? I find out tonight when and where, and we've got an early flight tomorrow.'

'I'm coming?' Aimee smiled.

CHAPTER 17

Antwerp

THE hotel room was full of period features, dark heavy wooden beams, and a large dark fireplace: ambient lighting, crisp white linen, a 50-inch plasma screen and music dock. In the corner of the room, there was a pre-ordered bottle of Dom Pérignon with Belgian chocolates.

Throwing her bag to the floor, Aimee jumped back onto the bed in delight, grabbing Harley's hand and pulling her down too. As she did, the tug nagged at the lingering ache left in Harley's body from the week before. Aimee sat up. 'Let me have a look.'

Yellowish black-blue bruising marbled along Harley's back; it was the same on her knees, neck, and wrists. 'Is this to do with the envelopes?' Aimee asked.

Harley pulled the woman's fingers away from her skin and held them tightly. 'How do you know about the envelopes?'

'Dad and Ben were whispering about them the other day. They forget I'm there sometimes.'

'What did you hear?'

'Nothing important, just Ben was asking Dad what was in them, but he said he didn't know. It's obvious whoever you're stealing off doesn't want the police involved, though ... don't you think? Otherwise, they'd have been called when you were caught.'

'How do you know the police weren't called?'

'I have friends. I'm not as stupid as you lot think.'

Harley studied Aimee carefully. 'What friends?'

'I just know there weren't any reported burglaries that night.' She smiled.

'What night? What exactly do you know?'

'The night you got these bruises. Why don't we open the champagne, have a shower and head out into the town to see what it can offer? Antwerp has fifty-five gay bars, you know!'

Antwerp: Diamond District

Antwerp: over 80% of the world's rough diamonds were handled and passed through its distribution channels. Harley internally trembled.

Leaning on the wall opposite the Railway Cathedral in the diamond boutique district, she studied the exits. If anything did go wrong, she had nobody to tell, no one to contact, not even Aimee. One wrong move would lead everything back to George.

The cigarette end flicked from her fingers into the kerb and rolled a spark against the grey concrete – her eyes followed it for a moment. Her skin tingled as she took a deep breath and strolled across the street. This job was different. Maybe it was because Eddie Ranking was involved, or perhaps it was because Aimee had caused all the mess. It was an exciting different – like a new drug to feed her system. She knew she should be scared: scared of things going wrong, of being caught, of being in a foreign prison, but she wasn't.

She walked casually inside the Railway Cathedral, her gaze scanning in every direction. Her eyes worked hard to find where mirrors hid cameras. Above her head, tiny dots of red light moved at different levels as digital eyes scrutinised every move made by visitors – too many even for Harley to remember.

And despite there being numerous diamond boutiques, all gleaming under the lights, she was only interested in one. Security guards – two – stood at its doorway, loaded with a range of equipment on their waist-belts. She strolled past them into the boutique, her heart drumming hard against her ribs. The air was cool, and a scent of fresh flowers hovered delicately from the glass vases that reflected under the jewellers' lighting. Everything shone. Glass cabinets, mirrors, marble floors, and chandeliers. It was a universe of tempting reflections.

A tall, striking woman in her forties with short blonde hair cropped into her neck stood motionless at the end of a counter. Anaïs. Other than the security guards, she was the person Harley needed to see. She knew her face, but Anaïs didn't know hers – yet. It gave her the edge, just a little: a moment to assess the coiled rigidity, the business-like detached smile. Anaïs' hazel gaze met hers as she stood before the woman and said, 'A friend in London suggested I come to you.'

'Did he recommend anything in particular?'

'Round brilliant-cut.'

'He has good taste. When was he here last?'

'July 18th.'

'What setting did he suggest?'

'He advised that you guide me on this.'

'Perhaps you would like to come with me?' Anaïs led her away from the boutique's public front and through a heavy metal door opened by a lever like the ones on an aeroplane. It shut behind them with a mechanical thud. Inside – under her skin – was a cocktail of fear and excitement. As they walked, a shiver prickled up her spine and into her head. Cameras silently followed them from every angle, and motion detectors smouldered red as they walked towards another door. In a room with no natural daylight, Anaïs told her to remove her jacket and shoes. Harley complied, and the woman passed them to a featureless shadow in the dark corner.

'Arms. Stretch them out. Open your legs wide.'

Well-manicured red fingernails ran coolly over every inch of her body, even between her thighs. Fingertips searched through her hair and into her mouth. There was no gentleness in Anaïs' hands. She was rough, purposeful. Despite being checked, her jacket and boots weren't handed back – they stayed in the thick heavy hands of the man holding them. It was all she could see of him, except a shadow of light on his nose.

Working through the double key locks and code, Anaïs opened the safe. She pulled out a black velvet pouch and emptied its contents onto a velvet-lined wooden jeweller's tray. The glimmer of their cut fell into the light, exquisitely – one by one: beautiful 10-carat iridescent droplets. Passing Harley a double lens jewellers' loupe, the woman told her to examine them. Between her fingertips, she marvelled at their beauty – flawless. Sparkling under the light, effervescent reflections. Prisms of colour. Harley held her breath.

'I'm told you haven't done this before.' The woman stated in perfect English. 'Buy a condom, wrap the diamonds in toilet paper, and put them inside the condom. Put the condom inside you. If you don't wrap them in toilet paper, they will split the condom and cut you, making you walk funny. With this many diamonds, you may walk funny anyway. One more thing, those big advertising screens you walk past … sitting behind them is security. You never know who is where. If you look suspicious, they will pick it up from the moment you arrive at the airport. Getting through the customs check is the easy part. Do you understand?'

★

Antwerp: Hotel Astoria

In a small, beautifully restored townhouse offering authentic cuisine and good Belgian beer, Harley found Aimee.

'Did it go okay?'

'All good, although she pointed out my bruises need to be covered tomorrow when we go through customs.'

'She may have a point.' Aimee's full mouth, about to encircle the waffle and ice cream, looked, for the first time in a long time, kissable to Harley and her skin tingled. The feeling went through her limbs as if she'd inhaled a line of cocaine and was sparkling its dust in her blood.

Catching her gaze, Aimee frowned. 'Do I have ice cream on my face?' She quickly rubbed her napkin over her mouth.

'I was just thinking about how I'd like to take you to bed.'

She smiled. 'About time.'

Harley placed a small, gift-wrapped box on the table.

The spoon, mid-motion to Aimee's mouth, stopped. Putting it down slowly, she picked up the box as if too nervous to touch it. Hesitating, it sat in her hand with anticipation, then, pulling the ribbon off, she smiled.

'Oh my god! Fucking hell! They're gorgeous.' When she glanced up, tears glistened around the edges of her eyes. 'What on earth have I done to deserve these?' she asked quietly.

Harley shrugged. 'Do I need a reason to buy you something nice?'

Aimee glanced back down at the diamond earrings. 'Can I put them on now?'

'You can put them on whenever you like. They're yours!'

London: City Airport

There were no customs checks on the way out of Antwerp. No one was interested in anything being taken out of the country even though Anaïs' had said, 'you don't know who is watching from where.'

Harley continued to clench the diamonds as she walked and waited to board. When the plane's engines started up, its tremors shuddered and pulsated against the diamonds inside – the most expensive vibrator in the world – and she could feel it.

City Airport and its green lane weren't so easy. A wave of anxiety rose in her stomach as customs officers sat on the sterile metal benches watching everyone. Acid burnt in her throat as she swallowed. The blood drained from her face. *They must know*, she thought, as her lungs hesitated in their breath. The pace of her heartbeat accelerated. Wheels from suitcases rolled on the marbled floor around her – they screeched in her ears. Everything moved in slow motion. Voices dragged like she was on LSD, tripping in a trail-back.

A little squeeze of her arm from Aimee as they walked made her smile. 'I could do with more champagne,' Harley said quietly.

Aimee grinned. 'It would be rude not to. This has been the best weekend ever.'

Harley half smiled as they walked through to the side of freedom, causing a gunshot rush to her head before hitting her bloodstream. She wanted to do it all again.

CHAPTER 18

Islington

SHE sat opposite Thomas at the kitchen table with a glass of wine and a tub of olives as he opened the handwritten ledgers.

'I can't believe you still use these.' Emily smiled as she traced her fingers over his tiny, almost illegible writing.

'No one can hack these.'

'Why are you showing them to me?'

'I need you to understand something, Emily. I was just your father's accountant, and I didn't judge. I didn't get involved with his business. I did his books. I shifted things around to protect every asset he had. Do you understand?' Thomas opened the second ledger. 'Everything in the first one was included in probate; everything in the second one was not.'

Leaning closer toward Thomas' small scribbles, Emily mumbled, 'Jesus.' Payments spanned back twenty years. Thousands every month: different amounts, regular names. Her fingers traced over each page as she held her breath – twenty years of small Thomas-scribbles: all leading to one final amount. Stepping back from the ledger, she looked at him.

'I know that name!' Emily tapped her finger down onto the paper. 'Why was he paying her money? Please tell me it wasn't true what she said about him?'

Thomas shook his head. 'No, sweetheart, that was *never* true.'

Relief swept through her so hard that she felt faint. 'Then why all the regular payments to her?' She asked quietly.

'Because the child *was* his. *Is* his. He never disputed it.'

'And the others? Who are they? Why were they all paying my father so much money every month? Why? I mean, offshore accounts. It's money laundering.'

'Every business involved was legitimate.'

Sighing, Emily lit a cigarette. 'Don't treat me like I'm stupid.'

'I didn't mean to.' He stood opposite her. 'Look, all I can say is that your father paid me well, and it's because of him that I was able to buy my little party mansion in Marbella.'

'I don't understand. Why would father pay you so much that you could afford such a place? And why was everyone paying *him*?' Emily paused – her mind racing ahead before Thomas could answer.

'Bloody hell.' She stepped away from the ledgers. The loose bun at the nape of her neck unravelled as she ran her hand through her hair. 'Jesus Christ.' She whispered. 'It was protection money, wasn't it?'

'Something like that.' Thomas replied quietly.

Their eyes met. Emily shook her head. 'No. No way. You're lying.'

'I wouldn't lie to you; you know that. The books don't lie, Emily.'

Emily stared at him. 'Well, they obviously can, can't they. And you can't earn money like that without being the main player. Oh my god! Is that what he was? The main player? Jesus Christ, Thomas, was father at the top of it all?'

The breath in her chest stuck like a claw holding her heartbeat. Shaking her head, she paced away from her old friend and towards the kitchen door. Her hair, now fully tumbled around her shoulders and face, was swept back by her fingers as she sighed heavily.

Slowly, she tried to breathe to get rid of the clench in her throat and the bile rising from her stomach. She turned to look at Thomas, then back at the ledgers. Staring at them, she kept her eyes on the woman's name she recognised. Over twenty years of payments – not one missed – from her father to the woman who had accused him of rape twenty-three years ago. And then there were all the other payments to him from men she'd never heard of.

What a fool.

Her entire career had been based on doing the right thing so he would respect her.

He was corrupt.

Thomas was corrupt.

Both had always been her moral compass. She'd admired them because of it. Her father had taught her to be ethical, to stand up for all the good things and do battle with the bad. It wasn't always what she wanted to do – to be. There were times when she wanted to bend the rules, to go against everything bloody moral – to be reckless. To enjoy the thrill. But her father pushed and moulded her with his own moral code. If anything, she'd bowed to his wishes because she respected him so much. When she'd enjoyed the rebellious moments of cocaine highs as a pupil barrister, it was her father's reproachful voice in her head that had eventually made her say no. And now … just fuck!

Now Thomas was proving that her father was everything he'd supposedly stood against. He'd been a complete lie.

'There's £30 million in payments there.' She whispered, '£30 million.'

'This is a lot for you to take in, sweetheart,' Thomas said as he touched her hand gently.

She pulled away. 'I thought seeing you tonight would bring answers to my questions, but it hasn't.' Her eyes glistened with tears as she asked, 'What do we do next?'

'We can't do anything unless we have the final bank account details, and that, my dear Emily, is something your father never trusted me with.'

'Nor me, it seems.'

'Did he leave you anything else other than the letter?'

'Yes, a key, but I've no idea what it's for. He didn't say.'

St Albans

With the two lazy old dogs lying at her feet, the housekeeper, Agi, snoozed on the kitchen sofa as Emily entered the room. They raised their heads, wagged their tails, and dozed off again. Torn about whether she should wake Agi, Emily gently popped a post-it note on the housekeeper's hand, warning her not to be startled when she woke.

Leaving the sleeping trio, she quietly made her way to the study and closed the door behind her. Emily stood in the middle of the room and glanced around. Agi had done a brilliant job clearing up after forensics had ripped the place to pieces, but she could still see where they had been.

Her gaze scanned. There were barely any places where things could hide. Books covered shelves. Shelves covered walls. Scarcely an inch of wall space was left. Behind her father's desk hung an oversized painting of the Cutty Sark at Greenwich. A gift to her father from her mother on their wedding day: the place where he'd proposed. Emily stood before it – fixated.

Every year, until the day her mother died, her parents would go back to the Cutty Sark and sit by the river with their flask of hot tea and homemade sandwiches. Maybe that's what she needed to do – to sit where they had sat. The thought made her jaw clench as the familiar ache inside her chest fluttered with nausea. Exhaling heavily, she stepped towards the painting. It had to be behind it, the place where the key would fit. Gently, her fingers touched the heavy gold-wooden frame and slid behind it to the painting's back. With cautious unease, she slowly eased it a fraction away from the wall and pressed her cheek against the cool plaster. Her nose pushed on the frame's edge as she tried to peer into the small space of darkness. The wall was smooth and intact. Nothing.

Stepping away, Emily turned to face the room and all its books again. One by one, she slid them out, looked and felt behind them. It was the only other obvious place.

An hour passed – methodical sliding and exploring. Book dust floated in the air – her nose tingling. Two hours. Then three. Sliding, looking, exploring with her fingertips. An afternoon gone without any success. When the last book was back in its rightful place, she slumped onto her father's armchair and rested her head on its high back. Closing her eyes, she fought the tears aching in her throat. There was an entire house to search. She sighed. Rooms full of memories, boxes, childhood books, clothes, papers – *stuff*. Stuff from thirty years ago collecting dust in the loft. Stuff she didn't want to have to hunt through for clues. Why the hell hadn't he just told her what the key would open?

Long summer evenings – that's what he'd said in his letter. Emily's eyes pinged open. Long summer evenings. Where they used to sit and study together for her exams. She shot up and raced out of the study, down the hall and into the kitchen. The sleeping dogs creaked up on their aged paws and gruffed with excited grumbles as she skidded past them. Agi jerked awake with a 'What the Jesus?'

'It's just me, Agi.' Emily called as she dashed through the back door and into the glass-walled terrace that they opened up for those long summer evenings … where they had studied together for her exams. Frantically, she began opening the drawers and doors of the cupboards.

'What on earth are you looking for?' Agi asked as she shuffled in her slippers to the doorway.

'I don't know yet, but I'll know it when I see it.'

Agi shook her head. 'Well, I'll be of no use to you then. Do you want something to eat?'

Emily stopped mid-search of a cupboard and looked up. 'Only if it's no bother.' She smiled at the housekeeper.

Another hour passed. Another hour of unsuccessful hunting. Sitting on the cold tiled floor, Emily looked around her at the mess she'd created. Garden crockery and barbeque paraphernalia were scattered around her like a burglary scene. She stared at it with frustration. What the hell had her father meant if it wasn't the terrace where they'd spent those evenings?

CHAPTER 19

East Ham: Nelson Street, The Primrose Estate

THE grip of Debra Evans's fingers dug into Joanna's wrists as she was flung backwards, away from the kitchen sink. Her backbone, nobbled and scrawny, smacked against the handle on the fridge, but she daren't let out a cry.

'That money ain't yours, remember. Ya can't buy a fuck load of books with it. That's what the library is for.'

Tears welled in the girl's eyes. 'I bought them before uni, from my pub wages.'

'Then why was ya hiding them under ya bed?'

'I didn't have anywhere else to put them.'

'Don't fucking lie to me, child. They ain't any use to a thick shit like you anyway. What grades ya getting? Eh? Can't be good if ya haven't told me.'

Wiping her eyes with the cuffs of her jumper, Joanna sniffed up the nose-snot she didn't want her mother to see. 'I don't know yet. It's too early to tell.'

'You'll fail. Ya always fucking do.'

'Can I have them back? Please, Mum, I need them for my homework.'

Her mother bent down her tall, slender body and picked the books up, throwing them across the room. They hit Joanna in the chest, the stomach, and her thighs. She flinched as each one thumped against her bones – she didn't try to protect herself. When all the books had thudded to the floor, she leant down and slowly picked them up – still stinging from their impact. Hugging them tightly, she quietly asked, 'Can I go now?

Joanna ran up the stairs – the books clamped to her chest. Sitting on her bed, she slowly placed each one of them on the faded pink duvet and inspected them: checking pages, spines, and for anything that may have been ripped out. Sighing deeply, the girl relaxed just a little; at least her mother hadn't actually been through them. If she had, she'd have kicked off even worse and probably ripped one of them in particular to pieces.

Tucking them all safely back under her bed, Joanna flopped face down onto her pillow and hugged it. She fought with herself to stop the tears, but she couldn't. Most of the time, she could. Most of the time, she didn't even feel like crying. Her life was beyond the tears. But to have her mother find her most precious belongings got inside her, making her skin cold and her stomach quiver.

Joanna's body trembled, but she daren't make a sound as she cried, or her mother would hear. The walls were thin in their two-up, two-down. Every noise could be heard. Even the neighbours going to the loo during the night woke Joanna up.

While she lay on her bed, her mother banged the cupboard doors in the kitchen, looking for another bottle of vodka, no doubt. The sound echoed through the floorboards. Maybe that's what set her off, Joanna thought. She should have got her some from the pub, from the customers who always offered her drinks, and the vodka tally she built up so she could take a bottle home at the end of a few shifts.

Closing her eyes, she wiped her face and snuggled into the soft pillow. There were only a few weeks to go, and she would get her first essay grades back. For the past two weeks, when she hadn't been at work or university, she'd studied until the early hours of every morning. More than anything, she wanted to show Professor Knight what she could do – and Harley – and her uncle Tom. She knew she wasn't intelligent, but she'd really tried and had worked harder than Harley ever would. It didn't bother her that she had to, as long as her new friend was proud of her, and Knight would see she wasn't as stupid as she behaved in class.

Leaning over to the side table drawer, she pulled out the well-used tube of cream and rubbed it on her wrists to ease the bruising. Before long, Joanna drifted off into sleep – a few stray tears still dampening her face as she gently snored.

CHAPTER 20

East London: University

STILL giddy from the adrenaline of the diamond smuggling, Harley found it difficult to concentrate on anything at university. She wanted more of the feeling that was like old times when she'd first worked for George. Her body was restless – edgy.

Zoned out from Joanna's white noise about a book she was reading, Harley's attention only came back to the conversation when the girl reached over to steal the cake sitting untouched on her plate and said, 'I take it you don't want this?'

Glancing down, Harley's eyes were drawn to the marks on her friend's wrist as the jumper sleeves moved up with the stretch. The white-on-white scars flashed starkly against the deep blue-purple bruises rising to the girl's skin.

'Have it,' Harley said softly. 'What have you been up to this week? I've barely seen you.' With a mouthful of lemon drizzle cake, Joanna shook her head as if to say nothing. 'Have you been out at all?' Harley asked. The girl shook her head again and took another mouthful. 'How are things with your mother? You said she was a bit stressed last time I saw you.'

Joanna glanced at the fork in her hand and paused. Her hesitation only lasted seconds before she smiled lightly. 'Oh, you know, mother is mother. Are you still coming round this week to mine to study?'

Harley gazed at her. 'Wouldn't miss it, and no doubt you've entered me into your timetable for the next three years. What colour am I?'

Smiling properly for the first time all morning, Joanna pulled a timetable from her bag and showed it to Harley with excitement. 'Gold, like autumn, that's what you remind me of.'

'What colour are you?'

Joanna looked at her timetable thoughtfully. 'I don't have a colour.'

'Then I nominate something pretty, like pink.'

The palest blue eyes looked up. 'You think I'm pretty?'

'I do. Don't you?'

'Mum said we can't all be blessed with looks.'

'Well, I think you're a pretty pink, so your name should have that colour.'

The girl blushed. 'Are you coming to the bar with us tomorrow after the lecture?'

'I totally am. I really need a drink today.' She glanced at her watch. 'Shit, we'd better go.'

★

Turning her chair back-to-front to lean against it, Knight glanced around the room. 'Today, we will be looking at the theory of correspondence in relation to *mens rea* and *actus reus*. Would anyone like to start the tutorial off?'

Every head in the room dipped. Knight's eyes scanned over them all and, for a moment, lingered on Harley. Heads stayed down, but it was a trick never to be used with Knight. 'Mr Masters, what do you think the correspondence theory is?'

Flicking his pen nervously against his thumb, James cleared his throat. 'I think it means that both the *mens rea* and *actus reus* have to correspond for a person to be convicted of a crime.'

'And do you think this is the case in practice?'

Blushing, he blinked rapidly. Knight moved her attention to Joanna. 'Miss Evans, what do you think?'

Joanna pulled her colourful notes closer to her body, searching for the highlighted answer. Harley wanted to push her one page of notes over to her friend, where the case name was at the top, but she didn't – couldn't. If she had, Joanna would have been even more embarrassed. Patchy red spots rose on her friend's cheeks, standing out on her pale skin as if a bee swarm had attacked her. Knight's attention on the girl stayed fixed. Silence hung in the room. Then, just as Joanna went to speak, Knight moved on, sighing. 'Does anyone know the answer?'

'I know it.' Harley answered. 'Joanna knows it too. We talked about it this morning in preparation; only you haven't given her a chance to say it.'

'Then please do tell us, Miss Smith.' The Professor's gaze coldly met Harley's.

With her head down, Joanna's face continued its deep blotching as Harley gave a clear and unwavering answer – the beat in her heart pulsing with irritation. If there was one thing she hated, it was a bully.

As everyone packed up their books and began to leave, the Professor stopped her at the door. 'I'd like to see you in my office. Now.'

★

In silence, Knight placed the bundle of papers on her desk and turned. 'Please sit.'

'I'd rather stand.'

Folding her arms over her chest, the woman studied her student. 'You did well with your answer, but as I've said before, your delivery needs some work.'

'Just because you're my professor doesn't mean I don't have to agree with how you teach.'

'Really?' Knight replied. 'And what don't you agree with?'

'Well, firstly, I have an unfair advantage over Joanna.'

'And what makes you think that?'

'We discussed the subject in our hour together last week. Unfortunately, someone like Joanna didn't have that chance since you're not her academic adviser.'

Knight's head lowered – eyes to the floor. Her hair fell forward around her face, dark in its tumble. When she finally lifted her gaze back up, Harley expected to see irritation, but there was nothing. 'I'm disappointed you view your subject knowledge as a disadvantage.'

Harley snapped. 'That's not what I said.'

There it was – a flash of irritation and a narrowing of the Professor's eyes.

'No, you said you had an unfair advantage. But if you fail to use the knowledge you have because of a misguided sense of loyalty to your peers, knowledge becomes a disadvantage. Do you understand what I'm trying to tell you, Miss Smith?'

'You're telling me there's no point in me knowing the answer unless I can use it, and I shouldn't avoid doing so because of my friends.'

'Indeed.'

Harley stared at the woman standing opposite her. 'You could have explained it just as simply.'

'I was explaining it thoroughly,' Knight replied with irritation.

'Do you think it's fair that some students, like Joanna, don't have the advantage of an academic adviser like you? You spend time explaining things in our hour together.' She didn't wait for the Professor's answer before saying, 'What you do creates an advantage for your advisees. Other students have advisers who don't give a damn. I've only been here several weeks, but it's obvious a lot of the academics don't even know who their advisees are, let alone spend time with them explaining things on a 1-2-1. So, when you come down harshly on other students in my group because they don't know what I know, maybe you should remember that they haven't had the same privilege as me. I'm not about to make them feel even more inadequate just to impress you.'

'Have you finished?'

'No. But I am very aware that I've probably said too much.'

'Did you know Miss Evans before starting here?'

'No. Why?'

The Professor crossed her arms. 'Your loyalty to her after just several weeks is astonishing.'

'I think you interpret my sense of fairness as an act of loyalty.'

They stood opposite each other in silence for a moment: an equalling of wills as they absorbed each other's position.

'And secondly?' Knight asked. 'You said firstly, so there must be a secondly.'

'You don't give Joanna a chance to speak. As a result, she's nervous in your class.'

'She can't be nervous in court. If she is, she'll never succeed.'

'And you were good, were you, when you started? Or have you forgotten what that feels like? Or maybe you weren't nervous and just breezed your way through it, only I don't think you did, based on some of the cases you lost in your first few years as a barrister.'

Turning her back to Harley, Knight stood by the window and slid her hands into the pockets of her trousers. Silently, she stared out across the campus, down to the canal where the narrow boats moored and a black motorbike was parked. 'My role is to focus on my own advisees, Miss Smith.' The woman turned to face her. 'Your bruises are almost gone, but I have to ask once more, do you need pastoral services?'

Harley shook her head.

'Good. You may go. I have a meeting to attend.'

Westminster

'Do you know The Temple Club in Mayfair? I followed the old man last night. He didn't go to The Eagle, just like Mum said.'

Sitting down on the sofa, she tucked her legs under her body, put the phone on loudspeaker and lit a cigarette. 'Yeah, it's an old boys club. He's not a member, though, is he? Do you think that's where he's meeting the client who wants the envelopes?'

Ben sighed. 'I don't know, but Mayfair isn't really his thing is it!' Harley heard the worry in his voice as he said, 'You know, he met Eddie again this week.'

'Where?'

'Down at the Ship. Mum told me.'

'That's Eddie's patch, isn't it? So why would he go there?' She flipped down the laptop lid and pushed it away.

'Exactly. That's what I mean; he's acting really odd since we got this envelope job and had to start hitting the Red List.'

'We need a copy of The Temple Club's members.'

'Why? And you do know how secretive these clubs are? They're like, full of generations of the bloody elite.'

'We can go in and take it.' Harley sighed. 'Ben, we need to know who he is meeting and who the client is.' Pausing to think, she blew a plume of cigarette smoke into the air before saying, 'You need to scope it out. I don't have time. Can't you get a job there or something?'

'Yeah, cos that's going to be easy, ain't it!'

'Well, the list will either be on a hard drive in one of the admin offices or, if they're still in the dark ages, there'll be a ledger … probably on the concierge desk where they all sign in. It might get locked away at night, but I doubt it; they're usually quite large and heavy.'

'And you know that how?'

'My friend's father was a member of a similar club. I went a few times with her to meet him.' She paused. 'What I don't get is why someone would risk meeting George at a club like The Temple.'

'I need to follow him again.'

'What if he sees you?'

Ben laughed. 'You have no idea how invisible I can be.'

After Ben said goodbye, she stood up, stretched her back and unravelled the knots in her neck with a slow circular motion. Mayfair and The Temple Club. It made no sense. He wasn't a Mayfair man. Consistent and habitual – George spent most of his spare evenings in The Eagle. It was where most of his business was conducted – where most of his associates drifted in and out. Whenever the police needed information, it was the place they headed to first. They accepted it was a pool of criminal knowledge, not just with the old school but with the new. In return for being left alone most of the time, the community occasionally shared small snippets of information, but there were unspoken rules about just how much and what kind of information they gave. It was George's world, a world where he was safe. Mayfair didn't sit right, and neither did his meetings with Eddie.

Harley scribbled down the names on the Red List. She knew them by heart – she always had, but she wanted to stare at them; to see if there was a pattern that she was missing, something that would give her a clue as to what George was getting them into – why he was being shifty.

Sidney Knight – Deputy Commissioner of Scotland Yard
Richard Seal – Dean of Law at Oxford
Ethan Edwards – Cabinet Secretary
Stuart McKenzie – Deputy Assistant Commissioner
Sami Khan – Political Editor
Lucas Orchard – Chief of Counterterrorism
Robin Goldsmith – Director General Nuclear

But the names meant nothing to her, even though she knew exactly who they all were. Seven – all high profile, all living in properties that had top-end security, except Sidney Knight's, who, in hindsight, had needed it the most. She stared at her scribbles; she didn't even know why the Red List existed. Sighing, she screwed up the bit of paper and burnt it in the ashtray, sniffing in the light scent of woody smoke.

She'd never asked who'd originally created the List, but it had existed all the time she'd been working for George. Maybe that was the key – what Ben needed to find out. Grabbing her phone, she quickly tapped out a message to him and sent it before packing up her schoolbag and heading over to Joanna's for the afternoon.

East Ham: Park Avenue, The Primrose Estate

Debra Evans shouted, 'Ya stupid fecking girl,' as she smacked the mug upwards out of Joanna's hands. Hot liquid splashed over the girl's face. Harley, standing by the kitchen door, watched as Debra

Evans' palm slammed into Joanna's face. Unable to watch any longer, Harley shot out of the doorway and thumped her shoulder into the older woman's chest, knocking her hard against the wall. Ramming her forearm into Debra's neck, Harley felt the woman's strong limbs struggle against the hold. She had a strength Harley hadn't expected, especially for some of her age and build. She whispered close to Debra's face, 'You're welcome to try that on me.'

'Get the fuck off me, you dyke.'

Harley released the pressure. 'Next time, I won't,' she replied quietly.

Rubbing her neck, Debra Evans moved away, swearing under her breath. Joanna darted into the kitchen. Saying nothing, Harley took the mug from her friend's hand, who collected an armful of rags from beneath the kitchen sink. Together, they dropped to their knees in the hallway and silently, together, cleared up the mess until it had gone. Years of old nicotine vapours wafted into the air – Harley's empty stomach turned over.

Shutting themselves back in the kitchen, they sat quietly for the first thirty minutes. The girl didn't mention what happened, and Harley didn't force the words. What happened, happened. They didn't need words. She knew what it was like to have a parent with no anger control.

When the rhythmical snoring of Debra Evans rumbled from the lounge, Joanna's shoulders relaxed. Harley's heart sank. She understood. But Debra Evans wasn't ill like her father – she had no excuse. And Harley knew that stepping in to help Joanna would probably lead to the girl being belted even harder – later – when nobody could offer her any kindness or protection. Maybe she should just go into the lounge and wake the woman, slap her hard around the face and throw hot tea against her cheeks as Debra had done to her daughter.

For the next few hours, they worked quietly together. Harley helped Joanna understand all the things Knight had questioned her on, all the things Joanna struggled to say in their tutorial group. She prepped her for the following week, asking her questions and encouraging her to speak her answers clearly – with confidence. It was obvious that Joanna understood everything they explored together. Harley wanted to be sure that when she left, Joanna knew everything she would be asked – that she wouldn't be made to feel stupid in class again. That was a secret promise to herself – to protect the girl. As she packed up her books, Joanna's gaze came to hers.

'Do you have to go already?'

Harley smiled softly. 'I have to meet a friend tonight, but I'll see you soon, okay.' Before leaving, she turned. 'You know, if you need a place to stay, I have a spare room.'

CHAPTER 21

Sevenoaks: Stuart McKenzie's Residence

SHE whispered, *'Fuck!'* as her ankle twisted under her leg. Ben turned and tugged roughly at her arm.

'Fuck! Get up! We've got three minutes.' Dragging Harley to her feet, he pulled her behind him. Tears burnt her eyes as she stumbled across the field towards their concealed bikes. In the darkness, they methodically stripped down their kits. The bows and arrows used to enter the estate snapped with systematic clicks until they were folded in half and back in their toolkits. Every piece of evidence was removed from their bodies, distributed in all the secret compartments within the saddlebags. Jumping onto their bikes, they gently pulled out from the bushes and headed side-by-side down the empty country lanes.

When they got back to Ben's flat, he yanked off his helmet and threw it to the floor. 'What the fuck happened?' He snapped.

Harley's damp hair fell around her face as it twisted with pain. *'You.* You *fucking* happened! You left your fucking bow on the ground and I stumbled on it when I jumped down.'

'I did not!'

'Fuck me, Ben, you did!'

'Bollocks. You need to sort your fucking shit out. You keep fucking up.'

Glaring at him, she quietly said, 'You need to fuck off before I punch you in the goddamn fucking face.'

He sighed, his fingers running through the mop of blonde hair that flopped down over his eyes. 'It's these fucking jobs; they're distracting me … does it hurt?'

'Like hell, you bastard!'

'I'm sorry.'

'You're getting fat and sloppy.'

Ignoring her, he emptied his kit-bag. 'I got the envelope; what did you find? Was there anything else there to give us some clues?'

'I've no idea if it's a clue, but it's a bloody big find.'

Ben paced. 'We've got three more of these fucking jobs, and I can't cope with seeing the old man so stressed out until we've done them all.'

'Well, if we've got to do another in the next few days, I'm going to need some ice for my ankle, or a heating pad, or both. Actually, I'm going to need both.' She slumped onto the sofa and groaned. 'I think it's going to burst.'

Sitting on the coffee table in front of her, Ben slipped the pump from her right foot and rolled up her trouser leg. 'Jeez, no wonder it feels like shit. Have you seen it?'

Harley glanced down at her ankle and grumbled. 'Just what I need. Is there ice in the freezer?'

'I'll get some.'

She rummaged in her knapsack, looking for the gemstone she'd thrown into it without hesitation or examination. Harley didn't know what it was, but she knew it was something she'd never seen before. Finding it, she held the gem up to Ben as he walked back into the room. 'What do you think?'

'Fucking hell!' Passing Harley the ice, he gently took the diamond from her – a respect for what he was holding. 'It looks like the Yellow Sun-Drop.'

'That's over £15 million, right?'

Sitting next to her, Ben studied it carefully, bringing it close to his eye. 'What the hell was it doing there?'

Pressing the ice against her ankle, she sighed. 'I don't know … but that's not all I got, there's a Klimt. I reckon it's worth millions too. There's a couple of other pieces that look like they're worth a fair bit.'

Unrolling the canvas, Ben bent over the painting. Harley watched as his fingers ran through his hair again. 'The police will be all over this,' he mumbled.

'None of the other jobs have been reported.'

'How do you know they haven't?'

'Aimee told me. I think she's got friends in the Met, although she hasn't said that exactly, and there's been nothing in the press, not even local papers, I've been checking every day.'

'Aimee's a bloody liability.'

'It makes no sense. Why would the Deputy Assistant Commissioner have the Sun-Drop and a Klimt? Don't you find that odd? I mean, someone on his salary couldn't afford one of these items, let alone all of them. What are we going to do with it all?'

'Put them in your safe for now. I'll tell Dad in the morning.'

'Have you sorted out a way to get into The Temple Club?'

'I'm working on it. I need a few more days.'

Harley sighed. 'It will be Christmas soon, and we only have three more jobs.'

East London: University

Joanna, red and puffy-eyed, scraped back the chair and threw her bag onto the floor. Harley had waited for over forty minutes while she'd picked up her marked essays from the law office. From her friend's face, it was obvious things hadn't turned out the way she wanted. Joanna sat silent – the red on her skin creeping up from her blotchy neck.

Standing up, Harley went to the cake section of the café and bought a double slab of Victoria sponge, along with a gingerbread latte. Placing the cake and coffee on the table, she sat down and waited in silence for over ten minutes until Joanna finally said, 'thank you.'

'I haven't got to dash off this evening. Do you fancy a drink at the uni bar?'

Joanna shook her head. 'I've got to get back and sort out tea for Mum. She ditched her job a few days ago and has been on a binge of cheap vodka and pizza ever since. I need to get some shopping in.'

'Do you need a hand?' Harley asked, but Joanna shook her head again. 'How about I take you for a ride on the bike then, back to yours?' The girl's face lit up, and Harley added. 'I could do with it myself, to be honest, blow the cobwebs away. Some of my grades were pretty crap.'

Joanna looked at her. 'I don't believe you.'

Harley pulled out the bundle of essays from the brown envelope and scanned through them. 'Well, I was expecting higher than what I got, that's for sure.'

'Mine were okay, except criminal law. I worked so hard on that one. Knight hates me.'

'I don't think she's unprofessional in that way.'

'You think I'm stupid then?'

'That's not what I said.'

'But it is, isn't it?' Joanna pushed the plate away, the cake still on it. 'I can't believe you think I'm that fucking stupid.' It didn't seem possible that Joanna's face could turn any redder than it was, but the rising colour was scorching her skin. Her gaze focused on something beyond where they were sitting. 'I need to ask her why.' Joanna said quietly.

Harley's gaze followed Joanna's. Knight stood at the café counter with Ammon.

'Not here, Jo. Maybe make an appointment to see her in—' But her friend was already up, gathering her things, including her latte and essay paper. Harley tried again, but the sound of the girl's name did nothing to stop her from moving across the open space and towards the Professor. Hobbling after her, Harley tried to catch up, the sharp stab in her swollen ankle shooting into her leg bones.

'Professor,' Joanna said as she shoved the essay paper at Knight. 'I deserve more than this.'

Knight stepped back, the pages thumping against her chest. Ammon thrust his arm behind her, stopping her from knocking against the display of bottled artisan drinks precariously lined up next to the cakes. The Professor rebalanced – her hand clutching the loose-leaf papers. Her voice wasn't as assured as it usually was when she said, 'I'm happy to discuss this in my office, Miss Evans.'

Joanna glared at her. 'You didn't even write any suggestions.'

'I marked so many essays and can't recall all their details.'

'That's a lie, and you know it. You know exactly why you gave me such a shit grade.'

'Now is not the time or the place.' Knight said.

Harley limped forward and touched her friend's arm. 'Come on, Jo, we need to get you home, remember.'

Shrugging off Harley's touch, Joanna stepped towards Knight. 'You've had it in for me since I started, and I want a second opinion.'

The Professor offered the essay back to Joanna, but the girl pushed it away. As she did, the latte in her hand flew up towards Knight with the movement. Harley watched in slow motion. The warm coffee spewed into the air, over Knight's face and neck. Joanna laughed. Knight gasped. Harley saw the same expression of Joanna's mother flash over her friend's face. The sticky-gingerbread liquid dripped from the Professor's eyelashes and chin – from her hair. Ammon grabbed a handful of paper napkins to dry her off. 'Are all your students so insane?' he whispered.

'What did you say?' Harley snapped.

'Well, between you two, can you blame me for asking?'

'Are you that dim you can't see it was an accident?'

'That's enough, Miss Smith.' Knight glared at her.

Harley flashed a glare back. 'He just called us insane.'

'And you think this is normal behaviour!' Knight replied in a low voice – coffee still dripping from her hair.

'It was an accident.' Harley retorted. 'Anyone with any sense can see Joanna didn't mean to do it.'

The Professor's jaw clenched as she wiped the remains of the latte from her neck. 'I suggest you both leave. I will deal with this later.'

Mayfair

Parked between two white vans, Harley held the Triumph between her thighs. With her visor down, she stayed within the shadows – watching.

There wasn't much to do sitting outside the Hare & Dog except watch and wait. Although she was used to casing jobs late at night in the freezing cold, she could never get used to the chill that crept into her bones, despite her leathers. There was no way to keep warm and no way to take a pee.

Drinkers came and went. Entering sober and exiting merrier. Hours passed. As she lit a cigarette, she saw George and another man push open the heavy wooden swing doors. There was no laughing. No back-patting. No handshake. George turned left as he walked down the steps, back towards the tube station. The other man stood for a moment with his phone in his hand. As he typed a message, the glow lit up his face. He was a little older than George – fatter, dumpier. There was an extravagance to him in how he dressed: a deep-blue cravat around his neck and a large gold ring on his finger. His features weren't clear from where she hid, but she got a general sense of his wealth and how he spent it. After sending his message, he turned and hailed a black cab. Harley watched George finally disappear. Which one should she follow?

Hanging back, she trailed the cab through the city streets, keeping herself and the Triumph always a few cars behind. The cab weaved down lesser-known roads, swung round corners, and arrived outside The Temple Club. Harley pulled in down a sideroad just opposite the entrance and turned off the engine. Waiting for the man to pay, she flipped down the Triumph's stand and slid off to get a better view from a shadowed doorway. The lights outside The Temple Club caught more of his detail, and she noted the leather of his shoes, tan and buffed. His coat, cashmere, pulled a little too tightly over his stomach. Before entering the building, he checked his phone.

Standing in the doorway, using its small space to shield from the cold wind, Harley stood frozen – the cold seeping further into her skin and bones. It was 21.30 – nearly three hours without a loo break, and she desperately needed a wee. Just as she was about to give up and drive back to Westminster, a woman walked down the street, towards the Club and up its steps. The activity stirred her interest. Women couldn't be members, just guests. The long chocolate-black hair fell over her shoulders, over the heavy winter coat. She was carrying a black leather messenger bag across her right shoulder. Her stilettoed heeled boots echoed as she walked up the steps. Under the same lights where Harley had seen the man's details, she saw the woman's.

The breath in her lungs stopped.

She knew that face. Bloody hell. She'd studied and admired it. Knight walked through the heavy doors as if she belonged there.

Watching the Professor disappear, Harley quickly darted out of the doorway and moved along the street to get a better view. With the large expansive windows and glittering chandeliers that hung from the high ceilings, rooms exposed their occupants. Harley slid into another doorway and waited. Knight moved through the lobby, through one of the front rooms full of bookshelves and books, and into a second room, dimly lit and glowing orange from a fire. The man Harley had followed stood up and opened his arms to the Professor, who entered his embrace: a long, hugging embrace that was familiar and warm. He kissed her cheek, and they sat down, out of Harley's view.

The Professor's affection for the man was confusing. More than just acquaintances. She showed the same affection to Ammon. Was she having an affair?

There was nothing to see since they'd sat down, but she watched anyway while she thought. There was a link she wasn't understanding. Gently, she chewed the inside of her cheek. One of them had to be the client. Was it Knight? Why else would she meet someone straight after they'd met George? That had to be it. She had a middleman. Why would a barrister want the envelopes? Was she being blackmailed? Maybe Knight was the blackmailer. There was only one thing to do – find out more about the man in the blue cravat.

CHAPTER 22

Soho: The Polo Restaurant

THE gold watch on his wrist glistened under the artificial lights as Zeb raised a glass of iced water to his lips. She watched her brother smile as she walked towards him, his gaze steady, like him.

Emily draped her coat on the back of a chair. She loved him without question, but as she sat down opposite him, she thought, at forty, she should be out having a different kind of fun. She longed instead for the occasional date: to have the sporadic flutter in her stomach. She wanted the anticipation of a kiss lingering in the air – an injected a fizz of excitement into her body. What she didn't want was to desire those things from her student – from an incredibly irritating student too.

The woman was frustrating but challenging – questioning and difficult – with a defiance for authority that made Emily hesitant when they spoke. When Harley was in the room, it made Emily feel stronger yet weaker. She'd never been challenged by a student before, not in the way Harley Smith challenged her. She questioned why the woman had taken so long to find her way to higher education – what she'd been doing before with her remarkable brain. Maybe that was it, the reason she was so unsettled in her student's company – a remarkable brain that even she couldn't match. But that wasn't *just* it, and her face flushed.

'You're looking brighter, Sis.' Zeb smiled as he poured a glass of wine from the chilled bottle.

'I feel it, I think. No wine for me tonight. I've got a busy day tomorrow prepping for court and lectures.'

'Good to hear. I've been worried about you since you lost that case. It's not like you at all.'

'I took my eye off the ball for a moment, that's all.' Gazing over the menu, she quickly chose and ordered, not wanting to waste any time before picking Zeb's brain. She leant her elbows on the table and rested her chin on the edge of her hands. 'Have you heard of The Domino Set?'

'Blimey. There's a blast from the past. Why do you ask?'

'A client mentioned them recently. I've heard of them a few times but don't know much about them. I take it you do?'

Zeb crunched an ice cube. 'I learnt of them years ago when they cropped up in one of the Ministry's investigations. I headed up some intelligence gathering where they were briefly mentioned. They weren't relevant to national security, so I passed the file onto Scotland Yard just before Dad retired.'

'Who are they? Did Dad know?'

Leaning in, Zeb lowered his voice. 'Nobody knows. They've never been caught. Rumour has it they have protection from the top, which makes sense because they're in a league of their own.'

Emily whispered. 'Do you know where the name came from?'

Her brother nodded. 'That bit, I do know. Years ago, fuck, it must be nearly thirty, I imagine, they used to leave behind a domino at each job. Like a calling card. Bit of a romantic notion of the old criminal gangs. They stopped doing it at some point, but I don't know why or when. It didn't mean they were less active – I guess the old boys had to hand over to the youngster, and the tradition got lost. Are you sure you don't want wine?'

Emily gave him her glass and laughed. 'Why can't I say no to you!' Watching him, she pondered what he'd said. She had so many more questions, but Zeb was astute, and if she pushed him too far she knew he'd pick up that her interest went way beyond a client's simple comment. Her brother didn't give her time to ask anything else before he told her about their sister's new tribulations at home. Although Emily listened, her mind drifted to the information he'd given her, trying to untangle it. Zeb continued: a white noise until he said that Rosa's eldest son Samuel, their nephew, had been suspended from school for selling nitrous oxide canisters to his friends. Her attention jolted back. 'What's Rosa doing about it?'

'She's has tried calling you a couple of times, Sis, but you don't answer.'

'I'm just busy and distracted. I'll call this weekend.'

Her brother emptied the wine bottle and ordered another. 'Please do. I don't know how much more I can take of her moaning about you.'

Emily rolled her eyes. 'Nothing new there, then.' She paused. 'Do you remember when we lived in that tiny house on the estate in East Ham? Dad was really happy, but then we suddenly moved to St Albans and he changed and became, I don't know, a bit…'

'Uptight?' Zeb replied.

'I guess, yes. Do you know why we moved? I don't think I ever knew why.'

'I'm not sure that I do either. I think it had something to do with that woman who accused him of rape.'

'Yes, but how could he suddenly afford to upscale like that? Had he been promoted by then, or did that come later?'

'Later, I think. I don't know. I haven't thought about those days for years.' He smiled. 'Do you remember the summer parties we had, when all of Dad's friends used to come and stay, and Thomas would make us laugh with his impersonations of everyone? They were good days.'

'Wonderful days. It's a shame they came to such an abrupt end.' She poured them both another glass of wine. 'I've been thinking a lot about that time. How one minute we were in East Ham, then suddenly in St Albans, and Dad being, as you said, uptight.'

'It was probably all to do work. I remember when I started at the Ministry and had to spend some time with him at Scotland Yard. That place was full of corruption in those days. I don't think Dad handled it well.'

Emily paused as the waiter delivered their food. The smell of garlic and roasted onion drifted in the air under her nose making her stomach rumble. 'What do you mean by corrupt?'

'You know what it was like back in those days – before accountability. Bribes and backhanders were happening in almost every station. Dad was even accused of it once.' He snapped his fingers and pointed at his sister. 'That was it! I remember. Dad never talked about it, but Mum did. I remember her telling me that summer, when the parties stopped, that Dad had been accused of tampering with evidence ... something to do with a stolen security van packed with cash.'

Emily sipped her wine. 'Do you remember where the robbery took place?'

'Mum never said. I don't think she knew to be honest, but I did do some digging at the Ministry once. It used to be easy in those days.' He frowned. 'Now they watch the watchers.'

'And?' Emily asked impatiently. 'What did you find?'

Zeb leant forward. 'Well, here's the thing, Sis, it happened in Clacton, not London. Dad wasn't stationed anywhere in Essex at any time during his service. So there's no way he could have tampered with the evidence. The appeal board agreed, and he was cleared. But ...' He leant in further. 'The two suspects were from where we grew

106

up, so I reckon that's how his name got connected.'

Gazing at her brother, she asked, 'Who were they?'

CHAPTER 23

London: Oxford Street

Ben kept his arm around her shoulder: an average couple taking a romantic walk. They strolled casually along Oxford Street, their kit-bags on their backs. The streets were quiet – just a few stray people enjoying a late winter night in the city. Harley tucked her freezing hands further into her pockets. Off Oxford Street, they turned into Park Street and headed towards Grosvenor Square.

The walk didn't take long. Within fifteen minutes, they were outside The Temple Club, which, although closed, still had one of its central chandeliers glowing a vibrant light against its crystals. They continued to walk past it, chatting, but their eyes took in every angle of the street around them.

'We get in through the back. There's a car park.'

'Cameras?'

'One. It'll be so empty tonight that a time-lapse will work.'

'Alarms?'

'Simple punch code.'

'Door?'

'Crowbar on the first, pick on the second and third.'

'Motion detectors?'

'Connected to the main coded panel.'

'Security guard?'

'Nope. The cleaner comes in at 5.00 in the morning.'

Ben guided them around the corner. At the back of the Club was a car park with pedestrian access. Harley's green eyes glanced up to find the camera as they walked past the car barrier. It was aimed at the rear door, screwed to the brickwork – simple. Grabbing her arm gently, Ben pulled her into a doorway.

'We need to get our kit on before we move into the camera's sight.'

Unbuttoning her warm winter coat, the icy winter chill bit through Harley's thin black clothes. She tucked the sleeves of her top into the thin leather gloves.

'This Paige you're fucking, was she just easier than you getting a job here?'

As he pulled the black balaclava over his head, he laughed lightly. 'She's prettier than the door manager I'd have to suck up to.'

'Didn't she think it was strange? You asking loads of questions about her job?' Wrapping her hair into a flat twist at the back of her neck, she tucked it all up into the woollen balaclava that gave her some warmth, at least. Rolling her coat into a tight bundle, she hid it in the dark doorway and clipped her kit-belt around her waist. Ben set up the camera time-lapses – they had thirty minutes to get in and get out.

'It's not just you who can use your tongue to make a woman talk, you know.'

Ignoring him, Harley slid the small black crowbar against the old wooden door and popped it with ease. Closing it behind them, Ben signalled for her to move to the second door – heavier: old metal, like a prison door. On it were two locks, top and bottom. She squatted down, her picks in her hand, as Ben reached above her. They worked as one, methodically, simultaneously, skilfully listening and feeling for microscopic clicks inside the locks until they were open. As they entered the dark, cold kitchen, Harley's eyes followed the line of Ben's hand pointing towards the double swing doors across the other side.

They ran: no noise from the soft pumps that were like socks on their feet. Harley spotted the alarm panel on the corridor wall as she lightly pushed open the swing doors. Her gaze caught Ben's, and he nodded.

From her kit-belt, she took out her code reader, magnetising the alarm's electronics so it could read its secrets silently for her. One by one, each number flashed silently on the screen, and her leathered fingers slowly pressed them in order on the alarm panel. Tiny touchpad sounds beeped as the motion sensor's red dots slowly shut down above her.

They were creaky stairs no matter where she laid her feet; if anyone had been in the building, they would have heard her movements. She climbed them steadily, with Ben following behind. When she reached the landing, she looked back at him again, and he held up four fingers, telling her to go to the fourth door on the right.

The round loose handle rattled as she touched it, but it didn't open – an old original door from the eighteen-hundreds hanging heavily on its hinges. Bending to her knees, she withdrew her picks again and put her ear to the lock, listening for the internal clunks. Ben stood behind her, waiting, his eyes scanning.

Once in the office, he walked to Paige's computer and typed in her password. Harley slid in a small silver USB and took over from him, her fingers working swiftly to open the main drive and begin a search for the members' list. There were numerous files to search through, and Ben wandered off – his gloved fingers tracing over random personal items on desks. Harley's eyes skimmed through folder after folder, trying to find the logic of Paige's filing. Folders for archives, folders for the current year, folders within folders, each document perfectly placed. What a waste of a life, Harley thought as she delved into them all, looking for the membership list for each year that it had been logged.

As she waited, she opened the accounts file and scanned through the names. It was the only spreadsheet not separated into years. With transfers from a paper ledger to an electronic ledger, it went back as far as 1950; her eyes scanned through multitudes of names, dates, and amounts of money. Looking for nothing in particular, and nothing stood out, she closed the file, stood up, and stretched.

'Are you just dicking around or doing something useful?' She teased Ben.

'Dicking around, why? What should I be doing?'

Harley scanned the room. There was no need to look for anything other than the membership list but instinct, or experience, drove her to explore. Unlike Ben, her mind was curious. In the far corner of the room, among the modern furniture, was an old wooden desk. Drawn to it, she walked around its edges, her eyes studying the chips and dents. Well-ordered and methodically laid out were a row of old fountain pens, a calculator, a pot of traditional wooden HB pencils, two used rubbers and a vintage pencil sharpener clamped to the side of the desk. The tools of an accountant, she thought, as she stepped back to view the scene. There was no computer on the desk. Whoever worked there did so with pencil and paper. Her gaze darted to the wooden side cabinet. Kneeling before it, she unravelled the small black pouch of her picks, and slowly, she worked the locks until they clicked.

Inside was a stack of brown books, leatherbound and dated with embossed years. Her gaze trailed along the spines, noting each year, each sign of wear; they were beautifully crafted old-school ledgers she wanted to explore. Years of history. Closing the door, she noticed that 1995 was embossed on more than one of them. Like all the other ledgers, the first one was dusty and almost perfect. The one next to it had been pulled out more often – its spine more torn and battered at the top. Harley whispered, 'Why would someone have two for one year?' But she knew why … and it wasn't dusty like the others. Softly, she eased it out from the grip of the two books on either side.

Ben came to her side. 'What ya found?' he whispered.

Harley didn't speak – too fascinated with what she was reading to articulate it. 'Did you bring the little digital camera? Please tell me you have.'

Smiling, he rummaged in his kit-bag and passed it to her. 'Not such a dick after all!'

She looked up at him. 'Says the man who brought his phone along last time.'

Page turned after page as she photographed each one carefully. There was a pattern developing in the ledgers, but until she downloaded the photos to her laptop, she couldn't follow it properly. Names flashed at her as she photographed. Names she knew. The beat in her heart raced – thumping so loudly she thought Ben might hear it. One name, in particular, was on every page, in every entry. It flashed at her like a glaring neon sign in the pitch-black of the night. Why hadn't she made the connection before? It could be nothing, but it could be something.

Ben tapped his watch. Placing the ledger carefully back into the cupboard, Harley locked it and checked everything was as it should be. Before leaving the office, she ejected the memory stick, closed Paige's computer, pushed the chair back in, and raised a thumb to her partner. Meticulously, they retraced their steps, checking nothing was left behind – closing and locking doors until they were back in the freezing London air. Harley returned to the doorway and pulled off the balaclava as Ben dismantled the time-lapses. They returned to their normal winter coats – their tools neatly tucked into the knapsacks. Ben offered Harley his arm, and they walked out onto the desolate London street.

Westminster

'Babe?' Resting her head on the palm of her hand, Aimee looked down at Harley.

'What?'

'Don't you feel like it?'

'I'm worn out … tomorrow?'

'I'm not going to see you tomorrow, you've got that school Christmas party thing, and I've got to have tea with Mum and Dad before I fly off to the Maldives.'

'Are you excited?'

'I wish you were coming.'

'It's good that all the girls are going … you won't miss me.'

When Aimee drifted off to sleep, Harley snuck out of the bedroom to the study. Opening the laptop, she plugged in the USB and waited. Ben was right. George was involved in something he wasn't being honest about, which made her uneasy. She shook her head – the irony of her thought, like a thief would ever be honest. But he'd never kept secrets from them, or had he? How could she be sure? Her fingers tapped the pencil on the desk with repeated dings as the spreadsheets loaded.

Waiting, she organised her thoughts. There were twenty-eight names in the ledger she'd photographed. George was on it. Eddie Ranking was on it. And so was Sidney Knight. The connections zapped in her mind, drawing lines between Sidney Knight and Professor Knight. The laptop fan whirred. Why the fuck hadn't she seen the connection before?

Flicking up The Temple Club spreadsheet, she began cross-checking the names from the membership list against the photographs of the ledger. At the top of each ledger page, TC was scrawled in blue ink. Every name on it was also on the Club's membership list. Harley sighed. That bit made sense but it didn't make sense why George and Eddie's names were on either. Why would they be members of such an exclusive club? How? She stared at all the names again. That was the question. How?

Sitting back in the chair, her focus turned to the numerous photos she'd taken covering each month, year on year, right back to 1995. Her gaze flicked to the membership list on the laptop screen. It went back as far as 1950 but 1995 was highlighted in yellow. She whispered to herself, '1995.'

She scribbled on the notepad as her free fingers traced over each ledger entry – muttering to herself – page after page of notes. Pencilled scrawls, lines, connecting arrows, figures, crossings-out, and annotations under annotations. Her fingers stressed into her hair when she paused, twiddling, running through it, until it stood up in little twists, then flopped down again, only to be twiddled upwards once more.

Every month of every year from 1995 in the ledger, George and Eddie's names were entered. Payments to Sidney Knight. Never late. Never short. Harley stood up and unravelled her hunched body. Were they the ones being blackmailed?

Moving to the kitchen, she laid the papers out across the floor and knelt on the cold tiles; with a highlighter, she struck through the names that appeared repeatedly. Names she already knew or was becoming familiar with. By 3.30 in the morning, her eyes ached under her eyelids. Still, she carried on, and by 7.30, the kitchen floor was covered with long rows of papers all taped together. They were colour coded – linking three crucial things: the Club's accounts, the Club's membership list, and Sidney Knight. She stood above them and stretched, her body aching from bending so long. Her arms rose above her head as she uncurled herself again. Sidney Knight – highlighted in pink – a name present all the way from 1995 to 2021. The man who got the money.

Her mobile phone vibrated on the countertop as a text message came through from Aimee: *Come back to bed. I miss you.*

Turning it on silent, then over, Harley headed to the bathroom and quickly cleaned her teeth. After throwing on her running shoes, she moved the mind maps to her study, locked the door, and headed down the ten flights of stairs. If she couldn't sleep, she needed to run; she needed a fresh mind before her long day started.

CHAPTER 24

Soho: The Bloomsbury Lounge

PROFESSOR Pelta – a modern-day Oscar Wilde – owned a small club called the Bloomsbury Lounge, where everyone headed after Christmas drinks in the Law School's reception.

From the outside, it was as if nothing existed except a small public loo, but underground there were two small bars and an array of sofas and lounge chairs – like traditional 1930s clubs where smoking cigars seemed appropriate. There was a small dance area and stage, with a lady singing soft jazz to the few guests already inside.

It was dark, ambient: a members-only venue with soft red lighting combined with luxurious velvets draped over the sofas and chairs. Harley ordered a single malt whisky and let her thoughts drift as she listened to the music.

She was shattered but finally, she felt like she could breathe. The tightness in her chest had eased, and she knew that for a few weeks, when her front door closed, it wasn't going to open again, with Aimee breezing through as if she lived there. That peace – that opportunity to exhale without interruption – lightened the tension inside her soul. All she had to do before returning to the Red List was get through the School's Christmas party, which wasn't hard as the whisky warmed her throat and eased her busy mind.

Friends from her tutorial group stood nearby as she leant on the heavy wooden railing separating them all from the dance floor. The singer rolled out her long, elegant fingers as she sang, and Harley listened to her rendition of 'Black Angel Blues' with her voice creamy and smooth. It reminded her of her mother – a song she played all the time, so much so that her father had to buy a new vinyl copy when the old one became scratched and worn out.

Behind her, Joanna and James laughed as they teased each other about how drunk they'd been the previous Friday in the union bar. As the laughter mingled with the music, Harley watched the academics move through the Lounge and find their places within their groups. Some stayed with the students, finding common ground to chat about.

A Professor they all called 'Toes' slid to her side: the ugliest man she'd ever met. Wearing faded khaki chinos tucked into his socks and a t-shirt with a starched turned-up collar, his arm brushed into hers. Excessively smeared, his glasses sat below an abundant monobrow. There was a similar amount of hair in his ears, nostrils and around his neck. He was like roadkill.

'You know, if you have any problems with your subjects this year, I'd be more than willing to work with you.'

As Harley was just about to answer, a voice behind them said, 'I believe it would be far more beneficial, Steven, if Miss Smith brought such concerns to me as her academic adviser, don't you?'

'Quite right, I was just offering additional support.'

Knight's eyes studied him. 'Indeed, I'm sure you were but I'd like a private word with Miss Smith.'

Toes skulked away. Knight's gaze followed him – her jawline tight. Once he was mingling, singling out another victim, she turned to Harley, her hand sliding into the pocket of her black trousers – her back straight. The Professor's pupils changed – narrow to dilated – a cat looking from light to darkness. 'He's always a little intense.'

An awkward silence came between them momentarily until Harley said, 'Toes is notorious for being a letch.'

The woman smiled ever so slightly. 'Toes?'

'He walks on his toes, haven't you noticed?'

The smile crept further across the woman's painted red lips. 'Do you have nicknames for us all?'

'Of course.' Harley waited for the question, but it didn't come. It was a beautiful and frustrating indifference that Knight had. 'Don't you want to know what yours is?' She asked impatiently.

'Do you not think I may already know, Miss Smith?'

'Oh.'

'You look disappointed.'

'I am!' Harley laughed.

'Really? And how would you like me to react when you tell me I'm called the Dark Knight?'

'I hadn't thought that far ahead.'

'How very unlike your wonderful brain.'

'I do believe you've paid me a compliment.'

'Intentionally so.' The Professor replied softly.

A whoosh pulsated in Harley's veins and across her tingling skin. It intensified as she rested on the railing and Knight's bare arm brushed against hers. A fiery yet familiar sensation. Forbidden – but as if it should always be that way. Silently, they gazed out ahead towards the stage.

The Lounge was full of activity, brimming with bodies, laughter, and the honeyed-sweet tones of the singer. The smoking ban was ignored, and blue-grey clouds drifted in pockets, floating, creating a haze. In her periphery, Harley saw that Knight had a glass of single malt too: long elegant fingers wrapped around the shining crystal-cut glass. Under the glow of the Lounge lights, with shadows gently caressing the Professor's face, she looked ethereal, haloed by soft whites and subtle purple blues that touched her skin. The woman's t-shirt tucked into her trousers – a thin black belt shaping her slender waist. High heels elongated her legs, and the curve of her breasts rounded into shapes Harley wanted to touch. She had never thought a woman more beautiful.

'I'd never have assumed you liked jazz.' Knight said, turning to face her slightly.

'It seems your assumptions of me are often wrong.'

'I think they often are. You always surprise me.'

Whisky ran warm through Harley's veins. Combined with a lack of sleep, she was dizzy with her thoughts. Pondering, she stood silent for a few moments, thinking about the words she wanted to say. Knight remained still, waiting. Face-to-face, they stood, their eyes exploring each other. Harley wanted to lean forward to kiss her. That's what she wanted – to lean in and softly taste the Professor's lips. Her eyes drifted to them, just for a second – or two; the power of the urge pulling her to do it. Glancing back up to the woman's eyes that were watching her, she could barely breathe. 'You confuse me,' Harley whispered.

Moving closer, Knight leant in towards Harley's face. Their cheeks caressed. The Professor's mouth came close to Harley's ear as if she were going to kiss her there. Their breasts lightly touched. A subtle, gentle touch from Knight's body sent its vibration to between Harley's thighs. A flow of warmth exploding. Knight's lips finally brushed against Harley's ear with a warm murmur, 'You confuse me just as much.'

Internally begging Knight not to move, Harley was fixed to the spot. She didn't want to lose the most beautiful sensation to have ever traced over her body. Soft. Delicate. Powerful. Lightheaded, woozy, she replied, 'I don't know why.' None of her limbs existed as their breasts pressed even closer.

Harley closed her eyes, the beat pulsating in her chest as she absorbed the feel of Knight against her. They fused together, their breathing pushing them deliberately closer – a little harder into each other – so they could consciously take each other in.

The Professor stepped a little closer. 'I like that you do.'

With her back against the railing she was leaning on, Harley felt the Professor's thigh touch her own. The woman enclosed her, something she wasn't used to, yet it excited her more than she knew it ever could. No one noticed their closeness in a cramped and loud club except Harley. Her entire body noticed. She noticed everything: how the woman's breasts pressed against hers so closely that she could feel the beautiful hardness of the Professor's nipples. And when the woman's thigh touched between Harley's, she noticed so much that she trembled.

'I can't move,' she whispered.

'I don't want you to.' The Professor whispered back.

'Are you two talking law? This is a party; we should be dancing!' James swung his heavy arm around Harley's shoulder and squeezed her into his chest. 'C'mon, Smithy, you promised me a dance, remember!'

Knight's heat pulled away, and Harley went cold. Within seconds, the Professor was lost in a conversation with another student and those who'd followed James over. Every so often, as Knight smiled politely at the jokes the boys made, her gaze found Harley's and held it for a passing moment. Harley's body ached, the warmth between her thighs pressing deeper inside. She was crumbling – she could almost feel Knight inside her. Taking a deep breath, she moved away with James and Joanna, but it hurt like hell to do so.

Reluctantly, she followed them as they pulled her through the crowds and onto the dance floor. Heaving, sweaty, drunken students bounced around as they tried to get into the middle of it all.

'You and Knight looked cosy.' Joanna shouted above the music that had turned from 1930s to club beats.

'I got stuck with Toes.' Harley shouted back. 'She came and saved me, not like you and James, you bastards.'

Soho: The Red Café

The streets of Soho were never quiet, and as she said goodbye to everyone, she was happy to be walking through the London she loved so much. It pleased her that James was taking Joanna home so the girl would get to spend some time with him alone. She smiled to herself – they looked sweet together.

'Miss Smith.'

Harley turned, tucking her cold hands into her jacket pockets. Knight was standing before her with her chocolate waterfall of hair, slightly dishevelled by the cold and the damp.

'Professor.'

'Are you walking home at this time of night?'

'I am.' The coldness of the air met her breath as she spoke – a wintery-cloud-mist wrapping around her words.

'Which way are you going? It's 2.30 in the morning, you know.'

Walking towards Knight so she didn't feel like she was shouting, Harley smiled. 'Are you showing concern for my safety?'

Knight laughed. 'Mine actually; I wondered if we were heading in the same direction?'

'Westminster, you?'

'May I join you for some of the way?' There was a polite innocence to her question, a coyness that made it endearing, almost vulnerable. Her cheeks flushed with the cold or the alcohol – a pale pink against the slightly olive skin.

'You do know it's about a thirty-minute walk, don't you? And you've been in those heels all day?'

'Now who's showing concern?' Knight smiled. The echo of the Professor's heels rang on the concrete – a reminder that the woman really was there, and Harley wasn't just dreaming her up.

The streets of Soho were still alive, with restaurants emptying their bins and small clusters of revellers leaving clubs. The flavours of Chinese food wafted on the chill of the air, and as they walked, lights began to turn off. London was shutting down. They walked at a steady pace, not a dawdle or a rush, just a constant, familiar pace as if they had always walked together, side-by-side.

'Can I ask you something, Professor?'

'I may not answer, but yes, you can.'

'Why are you always so … I don't know … professional?'

'I didn't feel particularly professional tonight.'

'You've been drinking, that's all.'

'Do you know, I'm actually rather hungry!' Knight stopped – the ding of her stilettos ceasing to exist. 'Do you fancy something to eat? There's a little all-night café I know not far from here.'

Not sure whether she was hungry but wanting to spend more time with the woman standing next to her, Harley said yes, and followed the Professor down a side street. Walking past the reflection of a shop window, Harley noticed a black motorbike pull into the opposite street, its lights turning quickly off. There was nothing unusual about it, yet the shine of the exhaust pipe caught her eyes. Although all black bikes looked similar, there was something familiar in the rider's posture; their black helmet shining under the streetlamp – the visor down. Harley paused at the window, her instinct stirred deep in her gut.

'Are you coveting the bike?'

Distracted, Harley mumbled, 'It's rather nice, isn't it?'

'I've seen it, or one like it, a couple of times recently. I prefer yours.'

'You know I drive a bike?'

Knight smiled and said nothing.

As they turned away from the reflection, Harley noted all its details: every aspect of its curves and every nuance of the driver sitting on it.

Just off Greek Street, they entered a tiny café where tables were covered in plastic gingham and red candles in jam-jars; it smelt of steak, chips, hot coffees, and baking. A dumpy woman in her late fifties came from behind a counter stuffed with all sorts of hot pies and pastries. Raising her hands into the air, she exclaimed. 'Emily, Emily. We've missed these late-night visits. My son said you haven't been in during the day either.'

'Mrs C, you look wonderful.'

'Bah. I wish my husband would say such things.' With delighted embarrassment, Mrs C darted back behind the counter. 'Who's your friend tonight?'

'A budding new lawyer.'

Mrs C smiled, her face wrinkled from too much sun and plumped from too many pastries. 'Do you want your usual?'

The Professor's eyes shone brightly as she glanced at Harley – her face relaxed – warm. She radiated happiness. 'My usual at this time of night is about three rounds of Marmite on toast with a rather large coffee. Would you like that or something different?'

Imagining Knight eating Marmite on toast at 3.00 in the morning in Soho was near impossible. Yet, it was taking place, and she was joining her. 'Marmite on toast sounds wonderful, and a coffee, black for me, please.'

'Smoke down there; no one will care at this time of night.'

There was no one else in the café *to* care, but they did as they were told and found a little corner at the back, where the lighting was only from the glow of the little red jam-jars.

'You've gone rather quiet.' Knight said as she tried to free herself from all her winter layers. One by one, pieces of clothing came off until she was back down to her t-shirt. It was warm enough at Mrs C's to be a summer's night.

'Well, I'm a little thrown. I'm out with my professor in the middle of the night, in a café in Soho, about to eat Marmite on toast. I'm probably drunk too. I'm not sure who wouldn't be quiet under these circumstances.'

From her handbag, Knight pulled out a packet of cigarettes.

Harley exclaimed, 'Oh, and she smokes too!'

Knight laughed. 'Harley Smith, you do surprise me. I never thought you'd be thrown by anything.'

Taking the cigarette she was offered, Harley leant in to light it as Mrs C brought over a large pot of freshly made coffee and two red mugs. 'You didn't answer my question.' Harley reminded.

Knight rolled her eyes. 'I'm always professional because I was taught to be that way. My father was a police officer. It's how he brought me up.'

'Did he teach you to stand like you do in your lectures? You don't move.'

'I must move. What an unusual thing to observe.'

'Not one bit. It's like you're challenging yourself to remain utterly still.'

'Well … I had a back injury when I was younger,' Knight said as she poured the coffee. 'It eases the pain if I stand on both feet perfectly balanced.'

It wasn't the exciting explanation Harley wanted to hear. She wanted to discover the Professor's technique so she could learn it to improve the one her father had forced on her time and time again. The candlelight flickered on Knight's face, its redness giving the woman an even darker look – a Flamenco grace.

'How did you injure it?'

'You've had quite a few questions; you owe me at least two.' Knight's chin rested on her hand as she leant her elbow on the table. 'How are you able to remember so much? I've never met anyone who can quote like you do.'

Shrugging, Harley replied, 'I've no idea. Books were my friend as a child. My mother used to buy me a new one every week, and I just kept reading them.'

'When did she pass away?'

'I didn't say she had.'

'Forgive me. I shouldn't have asked. I'm probably a little drunk too.'

A respectable silence hung in the air as Harley studied the woman sitting opposite her. 'I was sixteen when she died. Twelve when my father died. Although I found out later, after Mum died, that he wasn't my real father.'

'I'm sorry, I really shouldn't have asked.'

'It's okay. It's just been a long time since anyone has asked me something about myself.'

Holding the warm mug close to her lips, Knight gazed over the top of it. 'You have such a wonderful brain; do you know that?'

'Not really. I just remember pretty much everything I read.'

'Not everyone has the desire to read as much as you've obviously read.'

'Maybe, but I'm not the one who's been to Harvard or Cambridge or stood before the Court of Appeal and argued a case like you. In fact, I'm not sure what I've managed to achieve so far in comparison to someone like you.'

The biggest plate of freshly toasted doorstop bread she'd ever seen, with giant knobs of butter and pots of Marmite, landed like a magic carpet onto their table. For a while, only their knives scrapping on the toast sounded in the café as they munched with polite hunger.

'Do you mind being called the Dark Knight?' Harley asked as she prepared her third slice.

Placing her hand over her mouth, the Professor shook her head gently. 'Not at all. I used to have nicknames for all my professors.' She placed the toast down on the plate. 'Tell me, what did you do before uni? What's your profession?'

Harley stopped chewing. How the hell could she tell her what it was she did, had always done? Her brain wracked to find something that was near the truth yet a hundred miles away from it.

'I help a friend sell antiques,' she said quietly. In some ways, it was true; most of the jewellery she stole was antique.

The subject interested Knight, and for a moment, Harley breathed a little calmer and enjoyed the irrelevance of their conversation – the ease of their chat, but she knew she had to bring the woman back on track to find out more from her. When another pause came, she took the opportunity.

'How did you injure your back? It must have been quite an accident to still give you pain.'

'I was a dancer when I was younger, enrolled in ballet school. We were driving to a performance rehearsal when our car was smashed off the road by another one. My mother broke her leg, and I ended up with injuries that meant I couldn't dance again; well, not professionally.'

'So, you became a barrister?'

'I'd heard all the stories my father used to tell, and criminal law interested me. It was the perfect solution.'

'It must have been fascinating, having a father who was a policeman.'

'In some ways, yes, and in some ways, no. Things are never quite as simple as they seem. What did your parents do?'

'My father was a concert pianist, and my mother, well, she was my mother most of the time. When I was away at school, she used to sing locally, but my father didn't like her doing that much. I guess it wasn't what a concert pianist's wife should do.'

'Boarding school?'

'Until I was sixteen, yes. When my mother died, my father's parents decided not to continue with the fees, so I left. My inheritance was held in trust until I was eighteen, so for those two years, I slept on friend's sofas and picked up part-time work, doing bits and pieces.'

'If it was left on trust, then you could have continued with your schooling.'

Harley sighed. 'I know, but I was on a different path and didn't care.'

'Sorry, I didn't mean to bring it all back up.'

'Actually, it's quite a nice change to talk about something real with you.'

'I understand that,' Knight said softly. 'You always deflect me with a question.'

'Do I?' Harley smiled.

Knight grinned. 'So, what did you do those years after you lost your mother?'

'Cocaine.'

Knight's fingers, holding the toast, hesitated before she took a bite. Harley watched it, reading the pause as disapproval. The little red candlelight trembled its shadow on the woman's face opposite her and Harley caught the shimmer in her eyes. 'That's a frank answer.' Knight replied.

'You wanted to know something about me. I'm just sorry it's something you probably don't like.'

'You're assuming. What made you take cocaine at such a young age?'

Harley gazed at the trembling flame. 'Sometimes I think I have no excuses for doing it, and sometimes I think I had all the excuses a person could need. I don't know if I can really put all of that into words, but if I could, it would include things like grief, betrayal, loss, disappointment, excitement, adventure, anger, freedom and most of all, pain.'

'It took all the bad stuff away and left only the good.' It wasn't a question.

Their gazes met – an embrace of understanding.

'Do you miss dancing?'

'I miss the freedom of it; the way dancers can move their bodies and become absorbed in the music, but if I'd stayed in ballet, I'd be retired by now due to old age.'

'Well, you *are* forty.'

Knight went to say something with contrived shock but stopped and just smiled. 'I'm going to let you get away with that ... for tonight.'

Sitting back in her chair, Harley watched the woman spread more butter and Marmite on another piece of toast. 'Your father sounds interesting. What division was he in?'

'The Met. He must have spent most of his life at the Yard working his way up the ranks.'

'And you? You must have spent a great deal of yours there too. The daughter of a senior police officer doesn't get away from all the ceremony that easy.'

'What makes you think he was senior?'

'You remind me of a friend from boarding school. Her father was high up; she always had to go to charity concerts or functions. He had a chauffeur who'd pick us up in the holidays and take us shopping. At the end of the day, we'd collect her father from one of those old boys' clubs on our way home.'

Knight laughed. 'Oh, yes. My father had a driver. We used to totally abuse her, poor thing. Ours was the same lady for nearly fifteen years, so she became like an aunt to us. And he belonged to The Temple Club, which is probably the one your friend's father was a member of. Most of the establishment belonged to it in those days.'

'Is your father no longer a member?'

The woman sitting opposite glanced down at the half-empty cup of coffee she'd wrapped her fingers around for comfort. 'He passed away recently.'

Leaning forward to rest her elbows on the table and her chin on the palm of her hands, Harley gently asked, 'What was his name?'

Knight lightly smiled. 'Sidney. His name was Sidney.'

There it was, the confirmation Harley needed, only it didn't please her, nor did it surprise her. If only she had connected the names earlier, she would be further down the line in understanding what George was up to. The tip of her index finger gently tapped against her top lip. Had George put her at the same university as Knight for a reason? He'd helped her with the application, made suggestions, guided her choices. What the hell was he up to?

There was no way to tell the Professor she had witnessed her father's final moments and his death. Even if she could, would she? Who wanted to know about the final moments of their father intentionally walking towards a gun? She'd seen both her parents die – it did her no good to have those memories – not really.

'I can see how much you loved him.'

'I still do.' Knight sighed. 'He was murdered, but the police don't seem able to find any evidence.'

'Murdered.' Harley repeated. But he wasn't. Not really. Would she be better knowing the truth? Jeez. The old man had chosen his fate.

'I'm sorry, Professor. You've been through more than you should have,'

There were toast crumbs all over the table. The candles started flicking their death dance as Mrs C began scrubbing down counters. Mr C, every so often, came out to kiss her on her cheek to ask if she needed anything. Harley studied them as she considered the Professor and what her father had chosen. Silence hung in the air again until her gaze drifted back to Knight. There was a slight shine in the woman's eyes. Not tears. But there was emotion behind them that she was struggling to hold in.

The Professor glanced at Mr and Mrs C giggling behind the counter. 'They're so in love, aren't they? They've been here thirty years. I've known them for probably fifteen.'

'You've been coming here that long?'

'I used to live in a flat above one of the all-night sex shops, back when I was an impoverished PhD student.'

'Living in Soho isn't impoverished!'

Knight smiled. 'It's all relative. Besides, considering you're a student, you don't dress like an impoverished one.'

'I'm not the one wearing Louboutins.'

'But you like your Bvlgari, right? And the cufflinks you wear, let me guess, Zeb & Co?'

'Few people would know that.'

'Few people I know would wear them. You must have done well selling antiques.'

Shifting a little in her seat, Harley turned her attention back to the elderly couple. 'Why do they do work through the night at their age?'

'It's quiet, and Mr C can bake for the morning. It's busy in here during the day.' Knight's hand came to her mouth to stifle a yawn, and Harley smiled at her.

'Past your bedtime?'

'Way past, and I've got to go to Belmarsh Prison today.'

'It's Saturday!' Looking at her watch, she saw that it was 6.30 am. As she glanced to the front of the shop, winter morning was breaking through the dark night sky.

'Well, I hadn't planned on being up all night with one of my students.'

'I do believe you called me a lawyer when you were drunk.'

Smiling, Knight delved into her handbag and pulled out her purse; Harley tried to object, but the woman raised her hand. 'I'm now officially too tired to argue this one with you. I'm paying – end of.'

Wishing Mrs C a 'goodnight' rather than a 'good morning,' they returned to the streets of Soho. The air was just as cold as when they entered, yet time had moved on regardless of their glowing-red intimate bubble. Little street-cleaner carts brushed along – whirring – spreading water circles against the curbs. Newspaper vans were pulling up outside the clubs and throwing bundled papers against their doors. Harley didn't want to say goodbye as she hailed a passing taxi. 'I'm going to walk, but I think you need to get home as soon as possible.'

'Thank you. And thank you for a lovely few hours. I enjoyed your company.'

Harley smiled shyly. 'Go, or I'll freeze to death.'

The Professor leant in towards Harley, her lips softly touching against her cheek. 'Have a good Christmas, Miss Smith.'

Was she imagining things? The alcohol and the night were running through her mind as she walked along Oxford Street with a warm glow swimming in her blood but still, it looked like the same bike, with the same exhaust and the same shaped body under the leathers.

The phone vibrated in her pocket, and her fingers barely felt it in her hand as she put it to her ear. 'How did you know I was awake?'

'Why *are you* awake?' Ben asked.

'I'm just walking home. What do you want? Why are *you* awake?'

'Are you coming to mine on Christmas Day? Dad's coming; he keeps asking me if I've invited you. I thought I'd give Mum a rest this year and do it all.'

'Don't tell me you're actually cooking?'

Ben laughed. 'Fuck no. I've convinced Paige to do it. She's a domestic goddess and wants to impress the family.'

'So, you haven't dumped her yet, then?'

'She's got some good points.'

'What are you doing up so early?'

'I couldn't sleep. Dad was home late again last night. Mum texted me, going out of her mind.'

'I need to talk to him, Ben,' Harley said. 'Like really need to talk to him.'

CHAPTER 25

East Ham: Nelson Street, The Primrose Estate

JOANNA let James closer into her space on the walk from the bus stop to her house – his arm and shoulder touching hers. The feel of his hand in hers was like sparkles of glitter celebrating all over her skin. His fingers were warm and soft, and his touch tingled in her blood. Despite the chill of the December night, she didn't feel cold.

When James asked if he could take her home after the Christmas party, she thought he was joking. An embarrassed smile had blushed on her pale skin, and she'd giggled. James had blushed too. While on the night bus, he'd picked up her hand and hadn't let it go since. They didn't talk much after he'd done that, but their entwined fingers grew more comfortable and confident. They began to walk in harmony, merging with hesitant anticipation of when they would reach the house. It was on her mind – the goodbye. Joanna had never kissed a boy before, not even in the playground at school when all her friends had tried with the boys and giggled at the out-of-bounds delight; she'd never wanted to. But with James, she wanted to know if his mouth was as warm as his fingers. The idea that it might be made her quiver, and her stomach felt strange like it was flying around inside her body.

'Toes is a bit full-on, isn't he?' James said as they turned the corner into Joanna's road.

'Oh, he is.' Joanna replied, and a little laugh followed. 'Did you see him with Harley? He was all over her.'

'She can handle herself, that one.'

'I know, she's amazing. I can't believe she's my friend.'

James squeezed her hand a little tighter. 'She's got good taste.'

Blushing, Joanna lowered her head and smiled to herself. Everything was perfect. He was perfect. Even the fact the Knight had ignored her for the evening didn't matter because James was walking her home. Almost everything was starting to work out as she'd dreamt – a new friend and maybe a new boyfriend. Joanna's heart skipped inside her chest.

She stopped walking and held him back a little. 'I live just there.' She nodded over to her house.

'Then I shall wish you goodnight, my fair lady.' James dipped his head playfully.

Joanna giggled. 'I liked you walking me home.'

'I liked walking you.' James smiled. 'Maybe I could walk you home again sometime?'

'I'd like that.'

For a moment, they were silent – just their eyes talking to each other as they stood under the streetlamp, not wanting to let the moment go. James's ruddy face blushed an even deeper red.

'May I–'

Before he could finish, Joanna leant forward and placed her mouth on his. Her first kiss tasted of sweet coke and vodka. She liked it, especially on James. His mouth was as warm as his fingers, and she leant in a little further. James responded, his arms sliding around her shoulders. Everything about the kiss – the embrace – lifted the girl slightly off the ground and into the hold of the boy she'd been dreaming about every night for weeks. Joanna's body flew. She was lost.

'Get ya fucking grubby hands off my daughter.' Debra Evans grabbed her daughter's hair – yanking her backwards. Joanna jolted – yanked off James – and stumbled to the ground. The boy stepped forward, but Joanna put her hand up to him.

'I'm okay, James. You should go. I'll see you in class.'

Hand on hip, Debra stood over her daughter – owning her. As Joanna scrambled onto her feet, a sharp pain shot through the hand and wrist she'd landed on.

'Get inside the house.' Her mother hissed. 'Ya fucking whore.'

Looking over her shoulder as she walked to the front door, Joanna watched James walk away. What would he think? He wouldn't want her now, would he? James glanced back before he turned the corner. He was gone. The girl's heart lurched into her throat as her stomach dropped like a weight. Her world was over. How could she ever face him on Monday?

'I'm sorry, Mum. It was just a kiss.' She whispered as Debra Evans slammed the door behind them.

'Kisses lead to fucking, which leads to unwanted little shits like you.' Her mother pushed her further into the hallway. 'Get in the fucking kitchen and scrub ya face, look at the state of ya. Ya didn't leave the house with all that shit on it.'

Joanna was shoved down the hallway into the kitchen with her mother's hand on her back. Cigarette smoke and the smell of vinegar from soggy chips wafted in the air.

'Can I just go to bed?' Joanna asked quietly.

'Not until that shit's off ya face.'

'Please, Mum.'

Debra grabbed her daughter by the back of her head and dragged her to the kitchen sink. Cold water gushed from the lime-scaled tap. Holding her daughter's hair in the clench of her fist, Debra soaped up the scouring sponge with her free hand.

'Mum, *please*. Don't. I'll wash it off upstairs.' But her mother didn't hear her. Joanna's face plunged under the cold running water as the scouring sponge dragged across her pale skin. Scrunching up her face, the stinge of the washing liquid seep into her eyes. The gushing water flooded her mouth as her mother scrubbed. Soap lather dripped into her ears and hair as Debra Evans scoured the light makeup off her daughter's face. Joanna wriggled at first, then stopped. There was no point to the fight – she'd learnt that much.

Tugging Joanna's head backwards, her mother snorted a deep breath. 'There. No daughter of mine is gonna look like a fucking whore in front of the neighbours. Now piss off.'

Curled into a ball under the pink and blue duvet, Joanna closed her eyes. The taste of sweet coke and vodka, and the warmth of his mouth, killed the remains of the washing-up liquid. The salt from her tears dripped to the corners of her mouth. If he didn't want to walk her home again, at least she would always know what he tasted like.

CHAPTER 26

St Albans

IT was there again, the motorbike, lurking in the shadows.

As she got out of the car, her hands full of case bundles she'd brought to work on, the bike slipped into the bushes near the driveway of the house. It was too far away to see much of its detail.

Emily wanted to run towards it and shout at the coward hiding in the thickets of the hedge. Her jaw clenched, along with every muscle in her body, as she stood, staring into the darkness. What if it was her father's murderer? What if she ran at him? What if she got a knife … then ran at him? What if she got one of her father's old rusty shotguns and aimed that at him instead?

The leaves in the bushes stirred a little.

Agi opened the front door, and the slow paws of the old lazy dogs crunched on the shingle. Emily's concentration broke, and she turned her gaze to the woman who was more tired than usual – thinner and frazzled.

'I've made your favourite.' Agi smiled.

Clutching the bundle tighter to her chest, Emily smiled back. 'You're too good to me.' She patiently followed the slow, plodding dogs – with one last glance toward the shadow in the bushes.

'You need to eat before you work, Emily. Look at you. You've lost too much weight.' Agi lightly touched Emily's face.

It was a touch Emily wanted to move into – to feel the love of. A touch like any mother would give her child. It had been so long since she'd felt a touch so warm – so loving. In that split second of a moment, she felt her mother's absence. Her thoughts snowballed. The ache of loneliness rose inside her. It had been so long since anyone had touched her with love – made her feel safe.

'I'm fine, Agi, but I'll never refuse your goulash.'

Agi had covered the kitchen table with a feast for an entire family – the family she used to cook for when they were all together. Emily watched the woman who'd been part of her life since her mother had died. She was once a little plump, full-faced, and sparkling in the eyes. The past few months had been punishing – Emily could see that. Watching as the woman busied herself with all the crockery and cutlery needed to serve the Hungarian feast, Emily's heart melted with sadness.

'Did you get the invite from Zeb and Rosa for Christmas?'

'I didn't.'

'Zeb posted it a few weeks ago. They know you don't do text messages, so he used the old-fashioned method.'

Agi sat down on the chair opposite Emily, her eyes glistening. 'I thought I'd have to spend it on my own, here, without him.'

Picking up the housekeeper's hand gently, Emily squeezed it. 'I'm sorry we haven't been around much. It's hard coming here.'

'I know.' Agi lightly smiled. 'And I know you'll want to sell the house soon. I've been making plans to go back to Hungary to see my sister.'

'Oh, Agi!' Tears rimmed Emily's eyes. 'You daft thing. We're not selling the house until you decide you want to leave. And if you want to stay here for the rest of your life, then you can. Rosa, Zeb, and I decided that weeks ago. I thought Zeb would have told you.'

'I've not spoken to either of them recently.'

'Well, that's what we decided. There's absolutely no reason for us to sell the house. None of us needs the money. Besides, who will look after these two lazy old things?' She said sadly. 'Now, come on, eat with me. I can't manage all of this wonderful food without some help.'

Sitting peacefully together, they ate the deep rich flavours of the Hungarian goulash – a dish Agi had introduced them to on her first night as their new housekeeper. The agency had sent her to them when the first one had failed to turn up for her third shift. The early days were hard for them all. Agi's English was difficult to understand, and the woman struggled with Sidney's erratic hours and three grieving children. But Agi stuck it out through one of the worst times in their lives, and after moving in, she became part of their family. Emily glanced at the woman eating. There was no way they would let her down now.

As grumpy as her father was, he loved Agi too. Rumours had circulated in the village from time to time. How could a man and a woman live together without sleeping together? But Emily knew the rumours weren't true. The villagers loved to gossip, especially about Sidney Knight – the aloof policeman up on the hill.

It hurt to be in the house without him, particularly so close to Christmas. Decorations would have been up by now; her father would have opened the front door in an obligatory Christmas jumper bought for him by Agi. The house would have been laced and weaved with baubles, lights, candles, and fresh holly from the tree in the garden. He wouldn't have done it himself – money could buy almost anything.

She wasn't just missing her father; she was missing the idea of everything that came with him at Christmas: the smell of his new aftershave, the customary photo album of Christmases with her mother, snoozing next to him on the settee after lunch, and the leftovers on the kitchen table they all picked at while groaning they were full to the brim.

Spending it with Rosa and her wild herd of children at Zeb's house wasn't how Christmas was supposed to be. But her brother and sister wanted something different – they weren't even planning to cook a turkey. No wafts of roasting meat throughout the house. Everything was going to be strange.

'That's a big sigh.' Agi said as she stood up to clear the half-empty dishes from the table.

'I was also thinking about how much I'll miss him this Christmas.'

'I know parents shouldn't have favourites, but I always thought you were his. You were just closer to him than the other two.'

'I miss him, Agi, so much. I miss talking to him about everything. I think he was my best friend. That's sad, isn't it? Most people don't have a parent as a best friend.'

The housekeeper touched Emily's arm before leaning over to remove the last evidence of their feast. 'Two peas in a pod.' The woman said gently. 'I remember all the nights you'd sit talking until the early hours. Lord knows what about.'

Emily sat back in the chair and ran her hand over her full stomach. 'They were good days.' She sighed again. 'I'd never have qualified as a barrister without him.'

'That's not true. He just helped you, that's all.' Agi smiled. 'I'm not sure all the whisky you drank did much good, though.'

Emily smiled sadly. The whisky nights. They were the best moments they'd shared together. When the studying was at an end, and her brain was exhausted, her father would pour them the first measure of the night, and conversations would turn to other things.

Some nights, they would consume more than they should, and he'd send her down to the cellar to fetch another bottle while he foraged in the fridge for leftovers. The walk along the hallway and down the dusty stone stairs into the cool cellar room would fill her with joy. It was a walk that brought with it the knowledge they were going to ponder life together – debate the state of the world. Long summer nights while she studied, while they put the world to rights, and she got to spend time with her father. Happy memories.

Emily's chair scraped on the tiled floor – a shrill screech. *The whisky!*

'You're a genius,' she exclaimed as she rushed out of the kitchen and down the darkened hallway.

Agi called out. 'I'm off to bed. Leave the dishes til the morning.'

The cellar was cool beneath the house – a haven for old boxes, bottles of wine and the favoured whisky. There was also all the rubbish that her parents had collected over the years and the two old rusty bikes they'd enjoyed together when they were alive.

Emily stood at the bottom of the stone stairs and glanced around. The old fluorescent light flickered for a few minutes before it warmed up and stayed steady; its buzz familiar to her ears. Dust had settled on everything – a film of musty smelling powder-grime that pricked at her nose. Gradually she moved the boxes, one by one. If any other place in the house was part of their long summer nights drinking the whisky, it was the cellar. Her father had often joked that his life could be summed up by its contents – the memories it held.

Resisting the urge to go through each box, Emily methodically moved each one to an empty corner in the room until there was a clear pathway to the old dark wooden cabinet they'd hidden behind them. Kneeling before it, she opened the doors. Inside were more boxes – smaller ones – boxes full of sentimental knickknacks her parents had collected since they were married. She wanted to touch each one and learn its story. Such history, she thought, as she carefully took things out of the cabinet and laid them on the floor.

Somewhere. It had to be in the cabinet somewhere. But it wasn't. There was no hidden place that needed a key. Sighing, she tapped her curled fist against her mouth gently. Putting everything neatly back, she stood and stretched. If it's not the study, the terrace or the cellar, where else could her father's clue possibly mean? Why hadn't he just told her? Emily sighed again.

Tired, she left the boxes where she'd put them and moved to switch off the light. As she did, a small wooden panel built into the underneath of the first stone step caught her attention. No dust.

Kneeling again, Emily took the key from her back pocket and tried slipping it into the lock. It didn't fit. She tried again, turning the key upside down – jiggling it gently.

The lock clicked. The wooden panel opened. Cautiously, Emily put her hand into the narrow space and pulled out a manila folder.

CHAPTER 27

St Albans

THE phone vibrated in her pocket. Harley pulled it out to see Aimee's name and message flash on the screen. *'Hi babe, wish u were here xxx.'* Throwing it into the saddlebag, she turned to study the house and any movement within it.

She wasn't planning on mentioning her visit to Ben. She wanted time to find out more – on her own. The more she knew, the more she could tell George, and the more she could help him. If he'd been blackmailed for all these years, maybe, just maybe, she could get his money back. That meant treating Sidney Knight and his daughter, the Professor, as a job again, despite him being dead.

Quietly jacking the window open, she slid through the gap. She would have five minutes to get to the alarm system.

Just as she landed, crouched like a cat on all fours, a distant torch-glow was heading towards the alarm panel. The shadowy figure moved like a silent apparition. Harley's heart pumped under her chest. Moving along the hallway, she held her breath deeply in her lungs. She should turn back – avoid the danger – but she couldn't. She was bound by the intrigue of Sidney Knight and the Professor. From a dark corner, she watched the intruder walk past the alarm without needing to touch it; it was already off. Fear and excitement mixed like milk and coffee in Harley's veins. She didn't know exactly what she was looking for, but maybe the other intruder did. Perhaps they would lead her right to it.

The shadow ahead of her entered the study. That's what she'd look like if anyone ever saw her – a black phantom in the night.

Through the crack of the study door, she watched the intruder move straight towards the desk as if he knew what he wanted and where to find it. As she hid in the shadows, footsteps came up the stairs from the basement. Ducking into the darkness of the open doorway to the downstairs bathroom, Harley stepped back, wondering just how many of them there were in the house. It wasn't the housekeeper – the footsteps were coming from the wrong direction, but the steps pattered more freely than someone intruding – they were from someone who felt at home. They pattered right into the study – and stopped. Silence. No voices, no footsteps. Nothing.

Stepping silently back to the crack between the frame and door, where she'd stood and seen Sidney Knight slump to the floor, she peeked through. Professor Knight stood motionless with a gun pointing at her face. Not again, she thought. Harley's brain ran back and forth with thoughts she couldn't catch. They were too quick, like summer bugs, too fast to be squashed. Her gloved fingers came to her woollen-covered face as she tried desperately to think. *Think.* The intruder was on the other side of the desk. Even if Harley was an Olympic champion, she couldn't hurdle it in time. If she dived at Knight to bring her to the floor, the intruder would shoot her instead. Why wasn't he speaking? Why wasn't he demanding something from her, asking for what he wanted? If someone had walked in on her, would she ask or run? She'd run. And if this intruder wasn't there to kill Knight, he would want to run too.

Unable to speak or shout because Knight might recognise her voice, she whispered 'fuck' into her balaclava and hurled herself across the room, landing on Knight and bringing her to the floor with a thud. A gunshot blasted into the silent air as Harley covered Knight with the full extent of her body. She had no idea if either of them had been hit. The intruder stumbled over them to escape, but Harley grabbed his ankles, bringing him down to the floor. His feet kicked at her face, one catching the edge of her cheekbone while she grappled with them before grabbing hold and shoving his boots away. Dragging herself over Knight, who lay still beneath her, she pulled her way along the thrashing legs and onto the man's body, trying to escape her. Sitting on top of him, straddled, she gripped at his balaclava, trying to yank it from his face. His glove-leathered hands pulled at her wrists as he reared his hips into the air. They writhed against each other.

Within a flash, the man bucked her off, was on his feet and running. Harley hauled herself up, about to make chase, but Knight was still down on the ground. Harley glanced down. She wanted to ask if the Professor had been hit, but she couldn't. There were so many things she wanted to ask, but she couldn't risk it.

On the floor was a Manilla folder. Harley's gaze darted between the woman she wanted to protect and the thing she thought the intruder was after. As she leant down to pick it up, her heart took over, and she offered Knight her hand. The woman took it without hesitation, and for a second, they stood opposite each other: wide-eyed gazes locking together with panic before Harley realised it was time to run. The police would arrive any minute; the housekeeper would have called them when the gunshot had woken her. She swiftly bent down and grabbed the folder before turning and running.

Harley retraced her steps along the hallway and through the open window. Across the vast lawn, a single red light of a motorbike took off in the distance.

Westminster

Tony fiddled with the buttons on his heavy black coat. Yawning, he glanced up as Harley entered the building through the glass doors that slid open for her.

'It's cold this morning, Miss Harley.'

She smiled at him, pleased to see his craggy gentle face. 'Freezing. It's got to snow soon.'

'I'm just about to leave, but it looks like you've had a run-in. Your eye is smarting.'

She sat down on his chair and sighed. 'It's okay, honest.'

'Miss Davies mentioned she might move in when she's back.'

Harley glanced up at him. 'What? When did she say that?'

'She popped by while you were out the other night. She needed to pick up some things for her holiday.'

'Did you let her in?'

'I'd assumed you'd given her a key as she doesn't ask anymore.'

Harley frowned. 'No, I haven't. What exactly did she say?'

Tony tucked his hands into his pockets. 'Sorry, I just thought it was something you'd discussed by the way she said it.'

'I'm not that serious about her!'

'Well, she's here quite a bit, so maybe she thinks you are.'

'Jeez, I don't even know what serious feels like!'

He patted her shoulder tenderly. 'You will.'

'Why do you never ask when I come home so late?'

Burying his mouth behind the woollen scarf wrapped around his neck, he looked back at her softly. 'Would you like it if I did?'

'No … I wouldn't.'

'Then you have your answer.'

The file sat on her wooden desk, waiting to be opened. She had five hours to herself before meeting Joanna for their arranged Christmas cake and hot chocolate in Soho. As much as she needed sleep, she needed food and a shower and to open the file that someone else wanted as much as she did. Running her hands through her hair, she paced, unsure what to do first. Who else knew the file was there? Sitting down at her desk, she began to read. Her eyes scanned over the words of the first document – handwritten. The writing was beautiful, almost calligraphic, but she could see the pen had trembled in places. Hunching over each page as she turned them, she read:

My Dearest Emily,

You finally remembered our late nights drinking whisky while we debated the ethics of law and what kind of barrister you wanted to be. I was so proud of you those evenings. Your morals and ethics outshone mine every time. I never knew how I could teach you anything, considering the life I was leading or led.

I didn't want to place this letter with the first in case that was found by someone other than you. I wanted to give you time to take everything in that you were going to hear about me. If I'd told you everything at once, I fear you would have disowned me without learning the truth. I need you to forgive me so you can guide Rosa and Zeb through what you will ultimately need to tell them.

By now, Thomas would have told you about The Domino Set, but he won't be able to tell you everything, my darling. He was never a part of what we did, just the man who enjoyed playing with the money. Inside this file is a list of all the men and women who were part of the Set over the years. Names have changed, members have come and gone. Deaths, retirement, or imprisonments have happened. The founding members remain the same, except for me – I am now gone. Every job the Set has ever done is listed here. Everyone involved, even the periphery criminals – the Pips. Every job, Emily. I kept track of them all.

I asked you before not to go to the police. I needed you to use that extraordinary brain of yours before you did. I still need you to be measured when you decide to take this information to them – without damaging my name and losing the £30 million I have put offshore for you, Rosa, and Zeb. I don't fear the damage it will do to my reputation, but I do fear what this will do to all of yours. You three have been so successful in your chosen careers, and I know that what you will learn about me will damage you all.

The £30 million is in an account that no one can access except you. The account details are in a safe deposit box, along with a USB. All the information you are about to read in this file is copied onto the USB and more. It is your security, Emily – keep it safe.

When you are ready, and when you ask him, Angus, my dearest friend and your godfather, will provide you with the deposit box details. Everything you need is in there. He is instructed to only give you the envelope when you ask – when you are ready.

The details of every job we have ever done have been sent to six of my most trusted friends for your protection. They will never use the information against you, Emily, because there is a file on each of them in the safe deposit box, too, things they would never want anyone else to know. You'll understand when you read these names:

> *Richard Seal – Dean of Law, Oxford*
> *Ethan Edwards – Cabinet Secretary*
> *Stuart McKenzie – Assistant Chief Commander*
> *Sami Khan– Political Editor*
> *Lucas Orchard – Chief of Counterterrorism*
> *Robin Goldsmith – Director General Nuclear*

After reading the rest of the letter to the end, she put it down and slid her chair away from the desk. Lighting a cigarette, she turned the remaining pages and found names she hadn't expected to be there. Eddie's. George's. The Domino Set. Another twenty-six names were listed, too – all matching the names on The Temple Club's handwritten ledgers by TC.

Under a separate heading of Pips, she saw her own name with Ben's. The Domino Set. George and Eddie were part of it – part of the most notorious criminal gang in the country – that meant she was too. And Sidney Knight had known it. Her stomach fluxed. Did the Professor know too? Was that why she'd acted interested? Jeez, was that why George had suggested she study under Professor Emily Knight?

★

Soho: The Red Café

Freezing, Harley waited for her friend. She leant against the wall, her thoughts drifting with the passers-by as she rubbed her gloved hands together. Joanna was always late.

Lighting a cigarette, she studied the blue stream mingled with the coldness of her breath: cloud pockets rising into the air. She'd have given anything to cancel her plans so she could meet George instead, but when she'd asked, his text came back that he was busy until Christmas Day.

As she waited, thoughts turned to Sidney Knight's letter. If she could find this Angus, there was a chance she could get the money back for George and destroy all the damming evidence Sidney had collected over the years. She needed to destroy it as much for herself as for George and Ben.

Rushing towards her in the distance was Joanna – flushed and bothered. Without a 'hello,' she planted a kiss on Harley's cheek and linked their arms together.

'I've been looking forward to this all week,' she smiled.

Harley thought she resembled a marshmallow in her pale-pink sweater, pink gloves, and fluffy white coat.

'Where do you want to go?' she asked.

'My friend told me about this little place that does the best hot chocolate and homemade cakes in London. So, I thought we'd give it a go.'

Smiling to herself because the girl had a sweet tooth bigger than hers, she let Joanna lead them down the backstreets of Soho, where discreet clubs kept their doors closed, and men dressed in black stood outside with their earpieces on show. They chatted away about their mid-sessional exams until Joanna stopped. 'This is it.' She smiled.

'Here?' Harley asked in surprise.

'I know it doesn't look much, but seriously, my friend raves about it.'

Hesitantly, Harley followed Joanna in, wondering who the friend was because she'd never mentioned having any before. Mrs C and her husband, thankfully, weren't there; instead, two boys in their late twenties were behind the counter. The little red jam-jars weren't flickering their dancing shadows across the red gingham tables. It was all so different. Empty and no atmosphere in her opinion.

Joanna unravelled herself from the winter layers and went from plump to thin in seconds. 'I so needed to get out.'

'Things not good at home?'

'I can't wait to get back to uni.'

The café was a hub of music, voices, and clanking from behind the counter. Christmas cheer was pinging in the till every few seconds. Groups of people clustered around tables, chatting, drinking, and eating. Some sat alone, typing on laptops while servers moved between the tables. Fresh coffee and melting chocolate wafted to Harley's nostrils. It still felt empty though.

'So, what are you doing for Christmas?' Joanna asked.

'Going to a friend's, you?'

'Just me and Mum.' She explained that Christmas would be miserable until her uncles came over for a cold tea on Boxing Day. Part of Harley wanted to say that at least she had a family to spend it with, but the other part dreaded ever having to endure everything her friend mentioned, especially at Debra Evans's house.

'Are your uncles nice?'

'They're not my real uncles, just Mum's friends. She's known them since she was a kid.' The girl paused. 'Mum is on her best behaviour when they're around.' A tip of her blonde hair fell slightly into the hot chocolate as she took a sip. 'One is really fat and smells of cigarettes when he gives me a hug, and the other one is just as fat but short.' She laughed. 'Uncle Tom's got like this stupid Celtic tattoo on his wedding finger. He had it done when he got married, and then they split up two months later; he's a bit silly like that, but at least he buys me presents. I don't ever get them from Mum.' Joanna leant across the table and whispered, 'OMG, don't look now, but Knight's just come in.'

'How do you know?'

'The reflection in the mirror, doh.'

Harley flicked her gaze away from Joanna's flushed face and glanced over her shoulder. The girl was right, Knight was leading another woman through the spaces between the busy tables and searching for a place to sit. In a deep red coat that came up high on her long, elegant neck, the Professor was exquisite, her hair tumbling out from beneath a soft, black-peaked hat and her lips – perfectly painted – were a deep red. Her eyes were shadowed softly by makeup, but Harley saw she was tired beneath it. The woman behind her was slightly older. A faded, lesser version of Knight's beauty, but still beautiful.

Their eyes met. At first, there was a surprise in Knight's gaze and then a questioning furrow of her eyebrows. Embarrassed, Harley looked away. She didn't want to be in the Professor's café, not so soon after their night there together, and certainly not so soon after being in her father's house. Now the Professor would think she'd gone there on purpose, like a stalker.

Joanna whispered, 'Has she spotted us?'

Harley nodded.

'Shit.'

'She isn't coming over, so we're fine.'

'Don't you find her unpleasant?'

Pushing the empty mug into the middle of the table, Harley watched the colour rise on her friend's pale skin. It emphasised a bruise around her lips that Harley had noted earlier, making the purple almost pulsate on its own. She wondered why Joanna disliked the Professor so much. There was a tension between them that even Knight gave off when they were in the same room.

'Not really,' she replied quietly.

'That woman is one of the most unpleasant ones I've ever met.' Joanna twiddled the spoon in her hot chocolate as the top of her ears burnt an angry pink.

Harley sighed, 'Why do you hate her so much?'

The metal spoon clanked against the ceramic mug as Joanna released it from her fingers. 'Because she's rude. And I work hard. She just doesn't give me credit for it, unlike you!'

Harley's brain scrambled to find something to change the subject to, but Joanna was studying the mirror, which meant she was looking at Knight. The colour on her face rose to a deeper red.

Placing money on the table to pay the bill, Harley smiled softly at her friend. 'I was going to take you Christmas shopping so you could pick something nice. Do you fancy Covent Garden?'

The girl's expression lifted to a smile. 'Really, I can choose something?'

Thank God. Harley stood up. 'Come on. We can get something to eat there too.'

But Joanna walked ahead of Harley, manoeuvring herself towards Knight's table.

'Professor.'

Engrossed in a conversation, the Professor took a moment to

acknowledge them. The lady she was with smiled, but Knight looked tightly coiled. It troubled Harley that she was part of the reason there was tiredness under her eyes: hidden bags covered by makeup.

'Miss Evans, Miss Smith, a pleasure to see you both.' The smile on her lips was strained, as was the friendliness in her words. Maybe Joanna was right; maybe Knight didn't like her. It was painfully awkward, and Harley nudged her friend's hand as she said, 'We should go and leave the Professor to her conversation.'

Knight flashed a grateful gaze at her, and for a moment, there was a flicker of a smile in her eyes before they drifted to the bruise on Harley's chin. It was a bruise Harley hadn't thought about except to cover it with makeup. The kick from the other intruder at Knight's house had caught her face sharply, but it wasn't until Knight discreetly acknowledged it that the pain stung again.

Although it was just a brief acknowledgement, the gaze told Harley that Knight hadn't read the file she'd been carrying with her that night, which meant she had no idea of its contents or who Harley was. It also meant Harley had time to tell George what she'd found. She'd heard about The Domino Set over the years. Everyone in the criminal underworld had, but nobody knew who they were. The Set was revered amongst them: admired for the jobs they did, how they did them, and that they had stayed together for decades. It dawned on her as the Professor glanced at her chin that she too was also part of the Set – somehow – even if it was, as Sidney Knight had described her, a periphery, a Pip.

The bruises on Knight's right wrist made Harley's heart sink. She'd done that. She'd hurt a woman – stolen something from her that might have meant so much, something from her father. She'd done that. *What a fucking shit she was.*

Joanna's hand linked into hers, and the girl smirked. 'Have a lovely Christmas with your family, Professor.'

CHAPTER 28

East Ham: Pinnie Street, The Primrose Estate

'AIMEE'S bloody lucky to be missing this,' she said as she lit a cigarette.

'She's a selfish cow for dumping me in it at Christmas.'

'It's a holiday of a lifetime, Ben; how could she not go?'

Slipping his hand into hers, he said, 'You're the only girl I know who would ride a bloody racing bike wearing five-inch heels.'

Leaning on the wall next to her, Ben puffed his cigar: the scent and smoke wafting on the cold air; his pink lips even paler with the cold, and his blonde hair like snow had fallen on it – glistening in the winter light. His body was trembling, and his fingers were pinkie-red.

'Nothing's ever straightforward or simple with my sister; I don't know why you're with her.'

'It's easy.'

Stubbing the cigar tip onto the wall, Ben shivered. 'C'mon, we'd better go in. According to Paige, presents have got to be exchanged before dinner.'

'Why haven't you dumped her after the Temple job?'

'She's alright, you know.'

Alright, Harley thought. He must really like her.

It took two hours to unwrap all the presents, and Harley was starving. They were all starving, but they went around the room one by one, watching each person with embarrassment as Paige handed them their bundle from under the tree.

Harley's thoughts drifted to her mother on their last Christmas, trying to have a happy day despite knowing she would soon be gone. Her mother had handed her the last present – her wedding ring. The poignancy made the child dive into her mother's arms with uncontrollable sobs. She'd stroked Harley's hair so softly and shushed her with tender whispers, rocking her in her arms until the sobs subsided. They knew the day Elizabeth was diagnosed with ovarian cancer, that she would only survive one more Christmas. It was quick – too quick. Chemo hadn't worked, and cancer had riddled her body, from diagnosis to death – just months.

Harley had sat in the chair next to her bed at the hospice: refusing to leave, trying to feed her, massaging her hands and feet with creams to keep them moist. She dripped water from a lollypop sponge into her mouth so she could at least quench her thirst. Once full and agile, her mother's body turned into a skin-covered skeleton as the weight dropped off her. Her limbs became longer, and her movements … different. The tide would never turn back, and each day Harley watched her change. They no longer had verbal conversations; her mother's eyes would tell Harley what she wanted. When she could no longer keep them open, Harley asked her to keep moving her eyebrows so that she knew she could still hear her.

The cancer was quick, but the last few weeks were not; her mother's pain felt like it was going on forever. The incredible face, the face she'd seen every day of her life, the face that loved her, scolded her, believed in her, protected her, and listened to her, became a face twisted by the fucked-up journey cancer takes through the body.

The toxins backed up to her brain, and her hands plucked the air with her delusions. Her jaw dropped, and no matter how often Harley tried to close it, she couldn't. She made sounds in a tone Harley had never heard from her before, and despite all the bathing the nurses provided, there was a smell in the air that never went away.

The night she passed away, Harley had left for a few hours, needing to change her clothes – to eat. The nurses had said they would call if there were any changes; she trusted them, but they didn't call, not until it was too late. She'd wanted to be there with her like she was for her father, and she wasn't.

When the call finally came through, she got to her mother in less than twenty minutes, when she was still warm. Harley's fingers had brushed through her hair, and the tears had flooded her eyes, dripping onto her mother's face. She'd kissed her forehead over and over again, telling her she loved her, that she would miss her and that she was the best mother she could be. But she didn't look peaceful; she looked tormented.

The nurses had done everything else Harley had asked them to do when the time came; they'd opened all the windows of her mother's corner room and dressed her in underwear and her favourite pyjamas. She knew her mother wouldn't want to be removed from the hospice without her underwear – not her mother, a proud and private woman. The windows were opened to let her spirit fly free. They believed in that – believed that her father would be there to greet her. That night, Harley knew he was – that they were together again. The next day, she felt her mother fly around her, like a Tinkerbell ball of light, whizzing above her head, telling her she was there. She'd been there ever since, but Harley never stopped missing the silliest of things about her.

Paige stood before her with a large ribbon-wrapped bundle of gifts Harley hadn't expected.

'They can't all be for me!' she exclaimed.

Taking them from the orange-tanned girl, Harley felt herself become the centre of attention and wished for it to be over. Yet, one by one, she unwrapped the gifts, revealing toiletries, CDs, scarves, gloves, hats, socks, and books. The last two presents were from George and Ben, even though Ben had signed his name to all the other presents Paige had obviously bought on his behalf. Opening George's present first, beneath the lid of a black velvet box, was a platinum and onyx fountain pen. The tip of its cap sparkled, and she saw a 2-carot diamond embedded at its peak. Glancing up, she couldn't hide the tears in her eyes.

'It's beautiful, thank you,' she said quietly.

'Well, if you're going to be a top barrister, you need to look the part.'

Overwhelmed, she stared at it longer than the other guests wanted her to, and Paige suggested she open the last present. Her thoughts stayed with the pen as she quickly unwrapped Ben's. All she wanted was to write on the manuscript paper her father had always used.

Pulling off the ribbon, a different colour from all the others Paige had planned meticulously, she opened another black velvet box. Inside was a brilliant-cut diamond in a platinum setting, with twelve princess-cut diamonds on either side. It shone under all the Christmas lights that Paige had adorned the room with. Faces turned to Ben with panic – then to Harley, then Paige.

'Is that an engagement ring, boy?' asked his uncle.

Ben and Harley glanced at each other with feigned horror – then he laughed. 'She's a bloody lesbian, you Muppet!'

'Well, that doesn't mean anything, does it.' His uncle said seriously.

Ben shook his head in disbelief. 'It's to replace the ring her mother lost. It's an exact copy.'

As Paige opened her presents from Ben, Harley leant over to him and whispered, 'I can't believe you did it.'

'I always said I would.'

He had. When she'd told him the story of her mother losing her engagement ring, he promised that one day he'd replace it; she'd never believed him, even when he'd asked to see a picture of her mother only months ago, it never entered her head what he was up to.

'Go on, put it on; I want to see it next to her wedding ring.'

Slipping the wedding ring off, she glided it over her finger with ease – a perfect fit – and when she put the two together, she saw why her mother had chosen the wedding ring to match. They complimented and harmonised with each other's simple lines and beauty. They were nothing like the expensive antique jewellery she stole, but they were the most beautiful rings in the world. And although her mother had never worn the new one, it was the design she'd chosen to wear on her finger for the rest of her life.

'Now everyone thinks you two are getting married, and she ain't a lesbian.' George grumbled as they sat down in the kitchen with a whisky each.

Ben laughed. 'It was worth it just to see the look on Mum's face.'

George lit a chubby cigar, and Ben let Harley light a cigarette in the kitchen, too, seeing as it was Christmas. They sat together, smoking their chosen sins as the whisky warmed their tongues.

Leaning forward with her elbows on the table, Harley's voice was low. 'I know it's Christmas, George, but we need to discuss a few things.'

'Like what?'

She hesitated, wondering where to start. 'Well, what to do with the Klimt and Sun-Drop in my safe. No one will touch them at the moment.'

'We have to sit on them.'

'For how long? I don't like it being there.'

'Until everything calms down. I'm not happy about you taking them.'

'That's the deal, isn't it? We get what they want, and in return, we get what we want?'

'Usually, yes, but have you any idea how sought after the Sun-Drop is?'

'At 110-carats, I'm not surprised.' Ben grinned. 'Fuck'em. It only takes for us not to give them one of the envelopes, and I'm sure they'd back off.'

George sighed. 'It's not as simple as that. And Ranking's worked out it was you.'

Harley was desperate for Ben to leave them alone so she could ask George about what she'd found, but before her thoughts could take her further, George poured another shot into his glass and downed it. Wiping his lips, he said, 'There's things I can't tell you right now, not because I don't want to, but because I'm trying to protect you.' Harley and Ben remained quiet. 'It's me that needs the envelopes. I'm the client.'

Silence.

Harley and Ben glanced at each other.

Ben's expression turned from quizzical to a frown.

He's going to kick off, Harley thought. At some point, his chair would thump backwards, grating across the hard laminate floor with a screeching scrape that would send it flying against a kitchen cupboard, and then he would hiss 'fuck, fuck' several times before verbally lunging at his father for lying to them. It was rising in him – she could see it.

'Okay, this is okay. It's okay, isn't it, Ben? This means we know who we are dealing with and why, right?' Her gaze met his, and she silently begged him to calm down. She needed them both calm, so George would say as much as he thought he could. If he spoke, he might tell her more than she'd already found out – to fill in the gaps. They waited for Ben's reaction. Despite his criminal brilliance, Ben's temper made him dim sometimes.

Ben's chair *did* scrape backwards, but not with a screech. Instead, it was a slow drag, and when he stood, he turned his body towards the kitchen sink, his back to George and Harley. His hands momentarily gripped the stainless-steel edge before they went to his hair like they always did when he was thinking.

'I need a cup of tea. Does anyone else want one?' Without turning to look at them, he boiled the kettle, making three mugs of it – strong and sweet. There were no words as he did – a painful silence, dense. The mugs sat on the table between them with their steam-twirls rising in the air. The spark of the lighter grated, and the cigar crackled alive. Ben exhaled the smoke. 'Are you going to tell us why?'

George ran a hand through his already spiky-stressed hair. 'I can't tell you everything, but if I don't get those envelopes, we could all end up in prison.'

'Us and the rest of The Domino Set?' Harley asked, looking directly at him.

Ben glanced at her. 'The Domino Set?'

Without answering, she continued to watch George's face. The colour drained from the man she adored. Ben looked at his father. 'Dad, The Domino Set? Is that who we're doing this for?'

'George is part of The Domino Set.' Harley said quietly. 'And so is Eddie Ranking.'

Standing up, George downed the remainder of his whisky. 'That's enough. I need to think.' He walked out of the kitchen, leaving Harley and Ben in silence.

CHAPTER 29

East Ham: Nelson Street, The Primrose Estate

BOOKS sprawled over the kitchen table. Pens of all colours were scattered and strewn as she hunched over the criminal law book written by Knight. Her messy blonde hair fell around her face as she tried to hold it back in the grip of her hand. She was too focused to want to move, to want to run upstairs and grab the hairband she'd forgotten. Instead, words and theories belonging to Knight translated through her eyes to her brain and out again, down her arm and into her other hand that wrote manically on sheets of paper.

Coloured lines, perfectly organised for categories, and miniature mind maps took up the pages alongside her neat writing. Hours passed as she read, scribbled, read, fiddled with her hair, ate chocolate, drank glasses of fizzy drinks, paced, and read and wrote some more. She worked until the alarm buzzed on her phone. Her mother was due home in ten minutes. It was enough time to clear everything away and make the kitchen look like she'd never been there. Hitting the snooze, she continued to finish the chapter she was reading.

The clink of the key in the front door jolted her concentration. The noise made her heartbeat rise to the top of her throat and her stomach punch against her insides. Her hands scooped up everything on the table and threw it into the readied bag next to her on the floor.

The shuffles of her mother removing her winter coat, the sighs, the coughs, the usual routine of coming home and heading to the kitchen to demand a cup of tea made Joanna's throat burn. Her skin trembled as the door handle turned and her mother walked in.

'Ain't you fucking finished!'

'I was just clearing up. The kettle's on.'

Debra Evans sparked a cigarette. 'I need more than bloody tea. Get me the vodka from the cupboard.'

Joanna did as she was told and poured out the measure her mother liked, with the correct number of ice cubes in the glass she had to have. After placing it on the table, she slid over an ashtray. 'I'm just going to take my stuff upstairs, Mum.'

Debra ignored her daughter and slipped off her shoes. Joanna waited. There was silence as she stood, anticipating the permission –

or not. The clunking of the ice around the glass jarred Joanna right through to the roots of her teeth. Before being asked to, the girl raised the bottle and poured another. Her mother swallowed the measure again and lit another cigarette – the remains of the previous one melted down to its stinking butt: a smell that burnt Joanna's nostrils.

'Pour me another fucking one.' Debra mumbled – smoke exhaling from her nose.

Joanna fumbled to open the screwcap of the bottle and cut herself on its sharp metal. She whispered 'shit' under her breath and shoved her finger in her mouth to suck away the blood.

'Jesus fecking Christ, girl, can't you do anything right!'

'I'm sorry, Mum. I just caught myself, that's all.'

Debra eyed her daughter. 'God help me for giving birth to such a pathetic shit like you.'

Quietly, Joanna reached across the table and poured her mother another drink. A slight drop of blood dripped onto the plastic tablecloth. Debra Evans snatched the bottle from her daughter's hand and grabbed her bleeding finger. She pulled it hard, twisting it around until Joanna's slight frame was turning with it to stop the bones from breaking. She held back the squeal. Tears sprung to her eyes but didn't spill as she fell to the floor, her body crumpling as her mother pulled and twisted the bleeding finger. She couldn't scream. She couldn't. Instead, she held in the pain so her mother would get bored and stop. Holding her breath, she choked in the cries. Then, just as her body was taken to a literal breaking point, the pressure was released, and her mother threw her daughter's hand into the air.

'Stupid fecking girl. Get out of my sight.'

CHAPTER 30

Islington

AGI returned home after Boxing Day. As much as Emily had loved seeing her smile a little again, having her return to St Albans meant she could go home too, which brought peace and quiet again. Rosa's hoard of wild children were endless in their demands, and Zeb's incessant questions pushed her to almost breaking point. Free to spend the rest of her time off as she pleased, she returned to Islington, shutting the door with a deep sigh as she leant her back against it.

Her ex had called while driving home to see if she wanted to join the New Year's Eve party at the Blue Cat. Thomas had invited her to meet his new boyfriend, and Rosa had messaged five times asking her to come back to Zeb's as the children missed her. The phone buzzed again, and she sighed 'bloody hell' as she moved away from the door and slid off her coat.

Seeing the hallway plant pot toppled over, she rolled her eyes, realising the next-door cat had let itself in again through the old cat flap in the backdoor. Mumbling to herself what a 'little sod' he was, she propped the plant back up and wandered into the kitchen, noting that the small supply of cat biscuits she'd left out were still untouched.

It was too early for wine or whisky, so she made a mug of hot chocolate, kicked off her shoes, and made her way to her favourite room in the house – her study. As she passed her coat hanging on the bannister, she dipped her hand in its pocket and grabbed her relentlessly vibrating phone. It had gone so crazy with messages that it no longer told her who they were from. Staring at the screen while she walked, she saw there were thirty-six of the damn things.

Pushing a cushion to one side, she flopped onto her much-loved sofa-chair in the corner of the room and tucked her legs under her body. For a moment, she was in peaceful silence: her eyes closed as the warm mug rested against her cheek, and the smell of melted chocolate floated in the air under her nose. Her mind drifted to nowhere; she could have easily fallen asleep, but the phone buzzed again. Opening her eyes reluctantly, she picked it up and swiped the screen.

WHORE.

A punch hit her stomach, and she bolted upright. Text after text message – shouting at her – whore, slag, telling her she was being watched, that the sender knew where she lived, that she would pay for what she'd done. Her stomach lurched up into her throat, and her hands trembled as she re-read every message again and again.

She wanted to phone Rosa, or Zeb and Ammon, or Thomas, even her ex – someone – but she wouldn't be able to speak – she could just about hold the phone. The three little dots told her the sender was typing again as she stared at the screen. Throwing the phone to the floor, she stood up and slowly paced around the room – her bare feet repeatedly padding on the rug. Was it something to do with what Thomas had told her? The Domino Set? Did they think she'd found out how to access the money? Is that what they wanted from her? The money?

She needed to call him to meet him again. She had more questions than he'd given her answers and needed to tell him the file had been stolen from her, that someone had pointed a gun in her face. Why was he always away when she needed him?

Nothing made sense anymore. Everything that laid the foundations for who she was had been blasted into smithereens. Question after question in her mind. Why had her father gone against everything he believed in to run one of the most notorious criminal gangs? Why had they suddenly moved from their family home and never seen most of their old friends again? Was it money? She sighed as she paced. It was usually always money.

She'd never considered her father to be interested in the material trappings of wealth, but there could be no other reason. Her knowledge of him disappeared into a black hole. Everything about him was a lie, which meant everything he had taught her about morals and ethics was also grounded on lies. The phone buzzed again.

Finally, the wine glass stopped twirling between her fingers, and she lit a cigarette. She'd been staring at the same string of texts for nearly an hour. She'd stared at them every day in the same way when she wasn't marking mid-sessional exam papers or preparing a brief for court or notes for lectures. They were relentless and getting worse. She'd been used to abusive emails from partners of clients when things weren't going well in court or from victims of the defendants she took on, but they usually eased off after two or three attempts to freak her out. The sender of these was possessed.

Sitting in the kitchen, her mind turned back to the night of the burglary in St Albans, still unable to work out why there were two of them, whether they were working together or after the same thing, which must have been the file. When the police had arrived, they didn't believe that one burglar had saved her life or that she couldn't give them a description of either despite tumbling on the floor beneath one. Neither of them had spoken, and it had been too chaotic to gauge their heights or builds.

But there was no mistaking that the one on top of her, even though her body was strong, was finely boned like a woman. And there was a definite shape of breasts that had slid across her back as she lay shielded beneath. On reflection, they felt strange, not like soft breasts, but flattened. Even so, the shape didn't belong to a man. What kind of woman would break in during the middle of the night looking for something yet willing to protect her victim with her own life? So many questions buzzed in her mind as the stem of a wine glass repetitively rolled between her fingers.

Every night, as her body told her it was done for the day, her mind sprang into action like a child at a sugar party. She'd lay in bed imagining her father's last moments because she'd seen them for herself – had that fear. His life flashed before her eyes in a way she didn't think she could ever imagine.

The phone glared up at her under the bright kitchen lights – telling her again that someone knew where she lived. Taking another giant slug of wine, she stared at the number she'd become familiar with – sickness rose to her throat. Then Thomas' name flashed up, and she quickly took comfort – thank God.

Finally, Thomas answered her desperate texts, but it wasn't what she wanted to hear. Back in Marbella for a short while, he said he couldn't meet with her until a few days' time. Emily gulped the wine and frantically tapped a message back. The whoosh of it sending eased her just a little. At least someone else knew what she was going through. There was no one else she could tell. No one else that she could share her father's mess with.

The text exchange went back and forth, and Emily told him more than she'd been able to say to the police about the gunman. The shock was starting to fade, and her memory was clearing. Thomas' texts brought her a little more peace as he asked about the burglar on top of her, the colour of her eyes, and her height. He asked for detail about the one with the gun and what his build was like. Emily couldn't answer all his questions but the woman, she remembered, had green eyes. Even in the shadows of semi-darkness, she was taken by the woman's green eyes.

She told him details of the gun barrel that pointed at her face: its shiny steel and how the light from the study lamp had caught it with a gleam. She asked if he could shed some light on who was doing this to her – on who had murdered her father – because The Domino Set would surely know something about what was going on. Thomas promised to ask around for her, but she recognised the hesitancy in his replies after knowing him all her life.

Placing the phone down, she stretched her arms and legs out and stood up – unravelling the tight coil of her spine. She glanced at the clock on the wall – 3.45 in the morning – and yet somehow, she had to sleep. Students were returning, classes were starting, and Zeb had asked to meet her. The texts hadn't stopped since they started. It was in her mind to block the sender, but it made more sense to keep receiving them. The more she received, the more evidence she had if she needed it. At least while she was getting them, she knew what the sender's thoughts were and how they were escalating.

CHAPTER 31

Westminster

IT was eight days since George walked out on them in the kitchen, and he was still missing in action, although his wife knew where he was – she always did.

Harley was due to pick up the fifth envelope in Trier, Germany, in two days, and she needed to speak with him. She muttered how crap his timing was as she stood and waited for Aimee – back from her holiday and in need of some excitement. The last thing she wanted was Aimee's company when there was a crisis with George. Thinking about it, the last thing she needed was Aimee. Maybe it was time to finish it with her, but what would she do? She'd never be able to have another relationship with anyone again. How could she? And what would George think? He never wanted them together in the first place.

She sighed and stared out the balcony doors. Over the past few days, everything had shuffled into place a little more. From the pattern of payments and how George was being blackmailed, along with Eddie and all the other people named on the spreadsheet. She didn't care for any of them except George. If he'd lost millions over the years to Sidney's blackmail, she wanted to get it back. Maybe that's why he never moved from the East Ham estate.

Frustrated by his absence, she'd channelled her energy into working out all the figures and making an accounts spreadsheet for what George had paid Sidney Knight. As she'd methodically entered everything into it, questions rose in her mind, floating like oil on water. She knew the answers were easy to find. Everyone understood there was corruption in the force – why should Sidney Knight be any different. He must have discovered who George was, what he did, and who his contacts were. In exchange for protection, George, Eddie, and the others could stay active underground. There was nothing new in such a setup; it happened across the world, especially in the days when internal investigations were notoriously manipulated.

Her thoughts streamed endlessly as the pieces started to slide together. Finding out who the Angus was mentioned in Sidney Knight's letter to his daughter would take her one step closer to the truth. And although there weren't any entries for an Angus on the

Red List or in the hidden ledgers she'd found with TC's initials on every page, there were three on The Temple Club's membership list. She needed time to investigate – time to stake them out.

Harley stretched her neck from side to side. Her body ached. It was as tired as her brain. She understood George's behaviour now – he had everything to gain from Sidney Knight's death. Everything.

Dressed in heavy winter clothes, Aimee grinned as she entered the lounge.

'Where do you want to go?' Harley asked, irritated that her thoughts had been interrupted.

'School. I've not seen it yet, have I! Will the Dark Knight be there?'

'I've no idea.'

East London: University

Empty streets whizzed by as the frosty January air chilled through their layers of clothes. Snow-dust flew against their visors – melting into water droplets as the wind whipped behind them. London was crispy white.

Being the first working day after New Year, hardly anyone was around as the bike engine purred in the silence. As they reached the canal beside the university, the sound echoed in the empty space.

Their footsteps chomped on the thick fresh snow where only a few had made solitary trails since the snow had fallen. The canal – frozen over – was a white-green sheen of ice with bottles and wrappers floating beneath it like dead bodies in a horror film. Helmets in hand, they wandered into the School of Law. Although quiet, it was staffed and open as usual. Aimee wanted to see everything, so Harley took her floor-by-floor, explaining which room was which, where her seminars were … and her tutorials with Knight. They walked and talked, with Aimee asking questions as if she were in a place that overwhelmed her.

Finally bored, Aimee grabbed Harley's hand and tugged her back out into the open. They ran – laughing – down to the canal. Racing and skidding, picking up snow and throwing, their screams echoed in the hollow emptiness. Lost in the game, for a moment, the world didn't exist for Harley. Aimee moulded a giant snowball and threw it hard at Harley's head. Turning from the sting of the thump, she eyed Aimee with feigned annoyance and moulded an even bigger one. Aimee's hair fell from her knitted hat and down around her shoulders. Her face red and delighted, she skidded along the snow-covered pathway and grabbed Harley. Their breathing deepened as they fell into the thick inches of cushioned white padding. Aimee screamed, flinging herself on top of Harley and pinning her down while pushing a handful of snow into her face. She shrieked again. 'Come on. I dare you to kiss me.'

Harley tried to buck her off, but Aimee stayed straddled over her and leant down, whispering, 'I know you want me.' Their mouths met, but Harley didn't want them to.

'Aimee, stop it, not here.'

Fumbling in the cold to unzip Harley's coat, her fleece, Aimee's hand slipped under Harley's clothes, over her breasts, with cold, numb fingers undoing more buttons. She found Harley's skin, popped her bra and revealed Harley's breasts to the winter freeze.

'Pack it in.' Harley snapped and jolted her hips upwards.

Just as Aimee fell off laughing, footsteps crunched on the snow and stopped at their side. 'Am I to assume from your activities that you don't realise the university is open this week?'

Harley froze for a second, then felt the winter chill across her bare flesh and tried to cover herself. Aimee stood up, breathing heavily and looking a little wild.

'I think you need to stand up too, Miss Smith.' The Professor said.

There was nothing Harley could do but follow the instruction; she stood, her head down, her cheeks flushed, her hands trying to hold together all the layers Aimee had undone. Slowly, she turned to the Professor, dreading the look she was about to see. But the Professor's eyes were directly on Aimee – the rising and falling of her fastened breath. It was an expression that Harley thought was a little unnerved – or confused. For a moment, the two women studied each other.

Next to Knight was Ammon – flushed – carrying take-out lunch cartons from the campus restaurant.

'May I have a private word, Miss Smith?' The Professor's gaze left Aimee and homed in on Harley.

Leaving Aimee and Ammon silently in each other's company, Harley followed Knight. Covered in snow, she stood before the Professor – red-faced – with her heart beating so loudly she thought the woman would hear it. The Professor stood perfectly still, her arms crossed over her chest and her cream winter coat, her chocolate hair falling and tussling around her face, and her blushed lips brilliant against the cream scarf wrapped around her neck. Wearing dark-blue slim-fitting jeans tucked into fur-lined grey suede boots, she glowed wintery and beautiful.

'Perhaps you should take your activities elsewhere,' she finally said. 'And before you do, I think you need to cover yourself up.'

'I'm sorry, Professor.'

'This is not the place.'

'I know. It wasn't my intention.'

'Perhaps not, but you were party to the act.'

'I'm sorry, truly.'

'Unfortunately, I've not taught you about the laws of indecency. If I hadn't come along when I did, I might have been making a bail application on your behalf tomorrow at the Magistrates' Court. Do you understand?'

'Yes, Professor.'

'Good.' Knight almost smiled when she said, 'Now go; you are already starting to defrost.'

Westminster

'She said what?' Ben laughed

'That I was starting to defrost!'

'I can't believe you two were publicly going at it.'

'I wasn't!' Harley exclaimed.

Aimee grinned. 'We weren't far off it. I was ready if you know what I mean!'

'Woh, too much information for your brother to hear!'

Standing up, Aimee threw a cushion at him. 'You're such a dick sometimes. But, have to say, Joanna's right, she's a cold bitch that one. Right, give me ten minutes, and dinner will be served.'

As his sister disappeared into the kitchen, Ben smiled and asked, 'So what does this Professor look like then? Is she up my street?'

Harley laughed. 'You're such a tart! Do a search on your phone, and you'll see.'

Instantly, he found images of the Professor – from professional black and whites used for book covers to colour ones the university used for her bio and website. 'Bloody hell, she's well fit. How can you concentrate when she's teaching you?'

'Unlike you, I don't think about sex all the time!'

'I know you, Harley Smith, there's no way you ain't thinking about sex when she's teaching.'

The sound of Aimee entering the room with more champagne made them both look up from the pictures they were staring at. 'I thought you might like some before we eat.' She smiled.

'Cheers, Sis.' Ben took a glass and downed the contents within seconds. 'So, where's your tan then? Can't believe you spent all that money and came back whiter than when you left!'

Aimee feigned laughter. 'Fuck you, arsehole.'

After dinner, when Aimee disappeared to wash the dishes, Harley took Ben to the study. She didn't show him all her workings out; she didn't want him to see the name of Sidney Knight, highlighted in pink, across every page or the file she'd stolen from the Professor before Christmas. Instead, she showed him just twenty-eight selected names on the membership list of The Temple Club. Against those names, she'd compiled accounts of who was paying money to Sidney Knight, although she marked him as just SK so Ben couldn't make the connection. She showed him how much money had been paid over the years, when, by whom, how often, and when it had stopped. She'd calculated that over £100 million had been paid to Sidney since 1995.

Ben leant over the papers. 'So, each one of these paid money to this SK?'

'Yep.'

'And Dad's on the list?'

'Ben, he's been paying SK money every month for twenty-five years.'

Hunching over the papers, Ben studied them. 'And Ranking, he's been paying too, right?' Harley nodded. 'So, this SK, who is he?'

'I'd say he was blackmailing all the people on the spreadsheet.'

'Was?' Ben asked.

'He was murdered.'

Harley watched him as he stepped away from the desk and leant against the bookcase. His thumb rubbed across his lips, and then his hand went through his blonde mop before he started to pace slowly.

'So, SK is murdered. We do over the gaffs of people on the Red List to get envelopes. Ranking stresses out, Dad … I still don't get it.'

'Break it down differently, Ben.' Harley replied. 'Blackmailer is murdered. No one knows by who. George and Eddie are old rivals – we know that. They are part of The Domino Set – we also know that. So when SK dies, the Set isn't being blackmailed anymore.' She paused. 'But now the old top dog is knocked out, so maybe there's a race to fill his boots.' She stared at him. 'Do you think George murdered SK? I mean, that's a lot of money to keep handing over all the time. Or maybe SK was asking for more? What if George killed SK to take over or get all the money?'

Ben shook his head. 'Dad wouldn't do that.'

'You do know The Domino Set has been linked to several high-profile murders over the years, don't you?'

'Yeah, but Dad … What about Eddie?' He trailed off. 'What if Dad knows Eddie did the murder? I mean, they're both acting a bit strange right now.'

'I don't know, but what if Eddie knows about the envelopes and is putting the screws on George to hand them over?'

'It's possible. I still don't get it, though. Something ain't adding up.'

Filing the papers back into their bundle, she neatly placed them in the drawer and locked it. 'I can't believe your dad has agreed to me picking up more diamonds for Eddie while I'm in Trier.'

'Aimee's debt will never be settled. You know that don't you? Eddie doesn't let anything go.'

Sighing, Harley gazed at her friend. 'Sami Khan is our fifth envelope, so we've only got two to go after that and then George might deal with Eddie.'

'At least this one is easy, and you don't have to do a proper job.'

CHAPTER 32

East London: University

HER knuckles tapped on the door – it opened with no resistance. It was never left ajar like that, she thought.

'Professor.' Quietly, she stepped into the room.

Harley saw Knight startle then turn. 'Miss Smith, I didn't hear you. Please, come in.' Her hand indicated to the seat where her student usually sat, but as she did, Harley's gaze caught sight of something out of place on the typically uncluttered desk: a piece of paper that looked like text cut from a magazine had been stuck to it. Reading quicker than Knight's hand moved to cover it, the word 'whore' pulsated.

'How was your Christmas holiday?' Knight asked, her voice soft and distant.

Sitting down in their opposite chairs, Harley pondered the word she'd read and Knight's demeanour. 'It was okay. How was yours?'

'What would you like to discuss today?'

'Whatever it is that's troubling you.'

'That's not the answer I was seeking,' Knight said flatly.

'I've seen the note on your desk.'

Knight sighed. 'It's nothing – one of many.'

'It's probably just an irritated first-year trying to freak you out because they didn't like their exam grade.'

'You seem to have become an uninvited confidante,' Knight said quietly, her gaze directed down towards the entwined hands on her lap.

Harley knew the other students would relish the gossip if they knew what she'd seen. She wanted to reassure Knight that it would go no further, but how could she say that without making it seem empty? She pulled out her cigarettes, lit one, and passed it to the Professor, who took it with distraction without saying they shouldn't smoke in her office. Exhaling, Knight streamed out the smoke slowly – her profile shadowing against the evening sky seeping through the window. The woman has many faces, Harley thought. From a tussled wildness when she didn't expect to see students to the professional barrister – sharp and astute – with her hair pulled away from her exquisite cheeks and the glasses perched on the end of her nose.

Today's look was new – more tired than she'd ever seen. Dressed in simple black jeans, a plain black t-shirt, flat black boots and, more significantly, an oversized black cardigan. It was like she'd dressed for a day walking the dog rather than a day of lecturing. Without being able to tell Knight everything was okay, Harley didn't know what to do – except be normal.

'Considering your penchant for sex in the snow, were you able to complete your assignments?'

A blush rose to Harley's cheeks. 'I'm sorry you stumbled across that.'

'Really? It's my understanding that people who display such levels of intimacy in public places usually have the desire to be seen.'

'I doubt many would choose to be seen by their professor.'

'Indeed.'

'I thought you'd be angry with me.' Harley said quietly.

Knight didn't respond. Instead, she stood up and moved to the window, her favourite place when she was thinking. 'Does your husband know about your affair? Is that why he ...' Turning, she studied Harley. 'Is that why you are often covered in bruises?' Knight's eyes glanced at Harley's wedding finger, and for the first time, Harley saw what other people saw as she gazed down at the rings.

'I'm not married. This one is my mother's wedding ring; it was the last thing she gave me. And this one, well, it was a present from someone I wish I could marry, but he is a he, not a she if that makes sense?'

The Professor stared at her for some time before saying, 'The woman you were with, she's the one that likes to hit you?'

Furrowing her eyebrows together, Harley gently shook her head. 'I'm not sure how we got to this conversation, but no one is hitting me, not in the way that you think. We were talking about you, not me.'

Knight turned and opened a filing cabinet drawer as she said, 'I need a drink.'

Harley's blood whooshed through her body as the sound of glasses clunked against each other, and when Knight handed her a Jack Daniels, locked the office door and opened the window, she tingled all over.

'I need to smoke a lot more too.' Knight sighed, sitting down on the window seat and kicking off her shoes. She pulled her knees up to her chest, under her chin. 'What's her name?'

'Aimee.'

'And how long have you been together?'

'I don't know. Years.'

'Is she in love with you?' Knight asked.

Harley chewed her inner bottom lip and shrugged.

'Are you in love with her?'

'I'm not sure that's a conversation I should be having with my professor.'

The darkness of Knight's eyes met Harley's, backlit by the little desk lamp that always glowed warmth throughout their evenings together. Quietly, the woman said, 'I don't want to be your professor this evening.'

If she could have done, if it were possible, she would have melted into the chair after fainting. 'Who do you want to be?'

'Would you sit up here with me?' The question was yielding, inviting, and Knight's eyes were too gentle to resist. Harley moved, her legs vibrating, over to the window seat, to sit opposite her professor. The delicate vanilla of Knight's perfume was faint but enough for Harley to catch the scent of it – it was a smell she wanted to dive into.

'I've always thought you were married, therefore in love. One doesn't marry unless they're in love ...' She corrected herself. 'Rather, one shouldn't marry unless they're in love. Then I thought you were having an affair, and maybe it was her you loved.' Glancing at Harley, she said quietly. 'You are very confusing.'

'It's quite simple: I'm not married, and I'm not in love.'

Blowing out a blue stream of smoke, Knight asked, 'So, are you in an open relationship with her?'

'These are intrusive questions, Professor.'

Knight gazed out the open window. 'You're right; they are.' Their gazes came back together in the semi-darkness – shadows performing a ballet between them. 'I was confused after the Christmas party,' she said, with an openness that made Harley want to reach across and touch the Professor's face. 'Your wedding ring versus the way you said I can't move.'

Harley gazed at her. 'Did I sound married?'

'You sounded delicious.' Knight whispered. 'But ... I'm your professor.' She turned her gaze back to the window and the outside world. 'Someone seems to think I'm a whore, and maybe they're right. Maybe I am.' The Professor continued, 'I keep getting text messages saying it too.'

'Have you told anyone else? What about Ammon?'

'Ammon? I'm not sure he could help with this.'

It was in Harley's mind, on her lips, to ask who he was, but she stopped herself.

'You passed all your mid-sessionals, by the way.'

'Did I? Did I do well?'

'Top 5%, although you can do so much better.'

Harley wanted to tell Knight all the reasons she hadn't done better, but how could she explain such things? Part of her distraction lately was the Professor herself – personally and professionally.

If only she could tell Knight that it was because she'd been training late with Ben. If only she could say to her that when she wasn't working, she was running along the river Thames to keep herself fit for her work. Or how she'd been trying to figure out the Professor's role in everything going on with George and The Domino Set. She couldn't verbalise all the confusion building in her mind or tell her she was sorry for hurting her when she saved her life or that she'd read her father's last words to her in the stolen file.

How could she tell the woman she didn't know whether to trust her despite wanting her. How could she tell her she knew about the millions her father had blackmailed out of the biggest criminal gang in the country, which involved George, the man Harley loved the most in the world. And how she would have loved to tell her that she couldn't sleep because there were too many strands of thought springing in every direction that she found difficult to control. That there were live wires full of electric currents flailing around in her head.

She wanted to tell her that one of those wires was Knight herself, constantly sending restless torrents of wanting through her body. Restless torrents since the Christmas party that wouldn't go away even when she touched herself. There was no release. It was all going on inside. An undertow of emotions and activity she couldn't share with anyone, making her tired yet unable to let the tiredness wash over her enough to sleep. They weren't her excuses: she'd worked hard, and she was in the top 5%, but she knew her mind was never totally on her studies.

She couldn't tell her professor any of that, so she asked, 'How's your wrist? I noticed it was bruised when we saw you at Mrs C's.'

Looking down at her fingers, Knight held them up as if examining them. 'I was burgled, Harley. Well, my father's house was burgled. I was there doing some work.'

'And the burglar hurt you?' Harley asked quietly.

'One tried to, yes, but the other one stopped that happening.' Her hand rested on her lap again. 'I don't fully understand any of it. One wanted to kill me, and the other one protected me. And then she stole something from me that my father wanted me to have.'

Harley studied her carefully. 'You said 'she' – how do you know it was a woman?'

The Professor's gaze came to hers casually. 'She had breasts. They may have been strapped down or something because they felt different, but she definitely had breasts.'

'Are you sharing that whisky?' Harley asked, offering her empty glass to Knight. As the Professor poured them both another drink, Harley noted the darkness under her eyes.

'Your father … he was shot in his study, wasn't he?' Knight nodded as she gazed out the window. 'So, when you were burgled, I'm guessing you experienced a similar threat?' Again, Knight nodded. 'And I imagine you can't sleep because you don't know if either of the burglars will try again. And I'd put money on it that you can't get the image of your father out of your mind right now?'

Knight lightly wiped away a tear from her cheek. 'I'm sorry,' she whispered. 'This is so unprofessional.'

'It would be if you were my professor tonight,' Harley replied softly. 'But you said you didn't want to be that.' Sliding herself along the window seat, she moved closer to the woman. Gently, she brushed Knight's hair away from her face. The Professor moved into the touch, her eyes closing. The tears dropped silently onto her cheeks as her head lightly rested against the curve of Harley's neck. Silently, the cold tears fall onto Harley's skin – skin that was alive to everything in the room, even the air as it moved. Gently, her fingers drifted into Knight's hair. Rather than caressing it, she held her fingers – still – and breathed in deeply, inhaling the moment into her lungs so she could keep it inside her body for as long as Knight would allow her. She daren't move. If she did, she wouldn't be in control of herself – her urges – and she needed to be in control. She was honoured – privileged – to have Knight trusting her enough to reveal her pain. Despite her mistrust of the Professor, Harley melted into the beauty of having her so close.

'I don't want to move,' Knight whispered, 'but I need a tissue. I don't know you well enough to snot-dribble on your shirt.'

Harley laughed. 'I can't believe you just said that!'

As they moved away from each other, slightly laughing, Knight glanced out the window. 'Is that the motorbike we saw in Soho?'

Leaning towards the glass, Harley glanced down to the canal. 'Do you think you're being followed?'

'I've seen it a few times, so if I am, they're not very good at it.'

'If your father was murdered, and his house was burgled a second time, and you're getting threatening notes and think you're being followed, why haven't you told the police?'

Knight leant down for the whisky bottle and poured them both another drink before lighting two cigarettes and passing one to Harley. 'Things aren't that simple.' She replied. 'I wish I could tell you, but I can't. I don't know you.'

'What does your instinct tell you?'

'My instinct tells me you're trouble. Lovely trouble. But trouble.'

Harley smiled. 'I'm going to take that as a compliment ... but, on a more serious note, if you're in trouble, trouble I'm not the one causing, would you phone me? Or text me? If you feel unsafe or that you're being followed again? I can help more than you know.'

The woman's hand came to Harley's face, the fingertips on her skin, sending electricity pulsating through her nerve-endings like little butterflies.

CHAPTER 33

Mayfair: Browns

SHE tucked her scarf deeper into her coat and headed towards Browns of Mayfair. It was where she'd often met her father when he was in town, for a cream tea and a glass of champagne at the end of her day or after a big case she'd been working on. They were special moments she didn't have to share with her siblings, a place for just the two of them. Since he'd retired, her father was there so often that the doorman had got to know her just as well.

Already waiting for her, Zeb was sitting in a corner seat by the window. Before him were two glasses of bubbly and a bowl of chilli-salted olives he knew she loved. They embraced – his body warm against her cold face. As she removed her winter layers, he pulled a notebook from his bag and slid it across the table to her.

'Everything you need to know.' He smiled.

'What do you mean?' She asked, glancing at it.

'I don't work for the Ministry because of my looks, you know. I can tell when something is going on.' He sighed. 'Thomas knows what it is, doesn't he? Is that why you two met at The Temple Club?'

Sitting down, she pulled the notebook towards her. 'He's helping me, but he doesn't seem to know much.'

'Can you tell me what it is?'

She studied her brother's face. There was nothing more she would have liked – to tell him. His brain would have worked it all out so much quicker than hers. Zeb was like their father. Sharp minded. Always ahead of what was about to happen. Knowing him as she did, he would have pieced it all together and known how to handle everything she'd have found out. But her father would have told Zeb if he'd wanted him to know. As much as her brother would have worked it out, he would have been obliged to report it all to the Ministry too. His job was his life. And his loyalty to the Ministry always came first. It was bred into him, ironically, by a corrupt father.

And what if he knew and the person who'd attacked her at their family home attacked Zeb, too? She couldn't bear to lose him. Not now – not ever. How could she put him in danger like that?

'I don't think so, Zeb. Not yet. You're job ...' She sighed. 'Well, it makes it difficult.'

'I often think you care more about my job than I do.' He sighed and slid over the glass of bubbly. 'You look like you need this. You've been crying.'

Half smiling, she opened the notebook and scanned through the contents. Having him sit next to her after the day she'd had was more comfort than she could have asked for. There was a strength in Zeb she'd always loved. Unlike Rosa, he was calm and measured, more like her father than she or Rosa could ever be. Maybe that was why she hadn't always got on with her sister over the years. Zeb was strong-minded, just like Sidney – and exact. Sometimes they were both too exact and too demanding, with standards so high that very few could meet them.

She glanced over at him as he sat typing on his mobile and questioned if he, too, had the dark side her father had, the one she was discovering. If they were that alike, would Zeb go down a similar path in his life? What if he did, would he tell her? Would she want to know? Shaking the thought from her mind, she turned her attention back to the notes he'd scribbled and the names he'd put together small biographies for.

Glancing up, she asked, 'Who are these people?'

'It's a strange combination of names, don't you think? But I did a little more digging about The Domino Set after we last met. Although no one knows who they are, there's been a lot of suspicion over the years. They're a bit like Teflon. Then it struck me that some names sounded familiar. The summer parties you asked me about, and us all living in that tiny house on the Primrose Estate. Don't you recognise some of the names, Emily? Only some of those men that used to come to our summer parties are also Domino suspects.'

'These, these names here?' She pointed. 'So, they're from the Primrose Estate where Dad grew up, and we used to live?' Her gaze flashed to her brothers. 'And they came to our house?'

'Yes.'

'I don't remember them.' Sitting back in the chair, she called the waitress over and ordered another bottle. 'I wish we could still bloody smoke in here, like the old days.'

'I wish you would give up.' Zeb mumbled.

'I don't get it. How can people from the Primrose Estate fund and mastermind something like The Domino Set?'

'Because there's always been a rumour that The Domino Set is organised and protected from above. No one has looked into it for years, not since they came up in Operation Domino, which I mentioned, you know, when I handed that file to Dad. Seems it got lost at Scotland Yard and forgotten about. Keep reading, Sis.'

She flicked through the pages. 'This, where you've written Robert Ranking was killed under suspicious circumstances, that's not a petty crime.'

Zeb leant forward to look. 'He's just an interesting connection I had to look into when writing the report.'

'How did he die?'

'Hit by a train.'

'What's suspicious about that? Was it suicide?'

'It was reported as a misadventure by the coroner, but there was speculation he'd been pushed. The one eyewitness revoked her statement.'

'Wasn't there any evidence to support it? CCTV?'

'That's the odd thing; the first policeman on the scene noted at the time that there was a CCTV camera on one of the factories backing onto the line.'

'What's odd about that?'

'There's no record of the factory's statement or assistance. The CCTV was never recovered for the case.'

Emily scanned through more of the notes, trying to quickly absorb as much as possible. Her eyes ran over all the information until she reached a name that made her stomach flip over on itself. She looked up, her lips tightly pressed together.

'Debra Evans? Why is she here?'

'Not for the reasons you think.' He sighed.

'Is she part of The Domino Set?'

Zeb shook his head. 'According to police records, Debra Evans and Eddie Ranking were brought in for questioning over a security van packed with cash that was taken from outside a bank in Clacton in early 1995. Evidence against them was strong, but then much of it disappeared from the evidence room, and CPS decided they didn't have enough. So, there was an internal investigation into how it could get mislaid, and a new system was put in place. She's in the notes because she's linked to Eddie Ranking. We both know a brass like her wouldn't have the intelligence to be part of something like The Domino Set.'

'Does she have children?'

'One girl, Joanna Evans.' Zeb shook his head again. 'I know what you're thinking, but Evans was a prolific brass in those days. I met her when I'd just started at the Ministry. I was meeting Dad at the station, and she was being hauled in for something – absolutely vile woman. I'd never heard language like the stuff that came out of her mouth; it was so bad that the young PC couldn't handle her. It was Dad that calmed her down in the end.' He paused. 'I don't recall seeing that incident on her records.'

Emily pointed to Eddie Ranking's name. 'And him, what's he doing now, do you know?'

'Security. He has four legitimate branches to his company, selling all sorts of things like protection, alarms, bouncers etc.'

Emily nodded. 'And George Davies?'

'Antiques, he owns five shops, all in the prestigious parts of town, from Mayfair to Kensington, to Sloane Square. Looking at his client list, I'd say he's selling to the filthy rich.'

'And Thomas? Thomas is on the list, Zeb.'

'I know. It's hard to remember that Thomas grew up on the Primrose Estate, isn't it? He never talks about his childhood, does he?'

'This name, Elizabeth Bunting; who is she?'

'She was the witness who changed her statement about Robert Ranking's death. I believe she was his girlfriend. She died around twenty-five years ago. Left a daughter behind, and the husband died a few years earlier.'

Placing the notebook in her bag, she glanced at her brother. 'Thank you, this is really helpful.'

'You're welcome, and although I'm not going to ask, I'm just going to let you know that I don't believe your interest is spiked by a client's comment. This is about Dad, isn't it?'

Emily gazed at him lovingly. 'You're just like him.'

CHAPTER 34

Trier: Sami Khan

SAMI Khan, fifth on the Red List and a political editor, was on an assignment covering corruption at the European Academy. The pick-up of his envelope wasn't bothering Harley because George had called in a favour and all she had to do was take the envelope off the contact while sharing pleasantries over a coffee in a bar. The diamonds for Eddie – she wasn't so sure about.

When the bastard had found out she was going to Trier for George, he'd tagged on another smuggling job, using Aimee as his weapon for blackmail. When George told her the deal, Harley wanted to kick off and say not again, not for Eddie, but she couldn't. George would never ask her to do anything unless there was a need to do it, and she'd seen, by the expression in his eyes, that he didn't want to ask her. Whatever Eddie had on George, and it was something more than Aimee, was causing him to look drawn and pale.

Once off the plane, a car was waiting to drive her to Trier, arranged by Ranking. The stay would be short – thanks to him – and the only time she had to venture out of the room was to use the indoor pool, collect the envelope from George's contact, and get the diamonds for Eddie, who wanted them back within 48 hours.

After breakfast, she dressed, left the hotel, and walked for around fifteen minutes to Dr Günter's office in Weberbach. On arrival, she told the receptionist she was on holiday and suffering stomach cramps. After waiting for what felt like hours, the doctor came out of his office and beckoned her. He was plain, bald, around fifty-five: little hands and a large nose. Black glasses sat heavily on his face, making his eyes smaller than they were.

Looking at him, she wondered how a doctor had become involved in such a sequence of events. His office, just as ragged as the GP rooms in England, had mismatched chairs and peeling wallpaper, old posters half blue-tacked to walls, and information pamphlets in every space. The sterile smell permeated her stomach. It was a smell she was used to from all the doctor's appointments with her mother – old and musty yet scrubbed to an inch of its life with chemicals.

His voice was quiet. In broken English, he asked, 'You are from London, yes?'

'Eddie said you could help with my stomach pains.'

'Eddie was here last year. Ah ... what was the date?'

'18th July.'

With a nod of recognition, he shuffled towards a locked cabinet and punched a number into its combination lock. Following his fingers methodically with her gaze, she noted the code – an instinctive habit. Inside were two pouches: one he took out and one he left, almost hidden, in the corner. As he placed the larger pouch in her hand, its weight dipped against her palm.

She'd never held thirty 15-carat cushion diamonds before.

The doctor's little fingers pressed a button on the machine by his computer, and he spoke to someone at the other end in German.

Taking the pouch out of her hand, he tipped the diamonds onto blue paper towelling. With no ambient lighting, they were like pieces of glass – flat. The lamp he pushed towards her finally caught the gems' sparkling energy as they waited for her inspection. Methodically, with the jeweller's loop to her eye, she began. Hesitating at number eleven, she took a pen and drew a small dot on the notepad; placing the diamond on it, she leant her eye almost against its edge. A small circular reflection shadowed within its core, making her glance up at the doctor. At seventeen, she did the same. By the time she'd examined all thirty of them, five were in a pile to her right. The other twenty-five were returned to the pouch.

Sitting back in the chair, she studied the doctor; she couldn't show it, but she didn't know what to do. Eddie would probably have her seen to if she didn't turn up with everything he had asked for.

'These aren't real,' she said, pointing at five diamonds left in a pile. The little man's feigned surprise irritated her. 'It's all or nothing.'

The air sucked in through his hairy nostrils – flared with frustration – and he left the room. Harley glanced around, checking that there were no CCTV cameras and then shot out of the chair and to the safe. Punching in the code she'd seen his fingers enter just minutes before, her heart pumped in her ears. Grabbing the hidden pouch, she quickly swapped its contents with the five fake diamonds she'd left out on the table. Her hands worked quickly, but they trembled. As the footsteps in the other room got closer to the adjoining door, she skidded back to her seat. A deep breath in, a slow breath out. The doctor re-entered. In his hand was another small velvet pouch.

Harley watched five new diamonds tumble onto the blue towelling paper as the doctor emptied the pouch's contents. They gently rolled before her as she glanced at the other five diamonds from the safe, now sitting in a pile to the right where the fake pile had just been. In her grasp was so much money – money she didn't need but a thrill that she did. If she took them all and if Eddie found out, he'd probably kill her. Meticulously, she checked each new diamond the doctor had offered her and put them in the pouch with the other twenty-five. All that was left on the table were the five diamonds the doctor still believed to be fake.

'These are worthless.' She pointed at them. 'But I can use them.'

'£20,000.'

'Either you give them to me, or I'll tell Eddie what you just tried to pull.'

'£15,000.'

Picking up the pouch with the thirty diamonds meant for Eddie, Harley smiled at the doctor. 'You've met Eddie Ranking, I take it? I'm sure he'll have one of his colleagues get in touch as soon as he hears about what you just tried.' She turned to leave.

'Wait.' The doctor picked up the five extra diamonds and offered them to Harley. 'No mention to Eddie?' Harley nodded and took them from him, placing them in the inside pocket of her leather jacket. The doctor also passed her a small sachet. 'Take this. You swallow, then you poop.'

As she walked out of his office into the busy street, where buses and cars hummed in the traffic jam, Harley's stomach was close to hurling into her mouth. Her skin crawled alive, and her breathing pinched in her chest. She wanted to run. Everything, everyone, was moving too fast, and yet she had to walk as she'd normally walk. Between each of her footsteps, the pounding of her heart echoed.

Turning the corner, finally out of the doctor's view, a steady sound of footsteps followed behind her. Harley tilted her head – ever so slightly. Heavy and fast – the footsteps started to catch up – their presence creeping like shivers through her body. Passing a park on her right, she diverted into it. Abruptly, she stopped and turned. It was her only choice. A tall, muscular, unshaven man was looking at her with his hands in his pockets. Perhaps she should run. Maybe she could outpace him. But Harley didn't know the streets well enough to find her way back to safety before he caught her again.

The man moved a step closer – his glance darting around him before focusing right on hers. Harley dug her bodyweight down into her legs – tensing her muscles – preparing for what was about to come. And it came. Shooting across the space between them, the man knocked her to the ground. Hurtling backwards, she skidded along the grass. He landed on top of her, punching her in the chest with a knuckled fist. The impact knocked the breathing out of her, and she wheezed as she tried to breathe.

His entire body weight was on her, holding her down, crushing her. Seconds flashed by as she fought. His hands grappled with the zips on her jacket pockets, fumbling as she thrashed and struggled while her fists and arms flailed in every direction – getting her nowhere. Then she felt it, the rise of hardness between his legs – his erection pushing into her thighs – as hard as stone. Harley froze. At that moment, she couldn't think of anything except for what she could feel pushing hard onto her body. The world stopped – except for that feeling.

George's voice came to her and whispered in her head, *'You'll never win in a state of panic – you'll never win in a state of panic.'* He'd repeated it time and time again in her training after throwing her down to the ground and sitting on top of her, pushing her anger with verbal and physical prods until she couldn't breathe with the pain. Over months, he'd repeatedly taught her that anger – panic – had to be controlled. *It can only be controlled when the internal breath is calm; you'll never win in a state of panic.* Her eyes quickly darted in every direction as she prayed for someone to be nearby, that someone would stop and help her. But what if they did? What if they called the police? She had to escape.

Unsure of whether she could do it in reality, she tried to relax her body, to take slow deep breaths while her attacker wrestled in his frenzy. She blew out slowly, deliberately – repeating the slow breaths over and over – making herself limp. The tightness of his grip on her wrists released as she made herself appear worn out. As he relaxed, she yanked her arms away from him, from above her head, and brought them down to her sides. Calmly, she looked into his eyes, showing him she wasn't going to fight. His grappling stopped.

In that split second, with all her strength, she clenched his temples with the flats of her palms, pressing her fingertips into his temples and ramming her thumbs into his eyes. The muscles in her forearms shook as she pushed into the tear ducts and under his eyeballs.

Gripping her wrists, he tried to pull her hands away, but she ploughed deeper, curling her thumbs, burrowing them underneath his sockets until he gasped in pain. When he did, she raised her face to his and clenched her teeth to his nose, biting down so fucking hard that she felt the tips of her teeth dampen with his blood.

He rolled off and groaned as he grabbed his face.

Harley shot to her feet, her breathing taut in her throat. The sensible thing would have been to run, but the hardness between his legs made her bring her boot up before slamming it – with her entire body weight – right down into the crux of his groin. She did it again, ramming into his shrinking erection with such force she was thrown off balance. He doubled over, and she smashed her kneecap into his chin and up to his already bloodied nose, then kicked her heavy motorcycle boot into his mouth.

She stepped back. Feral. Uncontrolled. With quick sharp breaths heavy in her mouth.

Just as she wiped the blood away from her lips, a young couple walked towards the frenzy. Her gaze flashed at them before she ran – a run quicker than she'd ever done before in her life. She ran across the park, between the trees – as if she were still being followed.

She ran with every bit of adrenaline she had racing through her body, through streets, over pavements, between cars, until she reached the hotel. Sliding in the side door left open for smokers, she slowed herself down, walking along the hallway to her room as calmly as she could.

Throwing her belongings into the travel bag, she pulled the diamonds from her pockets and stared at them. For fuck's sake, she whispered, then filled two condoms with five diamonds in each to insert inside herself. The other twenty-five, she swallowed fast, dry gagging on each one until there were none.

The flight home was shit, uncomfortable, a total fucking wankstain of an experience, but she made it. She made it in one piece, just, with thirty-five 15-carat diamonds inside her – five of which she could keep, and no one would ever know.

Home safely, she took the dissolvable powder Dr Günter had given her. Within twenty minutes, she was in agony. The most horrendous stomach cramps she'd ever experienced in her life consumed her; hot sweats dripped down her spine and face as she prayed for it to be over.

By Sunday morning, all thirty-five 15-carat cushion diamonds were polished and sitting on the coffee table in her lounge. Pale and grey, she was safe and ready to meet Eddie.

East Ham: Ranking's Lock-up

Eddie laughed. 'Well, you're part of the family now.' A black canvas bag skidded across the floor to her, and she threw the pouch across the room to him in return.

'There's a little extra something in there for you.' He grinned.

She stared at the bag, then at him. 'Payment for getting the shit kicked out of me. Did you think I'd be an easy target to double-cross?'

'It had nothing to do with me.'

'Of course, it fucking did. If I didn't bring back the diamonds, you'd still have a hold over George and Aimee, wouldn't you!'

'Tell George it's not over yet.'

'Fuck you.'

'You sound just like your mother.'

'What the fuck did you say? What did you say?' Moving towards him, she shouted. 'What the fuck did you just say.'

One of Eddie's thugs put his arm across her chest.

'You heard what I said. Now get the fuck out of here.'

East Ham: Park Avenue, The Primrose Estate

'What the fuck did he mean?' Pushing her way past him into the hallway, she threw her coat and bag onto the kitchen floor. Pacing, she moved to the cupboard and pulled out George's bottle of whisky.

'Who?' George asked.

'Why the hell aren't you answering your phone?'

'What the fuck does who mean?' George snapped.

'Eddie fucking Ranking! Why would he say that? It makes no sense. Why would he say I'm just like my mother?' She walked as she smoked, her footsteps tapping repetitively on the lino flooring. 'I've never asked you anything, George, but things are getting messy, and you know it. Ben doesn't have a clue what's going on, but I'm starting to put pieces together. When are you going to tell me everything?' She put two glasses on the table and poured them a large shot each before she started to pace again. 'Jesus Christ, I mean … what the fuck is going on? Everything is falling apart. And why the fuck would he say that about my mother?'

George slammed his hand on the wooden table. 'Sit down … Just bloody sit down!'

Harley's pacing stopped, and she stared at him. He'd never spoken to her like that before, but she did as she was told and waited until George took a mouthful of his whisky. Lighting a cigar, he sighed. For the first time since knowing him, his expression made her feel queasy as he looked at her.

'Eddie knew your mother well. We all did.'

The palms of Harley's hands came up to the back of her head and scrunched her hair between her fingers. Tightly. Staring at him, she said nothing. He had taught her that. Silence is power. The smoke from his cigar made her want to gag. It had never caught in her throat before. Bringing her hands back down, she placed her elbows on the table and pressed her fingers into her cheeks.

'We grew up together. Elizabeth was part of it all, the group from the estate.' He paused. 'This one. This is where we all grew up. The Primrose Estate.' The inside of Harley's mouth caught between her teeth, and she chewed it.

'Aren't you going to say something?' He asked.

'How well did Eddie know her? You said he knew her well.'

'He liked her, once, when she was about fifteen. Your mother had more sense than to like him back, though. In fact, she hated him, but he wouldn't let it drop.'

Eddie Ranking liked her mother. She shook her head. 'No way.' Standing up, she began to pace again. 'No way, George. How the hell? I mean, what the fuck? How did I end up working for you? And now him? How the fuck did that happen?'

Leaning back on the chair to watch her, George brushed his hand through his hair several times. 'That night when I saw you trying to steal the car … I knew exactly who you were before you even said your name. You're the spit of her. We'd all thought you were okay. Your father was loaded, and you were at boarding school. None of us ever thought we had to worry about you ever again. Then I saw you … coked up and looking a bloody mess.' He sighed. 'I couldn't leave you like that, not Lizzie's daughter. She'd never have forgiven me.'

Harley stared at him, her jaw clenched as tears pricked her eyes. 'Why didn't you tell me? All this time. I could have asked you so many questions, learnt so many things about her, about my father.' Her voice broke as she said, 'I could have grieved with someone, not on my own like I did.'

George's pale slate-blue eyes moistened. 'I had to get you off the coke, Love, and then I just wanted to give you something to take your mind off things. We all loved Lizzie, some of us more than others, and all I wanted to do was bring you home, where I knew you'd be safe.'

Their eyes met – no words – yet they spoke to each other. 'Are you my father?' Harley asked, her voice almost inaudible.

George shook his head.

'Is Eddie?'

'Your mother wasn't that stupid.'

Harley collapsed back into the chair. 'Does Ben know?'

Shaking his head again, George added, 'And neither does Aimee. Only us kids from the estate knew Lizzie. We spent every moment together when we weren't at school.'

Her hands clasped together in front of her face. She could feel George's eyes watching her, waiting for the next question. Before she had time to ask, he said, 'Your real father … he was one of us. His name was Robert, Robbie Ranking; he loved your mother and was my best friend.'

'Was?' Harley repeated.

'He was killed.'

She stared at George. '*Killed.* I don't know what to ask first. How he was killed or whether Eddie Ranking is my fucking uncle.'

George looked up at her. 'I need you to focus on the last two envelopes, Love. We can talk about all of this after.'

'Did you really just say that? Fucking hell.' Harley glared at the man sitting opposite her, the man she had always trusted. 'Jesus fucking Christ, George. You've just dumped a shitstorm on me, and all you can think about are the fucking envelopes!'

'You know what I mean.' He snapped.

'Fuck you!'

179

Westminster

George's words stuck in her mind, just like the pain in her chest. Neither eased despite the painkillers she'd taken for the bruising she'd have to explain to Knight yet again.

The muscles behind her eyes trembled as she rubbed them. They were sore, puffy, and moved slower than she'd ever been used to. She tried to blink away the soreness as she nestled down into the sofa, curled under a soft fleecy blanket as she opened the laptop resting on her knees. It didn't take long for her to find information on Robert Ranking, the younger brother of Eddie Ranking and twin brother to Anthony Ranking. That made three Rankings she was related to, but all the photos she found were old and grainy. She had no idea if Robert, her father, was an identical twin or not.

Tears streamed from her already sore eyes as she read the news article twice that she'd found on the internet – her jumper wet around her neck. Robert was twenty-nine when he was hit by a train between Fenchurch Street and East Ham. As she read the blurred words of an article written way before things had been digitalised, she wished she was still in the kitchen with George, drinking his whisky and asking him questions.

Her stomach ached like hell.

She'd always thought her mother had got pregnant through a one-night stand, or her father was a man that didn't want to know her. But now, George had said he'd loved her. He'd loved her mother, and yet her mother had never been able to mention him, share him. All those years living with his death and never being able to share that love again. Would he have loved his daughter too? Did he know she was going to exist? So many questions she needed answers to. She hated George for all his lies.

CHAPTER 35

East Ham: Nelson Street, The Primrose Estate

As Joanna talked – white noise in the air – Harley found it hard to be with her, knowing that her mother was somehow part of the same twisted mess George had pulled them all into. She wondered if Joanna knew everything, anything, and that's why she'd tried to befriend her from day one. Did she know Sidney Knight had a file that included the details of her mother, Debra Evans? Harley looked at the girl as she spoke. Maybe that's why she hated the Professor so much.

Her thoughts drifted back to George. All her intentions to question him had been flung out of the window when he'd told her about her mother – about her real father. Every day since, she'd hunted more and more on the internet to discover anything she could on Robert Ranking, but there was nothing more there. She'd even researched through all the online law databases through the university. Her head thumped with it all, like an explosion about to happen. Everything was distorted in her thoughts – her poker face wanted to scream.

Joanna flopped her textbook down on the kitchen table. 'Are you listening to me?'

Harley's attention jolted back. 'I am. You said you needed me to run through *mens rea* and the correspondence theory again.' Leaning forward, she picked up the book Joanna had given up on. 'Come on, you can do this.'

'I know I can do it; I just can't get the fucking professor to see that I can.'

'What time is your mother due back?'

'Soon, I imagine. Unless she won at bingo and has gone to the pub.'

'I should head off; I've got some stuff to do tonight.'

Joanna lit a cigarette, a new habit she had picked up. 'You never agree with me about her.'

'Who? Your mother?'

'Knight. You never agree with me that she's an evil fucking bitch.'

Closing all the books strewn across the table, Harley glanced fleetingly at her friend. 'That's because I don't think she is.'

'So you think I'm lying?' Joanna snapped.

Harley stopped packing her bag. 'No … I think you have a different opinion to me, that's all. Why do you hate her so much?'

'Why do you like her so much?'

Half smiling, Harley shook her head gently. 'You know, I don't need this right now, Jo. I need to go.'

Joanna stood up, the chair scraping on the cheap lino floor. 'I don't want you to go. I'm sorry. Please, Harley, I'm sorry. Don't go. Please.' Joanna grabbed Harley's arm as she tried to leave. Her face was flushed, and her eyes pricked with tears.

'I have to.'

The Streets of London

Speeding off into the darkness, she drove on autopilot. It was only when she checked her mirrors that she saw the motorbike behind her.

Veering to a different route, she shot the Triumph around a corner into a deserted street and waited between two parked cars. As the motorbike came around, passing her, she pulled out behind it. Ahead, it swung wide on the corner and out of sight. Speeding after it, Harley revved the Triumph's engine to a boom that trail-backed behind her. She whizzed past parked cars, dead for the night, and leant to the right, taking the Triumph with her, sharply to its side. The motorbike was back in sight.

Bursting the accelerator open, Harley's body moved forward, her chin almost on the handlebars. The bike ahead coiled around another corner, smacking them both into a mid-stream of sporadic night traffic along Whitechapel Road. It weaved between taxis and nocturnal lorries delivering their goods, as green lights turned amber before Harley could reach them. Then red. She hissed 'shit' beneath her helmet and rested up on her feet, waiting for green to flash up again while keeping her eyes focused ahead – the distance was growing further.

The engine roared – she was chasing again. Between cars, with lights flashing against her eyes, she zigzagged, using her legs to control the Triumph into leans and dips that pushed her further, faster. A car bibbed as she cut across it on the late-night street, but she didn't care – slamming her Triumph through every space, trying to get back behind the other bike. Turns and twists led her off into side streets, down Plumber's Row, back to Whitechapel Road and through Aldgate. There was no sense to his direction, just streets hissing past as the powerful engines bellowed and resounded against small, terraced houses and glass shop fronts. Turning into the Minories, the bike suddenly careered around looming roadworks, its wheel slipping on the edge of a lean. Struggling to control the shake, the rider's knee almost scraped the tarmac as he twisted himself to bring his bike back up. Slowing down, shaken, he turned into Vine Street. Tosser, Harley thought, not so cool now ...

She followed – she'd got him; there was nowhere to go – a dead end that led onto the back of restaurants. The Triumph's engine purred as she slowed down to a stop at the street entrance. Holding the bike between her legs, she sat up from the handlebars and calculated the rider's next move. With his back facing her, she studied his leather jacket, its shape, and the small red logo on its arm – she'd seen it many times before on biker jackets – a common brand.

The engines quietly hummed after they had thundered against each other through the streets of East London. Waiting, Harley watched. The other bike turned around. Harley knew that the eyes behind the visor were weighing up the escape route, weighing up whether he could fly past her through the gaps on either side. It was a chance she would take herself. They stared straight at each other.

Her heartbeat pummelled – did his? Was his blood spiralling in his veins like hers? The rider on the bike was fast but not as experienced – his control was shabby. Chewing the inside of her bottom lip between her teeth, she opened the throttle of the Triumph. The engine's drum-firing blast smashed into the silence as the front wheel rose up to the sky. She span up on the back wheel towards him. When the front wheel came down to the road with acceleration, she contorted her body to the side, bringing the Triumph into a sharp lean. Her weapon was the back wheel; her aim was to clip it against the rear of her opponent – to cut his bike from beneath his body.

But he'd seen what was coming and spun his back wheel out towards her, clipping her bike beneath her and spinning her across the cobbled road. As she skidded, he accelerated a short spurt away from her.

Pulling herself up, she stood, the Triumph limp on its side. He paused, sitting back on his bike, and briefly, he watched her as she lifted the scratched Triumph back to its wheels. Then, when it was upright and by her side, his engine roared – a reverberation that boomed in her bones – and he sped off.

Pulling her phone from her pocket, she called Ben. His phone switched straight to voicemail. After leaving a rambling message about how she needed his help and that he had to hunt down the fucker on the bike with the red logo on his jacket, Harley lit a cigarette and sat down on the kerb of the street.

Westminster

'Just seen your bike in the car park; what the fuck happened?'

'It's nothing.' Harley said quietly as she pulled Aimee out of the corridor and into the flat.

'It never used to be like this; it's only since you started uni, d'you know that?'

'It's nothing.'

'At this rate, you could end up dead.'

'What are you doing here? It's gone midnight.'

Removing her jacket and breezing through the half-opened door, Aimee replied. 'I went to Claire's after work tonight for a curry, saw your light on and thought I'd pop in and say hello on my way home.'

'You must have good eyesight; I'm ten floors up.' Plonking herself onto the sofa, Harley sighed and lit a cigarette. Aimee wasn't who she wanted to talk to. She wanted Ben, but he still wasn't answering his phone.

'I can go if ya want.'

'Why do you have your night bag?'

'It was in the car, so I thought I'd bring it up, just in case. Shall we go to bed?'

'I need a hot bath, and then I have some work to do.'

'Fine with me. C'mon, I'll join you.'

Sitting at opposite ends of the bathtub, they sipped from the chilled glasses that trickled with condensation. 'You look gorgeous.' Aimee smiled and pushed her foot between Harley's legs.

She pushed it away. 'Have you seen your father lately?'

'Why are you following him?'

Harley sat up straight, water splashing around her breasts. 'What makes you think that I am?'

'You all think I'm stupid!' Aimee's glass clunked down on the edge of the bath rim. 'I meant what I said, all this shit has happened since you started at university.'

'That's got nothing to do with the jobs we're doing or why George isn't himself.'

'Really?' Aimee mocked. 'I don't believe your brain hasn't put it all together yet.'

'Put what together yet? What do you think you know that I don't?'

Aimee smiled. 'You know, maybe I should move in, then we could see each other more.'

East London: University

The bruises on Joanna's wrists popped against the whiteness of her skin as she reached out across the table for the sugar. The dark puffy circles under her eyes were darker than usual, and there was even less colour on her already ghostly face. Even her blonde hair was listless as she instinctively swept it away from her cheeks, so it didn't get in the sugar-coated doughnut.

'Am I allowed to sit?' Harley asked. 'Or are you going to have a go at me again?'

Mid-chew, with sugar around her lips, the girl glanced up. 'I didn't think you'd talk to me again.'

Harley sat down opposite. 'You look tired.'

'Mum's more stressed than usual.'

Watching Joanna tear off a chunk of the doughnut, Harley looked at her. 'Why, has something happened?'

'I don't know, she doesn't tell me anything, but Uncle Tom was round, and they were shouting.'

'Is Uncle Tom the gay one with the Celtic tattoo on his wedding finger?'

Joanna nodded, putting her hand over her sugary mouth as she said, 'Uncle Eddie's been round a lot too, so all three of them have been shouting at each other. I've not had any sleep. They seem to be round every night.'

Harley sat forward. 'Uncle Eddie? What's his last name?'

'Ranking, why?'

Ranking. Eddie Ranking. Harley looked at her friend – or her cousin – what was she to her? If Eddie Ranking was Joanna's uncle, who the hell was the girl's father? And who was Debra Evans in the scheme of things? Sugar rimmed the girl's lips as she bit into her second doughnut. Cousins. Wasn't it too much of a coincidence to be at the same university at the same time, in the same class? Is that why the girl wanted to swap into Knight's class with her, even though she hated the Professor so intensely? Eddie Ranking. The hunger in Harley's stomach swirled into nausea.

'And Uncle Tom's?' Harley asked quietly.

'Crowe, why?'

Thomas Crowe. TC. *T fucking C.* Shaking her head, Harley quietly said, 'No reason.' An electrical current in her head snapped back and forth. TC. Thomas Crowe. TC. Fuck. 'I bet they spoil you rotten. Do you have any photos of you all together?'

Joanna picked up her phone, smearing jam on its screen as she unlocked it. 'Just a couple. Here.' She flashed her phone at Harley. 'That was taken at Christmas.'

Uncle Tom's features were clear – she knew his profile from under the streetlights near The Temple Club. The man that met with Professor Knight. The man that had met with George just an hour before. TC. Thomas Crowe. The Temple Club's accountant. Joanna Evans's adopted uncle. Friend to Eddie Ranking.

'You don't look alike, you and Eddie.'

Joanna laughed. 'Thank God. He's not my real uncle, silly. He's like Uncle Tom. We're not related.'

'Is Uncle Tom close to your Mum, like Eddie is?'

The girl nodded. 'They all grew up together on the estate,' she replied before gulping a swig of her hot chocolate. 'I found old photos of them all once.'

'I'd love to see them sometime.' Harley smiled. 'It must have been nice for you to grow up with them all.'

'I didn't, not really. I think there was a massive falling out for a while because the photos stopped.' She flicked through her phone again. 'I have some on here somewhere. I took photos of the photos. I was going to make one of those digital frames for Mum's birthday, but she found out and had a go at me for going through her stuff.' She flashed the screen back at Harley. 'This is one of them all together when they were like, in their twenties.'

The faces were blurred, and the photo was badly taken, but Harley knew her mother's features by heart, even if she was younger than Harley had ever known her. Standing by her mother's side was a young man, maybe her father. Seeing them together for the first time made her heart drop a million miles into the depths of her stomach before it rebounded back up and grasped in her throat. With all her strength, she caught the tears in her eyes before they landed. She quickly cleared her throat.

'Do you know all of them in the photo, Jo? Is your father there?' Joanna pulled the phone back and closed the screen. Her face blotched to a deep red, and she quickly put the remains of the doughnut in her mouth. 'Mum doesn't keep in touch with the others. Like I said, there was some kind of falling out.'

Harley sat back in the chair, her heart slowing down – just a little. For a fleeting moment, it beat so loudly that she heard it in her ears. Questions flashed through her mind; did Joanna know who George was? If she did, she would know who Harley was too. If she knew Eddie and Thomas, she'd know Sidney Knight too, which meant Debra Evans must know who Harley was and what she did. What if Evans was a snitch? Harley whispered 'Jesus' in her head. What if Joanna was a snitch? She drew in a deep breath and exhaled it slowly.

At the opposite side of the café, James sauntered through the door and caught Harley's gaze; he smiled and made his way to them, his ruddy cheeks glowing even more from the winter chill outside. It took him a while to get through the battlefield of chaotic chairs dragged to different tables and huddles of students with heavy rucksacks full of books, laptops, and folders.

'Hey.'

Joanna glanced up at him before returning her gaze to the mass of highlighted notes she'd been working on when Harley arrived.

'You're leaving it to the last minute, aren't you!' He said, pulling a chair from another table and plonking himself down.

'I've been learning this all week,' she replied, blotching red.

'I don't get why you can't answer her questions; you do in all the other seminars.'

'What's that supposed to mean?' She snapped, her gaze shooting up at him.

'Nothing.' James and Harley glanced at each other. 'Sorry Jo, I was just saying how good you are in the other seminars.'

'No, you weren't. You were implying I'm stupid. I can't help it if the bitch doesn't like me.' Red turned to crimson on her white neck.

'Hey,' Harley said softly, leaning forward to touch her arm. 'You know more than any of us.'

'That's the first lie I've heard you tell. Why would you lie to me?' Standing up, Joanna grabbed her notes, crumpling them as she stuffed the bundle into her bag. 'I'm going. I need to read in peace.' When she left the table, scraping her chair on the floor as she went, Harley watched silently. The girl's mood was swinging back and forth over the past few weeks. Harley turned to James. 'How did it go when you took Joanna home after Christmas? She's not mentioned it.'

James sighed heavily. 'Have you met her mother?'

'Unfortunately, yes.'

'Yeah, that's what I thought too. She saw us saying goodbye to each other and came out of the house like a raging banshee. She dragged Joanna off me and told me to fuck off.' James blotched. 'I heard her calling Joanna a whore.'

'I'm worried about her.'

'I've been keeping an eye on her when you're not around, but she's gone all weird and distant like she barely knows me sometimes.'

Harley smiled at the boy. 'You like her, don't you?'

Blushing, he said, 'She's not easy to like sometimes.'

'I don't think she's used to being liked.' Grabbing her bag, she stood up, but before she left, she added. 'Do me a favour, keep an eye on her a bit more, will you? Something's not right with her at the moment.'

The boy nodded. 'Hey, how's your bike? Jo said you'd had a bit of an accident on it.'

Harley smiled. 'It's in bike hospital, but I'm off to pick it up right now.'

Leaving James sitting on his own, Harley left campus and headed back to Westminster, towards the garage where the Triumph was waiting for her. She needed it back in action. Days had been lost, and she needed to hunt down Angus McLellan, Sidney Knight's friend and Emily's godfather. Her thoughts turned to the letter Sidney had left his daughter, mentioning a safe deposit box Angus held all the details for. If she could find them before Professor Knight, maybe she could get George's money back. And maybe she could help him settle down again to the old George. All she needed was the Triumph back in her armoury and the dark hours of a late night.

CHAPTER 36

Covent Garden: Offices of Angus McLellan

Outside his offices, a small law firm based in Covent Garden, Harley sat on her bike between two vans and away from the streetlights. She waited. She'd sat in the same position for three nights, assessing the entry points, noting the comings and goings of staff, clocking the times, security, and cleaners. It wasn't long enough to stake the place out properly, but she was running out of time. There would be a new envelope job soon, and George was going more into himself – avoiding her as much as he could. She didn't like it, the fear he seemed to always have in his eyes.

At 11.30, in the darkness of a January evening, the City of London side street was almost silent. Offices had closed. Lights were switched off. Except for the occasional late worker hurrying down the street to catch the last tube or train home, she was practically alone. Harley slid off her bike, pulled a briefcase from the saddlebag, tucked her helmet safely away, ruffled her hair and straightened her suit. To go unnoticed, she looked the part because the only way in was through the front door.

Walking across the road, her heeled boots reverberated on the pavement as her eyes scanned in every direction. There were no CCTV cameras outside the law firm, but she had no idea what was inside – it was too risky to scope so close to breaking in.

Her skilled fingers picked the entry lock with ease, and she went through the main door, closing it gently behind her. The lights were off, but her eyes accustomed quickly to the darkness. Slipping her shoes off, she tossed them into the briefcase and quietly ran up the five flights of stairs to Angus' offices. Her gloved hands used the rail to propel her upwards with each step. At the landing, where Angus' name was sandblasted into the glass, she stepped into the darkest corner and studied the area for cameras.

Above her was a small red dot – discreet but obviously placed. Sliding a black balaclava over her face, she flipped off the spray paint lid and pressed her finger on the nozzle. There wasn't time to disconnect the camera. She had twenty minutes before the two night cleaners arrived, starting on the ground floor and working their way upwards. Twenty minutes was long enough when she knew where to look, but she didn't.

As her body slid into the offices, an alarm panel flashed on the wall, triggered by the motion. It was an old and familiar panel, but she knew never to underestimate what an alarm was hooked up to. Seconds flashed on her watch as she slipped across the room and dismantled the front panel to find the wires. Drips of sweat trailed down the back of her neck and in her hair. This was more like it … this was the excitement she'd been looking for, testing her skills again as if she had never done a job before in her life.

Deftly, she used the wire cutters to snip through the coloured wires in order – the seconds on her watch flashing as she worked. When the last wire was cut, she took a deep breath and looked around the office, scoping its layout in the dark with the streetlight shadows gently touching across all the shapes.

Five glass-panelled doors led off from the main reception: a large modern open space with splodges of artwork, reed infusers and cream leather sofas. Harley moved past each door one by one, looking for Angus' name. Door number four.

She knelt down on the oak floor and picked the double lock – the picks sliding and clicking as she pushed three in, one after the other, finding the mechanism, wiggling, until the latch clunked and the handle turned. Inside his office were three filing cabinets, two desks, and four paintings hanging on the walls. Standing still, Harley's eyes scanned the room. Her watch flashed – five minutes down.

She glanced at the wooden filing cabinets briefly, mumbling in her mind to find the logic of where Angus would hide the letter of his dearest friend to his daughter. She turned away from them and gazed at the pictures on the wall. Like a scanning computer, her eyes studied each one. She processed the images and walked over to the third picture, the only one that didn't have hardware screwing it to the wall. Placing her cheek against the cold concrete, she ran her gaze up and down the length of the picture frame to see if there were any wires behind it – where the hinges were placed. Her watch flashed. Seven minutes down.

Gently, with her gloved fingers, she eased the frame away from the latte-coloured wall and slowly opened it like a hanging door and pulled out the small magnetic reader from the briefcase, holding it against the safe's keypad. The digital screen spun numbers like a bomb timer until, one by one, numbers stopped and froze. When all six numbers were fixed then flashed, Harley punched them onto the safe's keypad in order. The door popped open. Eight minutes down.

Tugging out a bundle of envelopes, Harley scattered them over the nearest desk. There were over twenty, all identical except for a case number on the front. Methodically, she opened each one, looking for recognisable handwriting, and reading the top line. The ache in her back from hunching over – concentrating – made her stop to unravel and stretch. The watch flashed. Twelve minutes down.

Her hand moved across the envelopes, spreading them further apart on the desk. For a moment, she stared at them. Sighing, she continued. Opening Case 43-18 and unfolding the papers inside, she saw his writing. Sidney Knight. She knew it by heart. Without reading the words, she folded them back up and put them in her briefcase. Fourteen minutes down.

The muffled sound of alarm beeps from a code punched into a key panel stopped her mid-movement. Her gloved hands were halfway in the safe with the bundle of envelopes. Her breathing silenced – held in the depths of her lungs. Her watch flashed again. Fifteen minutes down.

They were early.

The beat in her heart pulsated hard under her chest bones as she listened for where the footsteps would go – but they were too far away.

Working fast, she placed the envelopes back in the safe as she'd found them, closed its door, and eased the picture back against the wall until the hinges clicked into place. Lightly moving across the wooden floors, not knowing where the creaks would be, the blood pulsed through her veins as if it were alive and on speed. With a quick glance back to make sure nothing was disturbed, she slipped out of the office and into the stairwell.

Laughter rang out from below, echoing up the empty void of the stairwell at the heart of the building. Muffled and distant, she figured they were still on the ground floor. Her watch flashed again. Harley ignored it and moved down to the third floor.

The footsteps below sounded on the stairs. They were on their way up. Her eyes scanned in the darkness. Why would they be on their way up already? The adrenaline raced into her blood. Stepping backwards, a metal handle prodded into her sharply. She jolted and turned. Bending down, with trembling fingers, she began to pick the lock. The laughter and the footsteps came closer. Sweat seeped into her skin behind the woollen mask. The second pick fell from fingers, chiming on the floor like a piano tuner. The footsteps stopped. Harley's life drained from her body. Silence came as everyone in the stairwell waited and listened.

The footsteps started again, and Harley slid the second pick back into the lock and silently opened it. She slipped between the door and its frame, closing it softly and turning the latch to lock herself in. The smell of paint and white spirits wafted to her nostrils, making them burn. Her feet touched the edge of a paint can, and she stopped – frozen. The chatter of the two cleaners came closer. Her watch flashed. Twenty minutes down.

'I swear, I heard something.' A woman whispered.

'You always hear things.' The other one giggled. 'There's no one here, ya silly cow. Come on, I'm starving.'

CHAPTER 37

Islington: Garden Square

SITTING on the edge of the bench, Joanna stretched out her legs. Her hands, warmed by red mittens, slid between her thighs. Her breath puffed out little chill-clouds, but she'd prepared for it – a flask of hot chocolate in her bag.

After being stationary for nearly fifteen minutes, she stretched again and moved backwards – the wood of the bench pressing into the bruises on her spine.

She watched, unseen, as the Professor fumbled for the keys in her bag. Maybe that was something she could buy her – one of those key alarms that beeped when whistled for. If she did something like that, would the Professor finally like her?

The key fumbling went on for minutes – long enough for Joanna to sit and study Knight even more. She liked the way the woman's hair tumbled in thick waves over her shoulders and her red coat. They both liked red. Joanna smiled. Even the way Knight brushed her hair from her face was something Joanna knew she would never have the style to do. She hated her own hair: it was thin and blonde, more like her father's than her mother's. So many times throughout the day, she would wonder what her father was really like. The stories her mother told of him were vile, but Uncle Tom – he never commented: just dipped his eyes and held his tongue.

Knight disappeared into her house, and Joanna sighed. Would that be it for the next few hours? Maybe she should sit for a bit longer. She had nowhere else she had to be. No one would miss her for hours.

The bruises on her spine thumped as the cold bench pressed against them. Lighting a cigarette, she coughed a little, then settled back into the pleasure of smoking it. At least it took her mind off the pain in her back and made her feel closer to Harley.

All she wanted was to escape – to have a life without her mother and a different kind of family. Any family. And normality. She wanted to feel normal, not like the unwanted freak her mother made her feel. Everything she did, everything she said, it was all an inconvenience to everyone – except Uncle Tom and Harley. The thought made her throat painfully close. An inconvenience.

Her mind drew into itself as she sat, with her red mittened hand trying to hold the cigarette tightly. Why was she even alive? The question sat with her most of the time; it was only when she was with Harley that she had some worth – and James; he seemed to still like her despite her mother. The corners of her eyes moistened, and she sniffed up the nose-dribble that needed a tissue.

Her attention jolted as an upstairs blind twisted to a close. Why would she close the blind so early in the afternoon? Joanna dug the cigarette into the grass and blew out the last trail of smoke mingled with a cloud of cold air. Had she been spotted? Glancing around, she looked in every direction. Her eyes rested their gaze on a shape at the other end of the public gardens opposite Knight's house.

The leather-clad body looked like Harley – how her friend always looked when she'd been on her bike. For a second, Joanna thought it was her until she saw the red logo on the biker's jacket sleeve. Sitting back, she sighed, not knowing if she was disappointed or relieved. The only other person in the gardens was facing Knight's house too.

Joanna leant down to her bag and retrieved the flask of hot chocolate. Despite her woollen mittens, her fingers were burning with the cold and her nose, momentarily warmed by the nose-dribble, was almost too cold to feel. She rested the flask's full cup against her cheek to warm her face before taking a few hesitant sips of the steaming drink. It burnt her tongue, then warmed her throat – all the way down into her stomach.

As she sat, she had no idea if Knight would appear again or move again within the house, but maybe, if she waited a little longer, she would be able to see a little more of her. Perhaps Knight would notice her in the gardens and come outside to invite her in. Maybe they would talk and laugh – get to know each other. She smiled to herself again. Getting to know the Professor would make everything right in Joanna's life.

Just as she brought the cup of hot chocolate to her lips to blow on, the leather-clad figure moved from its bench. Joanna saw it in her periphery. Her attention peaked as he walked straight toward her. The beat of her heart pounding in her ears as if her eardrums were vibrating next to a loudspeaker. The mug stopped in front of her lips, and she looked up, her eyes widening.

'You're Joanna, right?'

The girl nodded.

'Why are you camped outside Professor Knight's house?'

CHAPTER 38

Westminster

THE letter from Angus McLellan's safe sat on her desk, unfolded. Although she'd read it several times over, as she dressed in her biker leathers and strapped her kit-bag onto her body, her eyes scanned it again. Thomas Crowe. *TC.* His name had popped up in it several times, and she needed to find out more about him.

It was Wednesday evening, and if she'd judged TC right, he would be at The Temple Club until around 11.00 p.m. That gave her two hours to enter his home and rummage. She was going in blind again, but there was no other way. There wasn't time to stake his place out or watch his movements.

Harley sighed. The last thing she wanted was another late night. All she seemed to be doing was working either off the radar or on her law essays. Everything felt like it was coming at her from every direction. Aimee and her constant demands to move in. George and his continual disappearing act. Ben and his anxieties over his father's behaviour. Studies. Work. Envelopes. Harley froze for a moment – the beat in her heart fast and fluttery. She drew in a deeper sigh and exhaled it slowly from her lips. Pull it together, Smith, she whispered in her head.

Checking her straps were all in place and her knapsack secure on her back, she left her flat and ran down the ten flights of stairs. Tony – hanging his coat up as she entered reception – turned and smiled, his teeth slightly whiter against his tan and grey-white speckled hair.

'You've been on the sunbeds again.' She laughed.

He grinned and rolled his eyes. 'Well, the missus said I need to be tanned before we go away next week; otherwise, I'll look too English.'

'That's hilarious.' She laughed again and put a small package on the concierge desk. 'I got this for you.'

'What is it?'

'Open it and see. I saw it in a junk shop.'

His gaze came to hers. 'A junk shop. Is that right?' He teased.

She watched as his hands, well-manicured, tanned, and elegant, deftly open the brown paper she'd wrapped his present in. Then her gaze rose to his face, waiting to see his reaction. Harley's heart melted with delight as a smile lit up his face.

'Peter Pan. I love it.' He grinned and flicked through the book's pages. 'Bloody hell. Junk shop, my arse; it's a first edition.'

'Is it?' Harley smiled.

'It's perfect. I can't believe you remembered.'

'The most important birthday of the year, how could I forget!'

'I didn't mean my birthday.' Tony said quietly. 'I meant the book.'

'Well, I know how much the story means to you because of your brother.'

Tony glanced down at the faded, well-worn cover. 'It was his favourite.'

Knightsbridge: Thomas Crowe's Residence

Her stomach churned as she rode towards Knightsbridge on the Triumph. London houses were more complicated to break into than any others unless they were in the commercial district, above businesses that closed for the night. Entry cameras, neighbours, visitors, late-night returners, home workers, nannies, housemaids, cleaners, cooks, and delivery men all coming and going in the area – all uncontrollable factors that could mess up her plans at any given moment. She had to blend in.

Parked just around the corner, with his house in sight, she sat and watched to see if there was any movement within it. Her eyes trailed over the shape of the corner house: the levels of its structure, from the entrance porch to the balcony, the white brick wall running along its side, and the ground floor brick-built extension with the flat roof – except for the glass pyramid jutting from its centre.

Single glazed sash windows. A side brick wall. Side gate. Front first-floor balcony. Front door. Glass doors to the conservatory. Flat roofed garage. So many different ways in. His house was a burglar's dream, except it was in London. She desperately wanted to light a cigarette and ponder for longer, but she needed as much time as she could get inside the house. She didn't even know what she was looking for, but she needed to know him, to know Thomas – to know who TC really was.

From her saddlebag, Harley pulled out a brown box addressed to Thomas Crowe, 28 Trevor Square, Knightsbridge. She straightened her leather jacket and the straps on her knapsack. It was one last habitual adjustment before she walked towards the house in darkness and placed the box on the ground next to the 12 ft white stone wall. She stepped back. Stepped back a little further – a little further – glanced left then right, and with one fluid movement, propelled herself like a long jumper onto the solid box she'd strategically positioned. Her plimsoled foot pressed itself into the wall to thrust her body upwards as her gloved hands landed on the edge of the wall-top and gripped. Pulling herself up, she flipped her body over and down to the other side, landing on the gravel like a cat. Crouched. Poised.

Still and silent, she held her position until she knew it was safe to move. Swiftly, she removed her knapsack and strapped the toolkit around her waist. One single glass cutter and a suction cup worked deftly between her fingers as she cut a hole big enough for her to slide through in the conservatory glass. Once inside the house, she moved lightly across the tiled conservatory floor and into the open-plan kitchen. Next to the kitchen door, the alarm panel sat without any flashing. Harley chewed the inside of her bottom lip as she often did when thinking … or stressed. Why would he have it there and not by the front door? Her gaze darted around the kitchen to see if there were cameras attached or motion sensors, but there were none. She stared at it a little longer. Why weren't there any lights flashing?

Standing before it, she concentrated her gaze as if it were a rare thing not to be touched. Her magnetic code reader scanned over the alarm and found nothing – no signal. No electricity.

Harley moved out of the kitchen and into the hallway – her eyes still searching for the alarm panel that was connected, but there wasn't one – not even by the front door. Puzzled, she moved up the stairs, searching for the study. There had to be a study for someone like Thomas – an accountant. The stairs creaked beneath her feet. The sound reminded her of home, being with her parents, and their old house in Blackheath. Stairs creaking always made her feel sad – they were the sound of a family coming and going.

At the top of the stairs, she turned and went up the second flight – her eyes still scanning for motion sensors – for something. Anything. Up the sides of the staircase were black and white photos of Thomas Crowe with a young man. Typical studio photos. White backgrounds and laughing faces. All displaying happy-couple togetherness. She wondered where the young man was. Would he come back before Thomas? How long did she have? As she reached the last stair landing, she entered an open-plan space except for a small ensuite. In the corner of the room was a treadmill and a press-up bench. In the other corner, facing the window, was a desk similar to the one she'd seen at The Temple Club – leather topped, antique, and expensive. His taste was a mixture of predictable and bespoke to the exquisite.

Without moving further, Harley glanced cautiously around the room. There had to be something. Someone so involved in The Domino Set wouldn't leave his home unprotected. Tracing her gaze over every inch of the space before her, she saw a red flash of light on the bookcase. As it flashed, so did a small red dot on the chandelier above her. She traced the outline of the light fitting. That's where it would be, whatever she was looking for. Of course! Thomas Crowe knew Eddie Ranking, and Eddie would know how to hide a safe better than most.

Harley stood in thought. How would she get across the room without setting off the triggers? She'd no way of telling what was above the sparkling crystal chandelier droplets. If the safe was anything like hers, the only way to access it was from below, not above. The loft was of no use to her. Her bottom lip gently again chewed between her teeth.

'Damn you, Thomas Crowe,' she whispered and looked up to the ceiling.

On the wall was a long chrome loft-hatch pole. Harley plucked it from its brackets and raised it above her head, releasing the hatch and the sliding ladder. Climbing upwards, she popped her head slightly above ceiling level into the loft. In its centre was a safe, surrounded by a network of wires. Suspended above it was a cast aluminium case with four black canisters attached – all pointing down. Fuck, she muttered to herself and dropped her head quickly below the loft-hatch level. A fucking burglar blaster. Four canisters full of pepper spray – triggered by motion – within twenty seconds of sensing it.

Harley slid down the ladder.

She whispered 'fuck' again.

The pepper spray would linger for around forty-five minutes without ventilation, and she would be incapacitated for a similar amount of time if she triggered it.

Moving down to the first floor, she found Thomas' bedroom and began rummaging through his wardrobe and his drawers. It bothered her. She never rummaged. She wasn't a burglar – she was a thief. There was a difference. Her hands moved fast, pulling everything out as she went. There was no time to be considerate. The more time she spent being respectful, the more time she was losing. Shoe boxes emptied on the floor; drawer contents spewed out as her hands searched. Wardrobe doors remained open as she flicked through the hangers and emptied the shelves. There had to be an old pair somewhere. Everyone had an old pair.

Lying down on the floor, Harley slid onto her stomach and began hunting under the bed. Pulling out a dusty suitcase, she quickly opened it. Inside were crumpled shorts, garish shirts, swimming trunks, and goggles. Smiling, she threw them onto the top of the bed. Quickly, she grabbed one of the blue Hawaiian shirts and tripled it over itself to make a mask, tying it around her face to cover her mouth and nose. About to leave Thomas' bedroom, she caught a glance of herself with disbelief.

Raising her head above the loft-hatch for a second time, Harley threw a blue velvet slipper into the centre, just below the canisters. With every second that passed, she counted; the burglar blaster flicked a blue light. At twenty seconds, the canisters hissed. Harley dropped down the ladder and ran down the stairs. A thick heavy cloud blew through the hatch as if a building had just been demolished at its foundations, and Harley tumbled back against the landing wall in shock. The hiss was like a pressure cooker exploding, and the smell was nasty.

When the hissing stopped, Harley moved back up the stairs towards the loft, the swimming goggles covering her eyes and her skin tingling as she got closer. Despite the tripled facemask, she could smell the spray in the air – like someone had squirted rotten eggs into the room. If she held her breath, she had two minutes to find the right wires to cut and get out again. She set her watch. Two minutes started to count down.

★

Coughing, she ran down the stairs, through the kitchen, and stuck her head out of the hole she'd cut in the glass. The skin stung on her face – her nostrils burning. Groaning, she stood up. She had to go back. All the effort had to be worth something. Taking a deep breath to ease her lungs, she went up the stairs again and into the open-spaced study where the motion sensors had been disabled. Standing on a chair, she began to work. Within five minutes, she'd opened Thomas' safe and emptied its contents. She wanted everything there was. Having caused chaos in his home, there were no boundaries left. Everything he held as precious was shoved into a blue and yellow paisley pillowcase – letters, velvet pouches, ledgers, jewellery boxes and money. What he held dear to him would be in everything she stole, and everything she stole would tell her all that she wanted and needed to know.

★

Just as she slipped the pillowcase into the saddlebag on her Triumph, a voice behind her calmly said, 'I see you.'

Harley stopped. She didn't know whether to turn or run. It wasn't a voice she recognised, but she didn't know what Thomas Crowe sounded like. In the frozen moment, she tried to work out whether it was an old voice, a young voice, an official voice or an interested voice. 'I see you.' What did that even mean? She turned. Did she have a choice?

Before her stood an olive-skinned man in his forties. He wasn't the one in the photos with Thomas Crowe; she could work out that much.

'And I see you.' She replied calmly. 'What do you want?'

The man smiled. 'Considering what you've just done, you're quite bold, aren't you?'

'If you're the police, perhaps you can get it over and done with. I have things to do.'

'I'm not the police, Harley Smith. I am beyond them.'

'So, what do you want?'

'I want to make sure you take him down in a way that will hurt him the most.'

Harley stared at the well-dressed, well-manicured man. There was something familiar about him, something about the line of his jaw and the mop of dark hair that tussled slightly over his eyes. They were tired eyes, though, as if he'd been out heavily drinking the night before or not slept for weeks.

'You're asking me to take Thomas Crowe down?'

'I am.'

'What is he to you?'

'You don't need to know that.'

'Then why should I?'

Sweeping the mopish hair from his face, the man smiled gently. Why would he smile? And why would he do it as if he knew her rather than was about to threaten her? If someone wanted something, a threat usually came along with the demand – in Harley's world anyway.

'Because I see you,' he said. 'And I see George and Ben too.'

'Is that it? The extent of your threat?'

Buttoning up his coat, the man gazed at her. 'Would it serve me better to threaten you with violence? Only with everything I know about you Harley Smith, and I know a lot given the years you've been on my radar, I wouldn't have you down as a fool.'

She said nothing, although for once it didn't ring true that there was power in silence.

'You're going to need this,' he said, and handed her a USB stick.

CHAPTER 39

Islington

THE letterbox clanked. Emily's eyes pinged open. The thud of heavy booted footsteps outside her front door at 4.30 a.m. startled her.

The beat in her heart thumped as she flew out of bed and threw on a t-shirt. Grabbing the hockey stick by the bedside table, she darted out the bedroom door, down the stairs to the entrance hallway. On the doormat was a cream A4 envelope. Blank. Emily leant down and picked it up after checking the door bolts.

In the kitchen, she switched on the coffee machine, grabbed a knife, and sliced the envelope open. Inside were two pages of typed cream silk-weaved paper and numerous photographs from an accounts ledger. Either someone knew her father's choice of paper, or their tastes were as refined as his. The coffee machine gurgled its last bubble-blurb of coffee as she stared at the letter.

The word 'whore' wasn't on the first page; was it to come?

Did she want to read the abuse and hatred so early in the morning? She ran a hand through her tumbling bed hair and sighed. In her mind, there was no choice but to read the words, whether they were abusing her or not. She had to know what they said – at least then she would know what to do. Sliding out a kitchen bar stool, she sat down and began to read.

The second mug of coffee steamed in the cold morning air. The heating had yet to click on, and the chill seeped through to her skin. She'd read the letter three times. Uncurling herself, she stood, stretched, and retrieved a blanket from the sitting room before settling back on the stool to read the letter again.

The tone was different to the messages she'd been getting. There was nothing intentionally vile; in fact, it seemed to have been written by someone who cared. It made no sense. Emily read the words again. How could the author know so much about her father's murder and his involvement in The Domino Set? She sat back and stared at the typed words. They know, she thought, and there was only one person she could think of who would have had access to such detailed information that wasn't Thomas. The woman who'd saved her life. The woman who'd stolen the file she'd found in the hidden basement cupboard in St Albans.

Emily leant forward – the warm coffee mug pressed against her cheek. Staring at the letter, her thoughts tumbled in every direction. Why would the woman not just give her the file back instead of a letter and photos?

Sitting up straight, she thought, why would she? She's edited it down. There must be more in the file than she was being told, yet she was being told enough to ask Thomas more questions than he would be comfortable with.

Her legal training, her years of asking probing questions, woke up with the effects of the caffeine. As dawn birthed its light into the kitchen, Emily's stomach tightened. She wasn't being told information – she was being told to question. To question Thomas. For the fifth time, her eyes traced over the printed words.

Thomas Crowe isn't the man you think he is. I don't know the true nature of your involvement with him or The Domino Set, but I do know that he, unlike most accountants who have two sets of books, has three when it comes to your father. He'll be a little stressed when he sees you next because now, I have the third ledger – the one he'd hidden in his Knightsbridge house. I've studied it in detail and compared it to the second one (the first being irrelevant to anyone except the taxman). If he has shown you the third one, then you can disregard this letter, but if he hasn't, you need to ask him why there is a discrepancy of £70 million between the two unofficial ledgers. The amount your father left you and your siblings is £70 million more than I'm guessing Thomas Crowe is telling you. So if he's lying to you about such a thing, there must be more he isn't telling you … I know there is more. Ask him. You deserve to know the truth.

Was it true? It couldn't be, surely? Was this just part of the same sick game her obsessed stalker was playing? But that made no sense. And the tone was completely different. Who was she … the woman that saved her life.

For the first time, Emily looked at the ledger photos. There was page after page of them: organised and colour coded, taped together for comparisons between the second and third set of accounts.

Moving to the large, battered sofa against the kitchen wall, she sat, curling her legs under her body and tucking herself in the blanket again. Her eyes scanned over the numbers, the years, the amounts. Numbers were never her strong point, but the systematic highlighting directed her gaze, pulling her eyes to the pattern of skimmed payments. As the financial total declined in the second set of accounts, it accumulated by the exact same amount in the third.

Taking a deep breath, Emily breathed it slowly out. The clock ticked on the kitchen wall as the morning light drifted drearily through the windows. She gazed out to the garden, the sky like a heavily pregnant woman, full of rain, ready to give birth. Thomas *wasn't* the man she thought he was – whoever sent the letter had got that right. It was hard enough since her father had died, but Thomas had skimmed off millions from him, as well as her inheritance. Had he? Had he really done that, or was it some twisted woman trying to make her life hell? Her heart trembled. She closed her eyes as the turmoil battled inside. The shallowness of her breathing caught in her throat, and tears slid down her cheeks.

The alarm beeped on her phone, and she jolted. The rain burst through the morning skies and dripped its little thuds on the windowpane before trickling down to thud again on the ledge. Emily rubbed her face and glanced at the clock. Then, without thinking too far ahead, she typed a text that sent with a whoosh to Thomas. Hauling herself out of the soft chair, she dragged her body up the stairs to the shower.

Warm water mixed with shampoo and shower gel as her brain switched on again. What would she say to him? How would she say it? What excuses would he have? He'd definitely have some – that much she knew. What if he paid her it all back? What would she do with it? How would she tell Rosa and Zeb? Would he even offer to pay it back? There was no need for more money in her life. Everything she wanted – financially – she had. What the hell would she do with a third of £100 million? Sitting on the edge of the bed with the towel wrapped around her, water dripped from her hair and over her damp skin. She didn't know how to relate to the possibility of suddenly having over £33 million in her life.

Sluggish and foggy, she slowly dressed, her brain trying desperately to focus on reality. She didn't want it. Why would she? Rosa would give up work without question. Zeb – she wasn't sure. But work was her life. She lived to practise and teach. What would she do without those things in her life? Why would she want money her father had made by criminal means? Only she would know the truth; Rosa and Zeb could take it guilt-free. Would they want to know? She sat back on the bed and towel-dried her hair to a tussle of waves. Surely, she would have to tell them. They'd want to know … wouldn't they?

CHAPTER 40

East London: University

WHORE. That's what was sprayed in big, bold red letters on the window of the Professor's office. That's what Harley saw as the door she knocked on, left ajar, opened, and Ammon greeted her. Harley's jaw clenched – just a little – at seeing him.

Behind him, Knight stood with a man dressed in the dark blue of campus security. Drained of colour, the Professor turned and signalled Harley to come in. Everywhere, papers, books, files, and belongings were torn to pieces and scattered like garbage strewn across the floor.

Quietly, she asked, 'Should I leave?'

'Stay,' Knight replied. 'You have your essay grade to collect.' Ammon kissed the Professor's cheek and whispered something in her ear that Harley couldn't hear.

As she stood waiting for the security guard to leave, she studied the movements of Knight – slow and drawn. Had she contributed to the tiredness by writing the letter and telling Knight about Thomas? Of course she had. Harley wondered if she had told the Professor too much – or too little.

And then there was the safety deposit box Sidney Knight had mentioned in the letter she'd stolen from Angus McLellan's office. Should she have told her about too? But if she had, George would be at risk. Harley internally sighed. *What a fucking mess.* Even if she wanted to tell the Professor, now was not the time. And if she told Knight everything, Harley herself would be at risk too. It had to be the right thing – to tell the Professor about Thomas. It was ethical. *Ethical.* Harley watched the woman show the security guard to the door. *Ethical.* How could anything she did be ethical?

Knight closed the door and paused before turning. A composure pause, Harley thought, as the woman's shoulders pulled back ever so slightly. She dropped her bag to the floor and moved to the filing cabinet. 'Is it too early?' She asked as she pulled the bottle of Jack Daniels from a drawer.

Knight shook her head. 'Not today.' Sitting down, she ran her hands over her trousers and sighed. 'Your other essay grades are almost as good as your criminal one.'

'My grades are the last thing on my mind right now.'

A slight smile came to the Professor's eyes. 'I read your paper against having a written constitution; you were magnificent in your argument.'

Standing in the middle of the room, Harley tingled. Magnificent. One of the greatest criminal minds in Britain was calling her magnificent.

'What did security tell you about the break-in?'

'Not much. They're going to check CCTV.'

'And the police? Are you going to get them to fingerprint the place?'

'It wouldn't be worth their time; so many students come and go, along with cleaners and other academics. And there's nothing valuable to be stolen.'

'Your door was popped, so she didn't know your code.'

Knight's eyes rose to Harley's. 'She?'

'The foot that stamped on your computer has left the imprint of a shoe. It's small and not fully outlined, like a heel from a boot, not a trainer.' Absorbed in the chaos, Harley stood motionless, except for her eyes. 'See there?' She pointed at the window where the word 'whore' was sprayed in red. 'That's the first thing she did when she arrived. If you look up there, you can see she turned with the spray can still in her hand. That's when she saw your desk and everything on it that represented you. It's when her anger peaked, and it's why all the possessions on your desk have been destroyed, not just by the smashing and throwing of them but because of the red spray paint she's covered them in. The angrier she became, the more destructive she felt towards your possessions and you.' Her gaze came back to Knight's. 'Her intention wasn't to destroy your office because the thing she came to do was write the word on the window. The destruction escalated the more she thought about you.' Harley paused. 'Has anything been stolen?'

Knight shook her head. 'Not that I can see. Everything is such a mess, but nothing obvious stands out.'

'Your black and silver necklace? The one you take off and leave here at the end of the day. It usually hangs over there. It's gone.' She pointed. 'Do you notice anything else unusual?' Knight shook her head again. 'Well, when she'd spent her rage against you, she turned it to the books. She was calmer at this point and more organised because she wanted to send you another message. All the books left on your shelves have fraud in the title. Can you see it?'

Knight stood up, her eyes scanning every book spine, looking to see if Harley was right. She glanced at her. 'I hadn't noticed any of that.'

'People who do these sorts of things have reason and purpose. She had a pattern. Whoever she is, she has an issue both with you and something to do with fraud, be it criminal fraud or maybe fraud, as in liar.' She watched Knight studying the books and asked gently, 'Have you had any cases recently where you've been involved in some kind of criminal fraud, or have you irritated an ex, making them believe you were something you're not?'

'No, not in the past year, at least, to either of those questions.' Knight turned to Harley. 'How do you know all this? I mean ... how do you see everything you've just told me?'

Harley smiled. 'Too many sleepless nights watching CSI.'

'Do you have any plans this evening?'

'Nothing, I can't reschedule. Why?'

'I've got a difficult catch-up with an old friend after work, but perhaps I can, if you'd like, repay you with a meal afterwards and maybe a much-needed glass of whisky?'

CHAPTER 41

Islington: The Wine Rooms

His embrace was empty as he wrapped his short arms around her body and kissed her on both cheeks. Meeting him outside the tube didn't make her heart smile like it usually did. He looked different. For the first time, she saw his gaudy clothes and the bloat of his face – the swell in his tubby hands as they waved her over. As they walked, he talked, telling her about the weekend in Marbella with his young lover and the hours they'd spent on the yacht he'd just bought. Emily listened – absorbing. Didn't he realise just how showy he was? How little he could hide his wealth? Her father's wealth.

After they'd sat down at a table in the bar and ordered wine, Thomas slid an envelope across to Emily.

'What's this?' She asked.

'Tickets to the theatre. I thought you could do with a night out, maybe take someone with you.' He smiled. 'My dear Emily, you need some fun back in your life.'

'You're right, I do. In fact, I'm doing something I've never done before and am meeting a student later after seeing you.'

Thomas threw his hands in the air and grinned. 'A student. So it's not just me with a taste for the younger model!'

Emily shook her head. She didn't want to be compared to Thomas, not in any way. 'No, she's a mature student. I don't think I could ever be attracted to such an age difference like you.'

Thomas shrugged. 'Each to their own, as my mother used to say. So, what's she like, what's she called?'

'It's not a date, Thomas. I'm just taking Harley out to thank you for helping me today.'

Thomas' smile disappeared as he picked up the wine glass and took a swig. 'Harley,' he repeated as he put the glass down with a clunk. 'Harley. An old school friend has a niece called Harley. Harley Smith.'

Emily studied him. 'Then maybe they are one and the same. Her surname is Smith. Perhaps you know her.'

'Well, she must be an unusual student for you to take her for a meal.' He replied. 'And how did she help you today?'

'My office was broken into overnight. Harley was wonderful at providing me with a possible reason and how it might have happened.' Emily paused. 'Better than campus security, that's for sure.'

'A modern-day Sherlock.' He half smiled.

Sitting back in the chair, Emily gazed at the old, tired face opposite her. For a man who had spent the weekend with his young lover, he didn't look refreshed or high-spirited. Part of her wanted to delay the conversation she needed to have with him – not for his benefit but for the sake of their friendship. How was she going to ask? How was he going to react? If she hadn't planned to meet her student later, she would have ordered more wine and spent hours building up to the conversation, but she was running out of time. If she didn't ask now, it could be weeks before another chance appeared. He was always disappearing of late.

'I needed to see you this evening, Thomas.'

'And here I was thinking you just delighted in my company.' He smiled again. 'So you have more questions about your father? How is the case going with the police?'

'It's not that. Well … it is that … but not in the way you think. The case isn't getting anywhere. The DI phoned yesterday to update me on the fact there aren't any updates. Even the motorbike that was spotted hasn't been caught on CCTV anywhere along the route.' Emily sighed. 'No, it's not that. Thomas, I need to ask you about the £30 million in the offshore account.'

'Do you need money?'

Emily shook her head. 'No. No, I'm fine for money – you know that.'

'Then what is it?'

Leaning down to her bag, Emily pulled out the photographs of the account ledger that had been included in the envelope dropped onto her doormat.

'This.' She passed it to him.

Thomas slipped on his reading glasses. Silently, she watched him as he read. Poker-faced. But Thomas had no control over the draining of colour from his wine-flushed cheeks as he saw the photocopy of his own handwriting.

'It seems we have both been the victim of burglaries this week. This, along with other things, was stolen from my house.' He murmured. Pallid, he glanced up. 'How did you get it?'

'Someone posted it through my letterbox, along with typed

extracts from letters my father left me but have since been stolen.'
Emily gazed at him. 'Thomas, the amounts you've entered here are
over £100 million. You had a third set of books.'

Thomas raised his hand and called the waiter over. Ordering
another bottle of wine, he waited silently until it arrived before
pouring himself a glass. Emily shifted in her chair. 'Every accountant
has a set of books no one knows about.' He finally replied.

Leaning forward, Emily whispered, 'Yes, I know they do, but not
a third set, not unless they're embezzling.' She stared at him. 'You
were stealing from my father, weren't you?'

His ashen skin turned to a high red – creeping up from his shirt
collar to the beads of sweat on his forehead. 'I don't know how to
respond.'

'With the truth, Thomas.'

'I can't deny the evidence in front of me.' He said quietly. 'I
wouldn't insult you with such a thing.'

'Yet you insulted my father and his love for you by stealing from
him.' Emily replied.

'He didn't need the money. He barely spent the money he
accumulated. My life … well, my lifestyle, I needed more. Sid didn't
even notice money was going missing.'

Emily watched Thomas as he drank his wine, wondering how she
could have missed just how garish and brassy he really was. His fat
little fingers ran over the top of his almost bald head.

'Just because I stole from him doesn't mean I didn't love him.
You must know that.'

'I'm not sure what I know anymore. Don't you see? Everyone
around me has lied.'

'Emily, darling, forgive me. I would never hurt you intentionally.'

'But you already have.'

'How can I make it up to you?'

'If I'm ever going to forgive you, and I'm not sure I can, you'll
have to tell me everything.'

'I don't have time to tell you this evening.'

'I thought you'd cleared your diary for our drinks.'

Thomas flushed. 'It seems I was wrong.'

Emily glanced at her watch. 'That doesn't mean this conversation
is over.'

CHAPTER 42

Islington: The Wine Rooms

PARKED up outside the bar in Soho, Harley sat and waited. Knight wanted to meet her there at 7.30 p.m., but the Professor was already fifteen minutes late.

When Harley saw her leave the bar, it was with the man she now knew was TC. Thomas Crowe. Had the Professor acted on the note she'd slipped through her letterbox? Or was she as involved in The Domino Set as much as Thomas or her father was? And what about the man who'd caught her burgling Thomas' house? Where did he fit in with everything? She needed a cigarette, but the Professor was almost before her.

It was the first time she'd seen him up close, Thomas Crowe, rather than in a photo or as a silhouette under street lighting. He was shorter and fatter than in the photos in his Knightsbridge house. And his clothes were far more decadent than suited his body.

Sliding off her bike, she removed her helmet and walked towards the Professor and the man Harley knew was in charge of the money. If she knew who *he* was, he'd surely know who she was too. Connected to George and Eddie – connected to her father and the Primrose Estate. She studied him; he was even connected to her mother. That thought made her throat clench. Her mother. He knew things about her mother that she didn't know. The throat clench turned into distaste for the man. How dare he know more – a man like him.

Whatever he was, she was sure Thomas Crowe would know exactly who she was and what she did. And she wanted that moment, the moment where she would see the recognition in his eyes. If he was everything she assumed him to be, intelligent and cunning, he would connect the dots.

Thomas' reaction didn't fail her. As she approached them and Knight smiled, Thomas' glance momentarily flitted to Harley and quickly away. His face drained of colour. It was enough for her to know that he knew. That's all she wanted. She was the spit of her mother, George had said – and she saw it in Thomas' eyes. Fucking got you, she whispered in her head.

'Miss Smith.' The Professor greeted her. 'Thomas, this is Harley

Smith, the student I was telling you about.' Thomas dipped his head in a polite bow. 'Thomas thinks he may know of you through an old school friend.' Knight smiled. 'What is it they say, six degrees of separation?'

'Thomas Crowe, I believe.' Harley held out her hand courteously. 'I've heard a lot about you from my friend, Joanna Evans.' As she shook his hand, Thomas' skin was cold under her touch – his fingers clammy.

Knight's brow furrowed as she glanced at Thomas. 'You know Joanna Evans?'

'I believe she calls him Uncle Tom.' Harley waited for her words to unravel in Knight's mind.

'How do you know this?' The Professor asked.

'I have a memory for faces. Joanna showed me the photos from Christmas. It looked like a wonderfully festive time together.'

Thomas glared at Harley before turning his eyes to the Professor. 'Emily, I can explain.'

'I'm sure you can.' Knight replied coldly. 'But now is not the time.' Turning to Harley, she said, 'I believe we have somewhere else to be.'

Leaning over to the saddlebag, Harley rummaged for the spare helmet and passed it to the Professor, who whispered in her ear.

'Take me home. I don't think I'm going to be the best company tonight.'

'Jump on.'

Islington

As they reached the top of the three steps, Knight stopped – frozen. 'Someone's in there,' she whispered.

The door, slightly open, drifted a little in the breeze. Stepping in front, Harley pushed it with her elbow. Before moving into the silence, she whispered, 'Wait here' to Knight, but the woman didn't listen, and Harley heard Knight's breath behind her, heavy and fast. It was too late to tell the Professor a second time not to follow.

With just a glow from the orange streetlights to light it, the hallway echoed their footsteps on the parquet flooring. Scanning, Harley's ears listened for sounds as they entered the centre of the house. Touching nothing, she took Knight with her through each room, listening and scanning until they reached the bedroom. The light was already on, a message that someone had been in the most private of places.

The beautiful antique collection of solid mahogany wardrobes and drawers was sprayed red with 'whore.'

Sheets, once white, were sullied with 'bitch' crudely across them. Chaos and devastation, as if a tornado had stormed through – there were belongings all over the place.

Clothes were sprawling on the floor and sprayed red, like the kill on the side of a road. Taking everything in, trying to work out the room's pattern, Harley saw none – a disorganised mind. 'You should call the police,' she said quietly.

'No, I think I know who this is, and I can deal with it myself.'

'You can't let them get away with it. All this harassment needs to stop.'

With distraction, Knight looked around her. 'It will, Harley, but I'll deal with it tomorrow.'

'Well, I'm not leaving you here; you're coming home with me.'

Without any challenge from Knight, they looked through her clothes to find anything that hadn't been sprayed red or cut with scissors and packed a small bag she could carry on her back. The door to the house closed behind them, and as they walked silently back down the steps to the street, Harley saw a lingering shadowy shape in a doorway, dismounted from a parked motorbike. Taking Knight's hand, she led her to the Triumph; her concern for the Professor far greater than the problem lurking and looking on.

Westminster

'Evening, Miss Harley.'

'Tony, would you mind turning Aimee away if she comes over tonight?'

His gaze drifted to Knight, then back to Harley. 'You have my word,' he said quietly.

The blue illuminated lift button pressed under her fingertip, and within minutes, she was turning the key to her flat. 'I'm going to order pizza. There's whisky over there if you'd like to pour yourself one while I do.'

★

With glasses of alcohol by their sides, they sat on the floor, pizza and garlic breadboxes scattered between them. The lamp shadowed its warm glow in the corner of the room, creating traces of muted intimacy as the night sky failed to illuminate the room – the moon covered by clouds. Music turned to an almost inaudible low, kept their silences connected, peaceful, as they ate.

'Do you know you've been bruised nearly all the way through the academic year,' Knight said quietly.

'Is that the thing really on your mind tonight?'

'No, but it's on my mind often enough.'

Throwing a pizza crust into the carton, Harley ran a tissue over her lips. 'I just get caught up in things at the wrong time.'

'Why do you stay with Aimee if you don't love her?'

Leaning back on the edge of the sofa, Harley sighed. 'You do ask lots of questions sometimes.' She traced her fingers over the edge of the whisky glass. 'To be truthful, it's easy.'

'Is that what you want? Easy?'

'Does that mean loving someone isn't easy?'

'You want easy love?' Knight asked.

'Could we not do this right now?'

'I don't want to talk about what's happened today and this evening. I feel like my world is falling apart, and I don't know why.'

Harley gazed at the Professor. 'Tell me. I can't help if you don't tell me.'

Knight rolled onto her stomach, stretching out and resting her elbows on the floor with her chin on her hands. She sighed. 'Even if I tell you, you can't help, Harley. This is a mess I need to untangle all on my own.'

'Move over. I need to lie down too.' Shifting her body, Harley lay on her back, looking upwards; Knight shifted onto her back too, and they lay side-by-side, gazing up to the ceiling, the alcohol drifting in their veins.

'Rumour has it you had an affair at ballet school with your professor.' Harley wrinkled her nose and screwed up her eyes. 'Sorry. I shouldn't have asked that question.'

Knight's voice, calm and soft, replied. 'I did. I was sixteen. It should never have happened.'

'I'm sorry, I really shouldn't have asked.'

'I'm not embarrassed by it. I thought I was in love with her, but it was just infatuation.'

'I didn't know it was with a woman.' Butterflies fluttered in Harley's stomach.

'Rumours are never accurate. Apparently, I was pregnant, which is why I left, not because I'd had a bad car crash and couldn't dance anymore.'

'Do you regret it? The affair?'

'I regret telling her I loved her, but not the lessons I learnt from it all. I've never said it so easily since.'

'But you've said it?'

'Haven't you?' Knight asked softly.

'Never, not even to Lucè, the first woman I was with.'

'You've loved … haven't you?'

'I loved a boy. I still do love a boy, Ben.'

'Then why aren't you with him if you love him? There's nothing wrong with loving boys *and* girls, you know.'

Harley sighed. 'Because it's not the kind of love I want to feel. With Ben, it's like he's another part of me; he knows me, and no matter what I do, he still wants to know me, but my love for him doesn't consume me. I don't want to be with him physically.'

'Is the physical important to you?'

'So far, it's been the only thing I've wanted from a woman.'

'So, sex is all you want from a woman?'

'I'm shallow.'

When she turned her face to Knight's, the woman's eyes were closed: the silhouette of her mouth naturally curved in its fullness. They were lips Harley wanted to kiss, lips that drew her into wanting to lean forward. It was a sensation she struggled to resist – a battle of wills between her body and mind. The shadows created by the lamp didn't help because they played over the woman's profile, making it even darker – more kissable.

Knight whispered, 'I don't believe you. Your brain is too endless to be shallow.'

'You give me too much credit. I'm the shallowest person I know.'

Opening her eyes, the Professor turned her face – they were inches apart.

'One day, you'll want to let someone in.'

'I'd probably be too scared.'

'Fearless of everything except love.'

Harley closed her eyes and drifted to the touch of the Professor's arm against hers. The length of their bodies pressed together – a bubble of solitude, shutting out the world for those moments. Hair intermingled as they lay, the space around them pliable, soft.

Together, in the peaceful ease of each other's company, they remained silent for some time – eyes closed. Both were floating in their own thoughts until Harley rolled onto her side and rested her head upon her hand so she could look down at the Professor. Their eyes came together, a soft, haunting look from Knight as she waited for Harley to speak. It was a look that moved into Harley's body like a drifting shadow, gliding through her veins as if Knight's breath was kissing her skin.

Lowering her eyes to Knight's mouth, she fought not to let the impulse take control of her. She couldn't lean forward; she couldn't let the urges win. Bringing her gaze back to Knight's, she saw a look she'd never seen before; it was dark, searching – penetrating. A look that almost brought the woman to her lips. She couldn't draw her eyes from the Professor's face, from the shadows cast across her skin, from the curve of her neck and the roundness of her breasts that pressed against – under – her black shirt.

In her periphery, she was taking all of her in, her eyes tasting and feeling every inch of Knight she could see. With frustration, she went to move away, but as she did, her eyes ran down the woman's body and over her breasts again. A button on Knight's shirt was undone, revealing the smooth light olive curve that dipped into the roundness of her cleavage. The black lace bra was slightly revealed, mocking Harley's attempts at controlling herself, urging her to gently run her fingertips to it, so she could explore the soft firmness of Knight beneath her fingers. She ached to touch her – it physically hurt not to.

'You are slightly undone, Professor,' she said quietly.

'I am,' she whispered back.

'Your shirt.' Her fingers reached to the button – she couldn't stop them. Rather than doing it up, Harley gently popped the next one from its hole, then the next. Each release revealed more of the Professor's olive skin, more of the smooth full curves of her breasts hidden beneath the black lace. Without moving, Knight let Harley slowly expose her until the shirt was undone, and Harley could see the shadows of her shape. No words came as her fingertips traced a whisper over the Professor's cleavage that plunged beautifully to the centre of the bra.

Knight's hand came to Harley's, covering it and cupping them together, pushing Harley's touch a little firmer around the curve of her breast. In Harley's hand, she could not only feel Knight's skin, but the vibration of it seeping through her fingers, into her arm and around every part of her body. She was spiralling inside with all the sensations.

A long sigh breathed out from Knight's lips as she clenched Harley against her. It was sad, a sigh of resignation – regret.

Quietly, she said, 'I can't, Harley, I'm …' She paused and exhaled again as her fingers pressed Harley's a little firmer. The Professor's eyes slowly closed. 'You feel exquisite,' she whispered, 'but we can't.' As she said it, her hand squeezed again against Harley's – so hard that a hushed gasp flowed from both their lips.

Their fingers, wrapped together, pulled the edge of the bra away, fully revealing the Professor's skin. Her breast, in its roundness, was held in their embrace – their hands moving over it together. The hardness of Knight's nipple slid between their fingers until the woman's hands came to Harley's hair, twisting gently into it, leaving Harley to move without direction.

Knight quietly breathed her desire gently into the air, her body arching from the floor in her need. Her hand returned to Harley's, and she held it still, firm, a controlling clench of pleasure as she said, 'We have to stop … God … I don't want you to.'

Holding their hands together, Knight slid their fingers down her stomach and to the button on her trousers. Harley slowly undid them as the Professor muttered, 'There are things I need to tell you.'

Harley slid her fingers beneath Knight's underwear and gently into the warmth. Her touch was slow, deliberate as she glided between the woman's legs and into the velvet heat inside; she wanted to feel every movement, to remember it, to be able to recall it in her mind whenever she closed her eyes. Knight trembled as Harley's fingers pressed deeply.

They held each other's gazes, their eyes sealing them together, as Harley delicately fucked the woman beneath her.

Their lips, silently parted with hushed gasps, spoke their words as their pupils desperately pulsated the controlled craving they had for each other. Harley watched as Knight's eyes began to change, began to beg – but her rhythm stayed the same. She wanted to see every microscopic expression, every nuance, as the Professor silently breathed, silently groaned.

Exhaling slowly, Knight's eyes closed, weakening in the pleasure. Harley whispered, 'Look at me,' and together, they watched the orgasm emanate between them as the Professor's back arched from the floor. Harley gently pushed a little deeper until Knight's slow-rolling shudders released on her fingers.

Bound together, their eyes kissed in the silence.

Gradually, Harley slid herself from the beautiful wetness, feeling the tiny aftershocks in the Professor's body as she did. She lay back down next to her and touched the velvety chocolate hair splayed on the wooden floor. With the light scent of Knight on her fingers, she curled them into the thick strands and held them to her lips, waiting for the Professor to breathe herself back to speech.

'I want to say so much,' Knight whispered, 'but I can't.'

'Then say nothing.' Harley whispered back.

CHAPTER 43

East Ham: Nelson Street, The Primrose Estate

SHE sat in the middle of the bedroom floor: a once tidy pile of magazines now sprawling around her in chaos. Law books, usually hidden under her bed as far back as possible against the wall, were strewn around the room like they had fallen from above after a tornado. Spines were wrecked. In the middle of the mess were the shredded flowers James had sent her. Shredded and flattened by her mother's stamping feet.

Joanna sniffed, holding in the tears. She leant forward and gently touched the rose petals that covered Knight's textbook. She didn't want to move either the book or the flowers, even though they were broken. Unloved. Too fragile to move.

After tracing her fingers lightly over both, Joanna sat back on her haunches and glanced around. It would take her hours to undo the mess her mother had caused – *and for what?* Joanna's face screwed up. A small squeaky gulp caught in her throat. She didn't want to cry, but everything she treasured, as if made from glittering gold, was hauled from its safe place and trashed. She hated her mother. She hated her more than anything she had ever hated before in her life.

Even the contents of her pencil case were splattered around the room, and her favourite poster of the Suffragettes – half ripped from the wall. Joanna stood up and stretched over her bed to press the poster back against the sticky pads. It fell forward again. The squeaky sob ached in her throat. She wasn't going to fucking cry. She wasn't. Slowly, she peeled the remainder of the poster from the wall and gently rolled it up as if to protect it; but the damage was already done.

Bending down, she collected the law books one by one and stacked them on the windowsill. There was no point in hiding anything now – her mother had found it all.

In a rage about money, Debra Evans had gone hunting. Convinced her daughter was holding out on her or spending her student loan on books, she had pulled Joanna's room apart, looking for the evidence. Any evidence. The flowers from James, a secret Joanna hid in her wardrobe, catapulted her mother into a fury. And with the shoe she had in her hand at the time, she'd belted her daughter across the face.

For the first time in her life, Joanna had properly tried to fight back. The bunch of flowers from James were hers. They were sent to her. And James liked her. They were the most precious gift she'd ever received. Her mother's bony nicotine-stained fingers had been all over them, squeezing the life out of their blue and white petals, snapping their stems and crushing their beauty. She'd tried to stop her mother from touching them, but the more she'd tried, the more Debra Evans squashed the flowers in her hand.

When she'd seen what they meant to her daughter, she'd laughed. Each time Joanna tried to stop her mother, the woman belted her harder and the last punch smacked Joanna with such force that she'd landed against the bedroom chair, which toppled beneath her. The girl had stayed on the floor, trying to catch her breath.

As Debra Evans left the room and the mess she'd created, she stamped her foot into her daughter's stomach.

Bending to pick up the books from the floor, knife-like pains shot inside her ribs, and Joanna winced with each movement she made. But if she didn't clear it all up, her mother would be back, and the rage would continue. For hours, Joanna worked slowly until everything was back in its place, except for the flowers. There was nothing she could do to save them. Stem by stem, petal by petal, she collected the treasured gift from James and placed all the pieces in the oversized dish she used for her cheap beads and hairbands.

Sitting on the edge of the bed, she glanced around. Everything looked normal again, but it wasn't. Not this time. This time, Joanna's hatred for her mother snapped to a different level.

CHAPTER 44

Westminster

LEANING on the countertop, Harley stared at the coffee machine as it gurgled and spluttered. Whatever it was doing, she found peace in its sounds and tiny movements. At that moment, it was the best coffee machine in the world, and the coffee smelt better than it had ever smelt in her life. She breathed the wafting caffeine deep into her lungs and smiled. Knight was still in bed, her waterfall of hair splayed across the white linen pillow and her red lips slightly open as she breathed deeply with her sleep. Harley had watched her for most of the night.

How could she sleep when she knew she had seen the Professor's father die? Was it even possible to sleep when the most beautiful woman she'd ever touched was lying next to her, vulnerable and hurting? It wasn't possible, not for Harley. There were too many thoughts, too many questions and not enough answers as she watched the Professor drift into an exhausted slumber. But Harley wasn't tired. Now more than ever, she needed to find out what Sidney Knight had on George and all the others in The Temple Club ledgers. She knew she needed to protect George, but now she also needed to protect the woman who had whispered her pleasure against Harley's skin in the night's shadows.

'The coffee smells wonderful.'

'Well, I can't say I've actually made it.' Turning to face Knight, she saw her again like it was the first time, freshly showered and in a pair of jeans she'd borrowed from Harley's wardrobe. Wearing one of Harley's black roll-neck sweaters she usually used for her business, the Professor glowed all dark and chocolatey. Her wet hair tumbled in waves over her shoulders as she stood, makeup-free. 'You look incredible,' Harley said quietly, taken aback.

Blushing, Knight smiled. 'You have a beautiful flat, and I didn't know you lived in such a wonderful location.'

'Then perhaps you should see the view I never want to leave.' Gently, she took Knight's hand and walked her through the study to the balcony doors, opening them out to the view of London. Knight leant onto the balcony railing, her eyes scanning in all directions before she gazed back at Harley.

'So, this is where you stand when you can't sleep?' Harley

nodded. 'And this is where you stand when you want to gaze at the world?' Harley nodded again. 'I like knowing that.' Knight smiled. 'I want to know more about you. Where do you run when you go out?'

'It depends on how I'm feeling. If I need to clear my head and push myself, then it's down by the river Thames. If I just need to run for the sake of running, then it's around St James's Park or maybe Hyde Park. There's a little duck there called Betty – she's my favourite girl.'

Smiling, Knight leant her cheek against the heat of the coffee mug. 'Then I don't stand a chance, not against Betty and the river.' She teased. 'Are you going to tell me that you're a secret millionaire? You must be to live here.'

Harley laughed. 'Would you be suitably impressed if I were?'

An amused glint entered the Professor's eyes. 'I'm suitably impressed by your antique collection, Miss Smith. Everything you have here, the Edwardian desk, the Sheraton chairs, and Tufft table … I never doubted you would be a skilled antique dealer, but you must be in the top echelons, Harley.' It was said with admiration, but Harley knew what it must look like. To someone who knew about antiques, the value in just the one-room alone was millions.

'I have to go soon.' Knight said quietly. 'I don't want to, but I have to sort out this mess I seem to find myself in.'

'You're going to see her, aren't you?'

'I have to end this, so yes, I am.'

'Am I allowed to know who *she* is?' Harley asked, but Knight glanced away from her. For a moment, Harley stood unsure. 'There's nothing you can say to me that would shock me.'

Knight's gaze came back. 'I don't know you to trust you.'

Harley smiled slightly. 'I can't promise you much, Professor, but I can promise you that anything you tell me will stay with me as if it were my own secret.'

Knight sighed. 'How well do you know Joanna?'

Harley paused, studying the woman before her. 'Barely at all, really. I met her on the first day of uni.'

'Nothing more than these past few months?'

'Well, we've become friends, and I feel very protective of her. I don't know if you've met her mother, but she is the vilest woman I've ever known, and I know she beats her. Joanna is always covered in bruises.'

'Like you,' The Professor said lightly.

'No.' Harley replied. 'No ... not like me at all. Joanna is vulnerable and volatile, and I am genuinely not being abused in that way – or any way. I'm sure Joanna is ... I've seen her mother lash out at her a couple of times ...' Harley touched Knight's hand. 'In answer to your question, I don't know her well at all, but I do know what I see, and I find her as kind and warm as she is volatile. Why do you ask?'

'I met Joanna about two years ago at a Law School open day. She followed me to my car that evening and told me she was my half-sister.'

Harley kept her hand in Knights while she processed what she'd heard. 'Okay,' she said slowly. 'So ... by your father or your mother?'

'Father. According to Joanna, my father raped her mother.'

Harley said nothing. Whatever she said at this point, whatever she asked, would seem wrong.

Knight continued. 'I'm finding out my father was a lot of things I didn't know about, but a rapist isn't one of them, and when Joanna told me, my father was still alive.' Knight pulled away from Harley's hand and moved back into the study, trailing her fingers along the spines of all the neatly lined books. 'Dad said he'd had a drunken night with Debra Evans many years ago. I found out recently that they grew up together on the Primrose Estate in East Ham. He wouldn't speak about any of it to me, but I guess ... I don't know ... maybe they were childhood sweethearts or something, and it was for old time's sake.' She turned to face Harley again. 'She brought me a DNA test result. Somehow, she'd managed to get a sample from me, so she's definitely my half-sister. Ever since she's told me, Harley, she's everywhere I look and go. It's not normal. If she'd just let the information sink in when she told me, I might have reacted differently, but she didn't, and it's like she's obsessed with me. I have to go and sort this out today.' Knight paused. 'You've gone quiet.'

'I was thinking.'

'Does your wonderful brain ever ...' Knight stopped midsentence. 'Where did you get that paper from?'

Harley's eyes followed the line of Knight's pointing finger. On the top of her desk, next to the printer, was a reem of cream silkweaved paper. 'I have it delivered from Liberty. Why?'

Knight stared at her, the muscle in her lower jaw visibly working. 'How did you know who Thomas was?'

'I told you. Joanna showed me a picture of him. She talks about him all the time.'

'And my house. Thinking about it, you knew exactly where to stop the bike without looking for the house number.'

Harley smiled. 'That's not hard to do. You've got two giant silver numbers on your wall outside.' Her hand reached out and gently picked up Knight's. 'Hey, whatever you're thinking, whatever is going on, I'm on your side.'

'I've got to go.'

Harley felt the chill of Knight's hand pull away as it hit her stomach, the thought that she'd lost her.

East Ham: Park Avenue, The Primrose Estate

'What's so urgent?'

Ben grabbed her arm and led her through his father's house, through the kitchen, the back garden, and into the garage. Before she could ask again, he threw her a black leather jacket. 'This.'

'What is it?'

'Look at it closely.'

Holding it up, she saw a small red logo on its arm. 'It's like the one the guy following me always wears. Where did you get it?'

Ben pushed the jacket to her nose. 'Smell it.'

Sniffing in deeply, Harley recognised the faint smell immediately. 'You don't think … you do, don't you? But why?'

'Because she's a fucking nutter. And she's obsessed with you, don't you know that?'

Harley silently stared at him. Maybe he was right. Maybe she was a nutter. And maybe she was obsessed too, but Aimee didn't have a bike. Shaking her head, she handed the jacket back to Ben.

'The guy following me can ride properly, Ben, unlike Aimee. She's not even passed her test.' Harley paused before saying, 'And she was away in the Maldives when I came off my bike, remember?'

Ben leant back on the car covered by grey plastic – a project George had been working on for over twenty years. He sighed. 'How do we know she even went to the Maldives? When I rummaged in her room while she was supposedly away, it didn't seem to me like any of her usual holiday stuff was missing.'

'Why were you going through her stuff?'

'Because my sister is unstable, and ever since she did over

Ranking's gaff, things have got fucked up.' His hand ran through his floppy blonde hair. 'Did you know she passed her bike test six months ago?'

Harley stared at him. 'What! Why didn't she tell anyone?'

'Because she's been up to something. I know it.'

'You're wrong. You have to be. Where is she?'

'Upstairs. I'm coming with you.'

'No. I need to speak with her on my own.' Leaving Ben in the garage, she went back through the house and up the stairs to Aimee's room. He couldn't be right, could he? Aimee. How could Aimee be the person who had reared her off her bike or the person she'd seen lurking in the doorway near Knight's house? That would make her the person who'd done over the Professor's house last night. She chewed the inside of her bottom lip a little too hard as she stood outside Aimee's bedroom door. It made no sense. But Aimee had done over Ranking's place, and wasn't it Aimee herself that had said they'd all underestimated her? Underestimated her for what, though? So she'd proved she could burgle a place – badly. What else was there to prove? She rapped her knuckles on the door and waited.

'What are you doing here?' Aimee asked in surprise.

'I need to talk to you.'

'Sorry, my room's a mess.' Perfume bottles, makeup bags, boots, shoes, coats, clothes, and glossy magazines were scattered about. Sitting down on the bed, Aimee smiled at her. 'What's up?'

For a moment, Harley stood and stared. Where should she start? What should she ask? Just as she was about to speak, Aimee jumped up off the bed. 'You've fucked her, haven't ya?' She ran her hands through her hair. 'Oh my god. I knew it was coming, but fuck. Fucking fuck!' Before Harley could answer, Aimee kicked a bag across the floor. 'What the fuck d'ya find attractive about her?'

'I can't explain it, but I want to give it a go.'

'A go? A GO! Since when have you given anyone a fucking go? I've spent years waiting for you to give it a go with me.' The smack of Aimee's hand slapped against Harley's cheek; her head jerked backwards – a throb pulsating on her skin. Aimee muttered, 'You fucking bitch!' as her hand raised again towards Harley's face. Grabbing Aimee by the wrist, Harley tried to stop her, but their hands and arms flayed without direction until they fell onto the bed.

Aimee laughed. 'Come on then, fuck me. She'd never say that to you, would she, the frigid fucking whore.'

Harley stood up, backing away from the woman.

'She's fucked up.' Aimee panted. 'D'ya know her Daddy was a rapist?'

Looking down at Aimee's bright red face, Harley quietly asked, 'Who told you about her father?'

Aimee laughed. 'Your little airhead friend Joanna. The girl is the spawn of him, did you know that?' Smirking, she added. 'Or are you fucking her too because she's another total fucking screw-up?'

'When have you seen Joanna?'

Aimee stood up and smoothed down her hair. 'You know the girl is obsessed with her, don't you? She follows her everywhere.'

Harley's mind whirred. In that short moment, Aimee had said so much without saying much at all. 'When did you pass your bike test?'

'What d'you care?'

'You know what, Aimee, you're right; I don't care. In fact, I'm done.' She turned to leave, but before making it to the bedroom door, she was pulled back by a sharp yank of her hair.

'No fucking way!' Aimee hissed.

The yank stung against her scalp as Aimee wound her fingers tighter and pulled her head backwards. Reaching her arm back, Harley grabbed Aimee's wrist and rotated her body around, using its full weight to shove Aimee into the wardrobe door. The crash of their bodies thumped against the wardrobe doors. With all her strength, Harley gripped Aimee's throat and squeezed into her windpipe.

'Let me go, or I'll scream the fucking place down.'

Harley stared at the wild eyes in front of her – her fingers clenching into the woman's skin. As she pushed Aimee harder against the wardrobe door, a thin black laced necklace fell from the doorknob, catching Harley's gaze. She glanced down, recognising it immediately.

'You're hurting me.' Aimee cried. 'And all for that fucking whore.'

'It's you. It's fucking you! You're the one sending her all the notes!' Harley released her hand and began tearing through the magazines piled in the corner of the room. She pulled at the ones on the bed, the ones in the bin. Frantically, she flicked through them all. Pages were ripped out, and chunks of letters were missing. She threw them across the room at Aimee and sprang at her, grabbing her again – slamming her back against the wardrobe. 'You turned her flat over last night, didn't you! DIDN'T YOU?'

With the pressure of Harley's fingers in her windpipe, Aimee tried to laugh. 'You haven't got a fucking clue who she is.'

Harley released her grip. 'Get your coat. NOW! Get your fucking coat!'

'What are you going to do?'

'I'm not going to do anything … you are.'

CHAPTER 45

East Ham: Nelson Road, The Primrose Estate

THE door opened. Her eyes were sharp – her face a bursting red. Debra Evans stood before them wearing a battered fur-trimmed coat. 'Ya'd better sort out the fucking commotion going on in there before I get back.'

Harley pushed Aimee into the house, through the hallway and into the dining room where Knight and Joanna were facing each other – flushed.

Joanna turned, snot-bubbles dripping from her nose. 'I don't want her here. Make her leave.'

'We'll get this sorted, Jo, I promise.' Shoving Aimee in front of Knight, Harley snapped. 'Tell her.'

'Fuck you!' Aimee sneered.

Grabbing her by the throat, Harley pressed her fingertips into the softness of Aimee's neck and rammed her backwards, forcing her through the air and slamming her into the wall.

Knight gently touched Harley's arm. 'What on earth are you doing?'

'It was her.' Harley replied. 'The one that's been doing this to you. Not Joanna.'

Leaning her tiny frame against the table, Joanna's face drained of all colour. 'What's going on? Why is she her?' She swung her gaze to Knight. 'Why is everyone here and shouting?'

'Aimee's been sending the Professor abusive letters, Jo, and last night she broke into her home and sprayed 'whore' and 'rapist' everywhere.'

Joanna looked at Aimee. 'You're Aimee,' she said quietly. Her gaze turned to Knight, then Harley. 'You know, don't you?' she whispered, bringing her hands to her face as the tears sprang to the rims of her eyes. Releasing her grip around Aimee's throat, Harley moved to her friend's side, wanting to help her. Pulling Joanna's hands away from her face, Harley smiled softly. 'We can sort this out together.'

Aimee laughed. 'How fucking lovely, you all love each other.'

Harley's glare span to her. 'Fuck you, Aimee.'

'Oh, but you have!' She grinned and turned to Knight. 'You have no idea how Harley can fuck, Professor.'

Knight went to reply, but Harley stepped in front of her and scowled at Aimee. 'You actually know nothing about me.'

'I know everything about you.' Aimee crossed her arms over her chest. 'Shall I tell her? Shall I tell her about your late-night trips out into the country? Shall I tell her about Antwerp too?'

Moving closer, Harley stood face-to-face with her. 'Shut the fuck up.'

'Why the hell should I?'

'I'm asking you not to go there.'

'Oh, I'm going there all right. I'm going to tell her every fucking detail about who you are and how you like to fuck me.' Her gaze turned to Knight's, and she smirked. 'Shall I spill everything, Professor, the whole fucking lot?'

Harley's forearm slammed into Aimee's shoulders, the force knocking her back against the wall. Their arms and hands tangled as Aimee tried to wrench herself from Harley's grip.

Knight gently put her hand on Harley's back. 'Leave her. What's done is done, and now we know.'

'You know nothing, ya stupid whore.' Aimee said, bringing herself to a standing position and stepping towards Knight. 'You don't know your precious fucking Harley is a thief, do ya?' She laughed. 'I bet she didn't tell you that did she when you were all over each other last night?' She moved in closer. 'I bet she didn't tell ya how she sneaks into people's houses while they're asleep. How she steals from them in the middle of the night?' Her breathing was fast, rapid. Adrenaline coloured her face to a bubbling red as she spat. 'Did you tell her, Harley?' She said breathlessly. 'Did you tell her ya smuggled diamonds in from Antwerp and then fucked me afterwards?' Her laughter resounded in the room. 'Oh, I can see it in your eyes – you didn't, did ya? How fucking brilliant!' Enjoying herself, Aimee's smile twisted in pleasure. 'She doesn't know a fucking thing about you, does she?'

Harley couldn't take her eyes off Knight as Aimee's words poisoned the space around them all. 'It's not just me you're going to betray here, Aimee. Think about that.'

'I don't give a fuck. They don't give a fuck about me.' Aimee sprang forward. 'I fucking hate you.' She cried, her knuckles banging into Harley's nose.

Harley hands grabbed Aimee's wrists and threw her backwards again. 'I can't say I like you much either.' Harley hit back, breathless.

'Do you think she'd ever let you fuck her with a strap-on?'

'You need to shut up.'

'Don't fucking tell me what to do.' Aimee spat. 'Don't you ever fucking tell me what to do.' She turned her face to Knight, and Harley knew another tirade of foulness was about to spit from her mouth. She heard Aimee's laugh – distorted, unrecognisable. 'You don't know who the fuck she is. All those bruises Professor. How the fuck d'ya think she got them? She wouldn't have told you she got them when she was working, would she? She wants you to think she's something so fucking special. You should have been checking her back for the nail marks I left there when we were fucking. I was hoping you'd find them.'

'I know everything I need to know about Harley.' Knight said calmly.

Turning to look at her, to thank her with her eyes, Harley saw Knight turn hers away. Rebuked. Her heart yanked out.

'Yeah, but does she know everything about you, Emily Knight?' Aimee grinned. 'I bet she doesn't know you like fucking in the loos of the Blue Cat, does she?' She laughed. 'What a whore you've fallen for, hey Harley.'

Joanna had stood silently in the corner of the room. When she spoke, her voice came so quietly that they all turned. 'I don't understand what's going on,' she said.

'We thought it might have been you, Jo, sending the letters and texts to the Professor because of her father.' Harley replied softly.

'You thought I could do that?' A flush rose to her cheeks and her bottom jaw clenched. 'I can't believe you actually thought I could do that.'

'You always got so angry when I mentioned her name.'

'You're unhinged,' Aimee muttered.

Joanna looked at her tearfully. 'Why would you say that? I thought we'd become friends.'

Aimee rolled her eyes. 'Jesus Christ! I met you once while you were stalking the fucking Professor outside her house. You're off your fucking head; it's obvious the apple didn't fall far from the tree. Why the fuck would you want to study where she is? You're obsessed.' She turned to Knight. 'Your little sister, Emily Knight, is a total fuck up.'

Steadily, Knight gazed at Aimee. 'And yet you are the one breaking into my home and sending me notes. And you're the one properly stalking me. What is it? Do you want more of my attention too?'

'You think you are so fucking smart, don't you, but d'ya think someone like you could ever satisfy someone like Harley in bed?' She leant in closer to Knight's face. 'D'ya think I'll let it all be taken away by a frigid bitch like you? I know how you fuck, remember.'

Moving between them, Harley touched Aimee's arm. 'Stop it, Aimee. You're not making any sense.'

'Ask her who the blonde was that she fucked in the loos at the Blue Cat. Go on. Ask her.'

The beat of Harley's heart spasmed as the breath in her throat caught. Between her teeth, the inside of her cheek bled. 'I didn't realise just how sick you were,' she said quietly.

'I had her before you, didn't I?' Aimee laughed. 'Oh my god! Well, from my experience, she doesn't quite reach the spot.' Her voice softened. 'You were supposed to love me, Harley.'

'I never told you I love you.'

'Jesus, just because you never said it doesn't mean ya didn't feel it. What was Antwerp all about? The fucking diamond earrings? And the sex we had when we got back? What was all of that if it wasn't you telling me you loved me?'

Harley's heart pounded in her ears as she stared at Aimee. What the hell was she saying? Things were unravelling, and she didn't understand. What the hell was she saying? The woman she'd once cared for, not loved, was standing before her with spittle at the corner of her lips and an expression on her face that Harley couldn't read. Had she ever been able to read her? Had she even tried? 'You know what, Aimee, you're right. I've been a bitch, and because of me, everyone in this room is hurting.'

Aimee glared at her. 'What gives you the right to treat me like a piece of shit and just toss me to one side because you've fucked me as much as you wanted to.'

A punch smacked on the side of Harley's head, and she stumbled, falling to the floor. Aimee threw herself on top of her, and their arms and legs thrashed into a struggling mess. Fingers grabbed at hair and limbs as they tussled – their feet kicking and their hands punching.

'Fucking stop Aimee, this is insane,' Harley shouted, but Aimee didn't. Instead, she struck her fist into the edge of Harley's nose. The pain seared in Harley's eyes as the blow hit a second time. Leaning upwards, her neck straining, she clamped her teeth into Aimee's arm, sinking them deep into the skin. But before Harley could free herself, Aimee's body moved swiftly over and then back – a motion so fast that Harley didn't see its consequences – but she felt it.

CHAPTER 46

East Ham: Nelson Road, The Primrose Estate

THE cold steel pinched into her throat. She froze. Aimee sat over her, breathing rapidly; the gun in her hand pressed into Harley's skin. Anger-red eyes glared down at her. The room was silent except for their ragged breathing. Without moving, Harley closed her eyes. Breathe, breathe, breathe, Harley ... breathe, she whispered in her head. Her eyes flashed open, and she gazed up at the woman sitting on top of her. *Breathe.*

Aimee's spit dripped from her mouth as she said, 'I'm the one you fucked the way you did; you can't do that if you don't feel something for me.'

'It was just sex.'

Aimee shook her head. 'No. What about the earrings? Why would you buy them if it was just sex?'

'I wanted to do something nice for you. That's all it was.' The cold metal pushed harder into her throat. The bile from her stomach burned on her tongue. She whispered in her mind, *breathe*, just breathe, then said, 'Why are you doing this?'

'Because you've taken everything I ever wanted away from me.'

'I've taken nothing, but if you want to shoot me, Aimee, then do it.' She gazed at her – poker-faced.

Joanna's sobbing pulled Aimee's gaze away.

'Go on, pull the trigger. Do you think I'm scared to die?' Harley asked, wanting the attention back, away from anyone else in the room. 'Come on, Aimee, pull the fucking trigger.'

'Shut up.' She hissed. 'Shut up. I hate you.' Tears formed in her eyes.

'You love me,' Harley whispered.

'I hate you. I fucking hate you.'

'If you hate me so much, then shoot me. I've nothing to lose.'

'You have her!'

Harley laughed. 'You've just taken that away from me, so maybe we are quits.'

'I've seen the way you look at each other.'

Harley put her hand slowly on the end of the gun. 'I promise you, on my love for my parents, that what we shared is never something I want to share with Professor Knight. I promise you.'

She couldn't be more honest than she was at that moment. She spoke with meaning, and Aimee heard their truth the way she wanted to hear it. Her hold on Harley's neck loosened just a little. As the pressure released, Harley grabbed the gun, pulling it away from her skin and skidding it across the room before she toppled Aimee off and scrambled to her feet.

Standing up, Harley turned to Knight. The woman's eyes were full of tears, the colour gone from her beautiful face. Harley was desperate to tell her everything would be okay, but her relief at being free from the gun lasted seconds as she heard Aimee's voice say behind her, 'You know she's married, don't you?'

Harley turned back, seeing Aimee's shaking hand holding out her mobile phone in one last desperate attempt. 'Him, she's married to him. They were always together, so a friend checked him out. They've been married for ten years,' she said as if she'd discovered something wonderful. 'She's been fucking with your mind. I knew it, and Jo knew it, but you've been too wrapped up in her to see any of it.' Tears smeared her makeup. 'I'd never do that to you.'

The photo said it all. It was a face Harley was familiar with. Ammon. The Professor was leaning into him, kissing his cheek. Harley moved away to the edge of the room where no one could touch her. Blood seeped inside her mouth as she chewed her inner cheek. The tears stung the rim of her eyes as she turned to Knight, her expression telling her what she needed to know.

Aimee was telling the truth. Harley's chest tightened. She couldn't breathe. She put her hand to her chest and resisted the urge to double over … she couldn't breathe … *she couldn't fucking breathe*. A retch came from her throat and loaded into her closed mouth, but she held it back so no one could hear.

She'd known, she'd always known; but she'd hoped it wasn't true. She'd hoped her mind had been playing with itself. She'd known, and she'd ignored it. Pulling herself up straight, raising her chin just a little too high, she looked at Knight and breathed quietly in.

'I told you she'd get inside your head,' Joanna whispered, the gun sitting in the tips of her fingers.

'It's okay, Jo.' Harley said quietly, still looking at Knight. 'She didn't quite manage it.'

Their eyes came together, Knight's silently searching as she said softly, 'He's my brother's boyfriend, Harley.'

'Liar!' Joanna exclaimed.

'It's a marriage of convenience so Ammon could stay in the UK for Zeb, my brother.'

Harley whispered. 'Is that all it is?'

Before Knight could reply, Aimee stood in front of her. 'Did Harley tell you she was there? The night your old dad popped his clogs. Did she tell you that, Professor?' Aimee asked. 'No, I didn't think she would. She told me not you! And what about the night you were shot at?'

'I didn't try to shoot her.' Harley snapped back. 'And I never told you about that night.'

The new information slungshot into her brain. 'It was you? Oh my god, Aimee. It was you? You tried to kill her!' Her hand ran through her hair as she tried to take it in. 'Please tell me you didn't murder Sidney Knight too?'

Aimee leant against the table next to Joanna. 'It wasn't me; I wasn't there the night the old man got bumped off.' She paused, her smile mocking Harley as she said, 'But it was me who broke in and gave you a bloody good beating the night you saved your precious Professor.'

Harley stood motionless. Aimee was there. Why would she be there trying to steal the file that Knight had found – the file Harley had stolen? She glanced at each of the women's faces in the room. Who were they? Her mind raced to try to unscramble everything she was hearing. The confusion blocking her logic – clogging her ability to unravel it all. *Who were they?* All three of them had lied to her in some way. Was she the only one who hadn't lied? But she had? Or had she just chosen not to tell the truth?

'What does she mean, you were there the night my father was killed?' Knight's eyes brimmed with tears. 'Is Aimee right? You were there?' Her head dipped to her chest, and her dark chocolate hair tumbled around her face. There was no sound for a moment in the room until Knight looked up, her eyes damp and her expression unreadable. 'Was it you? Did you kill him, Harley?'

'No! God, no.' Harley started to pace. 'Jesus. This is all such a bloody mess.'

She stopped and looked at Aimee. 'If you weren't there the night Sidney Knight was shot, why were you there the night when the Professor was shot at? Were you following me?'

'Eddie sent me.' Aimee grinned. 'Good old fat Eddie Ranking.'

Joanna stood up straight, pulling her shoulders a little too far back. 'Uncle Eddie?'

Harley raised her hand to hush the girl. 'Hang on, Jo.' She turned back to Aimee. 'Why would Eddie send you?'

'Because the person who shot the old man wasn't supposed to, and they didn't get what Eddie wanted.'

'Which was what?' Harley snapped.

'Whatever was in that file, only you stole it, which pissed Ranking off no end.'

Knight bent over again and whispered. 'This is too much. Too much.'

'Too much.' Joanna repeated. 'Seriously, too much? Our father is killed, and you think it's too much to hear how it happened.'

Aimee rolled her eyes. 'Oh for fuck's sake, fruit-loop, your father was a rapist. You can't pretend to grieve for the man who fucked your mother like that.'

Knight straightened – her jawline hard as she glared at Aimee. 'My father wasn't a rapist.'

'No? Then why won't you have anything to do with your half-sister, heh?'

Harley stared at them all, her brain zigzagging back and forth, the connections sparking electricity as all the dots began to join. So Eddie knew who killed Sidney Knight. Did that mean Aimee knew too? And Aimee was the one who'd tackled her to the floor and been the one who slammed her bike the night of the chase. Jesus. That meant Aimee had known all along that George was in trouble, surely? She whispered 'fuck' to herself as she realised that Eddie knew what was in all the envelopes … so he'd got Aimee to stalk Knight, or was that Aimee's choice? Aimee's choice, Harley thought as she looked at her across the room with her face red and the sweat dampening her hairline. And Knight, what did she know about any of this. What did the Professor know…

CHAPTER 47

East Ham: Nelson Road, The Primrose Estate

KNIGHT turned her gaze to Joanna. 'We need to talk away from here, and I promise I'll explain everything.'

Joanna shook her head, the tears smearing her cheeks. 'You've had years to talk.'

'I'm here now.' Knight replied softly.

'It's too late. You hate me, but I didn't ask to be born. I didn't ask to be his child.'

Knight whispered, 'I've never hated you.' Stepping towards the girl, she added, 'I just didn't know how to deal with everything.'

Joanna's breath caught in her throat. 'Deal with everything?' she repeated. 'I'm your sister, not something to deal with!' Wiping the sleeve of her sweater under her nose, her hand rubbed across her face as it scrunched into a tearful red mess. 'We could have been family.' She sobbed. 'And you took that away from me. It's all I wanted, just to have a sister, someone who loved me.'

'I'm sorry.' Knight said quietly.

'Why?' Joanna cried. 'Why couldn't you just love me? Am I that unlovable? We could have helped each other.' The tears flooded her eyes – washing her cheeks and dribbling from her chin. 'You could have helped me. Instead, because of you, I have nothing. No one.'

'I never wanted to hurt you, and I'm so sorry that I have. And I didn't want to interfere. I didn't know how much you knew.'

'Don't fucking lie! Do you know what it's like to know that whenever your Mum looks at you, she sees him?' The girl's skin flamed into a neck-blotching red. 'I see him when I look in the mirror; I know I look like him, my fucking mother tells me every day.' The gun waved in the air as the tears dropped off her nose, and she tried to wipe them away again. 'But you don't look a thing like him, do you?' Joanna snorted up the snot from her nostrils. 'I got all the fucking shit. He loved you, didn't he? But not me. Nobody has ever loved me.' Her voice wailed as her face crumpled.

Harley gently touched her friend's arm, but Joanna pushed her off. 'Don't fucking touch me! This is all because of you ... because you couldn't keep your hands off *her*!' She cried. 'I trusted you. You were supposed to be my friend.' The gun shook in her hand as she raised it up before Knight. 'How can Mum love me when all she can

237

see is him?'

Quietly, Harley said, 'It isn't her fault, Jo – just let her explain.'

'Everything I tried to do to make you notice me, Professor, and you never did. Everywhere you went, I tried to go too, but you only ever noticed Harley!'

'Then I'm the one to blame, not her,' Harley said. 'Please, Jo, give me the gun or aim it at me. This is all my fault. You even just said it is.' Harley tried to touch the girl's arm again, but she shoved her off, her elbow hitting Harley's chest, knocking her backwards. As she stumbled, Harley heard a loud ricocheting bang echo in the room, smacking the air and rumbling around them. There was a solid, dull thud.

Knight fell to the floor – blood leaking from her stomach.

The air moved against Harley as she tried to get to Knight's side, fighting against the space between them. Knight's hand rose to the pain. Harley kept trying but was going nowhere: slow motion pulling her backwards.

Aimee screamed, 'Jesus fucking Christ!' as Harley's knees finally thumped to Knight's side. Frantically ripping off her sweater, she pushed it against the small circular wound running red. 'Don't do this,' she cried, 'don't do this, don't do this.' Tears dropped from her eyes onto her face, but she didn't feel them.

Knight's blood pumped onto Harley's hands, and she screamed, 'Call an ambulance. Aimee, call a fucking ambulance.'

Debra Evans barged through the door. 'What the fuck?' Her hands grabbed at the gun, but Joanna snarled. 'Don't fucking touch me.'

'Don't be so fucking stupid!' Her mother snapped back.

The gun swung to Debra Evans's face. 'This is your fault!' Joanna cried. 'You should have got rid of me!' Her body doubled over, and she screamed. It was a scream that projected from her mouth with such force that her face turned crimson.

Debra tried to catch the gun as it waved in the air, but Joanna gripped it with all her strength. Through her sobs, she wailed, 'I fucking hate you. You've never loved me.' She brought the gun to her mother's face. 'All my life, you've treated me like shit.'

'Ya weren't supposed to happen.' Debra Evans shouted. 'Ya weren't supposed to fucking happen.'

'Then why did you keep me?'

'Because you made me money, ya stupid fucking girl.'

Harley's fingers pressed into Knight's body as the blood seeped onto her skin, staining her hands and clothes. She glanced up at the mother and daughter, begging them to stop – to see that Knight was dying before them. But Joanna was fixated on her mother. Harley pressed her fingers deeper into the wound to plug it as the colour drained from the Professor's face.

'Money.' Joanna whispered. 'What did you do? Did you blackmail him? My father?'

Debra Evans smirked. 'He paid a lot of money to keep the photos of him and me away from his wife.'

Joanna shook her head, 'That makes no sense. Photos of him raping you?'

'Use your brain, ya stupid girl. Men like Sidney Knight don't rape women. We made that bit up after getting him too drunk to remember what he'd done. How else were we going to get money out of him, eh? The big police chief that thought he was fucking better than all of us.' Evans laughed. 'He wasn't that fucking smart, though, was he!'

'We, who is we?' Tears streamed down Joanna's face – her voice breaking.

'Ya Uncle Eddie. Who else do you think would come up with such an idea heh? Bloody worked until the old man got cancer and wouldn't give us any more money. Stupid self-righteous bastard. That's why I ...' She stopped herself, but Harley heard it; her glance shot up.

'You what?' She snapped.

Evans turned to her. 'Precious little Harley Smith.' She said. 'Ya mother thought she was better than us too. Fucking little princess, she was.'

Torn between punching Debra Evans in the face and staying with Knight, Harley's eyes narrowed in on the woman. 'She had every right to think she was better than you. Look at you. Look at what you've done. Look at your daughter.'

'I didn't fucking kill him, alright. The stupid git walked into the gun. I wouldn't fucking kill the bastard supplying the cheques, would I!'

Joanna half-collapsed against the wall, letting it take her body weight as her legs shook under her skin. Before Debra Evans could say anything, the gun rose into the air again. 'You deserve to die.' Joanna whispered.

Harley wanted to stand up, but she couldn't. She couldn't leave Knight – her hands needed to be where they were, on her body, in the wound. She was the only thing keeping the Professor alive. Her voice reached out to her friend.

'She does, Jo. She deserves to die, but not by you. Don't let her ruin the rest of your life. You know the truth now, and Professor Knight will know it too if we get her to the hospital. Then, you two can sort it out. If you shoot your mother now, you'll end up in prison for life, and your sister will die.'

'My sister.' Joanna whispered.

'Your sister.' Harley echoed.

Aimee laughed. 'Fucking kill the evil bitch and let the Professor die too. Come on, Jo, they've both treated you like shit. Get rid of them, or haven't you got the balls. Maybe you're what your Mum says ya are, a pathetic waste of space.'

Joanna turned her gun towards Aimee. 'Shut up. Just shut up. I need to think.'

'We don't have time.' Harley said urgently. 'She's dying, Jo. Look at her. Look at your sister.'

Debra Evans stepped closer to her daughter. 'Let her die.' She whispered. 'We can sort this out.'

'You killed him, my father, you killed him.' The gun waved back to Evans. 'You told me he was a rapist, and you killed him. What kind of fucking mother are you?'

The girl's body straightened – a lengthening of her spine – her chin rising as her jaw clenched. She levelled the gun in the air, and with a calm, measured motion, she pulled her finger back on the trigger and fired a shot right into Debra Evans's chest. Evans fell to the floor with a thump. Aimee jumped back, smashing into the table behind her. Harley watched the girl, wondering where the gun would aim next. The expression she saw on her friend's face was different – she'd found something inside herself, something that made her Sidney Knight's daughter and the Professor's sister. For a moment, in the chaotic reality, she was proud of her friend for finding whatever she needed to survive, even if it was the wrong thing – ethically.

★

With the ambulance came three police cars and a van of armed officers. The blue flashing lights pulsated into the darkness of Debra

Evans's front room from outside as Harley sat with her fingers pressed into Knight's stomach. There was a bustling of uniforms around her, but she didn't see or hear them; she stared at the blood on her fingers – the paleness of Knight's face. She'd listened to every laboured breath escape Knight's lips, but as the paramedics pushed Harley to one side, their hands took over. They were hands that might save Knight's life, hands that were already as red as the blood on her own.

Slumped on the paramedics' trolley with bags and wires running into her veins, Knight left the room. Harley's stomach twisted – vomit rising to her mouth. A police officer's hand rested on her arm. 'You need to be checked over, Love. You're bleeding.'

'It's not my blood.' Harley whispered. Her gaze drifted to her clothes; the white t-shirt covered stained red, her hands wet and slippery. She retched. Tears erupted, turning into sobs. Collapsing, she fell to the floor. The arms of the officer slid under her armpits, catching her. He placed her on the sofa and sat down next to her, asking questions, but his voice was distant – odd – like a muffled slow whir in her head and a language she didn't recognise.

Unable to answer, the officer guided her through the house and into the small front garden of Debra Evans's house. Neighbours stood at their gates as she was placed in an ambulance. Lights flashed, but Harley could see nothing except Knight's pale, ashen face, her closed eyelids and the blood.

CHAPTER 48

Newham Hospital

GEORGE sat down next to her, his face paler than she'd ever seen. Dark circles shadowed his eyes. Without speaking, he picked up her hand and squeezed it. For those moments of silence, she treasured him – treasured his touch – until she withdrew.

'You knew all of this, didn't you?' She asked him quietly. In the distance, the surgeon talked to Knight's sister and brother. As she watched the conversation, she studied them both. They were familiar to her – both of them. The sister, Rosa, was easy to remember – the woman who was at the Red Café with the Professor the day Joanna decided she'd wanted a hot chocolate there. But the brother, he wasn't just easy to remember, he was impossible to forget.

And then there was Ammon by the brother's side, just as drawn in the face as his partner. They'd both seen her. One glanced at her as an acknowledgement, the other one just glanced – impassively.

Harley wanted to stand amongst them, to tell them it was all her fault. She needed to tell them so they would hate her like she hated herself.

George's fingers rested gently on her hand again. 'I didn't know Debra killed Sidney,' he said quietly. 'Or that Aimee had been following you and the Professor.' He sighed. 'I didn't know any of that, Love. I promise.'

She withdrew her hand again. 'You should have. That was your job.' Pausing, she asked, 'Where's Aimee?'

'In the nick, for possession of a firearm.'

'She deserves to be there.'

'I blame Eddie.' George sighed.

Harley turned to look at him. 'Eddie? How can you blame Eddie for your daughter's messed up head?'

'This is exactly what he does. He picks on ya weak spots and uses them to his advantage. I confronted him about it a couple of weeks ago – all the time she was spending at his. I knew something was up.'

'And you didn't think to tell Ben or me!' Harley tried to stand up, but George put his hand on her leg.

'I thought he was trying to get her to do jobs for him after he'd caught her doing over his gaff months ago. I didn't know he was getting her involved in any of this crap.' George sighed sadly. 'I never thought he would go as far as turning her against me.'

'Jesus, George. Didn't it ever occur to you that they'd be feeding off each other? Aimee would do anything to get you to see her as an equal to Ben ... and to me. You should have seen it coming.'

'Of course, I did. Who'd'ya think paid for the Maldives so I could get her away from him.'

Harley laughed. 'Yeah, well, worked out well, didn't it.'

'I didn't know until Ben told me last night, Love. I'd no idea she was on some weird stalking trip.' George ran a hand through his hair. 'Honestly, Harley. I didn't know she was that obsessed about you.' George sighed again. 'How is she? The Professor?'

'I don't know. I'm nothing and no one to any of them. They haven't told me anything.'

'Debra's in surgery, but the Yard are hanging about outside waiting for her to come round.'

'And Joanna?'

'Still at the station, they've charged her with attempted murder on two counts.'

'She needs a lawyer, George. Even if all they can do is get both charges down to attempted manslaughter.'

'You want me to help her after what she's done?'

Harley turned to face him. 'None of this is her fault. Do you think she'd have been so volatile if she'd known the truth?'

'I know ... you're right. Look ...' He ran his hand through his mop of silver hair. 'Sidney told me about Joanna years ago. There's a trust fund he set up for her. I don't know the details, but Sid's accountant does. She gets it when she's twenty-five and mature enough to get away from her mother.'

Harley snorted. 'Thomas Crowe! You know he's been syphoning off money, don't you?'

'How do you know about Thomas Crowe?'

'You've been acting so bloody strange these past few months, George, so I followed you. You met him at a bar, and I followed him after you left. He went to The Temple Club and met the Professor.'

George muttered, 'You followed me.'

'We had no choice. We broke into the Club just before Christmas and got copies of the membership list and accounts. Thomas had a third set of ledgers, George. You were in it, along with Eddie. All the money you were being blackmailed for, Thomas was taking most of it before giving the rest to Sidney. Did you know that?'

'Blackmailed? Me?'

'That's why you were paying him, right? To keep him quiet?'

George shook his head. 'No. No. That's not how it was. There's so much I need to tell ya, but that ain't how it played out.' He looked at Harley sadly. 'Sidney was my friend.'

'Why did you want the envelopes then? You've never told me.'

'Me and Eddie, we're not like Sid. We never had his brains.' George half smiled. 'Mind you, he could never have pulled off what we've pulled off. Anyway, I've never kept a record of all our jobs. I know you have it in ya head, but I started doing what I do way before you were even born. Those records, they listed everything from day one. Sid wasn't stupid. He wrote everything down. He told me, not long after he was diagnosed with cancer, that he would protect his family like he always had. He said he'd call in the favours even after he'd snuffed it.' George fidgeted in the chair. 'Eddie's been itching to take over Sid's role. Ever since Sid made a success of The Domino Set, Eddie's been at his heels. If Eddie had gotten hold of those files, you, me and Ben, well, we'd have been working for Eddie for the rest of our lives.'

Harley studied him. 'They'd incriminate Eddie too, though.'

'They would, Love, if Eddie wanted them to. Anything can be faked, you know that. Eddie may be stupid, but he's a bloody crafty shit, and I never wanted him to have a hold over us.'

'You could have told me all of this months ago.'

'I hadn't planned on ever telling you what happened to ya father, and I knew that if I opened that can of worms, it would all come out.'

Harley's gaze drifted to the surgeon talking to the Professor's family. 'Will she talk?' Harley asked. 'Debra Evans, will she talk?'

George looked down corridor. 'If she survives, she can't talk. None of us can. We're all bound to silence by—'

Harley stood up. Ammon had turned and caught her eye before walking towards her. Her heartbeat pummelled in her chest, and she stood waiting, trying to gauge the expression on his face, but there was none.

'Is she awake?' She asked impatiently before he fully reached her. He shook his head, but before he could answer, she blurted, 'Is she dead?'

George stood up. 'Let him speak, Love.'

Ammon smiled slightly at him, then Harley. 'She is neither.' He paused. 'The bullet smashed her pelvic bone to pieces and lodged into her liver. She's still in surgery.'

George put his hand on Harley's arm and took her weight as her legs buckled. He held her straight – kept her standing. Ammon nodded politely and went back to his family.

'Do you know him?' Harley flicked her gaze at Knight's brother. 'No, should I?'

She shook her head. 'We need to talk, and we can't do it here.'

East Ham: Park Avenue, The Primrose Estate

George sat across the table from her, his silver-grey hair sticking up as it always did when he was stressed or thoughtful. The silence between them was something they'd never had before. Heavy and distant. Harley felt it in her heart – on her shoulders.

'I don't know where to start.' George poured them both a double whisky.

'Well, I already know Eddie is my uncle and that I have another one somewhere. My father's twin.' George nodded. 'So, where is he? This other uncle of mine?'

George downed the contents of his glass and looked at her. 'He changed his name.'

'That doesn't answer my question, George. Where is he?'

'Right now, he'll be doing his night shift as a concierge.'

Harley sat back in her seat and stared at the man she had adored for nearly half of her life.

'Tony King. You're kidding me, right?'

All those years, he'd been right there, under her nose, never asking her questions about what she did, why she was home late, who Aimee was, where she'd been. Instead, he always showed her interesting articles about diamond heists and daring burglaries – some that she had secretly committed. And he never finished his shift until she was home safe.

Harley sighed heavily. 'Fucking hell, George.' She ran her fingers through her hair and shook her head. 'What the fuck am I supposed to make of that? And what about Eddie? You said he killed my father, but that was his brother too, are you sure? I mean, why would he do that?'

'I was there, Love. We all were.' George sighed. 'We were coming back from a night out at the R&R. All of us were pretty stinking by the time we'd left the club.'

'Yes, but why would he kill his brother?'

'It wasn't intentional. They were scrapping. Then we were all scrapping, trying to get them to stop beating the shit out of each other.'

'And Sidney Knight. Was he there? Is that what Eddie had on him?'

'Not just that. Although it was enough on its own.'

'I don't get it; Sidney could've easily dealt with Eddie. He was a policeman; he would have found a way.'

George shook his head. 'Sid was tight with the Rankings back then, especially Eddie. They'd grown up living next door to each other.' He poured himself another whisky. 'They were like brothers. More than Eddie was ever a brother to Robbie or Tony.'

'That's not a reason to let Eddie blackmail him into doing something that would ruin his career, though, is it.'

'Not to someone like you.' George murmured. 'But these were the Primrose Estate days. Things are different now.'

'So you're telling me that Sidney Knight let Eddie Ranking blackmail him into setting up The Domino Set just because Sidney witnessed Ranking accidentally murdering his own brother? I don't buy it.'

'You're forgetting Sid had a daughter by Debra Evans. He didn't want Eddie fucking up his marriage.'

'Yeah, well, being accused of rape by that woman would have fucked it up, surely. Didn't Sid's wife know about Joanna?'

George shook his head. 'Nope. As long as Sid covered for Eddie in those early years, Joanna was kept a secret.'

'I still don't get it, though. Why did Evans accuse Sidney of rape?'

'That wasn't their original plan. Debra recorded it all, the night she and Sid, you know. He was shit-faced, Harley. We all knew Sid couldn't handle his drink.' George glanced down at the half-empty glass of whisky. 'He never could, and they knew that, so they were going to blackmail him.'

'So, what went wrong?'

'Debra Evans. You've met the woman. She can't hold her mouth even when she's sober. The cops hauled her in for prostitution. When Sid refused to help her, she let rip and accused him of rape.

Eddie was in a rage for months about it as it messed with his plan, but then they found out Debra was pregnant.'

'Joanna.' Harley mumbled.

George sat back in his chair and sighed. 'Eddie had his Plan B with Joanna. Sid had already been through so much shit with the rape claim and didn't want to put his family through it again.' He gazed at Harley. 'He was a good man. What he did, he did to protect his family.' Leaning forward, he said, 'Sid protected Eddie over your father's murder too. If that'd got out, he would have lost his job, and we would've all gone down. It was all or nothing back in those days.'

'Like a set of dominoes.' Harley stated.

'Exactly.'

'Who was there that night, George? The night my father was killed.'

'All of us – all the gang.'

'I want to hear their names. I want to know.'

The whisky bottle clunked against the crystal glass as George poured himself another drink and knocked it back in one. He wiped his mouth. 'Ya mother and father, ya uncle Tony, Eddie, me, Sidney, Debra Evans, and Thomas Crowe.'

'Why were you paying Sidney money every month if he wasn't blackmailing you?'

'We all paid him. Paying him kept us safe. It kept us in the loop. How d'ya think we all got job info and stayed out of prison.'

'And the Red List? Who are they?'

'Sid called them friends, but I'd call them mutually interested parties.'

'I don't understand.'

'He knew stuff about them, and they knew stuff about him. It's the way the world works.'

Harley stood up and looked down at him – he looked smaller. 'Give me your car keys.'

'You've been drinking.'

Her hand stretched across the table. 'Give them to me.'

'What are ya going to do?'

'I don't know yet, but right now, I don't think you have the right to ask.'

CHAPTER 49

North Essex

How could she go back to Westminster knowing he was there, her uncle? Tony King. Anthony Ranking.

It had been forty-eight hours since she'd been back to her flat. There was no question in her mind that George would have told Tony everything by now. She wasn't ready to face him; how could she be? What the hell would they say to each other after all this time? And how would she control her hurt? Because she *was* hurt. All the years he'd been part of her life, with a family she could have been part of too, and yet he'd never truly included her. Yet he was her uncle. Didn't he want her? Or was it that he didn't want his family to know? But that made no sense in Harley's mind because he'd taken the job to be closer to her; that's what George had said. So, no, she wasn't ready to face him. And she had work to do.

Instead of picking her bike up and going home when she left George, she drove off to a place she'd only ever visited once before. It was a place she'd scoped from top to bottom with Ben while being in a ditch across from the expansive lawn. Eddie Ranking's house in North Essex. With everything going on in London, she knew he'd be in the Abney Park house, not the decadent one Aimee had done over in the posh part of Essex. No, Eddie needed to be near the biggest threat to his existence, Debra Evans.

With no one home, she made her way through the gated driveway, along the lawn's brick wall, and up the drainpipe into his study. She knew what she was looking for, and within minutes she'd found it, shoved it in her pocket and driven off back into London.

She'd warned Jude, her contact, in advance that she'd arrive during the night, so he was awake, waiting for her. While he worked, using her exact words scribbled on a piece of paper, she sat on his futon and chewed the inner part of her bottom lip. She needed what he was doing done within the hour, and she wasn't going to let his scrawny undernourished body out of her sight until he'd created his masterpiece.

When it was finished, she swapped cash for an envelope from him and sped off towards East Ham.

★

East Ham: Nelson Road, The Primrose Estate

The house was in darkness, and despite two shootings taking place within it, the police had all left – their tape over the front door the only reminder of a crime scene. She made her way down the back alley and vaulted the fence leading into the small concrete yard of Joanna's house. The one thing Debra Evans never invested in – with nothing to steal – was any kind of security.

Harley popped the kitchen window. Knowing her way around, she went straight to Debra's bedroom and scanned the small room. What she needed was somewhere obvious, but not somewhere the police would have immediately looked. After rummaging around, she found a small wooden box in the corner of the wardrobe – covered in dust and unopened for years. Harley quickly wiped it over with a scrunched-up blouse she found on the wardrobe floor and put the envelope inside.

She left the house and drove towards the home of the sixth name on the Red List, Lucas Orchard. There were three hours before dawn would break; she needed to be fast if she was going to get the last two envelopes and finish what George had started. The first of the two was easy. The usual security in the familiar places. Unimaginative and open to cracking by even the most uneducated thief. With no one home and a safe hidden behind the typical bookcase, she'd slid in and out within fifteen minutes. Envelope six was now in the secret compartment of her saddlebag.

West Hampstead: Director General Nuclear's Residence

It was the last name on the list that she dreaded. The seventh. The Director General Nuclear. She was under no illusion that his home would be covered in security, and she was far from prepared. Ben had only scoped it once, and his information was sketchy. And although she remembered the detail from when she'd snuck in for a sneaky look years ago, the alarm system would have changed. Going against all of George's methodical planning, she pulled into the darkest place on the West Hampstead street.

Her gaze scanned over the Director's house before she checked her watch. It was 3.36 in the morning. Anyone in the house should be fast asleep, in the deepest of sleep, but she only had about thirty minutes because she knew that between 4.15 and 4.45, people drifted into the lighter sleep where noises would stir them – or wake them. It was the time that brains switched on or anxiety took hold. People would get up to smoke, eat, drink, or scribble their thoughts down so they could go back for that hour before the alarm would beep them awake again. Thirty minutes didn't seem long enough when she wasn't sure what she was up against.

Sliding her hoodie, she made her way to the front of the house. In a built-up area with no back entrance she could reach, her only way in was from the front. It meant that people in the houses on either side might wake and hear her too – or see her. Glancing up at the flashing lights, she sighed. She was right, and it was the last thing she needed – the security system had been updated. State-of-the-art, high-end, the same company that served the Royal family. She would have to breach it without knowing precisely what it was until she met each level as she entered. Her gaze trailed down to the basement level.

Swiftly, she jumped over the old Victorian iron gates that would have squeaked if she'd opened them. As soon as she was out of street-level view, she pulled down the hoodie and slid the balaclava over her face. Rolling the hoodie and jacket into a bundle, she propped them in the corner so they were hidden and pushed her hands into the soft leather gloves that moved with every nuance of her fingers. From her kit-bag, she pulled out the small glass cutter.

Motion detectors on the window frames meant she couldn't pop them. The red dots in the corners of the room she was looking into meant there were more of them inside. The breath trembled in her throat as she cut through the glass and silently suction-cupped it out. Her hands, steady and methodical, waited for each flick of the infrared, which refreshed every twenty seconds. She counted each second and the pattern twice before gliding two mirrors on either side of the window frame and sticking them down with double-sided sticky pads.

Waiting, she held her breath to see if the rebound of infrared would set off the alarm. It was a trick Ben used, but she didn't know whether it worked: he knew more about alarm systems than she ever would. The next twenty seconds passed, and the alarm remained silent. Sliding over the cut glass, she slithered into the room, her feet landing softly on the wooden flooring of the downstairs gym. Giving her eyes time to adjust, she saw the shapes of the gym equipment.

Slowly, she made her way through the unfamiliar obstacle course.

Once on the other side of the first door, she gazed up the staircase and calculated the wear on the carpet to see where the pattern of footsteps fell. To avoid the creeks, she crept along the edge near the wall, one step at a time, assessing each step and the signs of someone walking on them. Glancing at her watch, she was eight minutes into her thirty.

Ben had already scoped where the safe was, using his contacts in security to find out as much as he could. Her biggest challenge was the iris scanner on the front of the safe. Had she prepared with Ben, they would have bypassed the system using a high definition print out of the Director's eye, but she didn't have it. All she had was her phone and a downloaded picture of his profile from his professional bio. If the light wasn't right in the photo, the entire system would set off, and she would be trapped in his house.

Before arriving, she'd brightened the photo so that when the iris scanner sent a beam of light to trace the eye, it would be bright enough for it to find the detail.

She could taste the sick rising in the back of her throat as she reached the top of the stairs to the ground floor. Moving along the hallway, she passed the sitting room with its dim nightlight and found the alarm panel. She studied it – the sweat-beads dripping down the centre of her spine. Silently, she placed a magnetic strip along its side that interfered with the electric current running to the number panel. A minute passed as the magnet did its work and gave her a seven-digit code to enter. The red dots of the infrared flashed, then stopped. Off.

Internally, Harley sighed, the sweat dripping on her face under the balaclava. She was desperate to pull it off and wipe her skin, but she continued to move silently down the hallway to the office door. Footsteps came with a thud from above – she paused, pulling herself into the downstairs loo as she waited. The sound of a heavy drawn-out wee from the toilet overhead echoed. She looked at her watch – fifteen minutes into the thirty.

The loo flushed, the tap gushed, the light switch clicked off. Would they notice the lack of red dots flashing? Her breath held deeper in her lungs. The footsteps thudded back along the upstairs hallway, and it went silent. The rebounding mirrors would only hold for another fifteen minutes before the downstairs infrareds set the alarm off by an error default. Ben had taught her that.

Silently, she moved out of the loo and tried to hurry her soft steps along towards the office. With the door slightly ajar, she slipped through without touching it. Above the mantle was the picture she knew hid the central safe, but there was another one, the one that most thieves would never bother to look for. It was hidden behind the first edition of Halsbury Laws – a masterpiece for legal brains and worth a fortune on the right market. Sliding it off the shelf, she placed it in her kit-bag and pulled out her phone. This was it, the pivotal point of her criminal career where she'd either go home or go to prison.

Standing before the safe, she pulled up the image of the Director and enlarged the photo so his right eye was the size of a normal one, whatever that was, she thought to herself as she held it in front of the iris scanner. Seconds passed as a violet light moved over the picture not once or twice but three times. Time stopped. Sweat dripped down her neck and between her breasts like she'd run a 10K.

The safe beeped – it clicked – it opened. Her hand dived in and grabbed the entire contents without looking – shoving it into the kit-bag. Before she turned to leave, she removed a fine grey hair from a zip-lock bag and placed it on the black velvet base of the safe.

Tracing her footsteps back, she made her way to the basement and the escape route she'd cut into the glass. As she entered the gym, a shadow stood in front of the window. Her heart stopped. Every internal organ jumped under her skin. What the fuck, she whispered under her breath. She froze. Why hadn't she heard the footsteps? What the fuck had she missed? Calculating her next move, she could only think of lunging directly at the shadowed figure standing between her and the way out. Her only weapon was her glass cutter, which was in her kit-bag. The black figure stood silent. Imposing. 'Have you lost your fucking mind?' It whispered.

'Jesus fucking Christ, Ben.' Harley whisper-hissed back. 'You scared the fucking life out of me.'

'We need to go. Now! You didn't turn the silent alarm off to the police station, did you? The one attached to the book in front of the safe. It's flashing like a beacon outside.'

Without faltering, Harley followed Ben through the window and over the Victorian iron gates. Shoving her kit-bag into the secret compartments of her saddlebags, she slid herself free from the balaclava and ruffled down her hair. 'Fuck. Fuck, fuck, fuck!'

He glared at her. 'What?'

'My hoodie and jacket, they're the other side of the gate, in the corner.'

Ben turned his body round in a flash and jumped over the gate again, grabbing her clothes and throwing them over. Just as he jumped back, the police lights flashed their blue around the corner. They had nowhere to go. Nowhere. Grabbing her bundle of clothes, Harley ripped the sleeve of her t-shirt and pushed her body and bundle at Ben. As the police got out of the car, she screamed at him.

'You fucking bastard. You fucking lying cheating bastard.' She threw her clothes at him. 'Fucking go, go on, fuck her for all I care, you fucking piece of shit.'

Ben picked up the hoodie and jacket. 'It's not what you think, I swear.'

'Are you okay, Miss?' A policeman asked.

Harley turned to look at him, her face red from the sweat that had dripped down it. 'He's a fucking piece of shit that's slept with my sister.' She shouted.

'Is he threatening you in any way?'

She laughed, her nerves filling her with so much anxiety she sounded almost drunk. 'He's too much of a fucking girl.'

A female police officer got out of the car and headed towards the fracas. 'If he's not threatening you, then I suggest you both go home and sleep it off; otherwise, we'll have to write you up as disturbing the peace.'

Ben picked up the clothes strewn across the pavement and grabbed Harley's hand. 'Babe, I swear, I haven't slept with ya sister; come on, before we get in trouble.'

'You're already in fucking trouble, you knob.' Harley muttered as Ben pulled her along the road and towards their parked bikes around the corner. She turned briefly to see the police knocking on the Director's door. 'How did you know where I was?' She whispered as they turned the corner.

'Dad sent me looking for you. I picked you up outside Joanna's house, pulling away. Come on, let's go back to mine.'

'I haven't finished yet, Ben. I've got two more things to do. You can either come or let me go so I can finish what I started.'

CHAPTER 50

Newham Hospital

THE pain thumped so badly in the centre of her body that she wanted to let out a loud groan – one that would somehow take the pain away. Something was in her mouth, trying to choke her. Gagging, her fingers rose to her face. Before she could rip out the tubes, a pair of hands came to her wrists and grabbed them gently. She heard the gentle 'shh' of a voice she recognised as the familiar touch brought her hands back down to her chest.

'You're in the hospital, Emily.' Her sister said softly.

Unable to speak, Knight opened her eyes, trying to communicate. Too dazed to make sense of where she was, she tried to pull at the tube again, but her sister stopped her. Within minutes, the room was full of other people, people in white and dark blue. They were wearing gloves and twiddling with the pipes and machines surrounding her bed. Slowly, they pulled out the tube from her throat, and she gasped a cough. Gently, a nurse sponged a dribble of water to her lips, and she sucked it like she'd never had a drink before. She wanted more, but the nurse said she was only allowed a sponge every ten minutes for the next hour.

Rosa squeezed her hand almost too tightly, and Emily felt the wetness of her sister's tears on her skin. She tried to speak, but her lips were stuck to her teeth, and her throat was so dry she wanted to hack like the stray cat she fed when it had a furball. She tried to say the word 'Harley,' but nothing came out. Ammon saw the movement of her lips and stepped forward, running his fingers across Knight's damp hair.

'She's not here.' He said gently. 'She was, but she left with someone called George a couple of days ago and hasn't been back.'

Knight stared at him, not sure what to make of what he'd said. It repeated in her drug-fogged mind. She'd left with George and hadn't come back. It kept playing on a loop until her eyes closed again, and she drifted back into the pool of heavenly morphine.

CHAPTER 51

Newham Hospital

HARLEY stood with her forehead resting on the cool glass of the hospital room window. Closing her eyes, she took a deep breath. How the hell did she get here? What would her mother say of the mess she'd made of her life? She couldn't believe that everything she'd been taught as a child, all her education and private schooling, all the ethics her mother had instilled in her, were thrown out the window through bad choices and a love of cocaine. Because they were the reasons she'd ultimately met George and ended up living the life she'd led. And now, because of those choices, Knight was in a hospital bed, slowly recovering from being shot.

'Recovering,' Harley whispered to herself as she opened her eyes and gazed into the room where Rosa and Zeb slept at Knight's side. At least the tubes are all gone, she thought, then shivered as the tiredness of seventy-two hours without sleep finally started to affect her body.

The clock on the wall said 5.30 a.m. It was time for Harley to go home and finally face him – her uncle. Besides, there was nothing more she could do; everything was set in place. The one final piece of the jigsaw had gone where it needed to go, and the police had been tipped off. It was her job to protect them all like George had always protected her.

But most of all, she wanted to protect the woman she'd fallen in love with – the woman who had made her feel something she'd never felt before. As she turned to walk away, a heavy weight pushed down on her; she hoped she'd done enough.

'Before you go.'

She'd only heard the voice once before, at Thomas Crowe's house, but it was as calm and as smooth as the first time. She turned to him, Zeb. 'You should have said you were her brother.'

'You should have worked it out.' He smiled slightly.

'What do you want? I'm going to do what you asked.'

'I want you to work for me. Properly.'

Harley shoved her hands in the pockets of her leather jacket and sighed. 'As what? What is it exactly that you do?'

'You'll go away and find that out for yourself now, won't you.'

255

He stepped closer to her. 'I don't want you to work for my day job, Harley Smith; I want you to help me take over my father's business.'

Harley stared at him. 'The Domino Set?' She whispered, 'Are you mad? Haven't you learnt anything from what's just happened?'

Zeb grinned. 'You've cleared the way for a new start. George said you'd sort it, and you did. What came next wasn't down to The Domino Set; it was down to messy obsessions.'

'You're the client.' She nodded to herself and half laughed. 'George lied ... again. Jesus Christ.' She turned away from him and ran her hands across her face, then through her hair, whispering 'Jesus Christ' again under her breath. What the hell else had George lied about? Turning back to face him, the heaviness of the lies pushed on her chest – suffocating.

'I don't get it; why did you want all the envelopes? You must have already known what was in them.'

'I didn't.' He smiled. 'I wanted you, and your name was in them.'

'You got me to steal envelopes so you could protect me?' Harley said, her voice a little raised.

'No, Harley, I got you to steal them so I could protect my best asset. You.'

Harley gently chewed her inner bottom lip. 'Well, aren't I privileged.'

Zeb gave her a small business card. No name. Just a phone number. 'George wants to retire. I can't let him do that unless someone else is in place. We both know that Ben isn't up to it, but you have something quite unique.'

She stared at the card. Should she take it? Did George deserve her loyalty – her freedom?

'When did you know? About your father? All the letters were addressed to Emily.'

The man tucked his hands into his trouser pockets and gazed at her. 'When you discover what I do, you'll realise that none of this is new to me. My father didn't have much of a choice, but I do.'

'And your sister ... does she get the right to choose what she wants? Or do I have to give up any hope I might have?'

Westminster

Pushing the door open, she saw him standing with his back to her, the heavy winter coat hanging on his sloped shoulders as if he were more tired than he had ever been. Hope and sadness passed over his eyes when he turned to look at her.

She could see he wanted to speak, but Tony was always good at being measured, at waiting. Without thinking, she walked towards him, dumping her kit-bag on his desk to free her hands. As she reached him, her arms opened and wrapped around him. It wasn't a time for words. All she wanted to do was hold the man that was part of her father. The anger, or the hurt, was still inside her, but she was too tired and weary to let it have its moment. It wasn't what she needed, and she knew it because there was no control over her actions as her arms opened and her head nestled into his shoulder.

There was no control over her emotions either, which came without permission as the tears rolled from her eyes onto his coat. Did he smell like her father? She wanted to know. She wanted to know everything about him. She wanted to feel his rough morning stubble on her soft cheek and breathe him in. He was her flesh, her blood, her DNA. It was DNA she thought had disappeared with her mother, and when he pulled her in closer, she felt it fizz between them. Her uncle. Her father's twin. She already loved him for who he had always been to her, but now she loved him differently.

'I'm sorry.' He whispered.

'I'd heard you'd flown back from your holiday.' She mumbled between the sniffs.

'I knew you needed me.'

She closed her wet eyes and absorbed him. He was half of her father and the closest she would ever get to him. Her arms squeezed him like it was the last time she would ever be allowed to hug him. Every cell in her body was consumed by emotion, and if she let it take hold even more, she would never stop it.

Stepping away, swallowing the pain in her chest, she smiled slightly. 'You have so much to tell me, Tony, or is it, Anthony?'

A gentle grin crept to his lips. 'Everyone calls me Tony.'

'I have a lot to sort out in the next few days … a lot to take in. Would you mind if we just carry on as normal until then? I'm not sure I can take much more until I've had some sleep.'

Tony nodded. 'We can take it slowly, and when you're ready, you can meet the rest of your family.'

'Family.' She repeated quietly. Her heart warmed. As she picked up her bag and walked towards the lift, she turned to her uncle.

'Eddie will be in trouble today. I thought you should know.' She entered the lift, but her hand quickly stopped the door from closing. 'Do you look like him, my father?'

Tony smiled. 'Identical.'

'Tell me.' She said quietly. 'Was Peter Pan really his favourite book?'

CHAPTER 52

H<small>E</small> glared at the clear evidence bags spread across the table before him.

'I'm telling you, I didn't write the bloody thing, and I've never seen that money before.'

The Detective Inspector swept hair away from her face. 'It looks like your handwriting Mr Ranking.'

'Then get it checked by one of your bloody experts because it ain't me that wrote it.'

'We already have, Eddie. Our expert confirms that it's your writing. So, you see, we've already got enough to charge you.'

'That ain't my writing! I'm being set up.'

The DI leant forward. 'You and Debra Evans go way back, don't you? Kids on the Primrose Estate, the same estate that Sidney Knight grew up on?'

'No comment.'

'Why would you pay her £100,000 in cash to kill him?'

'It ain't my writing.' He snapped. His solicitor tapped his thigh.

'Let's get this straight, Eddie. We've got a note in your handwriting to Debra Evans which says, 'For SK,' and the envelope it came in has your fingerprints on it. They're the only ones, in fact.' The DI sat back and looked at him. 'We have Evans' statement too.'

'No comment.'

'When did you decide you wanted him dead?'

'No comment.'

'He was dying of cancer, anyway, so why did you conspire with Debra Evans to kill him?'

'No comment.'

'Where were you this morning, Eddie? Between 3.55 and 4.45?'

'No comment.'

'For the purposes of the tape, I'm showing Mr Eddie Ranking evidence bags three, four and five.' She placed them on the table in front of him. 'These were taken from the Director General Nuclear's house this morning. Evidence bag three is a hair. Your hair. Would you like to tell us how it got there, in the DGN's safe?'

Eddie glared at the evidence bag. 'No comment.'

'Evidence bag four. You'll see that inside it is the first edition of Halsbury Law. This was stolen from the DGN's property in West Hampstead in the early hours of this morning. At 13.43 today, this item was recovered from your North Essex property. Can you tell us how it got there?'

'No comment.'

'Does anyone else have access to your property in your absence?'

'No comment.'

'Evidence bag number six.' It slid before him. Flat. Its contents were easy to see – the Klimt painting brazenly staring up at him. Eddie began to laugh.

CHAPTER 53

Bond Street: The Bank

LEANING on the wall outside the bank, Harley blew the smoke from her cigarette into the air – its blue trail twirling in the winter sun. George walked towards her, his head dipped, like the first time she'd seen him when she was just eighteen.

'Why are we meeting here?' He asked as she pushed herself away from the wall and flicked the cigarette to the kerb.

'This is the last thing we need to get so this can all end.' She handed him the last two envelopes she'd stolen. Before he could speak, she passed him the letter she'd taken from Angus' office.

'What's this?'

'It's instructions from Sidney Knight to his daughter. You didn't know it existed, did you?' She sighed. 'You can read it inside; we need to go.'

George hesitated. 'We need ID.'

'You're right, we do … I've been keeping Jude busy. Here's yours.'

The bank clerk met them with a beaming smile, her white teeth gleaming beneath the coral shade of her lipstick. Harley shook her hand and smiled back.

'Father said I should call you as soon as I was ready.'

The clerk nodded. 'I appreciate this will be hard for you, Ms Knight, so I've set aside a private room for you and your godfather.'

'That's very kind of you. Would it be possible not to be disturbed? I'm not sure how I'm going to feel.'

'Of course,' the clerk replied sympathetically. 'Follow me.'

The safe deposit box was already on the desk in their private room. A tray was next to it with two glasses and a bottle of still water. A notepad and pen had been thoughtfully left, too, along with a box of tissues. When the clerk shut the door, George stood in the middle of the room and turned a full 360°.

'Where are the cameras?'

'There aren't any. They're not allowed to see what's in a customer's deposit box, you know that George.' Harley sat down.

'But we're on camera from the moment we walked in.'

'We're not stealing anything.' Harley sighed. 'Sit down and

watch.'

While he'd been scanning the room for cameras, Harley had set up her laptop and opened the safe deposit box using the numbers in the letter Sidney had written. Inside the box was another letter and a solitary USB stick. Slotting it into the laptop, she glanced at George. 'We need to see this.'

Together, they sat behind the screen and watched. Grainy CCTV footage played – shot from a distance. Black and white, coarse and rough, the footage played until the end. George leant forward, his hands resting under his chin, his back slouched in concentration. 'I didn't know this existed.' He whispered.

'No one did, except Eddie and Sidney.' Harley rewound it.

Nausea bubbled in her stomach, but it was something she had to do. Seeing it all play out, even from a distance, made her heart thump louder than it ever had. It was hard to keep its beat under control.

The train sped through the scene, and she saw them all, the Primrose Estate gang, step back from the tracks, except the one that got hit – her father. There were no graphic details – everything was too fast and blurred for her to see his body being dragged. But she knew.

'It doesn't show anything.' George mumbled.

'It wouldn't back in those days. So Jude set my laptop up with some software to run it through. Give it a minute.'

George sat back in the chair. 'If Sidney had this, how could Eddie blackmail him all those years ago? Why didn't Sid just take it to the police and get Eddie off his case.'

'There's a letter to go with it for Professor Knight.' Harley carefully opened the envelope and slid out the sheets of A4 paper. Cream silk-woven, like the paper Knight had noticed in her study. The writing was familiar to her now, and although she didn't want to read it when she saw the opening line, her eyes continued to scan his words. They were probably the last ones he'd ever say to his daughter.

CHAPTER 54

Sidney Knight
The Final Letter

Dearest Emily,

You are finally here, and your knowledge of what I have done and what I have been is almost complete. Although I never wanted you to find out any of this, I knew you would need the truth when Thomas told you about the £30 million I had in the offshore account.

The internal battle I've had these last twenty-odd years has often been too great to bear, but I've done so because of my love for my family and my loyalty to my friends. As you read this, I may not seem like an ethical man to you, but I always was deep down. What I have done – what I have had to do – has all been to protect others, not to make money. The money was a hollow bonus.

My life – our family's happiness – changed in a way that became so tangled that I found it impossible to break free. The more I tried to protect everyone, the more I felt the tentacles of the world I'd entered suffocate me. Every decision I made seemed like it was the wrong one. I was never a bad man – just a stupid one. I tried to do some good along the way, giving money to charity and setting up a trust for your half-sister, Joanna. But those things never made me feel any better for breaking all the moral and ethical codes I held so dear, as I know you do. Those conversations we had on the late nights when you were studying were all true. They were true to my thoughts but not my actions.

Everything started so long ago that it's hard to remember the truth of it all. Thomas will be of no use to you in remembering; I recall him being so drunk that night. But there were others there, back in 1995. We were out celebrating – I'd just been promoted, and Thomas had passed his accountancy exams. It was a wonderful start to the celebrations. We'd spent the night drinking and dancing at the R&R Club (it no longer exists, by the way) and were all laughing and joking as we walked home along the railway track. It was always our shortcut back to the estate.

Eddie Ranking, who you must now be familiar with, was never

the easiest amongst us to get on with. I have never known such a difficult or angry man. Yet, Emily, he was the brother I never had. We grew up next door to each other, and despite his foibles, I loved him for most of my life. That night, he was in fine spirits until his brother, Robbie, told him he was about to become a father. Elizabeth, his fiancée, was with us that night, too – another part of the Primrose Estate gang that we loved. She was like a sister to us all, and the news raised our spirits even higher when we heard – except for Eddie's. I will never know the reasons why Eddie took it so badly. I often wonder if he was in love with Lizzie. Who could blame him – she was a beauty that we all admired.

Eddie erupted when he heard the news, and a row broke out between him and his brother, Robbie. We all tried to stop it – to calm Eddie down, but the more we tried, the more irate he became. Shouting turned into a physical altercation, and everything became messy. It's hard to understand what happened because we all got involved. There was so much pushing and shoving, and the girls were screaming.

None of us heard or saw the train until it was too late, and by that time, with all the physical to-ing and throwing, Robbie had fallen back onto the tracks. The train took him from us so quickly that we all stood in disbelief for some time – until the reality came.

Looking back, it seems so immature, but as a group, we always called ourselves The Domino Set. We used to play it as kids when there was nothing better to do on the estate and would bet our pocket money, or bags of sweets, as we played against each other. The older we became, the more we relied on the saying, 'if one goes down, we all go down.' It became our motto – our way of living. We believed we were the East End gang, but we were just kids playing around – getting dirty on the streets before being called home for tea. You may be wondering why I am telling you this, but what comes next is essential for your understanding of why I did what I did.

Police procedures were slow in those days, and although I wasn't allowed to work on Robbie's case because I was part of it, I'd been told that Elizabeth had blamed Eddie in her statement. None of my colleagues thought to seek out any possible CCTV of the accident until several days later, so I took the opportunity to find it myself. I wanted to know what had happened that night, for I, too, was a little worse for wear from the celebratory alcohol at R&R.

There was only one factory near the railway line that had CCTV. Back then, it was rare, but they'd installed it to find out who kept graffitiing their walls late at night. When I first saw the footage, I couldn't make sense of it, but I took it away and played it over and over again, in slow motion. Then it became clear. Robbie didn't stumble. In the chaos, he was pushed.

I knew that if the police found the evidence, one of my dearest friends would be convicted and charged with manslaughter. I always knew he wasn't an upstanding member of the community – few were from the estate – but he was a good man, and I needed to protect him. So, I hid the evidence. After Elizabeth accused Eddie of manslaughter, he set about trying to clear his name, so he, too, went looking for evidence. He found none, but he also found out that I had removed the footage from the factory. The only place I could keep it safe was here. It's been in this safe deposit box since 1995.

I thought I was doing a good thing in protecting my friend, but when Eddie discovered what I had done and what I had illegally taken, he threatened to expose me. He never saw the footage because I told no one where it was, but he had enough on me to ruin my career. But Eddie didn't just threaten my career, Emily, he threatened my family too. Despite being in the force, I didn't have the leverage to use it for protection in those days. Yet, Eddie, he'd built up a big enough network to sabotage everything in my life, including my career and the life we had built as a family.

Later in 1995, Eddie and Debra hit a security van in Clacton. Neither of them were bright enough to tackle such a job and not get caught, so when they were, Eddie called on me to help them out. I had no choice. Not only was I still protecting my friend, but I was now trying to protect my family too.

One blackmail led to another and another. By the end of the year, I had to cover more and more for Eddie and Debra. I knew there was no way out the deeper I found myself, so I made a decision. If I was going to be part of the criminal world, I would do it on my terms and in a way that benefited us as a family and those I cared for. The Domino Set grew and grew. Mutually convenient relationships of trust ensued, and despite knowing it was against everything I believed in and why I wanted to be a policeman in the first place, I always tried to remember that I found my way into the mess for the love I had for one of my dearest friends, and to protect my family.

So here it is, my dearest Emily. These are the reasons that your father became probably the most corrupt policeman in the Met during your lifetime. If I could turn back the clock, I would do it all again to protect my friend yet saying that fills me with conflict. I know by now that I would have lost your trust, admiration, and respect. They are, and were, worth more than anything I could ever imagine.

As I sign this letter off, I know I need to say goodbye for the final time. I will never see your beautiful face again, and you will never see my old, haggard, and grumpy one. My heart breaks to leave you, Rosa, and Zeb. You have been the world I have lived for, and every day, watching you grow and watching you achieve have been the happiest times in my life. My heart feels so much joy and hurt that it aches to the point of bursting. You are the beat between my heartbeats, and you have always been the reason for taking each and every breath.

Your loving father,

Dad

CHAPTER 55

Bond Street: The Bank

HARLEY quietly said, 'The software's finished, George.'
'I'm not sure I want to see it.'
'We've come this far.'
'I know.'
Trembling, her fingers tapped the keys on the laptop, and she began the footage again – the software giving her the chance to zoom in and slow things down. Sitting next to each other, they leant forward and watched. Harley shivered. Before her eyes was her father being pushed backwards and the train smashing into his body, taking it under until it was out of sight. She didn't know him – knew nothing about him – but the image she saw crashed into the centre of her heart, and the tears dripped unconsciously down onto the desk. She rewound and froze the frame, zooming in to the hand that touched him last – and the face it belonged to.

George sat back in his chair. Silent. The air sucked out of the room. In its place came a heaviness that could have crushed them if they hadn't already been crushed. Sitting close together, they were a universe apart.

'It was me.' George whispered. 'It was me.'

Harley stood up and moved to the window. There was nothing she could say to him – yet there was so much. Nothing came out. There was no energy left inside her body – no sense of thought or emotion. The numbness struck through her as her fingers pressed into the windowsill. She stared out into the industrial backyard of the bank, with its air conditioning units, brick outhouses and large metal bins. A cat sat on the top of one and stared back at her before raising its leg and washing its private parts.

George's body doubled over – his head squeezed between his palms as his nose touched his knees. He stayed there, motionless, for an eternity. Silence.

Wiping her face, Harley turned. Her heart was breaking into pieces as she watched him. 'I need to wipe the USB.' She said quietly and sat back down next to him.

'I did this.' George murmured, sitting back up. He was small, hunched into himself. Smaller than she had ever seen him.

'We need to wipe it, George.' The sound of her sniffs gave her away, and George touched her hand.

'Do you want me to give myself in?'

Looking down at his manicured, tanned fingers as they spread across her own, she felt the conflict of what she had seen against what she had always felt for the man who had taken her in and given her a purpose again – even if it was the wrong kind. Pulling away, she whispered, 'no,' and slowly started the process of shredding the evidence on the USB.

The Temple Club

Sitting opposite him, she noted his golden silk tie and the extravagant diamond pin that sat in the middle of it. He was nothing like the humble, understated George or the fat boar-like Eddie. To her trained eyes, he was dripping in vulgar excess. As he sat in the leather chair at The Temple Club, she instinctively disliked him even more than before, especially when his chubby little hand, with its Celtic wedding band tattoo, reached for the glass of champagne.

'I've known Emily for her entire life.' Thomas stated smugly. 'Did George mention that he has, too? Hard to say with George, though, isn't it? He doesn't say much.'

'He says what needs to be said.' Harley replied quietly.

'How is the old boy? I haven't seen him for years. We used to have some fabulous parties at Sidney's house when we were younger … before Eddie started to get up to no good.'

'Is that how you'd describe it?'

Thomas shifted a little in the chair. 'So, Elizabeth's daughter, what do you want from me?' His plump hand placed the champagne glass back on the table. Harley recoiled as she watched him. The diamond and rhodium ring on his little finger glittered under the Club's lights as he moved his hand to rearrange his tie. Harley noted the Breguet Tourbillon watch – over £150,000 strapped to his wrist.

'Tell me something, Thomas, or do you prefer Tom?' She didn't give him the chance to reply. 'How long have you been the accountant for The Temple Club?'

Thomas smiled uncomfortably. 'I prefer Thomas when I'm working. And I've been the accountant for around twenty-three years. Why do you ask?'

'I have the numbers to access Sidney Knight's account.'

Thomas uncrossed his legs and sat slightly forward in his chair. 'I thought Emily had them.'

'She never had them; Angus did. But now I do.'

'And what do you propose to do with the £30 million?'

'For an accountant, your maths is pretty shit, isn't it. Try £100 million, but you already know that I know, don't you.' She watched him, her eyes firmly fixed on the nuances of his reaction. If he was who she assumed him to be, he was quickly connecting the dots. In seconds, he would have worked it out.

And there it was – the reaction she'd expected. Thomas' face flushed red, then drained to grey. His eyes widened and narrowed as he glared at her. Beads of sweat sat on the brow of his balding head. So now they both knew it was her who'd been in his home and stolen the ledgers. And he now knew too that it was her who'd told Knight about his embezzling.

A waiter came to Thomas' side with another glass of champagne and quietly whispered as he bent down to place it on the table next to Thomas. 'There is a call for you, Mr Crowe.'

Thomas flicked his hand dismissively. 'Take a message and tell whoever it is that I'll call them back.'

'Sir, it's a new member who says it's urgent.'

Thomas glared at the young man. 'I said take a message. Actually, get my PA or the manager to deal with it.' Looking back at Harley, he said, 'You have my attention, Harley Smith.'

She studied him thoughtfully. An accountant. Just an accountant of the Club. 'Has it always been called The Temple Club?'

Thomas rested back in his leather armchair. 'It used to be called the Dunstan Club until 1995. Why?'

Harley half smiled. 'And then you changed it to The Temple Club to match your initials, TC?'

'You're even brighter than your mother, aren't you?' He said quietly. 'I wish we'd met under different circumstances.'

'Do The Domino Set know you have owned it all this time?'

Thomas smiled. 'How do you think their proceeds are laundered? We all have our legitimate businesses, Harley.'

'But do they know you've been syphoning off their payments, Thomas? I can't imagine Eddie would be very happy to hear that he's been paying into your bank account without him getting a cut of the action.'

Thomas leant forward, the pallor of his skin clammy and pale. 'What do you want from me? You've already done your worst by telling Emily.'

'That depends.' She replied. 'I have access to the money. Maybe we can mutually agree on some terms. But, before I trust you, you need to give me something ... I need you to tell me how you managed to launder and embezzle all that money without anyone ever finding out.'

Thomas laughed. 'You expect me to tell you the secrets of my trade?'

'Your choice, Thomas. I can walk away now and find someone else to help me.'

★

The Temple Club

Kicking the bike stand up, she held the Triumph between her thighs and put her helmet on. Sitting in the darkness, she waited. Watching. He'd leave soon. She wanted to see him leave. There wasn't a solid reason in her mind as to why, but she still sat, waiting. One hour later and Thomas Crowe exited The Temple's heavy double doors. The short, plump little man.

He'd agreed to all of her terms – ready to receive a third of the £30 million without a measure of remorse. Spilling his secrets – once he'd started, he couldn't stop. She knew that an excessive and inflated man like *Uncle Tom* wouldn't be as shrewd as he thought ... not when a £10 million golden carrot dangled before his eyes. Greed would be his downfall, she thought, as she watched him and wondered what he could have possibly done with over £70 million that he'd syphoned from Sidney Knight's offshore accounts.

Thomas stood on the steps for a moment, buttoning his coat – arranging his deep-blue and gold cravat. Watching, she started to digest all the information he'd given her. Somewhere within it, there was a way to punish him for his betrayal of Emily. The inside of her cheek pressed between her teeth as she sat in motionless silence. Thomas lit a cigar and then walked down the steps and into the evening streets of London. Her gaze followed him until he became an unrecognisable shape within the crowd.

★

Mayfair: Thomas Crowe's Offices

Removing his helmet, Ben ran his hand through his hair away from his blue eyes. Harley smiled.

'Thank you for coming.' She said quietly.

'How could I not? Seems to me that this will be our last job together.'

Harley turned her gaze to Thomas' offices. How could she tell him that it wasn't the end, not yet, that Zeb was taking over, and George was retiring?

'Are you sure you can trust this guy? I've never heard of him before.' She whispered.

'He's never heard of you either. That's how we all survive, right?'

'Where is he?'

'Waiting. He'll know when we're ready.'

Sliding off his bike, Ben organised his kit-bag. Harley did the same, and silently, they prepared themselves. Until they were inside, there would be no more words between them. Harley led Ben down the side alley to the backdoor of the offices. In seamless synchronisation, Ben inserted the tension wrench and rake into the bottom of the keyhole while Harley raked the mortice lock beneath it. The door glided open, and they moved inside the building.

As they did, a third shadow slipped in behind them. Through the darkness, the three of them made their way along the narrow corridor until they reached the next door. Harley silently pointed upwards to the door alarm. Sliding a small jammer out of his kit-bag, Ben reached up and held it close to the alarm. They waited, counting the time in their heads that it took for the wireless radio frequencies to enable them to open the final door. At the flash of a tiny blue dot, Harley knelt down and raked the lock. Leading them through the maze of corridors and interconnecting rooms, they reached the official office of Thomas Crowe & Co. Three locks. One door motion sensor. One internal room alarm connected to the managing security company.

In an unbroken fluidity of motions, Ben and Harley worked together. The third shadow leant against the wall – waiting. Tools slid from their kit-bags, pouches with rakes and levers gripped between their teeth. Harley turned the round knob and ushered the other two in before softly closing the door behind them. Immediately, Ben went to the window and peeped through the closed slatted blinds. Turning, he nodded at the third shadow, who quickly sat at Thomas' desk, and in front of his computer. Black latex-covered fingers began to connect wires to a small laptop. Harley moved to Ben's side. 'Who is he?' She whispered.

'They call him Mouse.'

'What kind of name is that?'

'That's how he does it – he jacks the mouse.'

Silently, they waited. There was nothing else to do until Mouse found what they needed – what she needed. Ben kept a lookout through the slatted blinds as Harley watched everything the mouse-jacker did. Ben might have trusted him, but there were millions of pounds at stake – no one was that trustworthy when it came to money.

Finally, Mouse motioned for her to join him, and she moved to his side, leaning over his shoulder. She could smell a mix of soap, garlic, and cigarettes; it wasn't pleasant, but the garlic made her feel hungry and nauseous at the same time. It had been days since she'd eaten.

'There's ten accounts that I can access.' Mouse whispered.

'How many that you can't?'

'None.' His fingertips touched the screen of the small laptop. 'That's why you're paying me millions. Right?'

Harley studied what he was showing her. Quickly, her brain added everything up that she could take from Thomas. She walked away and whispered, 'fuck.'

'How much?' Ben whispered.

'£152 million.' She stopped pacing. 'I can't leave him with anything, Ben.'

'Then we won't.' Ben watched her. 'The sun's coming up. We don't have much time left.'

'Do it.' Harley whispered to Mouse. 'All of it to the six accounts I gave you.' She stood to his side and pointed. 'That one there. That one's for you.'

East Ham: The Caff

'You look tired.' Harley said softly.

'Aimee was up before the magistrates yesterday.'

Desperate for a cigarette, Harley picked up the torn-off top from the sugar packet George had used and began to twiddle it. 'And?'

'They've committed the case to Crown. So she's going down for longer than the Mags can give her.'

She understood straight away, and from George's expression, she assumed he did too. If the Magistrates had sentenced her, it would have been a maximum of six months, but at Crown, it could be up to ten years for possession of a firearm.

'She pleaded guilty, right?'

'Yeah, but that ain't going to help. Two people were shot because of her.'

'Did they send her to Bronzefield on remand?' He nodded. 'She'll be there with Joanna then.'

Ben stumbled through the caff door with his blonde mop of hair flopping over his eyes, dampened by the fine misty rain drizzling down the streets of East Ham. He grinned at her as if he didn't have a care in the world and plonked heavily down next to his father. The three of them were together again, only with less energy, more worries, and less certainty about their futures. None of them spoke until after another round of coffee was delivered. George broke the silence. 'I've decided to give it all up and retire.' He said quietly.

'I'm not.' Ben stated. 'I enjoy it too much, and it's all I know.'

Harley continued to twiddle the paper sugar top. For years she'd wanted to call it a day and do something different, something she could share with a partner rather than hide in fear of judgement or exposure. Now she was faced with the final decision. If she didn't continue, George would have to.

'What about you, Love?' He asked softly – hopefully.

'I should go. I have some things I need to do.'

George gently grabbed her hand as she stood up. 'Are we alright?'

Harley's throat throbbed with pain as she fought the tears. 'Family is family,' she said quietly. Her decision was made.

CHAPTER 56

Newham Hospital

THE pain subsided as morphine slowly dripped into her veins with the push of a button. Propped up, she had an hour or so to herself while Rosa and Zeb returned home to go about their own needs. She was relieved to have silence in the room. Despite being drugged up, she could still hear all the chatter around her. It was like a distorted dream of being pulled and then pushed back – her mind and body battling with consciousness and sleep. Yet, for the first time in over a week, she was awake enough to see the room.

Emily smiled at the nurses as they brought her fluids, checked her vitals, and delivered her barely edible food. Just before she'd woken properly, a nurse left an envelope on her bedside cabinet. The movement and rustle disturbed her but not enough to stop a few more hours passing before she was awake enough to turn her eyes to the plain brown envelope waiting for her attention.

It took most of her energy to pull the envelope's seal from its glue – her fingers shaking with the effort. Inside was a typed letter and hidden behind it were pages of her father's handwriting – letters dated months before. Confused, she tried to pull herself up a little straighter, but the pain stabbed like a dagger in the lower part of her body. Releasing a cry, she screwed up her face and took a sharp breath. Jesus Christ. The papers flopped onto her lap as she tried to compose herself.

With another click of the morphine button, she held her position until she felt the drug swimming in her veins again, through her body, with a warm floatation that hit the back of her eyes – they rolled. Fighting with the sensation, she prised her eyelids open and picked the letters up. Blurred words floated off the pages at her. Her eyes were scanning across the lines and downwards as she read each one, slowly, repeatedly. An hour passed, then two.

Consciousness mingled with the legal high in her brain – she was clear-headed yet fuzzy. The reality of her father's battles was reaching through the morphine – electric synapses of truths she tried to grasp. Tears rolled unknowingly down her cheeks as she read each sentence of his story – each declaration of his love for his family. Emily's hands clutched the sheets of paper so tightly that they cramped when she tried to move them.

His last words. There weren't going to be any more. The reasons – his justifications – had been spilt, finally, to her. But she didn't want it to be over. While it lasted, while she was trying to find out what he had done and why he had done it, he was still alive. People were still talking about him. Even the DI was still calling her and mentioning his name. In a couple of weeks, all of it would be forgotten. Everyone would have moved on and found something else to focus on – except her, Rosa and Zeb. Even Harley Smith, she would have moved on too.

Closing her eyes, the letters floated back down to her lap again. Harley Smith. The night they had spent together – the morning they had woken up together. Emily drifted back to those moments and the past six months of Harley Smith. She'd been there when her father was shot. She'd seen him fall, yet she'd not said a word – pretended she knew nothing. Did she know nothing? Emily's mind drifted deeper back. Is that why, after never being interested in university, she finally decided to go, to get close to her? To use her so she could find the information for George. The morphine heaviness dragged her eyes down harder – too heavy to fight with. In the hidden darkness of her brain, Emily continued questioning. Her green eyes. *Green eyes.* Why hadn't she connected them before to the woman who had saved her life?

Their night together. Was she that good she could fake such intensity in her eyes? Emily's breathing – heavy and rhythmical from her nose – slowed down its pace even more. A blanket of weight pressed on all of her limbs, like a warm comfort that eased her further into the softness of the bed.

Harley Smith. She was the girl who questioned her ethics and morals, who stole her father's letters and then gave them back. She was the girl who watched her father die and yet touched her in such a powerful way. Harley Smith. She was a thief. She was the one who saved her life – twice.

Like the siren of a mermaid calling out to sailors in the night, the morphine hypnotised Emily into darkness – her thoughts crashing on its rocks until they died, and Emily slept.

CHAPTER 57

Newham Hospital

THE Night Sister came to Harley's side with a plastic cup of steaming tea.

'You look like you need this.'

'How is she?'

'Doing better.'

'It's because of me she's here.'

The Sister smiled gently. 'It's because of you she's alive. She'd have bled out within minutes if you hadn't kept the pressure on. From what I hear, you didn't give up even when the gun went off.'

'I'm not who she thought I was.' Harley whispered despondently.

The Sister sighed. 'My dear girl, if we were everything people thought we were, we'd be a million different people and nobody at the same time.' She paused. 'I have to wake her for medication. Would you like to come in?'

Fighting back the tears, Harley sat down next to the bed. She wanted to reach out and touch Knight's face, but she daren't. Instead, she waited patiently for the Sister to gently wake her – for Knight to drift into consciousness.

Knight's eyes slowly opened, and she lifted her head from the white hospital pillow as the pills were placed to her lips. As the Professor swallowed then slowly lowered herself back down, her eyes rolled to almost closed until the Sister said, 'She's here, Emily.'

Harley slid forward to the edge of her chair so Knight could see her. Finally, after ten days of being in the periphery, too scared to face her, Harley was able to look into the eyes of the woman she had fallen in love with.

'You came.' Knight whispered. 'You look tired.'

'I've been busy making sure everything is as it should be.'

Knight closed her eyes, hit by the morphine the Sister had pumped through the intravenous line. 'Nothing is going to be as it should be.' She mumbled.

'I should go and let you sleep.'

Knight's hand reached out and touched Harley's. It was a slow, heavy touch as the morphine began its work again. 'Stay a bit longer.'

'I'll stay as long as you need me to, Professor.'

Knight's voice drifted towards the oppressive morphine sleep as she murmured, 'It's Emily. My name is Emily.'

★

The End

Acknowledgements

Thank you, Tanya D and Vicky N, for starting the journey with me in the early days, supporting me and listening to my constant ramblings as the story unravelled in my mind. You carried me through those first drafts, and I am forever grateful.

Thank you, Aga J – your passion and belief were a gift. I will always cherish the days we spent getting excited about what was coming next.

Thank you, Andrea C, for always believing I would finish and enjoying every word I wrote.

Thank you, Sally-OJ and Carrie O, for being two editors from whom I have learnt so much.

And to The Rebels, you know who you are, thank you for always being the most supportive group of women in my life.

Printed in Great Britain
by Amazon

11117825R00163